Return of the Nyctalope

IN THE SAME SERIES

Jean de LA HIRE
The King of the Night
translated by
Brian Stableford

Jean-Marc & Randy LOFFICIER
Return of the Nyctalope

BLACK COAT PRESS

ISBN 978-1-61227-211-5. Printing. September 2013. Published by Black Coat Press, an imprint of Hollywood Comics.com, LLC, P.O. Box 17270, Encino, CA 91416. All rights reserved. Except for review purposes, no part of this book may be reproduced or transmitted in any form or by any means, electronic or mechanical, including photocopying, recording or by any information storage and retrieval system, without permission in writing from the publisher. The stories and characters depicted in this anthology are entirely fictional. Printed in the United States of America.

TABLE OF CONTENTS

Jean de La Hire

Le Roi
de la
Nuit

24ᶠ

Éditions
du Livre Moderne
Paris

Introduction

Le Roi de la Nuit (translated here by Brian Stableford as *The Nyctalope on Rhea*) is something of a publishing mystery.

In his entry on Jean de La Hire in the *Encyclopédie de l'Utopie et de la Science-Fiction*, Pierre Versins claimed that it was originally published in 1923 and included a reference to Cavorite. (La Hire having previously referenced Wells in *The Nyctalope on Mars*, this was no surprise.)

Genre scholar Jacques van Herp further claimed that *Le Roi de la Nuit* had been serialized in *L'Ami du Peuple* in 1923. This statement was bolstered by the fact that the book version, published in October 1943 by Editions du Livre Moderne, the "aryanized" successor of publisher Ferenczi, ended with the mention: "Novembre-décembre 1922, Paris & Le Breuil."

There are, however, several problems with this history.

The first is that *L'Ami du Peuple* didn't start until 1928, so a prepublication in 1923 would have been impossible. Further examination of both *Le Matin*, the newspaper which usually serialized La Hire's novels, for the year 1923, and of *L'Ami du Peuple* for the years 1928-30, does not reveal any pre-publications of *Le Roi de la Nuit*, or any similar story by La Hire under a different title.

To add to the mystery, the 1943 book version, which is translated here, does not mention Cavorite and features the characters of Gnô Mitang, Vitto and Soca as Leo's sidekicks. Yet, Gnô first appeared in *L'Antechrist* in 1927, and Vitto and Socca in *Titania* in 1929. So they couldn't possibly have been included in a novel written in 1922 since they hadn't yet been created!

We are left with several puzzling possibilities: there may have been an earlier version of *Le Roi de la Nuit* published somewhere in 1923—but if so, we don't know where—which mentioned Cavorite, but featured other supporting characters.

7

If so, that version was substantially rewritten by La Hire for the 1943 book edition to remove Cavorite (perhaps because of its English provenance, something that would have been unwelcome during WWII)[1] and update the cast. Or perhaps there was no earlier version, and *Le Roi de la Nuit* was first written in 1942. If so, then either La Hire lied, or the printer made a mistake, in that end note that should have read "1942" instead of "1922."

We may never know the truth.

Oddly, the 1943 version makes no reference to the context of the times. In early 1941, Jean de La Hire and André Bertrand had been given editorial control of publisher Ferenczi, which had issued paperback editions of many of their serial novels, as the result of the Nazis' efforts to "aryanize" French publishing and expropriate Jewish owners. In April 1941, Ferenczi was renamed "Editions du Livre Moderne." La Hire proved to be an incompetent publisher and was fired in December 1941. But since he did not avoid references to the German Occupation in *L'Enfant Perdu* (1942; translated in *The Nyctalope Steps In*) and *Night of the Nyctalope* (1944), why did he do so in *Le Roi de la Nuit*—unless, of course, the book was indeed written before the War? (It is, in fact, rather pacifistic in its approach to conflict.)

Again, we may never know the truth.

Because *Le Roi de la Nuit* appears, at face value, to take place before the War, Nyctalope scholar Emmanuel Gorlier decided to locate the story in the period ranging from June 1934 to December 1935. The Nyctalope's third wife, Sylvie

---

[1] In the novel that follows, we have assumed instead that Professor Olbans' spaceship was powered by "heliose," a substance discovered or rediscovered by Engineer Korridès in La Hire's *Le Trésor dans l'Abîme*. (1907). Héliose, indeed, might have been a type of Cavorite, or possibly a sample of the mysterious Doctor Omega's stellite.

MacDhul,[2] presumably died soon after *Les Mystères de Lyon* (1931), since Leo is single again in *Le Sphinx du Maroc* (early 1934). And Veronique is no longer mentioned in stories taking place in 1936 and 1937.

There is no doubt in our mind that La Hire intended for Leo to return to Rhea someday. We believe that, just as a shroud of darkness and evil was threatening to engulf the world of his birth, the Nyctalope indeed made a second, desperate trip to the wandering planetoid.

But this is not the story of that trip. Instead, this is the story of his third and final trip...

Return of the Nyctalope stands on its own, but readers might want to read, or reread, *The Nyctalope on Mars* and our story "The Ides of Mars" published in *Night of the Nyctalope*, which foreshadowed, to some extent, the events contained therein.

Jean-Marc & Randy Lofficier

---

[2] The Nyctalope's wives are: (1) Xavière de Ciserat; (2) Laurence Païli; (3) Sylvie MacDhul; (4) Véronique d'Olbans.

PLANÈTE SANS FEU
JEAN DE LA HIRE
FANTASTIC
Editions André Jaeger

Jean de La Hire: *The King of the Night*

To my dear friends Madeleine and André Chenue,
the first people to whom I talked
about this novel before writing it,
and their four children, for when they are grown up,
I dedicate this work in testimony
of my longstanding affection.
Jean de La Hire

Chapter I
The Nyctalope's Idea

It was two or three minutes after 8:30 p.m. when it happened—something unexpected since the world's beginning, which was very soon to produce the most extraordinary consequences.

Véronique d'Olbans had just said to Leo Saint-Clair, in a light tone not habitual to that passionate young woman:

"My dear Nyctalope, we're walking as if the Devil were on our heels. Look at my watch, which is always right: it's only 8:30. We're not late; we won't be sitting down at table for 30 minutes, and we'll be at the château in less than 15, as you know!"

"Very true, my dear," Saint-Clair replied, smiling.

The road was, in any case, quite steep; even without Véronique's remark, it would have been necessary to slow down. A hundred meters ahead of the walkers, between the woods of tall trees through which they were moving, an abrupt ridge was outlined against the flamboyant crepuscular sky.

It was then that a man appeared on that summit. His thin black silhouette rose up, soon visible in its entirety, upright on the saddle-back of the road.

"Who can it be?" Véronique murmured. "No one comes this way at this hour, except for the château's people, and I don't reco... Oh!"

Her speech was cut short as the man up above uttered a cry, abruptly raised his arms, staggered and fell...

Véronique and Saint-Clair were soon to recall that at that same instant they had heard liquid, silvery and limpid sounds vibrating in the air.

They ran forward and leaned over the body, which was lying face down, from either side. A gray felt hat had rolled a few paces away. The summer jacket that the man had been carrying over his arm was partly hidden underneath his abdomen.

"Uh oh!" said Saint-Clair. "What this?"

The shoulders, the nape of the neck and the back of the skull were dotted with minuscule holes; blood was spreading over the surface of the thin shirt, and swelling in droplets on the neck and the head, in the short-cropped hair.

"It's like a charge of lead pellets fired from 20 meters—but we didn't hear any rifle-shot."

Carefully, Saint-Clair turned the upper body over, almost completely. The throat and face were also speckled with bloody holes, larger than those at the rear.

"The exit holes of projectiles," said Saint-Clair. "It's not the lead-shot hunters use; that wouldn't have gone through. Truly bizarre... but what's certain is that the man's dead. Do you know him, Véronique?"

"No, I've never seen him before. This road only leads to the château, and only comes from the château. Unless the man's a hiker who's made a long detour through the forest paths from the village of Longpré? But that's a long way..."

Véronique fell silent, perplexed.

Saint-Clair's perplexity was different in kind.

"By what was the poor devil killed? That's even more inexplicable than his presence here..." He came to an abrupt decision. "You're strong, Véronique; help me. Grab his ankles; I'll take his armpits. Let's carry him to the ditch. Then we'll hurry on to the château, and we'll come back in my car..."

"Yes."

Saint-Clair learned over the bloody shoulders, neck, face and skull, and added:

"The tiny projectiles that hit him laterally didn't come from the undergrowth to the right or the left, but from the line of the road. The man was standing on the summit of the ridge; the road is steeper on the side behind the man than on the side he was facing. Fired from the road by a person standing up, the projectiles should have gone through the man diagonally— but the trajectory the projectiles followed through the shoulders, neck and head is very nearly horizontal. And first of all, what projectiles, fired by what weapon? We didn't hear any gunshot..."

Gravely, Véronique said:

"I heard... all this is really too strange... how shall I put it?... in the air, not far above us, a sound, or rather sounds, thin and silvery, very brief... for a few seconds. What about you?"

"That's true," said Saint-Clair. "I heard that too... at the exact moment when I saw the man raise his arms, stumble and fall."

"Yes."

The Nyctalope and the young woman bent down. They took hold of the cadaver at the ankles and armpits, and lifted it up easily—for the man who had just died so enigmatically was of medium height and girth, and weighed no more than 60 kilos.

They carried him to the ditch on the right and laid him at the bottom. It had been two weeks since a drop of rain had fallen in the locality; the ditch was quite dry. The jacket had been carried with the body; Saint-Clair went to retrieve the hat and dropped it on the body. Then he arranged the long grass on the edges of the ditch in such a way that the recumbent body was entirely covered and hidden.

"Come on, let's get back quickly," said Saint-Clair. "We'll come back in the car with your uncle. Together, we'll search the area. We'll try to find something to explain it."

Side by side, the Nyctalope and Véronique returned to the middle of the road. With an instinctive tacit accord, they stopped at the spot where the man had fallen.

In front of them, between the two continuous ramparts of verdure erected by the trees of the upper region of the vast forest domain, the narrow road ran down a steep slope to the depths of the valley, where there was an old stone bridge over the fast-flowing stream of the Miambe, a tributary of the Loir, which ran two kilometers away to the north, behind the hills, between Vendôme and La Châtre. Beyond the bridge, the road climbed again, just as steeply, to terminate in a semicircle in front of the large gate of the château. The descent to the stream and the ascent to the gate were almost the same length: between 500 and 600 meters.

Beyond the gate, the path, still climbing, was a driveway bordered by two sections of the grounds comprised entirely of pine trees—pines that were hundreds of years old, tall and straight, with vast magnificent green crowns. They gave their name to the place and the dwelling: the domain of the Château des Pins.

At the top of the 200-meter drive stood the château: a large rectangular building with two upper floors, its main façade facing south-east, flanked to the south by an enormous square tower whose rounded roof had been replaced 20 years before by the cupola of an astronomical observatory.

Less than a quarter of an hour after depositing the body in the ditch, LeoSaint-Clair and Véronique d'Olbans arrived at the château.

Rapidly, the young woman said:

"The dinner-bell hasn't rung yet. My uncle will be in the laboratory."

"Undoubtedly," said Saint-Clair.

Instead of going into the old house via the steps of the main façade or the tradesman's entrance on the north-east side, they went directly to the stout southern tower.

It had one floor more than the rectangular building. The ground floor and the second floor were libraries. The third, fitted out as a physics and chemistry laboratory, was also partly arranged as an astronomical study, the roof of that floor comprising the mobile cupola with multiple sections.

The zigzagging interior staircase connected the superimposed galleries of the libraries and the other floors. On the third floor, it opened on to a narrow landing. From there, in order to get into the laboratory, one had to go through three doors, two made of wood lined with thick sheets of cork and one made of steel, as heavy and massive as the door of a large safe. The system for opening and closing the first two was banal, but a bell and a secret mechanism controlled the third door.

Certain that her uncle was in the laboratory, Véronique rang the bell. Moments later, a red lamp lit up in a narrow corridor continuously illuminated by an ordinary electric bulb. Only then did the young woman turn the graduated handle that, in accordance with a number that was changed every day, was the key to the laboratory. The heavy batten pivoted slowly on its invisible hinges.

"How are you, Uncle?" Véronique exclaimed, immediately.

"Maxime!" called Saint-Clair.

At the other extremity of the immense square room, a large set of French windows opening on to a balcony was wide open. In front of that bay was a squat, or rather low table covered with a thick plate of glass. Sitting on a stool, his two arms stiff at one side of the table, his hand clutching the edge, was a man whose clean-shaven, livid face, streaming with sweat, his eyes staring, expressed violent and terrified surprise.

He did not react to Véronique's question and Saint-Clair's call. Had he heard them?

Gripped by the hands by his niece and by the shoulders by his friend, Maxime d'Olbans shivered abruptly, his entire body quivering. Raising his head, turning it to the right and the left, he stammered in a hoarse voice:

"It's... unimaginable! If I'm not mistaken, the consequences to be envisaged are... are..."

His mind in disarray, he would not find the word.

"Wait, Uncle," said Véronique, wisely. "Don't try... calm down..."

Swiftly, she went to a cupboard, opened it, took two bottles and four glasses out of a drinks-cabinet, and came back.

A few minutes later, his composure restored as much by the presence of his friend and his niece as a strong dose of old Ameragnac, the scientist was able to think clearly and speak with his customary ease.

"Do you see this sheet of lead?" he said.

On the glass plate of the table there was only one object, a thin sheet of lead, awkwardly unfolded, which still retained the lines and right angles indicating where it had been creased, clearly marked out.

"Do you recognize it?" added Monsieur d'Olbans.

"Yes," said Saint-Clair.

"Yes," said Véronique, adding: "You wrapped it around the little piece of the new metal that you'd succeeded in producing, the Z-4."

"Very good. Now listen to me!"

The instruction was surely unnecessary, but it was what the scientist always said when he had important things to impart.

"A little while ago, I had the idea of submitting the Z-4 to the action of three acids in combination—an experiment I hadn't yet carried out because I'd run out of one of the three acids. I received a demi-liter this afternoon. *I have the time*, I said to myself. *Véronique won't be back before dinner*. And I went to that cupboard over there to fetch one of the two packets, each composed of a large sheet of lead folded several times, enclosing between its median folds a kilo of grains of the Z-4, which I'd finally been able to obtain, as you know, last week... after years of research..."

He shrugged his shoulders and, mocking as much as marveling:

"Research! One thinks that one has invented, discovered, found something... and then, all of a sudden, *bang!*—an unexpected phenomenon informs you ironically that what you thought you knew is perhaps only the ten-thousandth part of what your discovery reveals to be still unknown..."

He struck the table with his hand and continued, in a sharply insistent tone:

"So I brought one of the two packets here, to the table. The windows were wide open, as they are now. And before even going to look for the test-tubes and the three acids, I started unwrapping the lead packages, impatient as I was to see the Z-4 again. And then... it was as rapid as lightning... rapid, yes, but all the same, absolutely immediate. You know that my faculty of observation is automatically exercised in a continuous manner, and that, even if I'm thinking about something else, the diagram, so to speak, of everything that strikes one or more of my five senses is automatically inscribed in my memory. I'm therefore quite certain of not being mistaken in affirming, firstly, that the phenomenon was not produced immediately after I had unwrapped the lead sheet completely and uncovered the mass of particles of Z-4; secondly, that the time elapsed prior to the production of the phenomenon was approximately one minute; thirdly, and finally, that the phenomenon was as rapid as a lightning-flash..."

He sighed, and passed a hand over his broad and high forehead, where an emotional sweat was pearling again.

Then Saint-Clair, with the serene gravity that he maintained in important circumstances, said:

"Yes! Streaking through the air with a scintillating, metallic, almost imperceptibly sonorous fulguration, the grains of Z-4 suddenly tore themselves away from the surface of the lead sheet and disappeared from your sight through the open window..."

Maxime d'Olbans started, his eyes widening, and exclaimed in a strangled voice:

"Oh! How did you know that?"

The Nyctalope lost none of his serenity in replying:

"You pronounced, my dear Maxime, the word *ironically*; I'll add: *tragically...*"

He broke off. There was a pause.

"Tragically?" stammered Monsieur d'Olbans. "What does that mean?"

"The Z-4 grapeshot, my dear friend, shot out of the window on an almost-horizontal plane—and over there, almost grazing the summit of the hill, the several dozen minuscule projectiles passed through an obstacle like a charge of leadshot going through a leaf. The tragedy was that the obstacle in question was a man who was walking along the road."

Taking the astounded Monsieur d'Olbans by the arm, Saint-Clair led him on to the balcony. In front of them, beyond the driveway through the park and the gate, the road sloped downwards to the river and rose up again to the saddle-back, which was indeed on an imaginary horizontal line extrapolated directly south-eastwards from the laboratory window.

The "reckoning of science" is often as powerful in its effects as the "reckoning of the State."

The public remained entirely ignorant of the real circumstances of the sudden death of a certain Lucien Demonpel on the territory of the commune of Longpré (Sarthe), more precisely on a private road in the forested domain belonging to Monsieur Maxime d'Olbans, physicist, chemist and astronomer, member of the Institute and Commander of the Légion d'honneur.

On the night of June 19-20, Vitto and Soca, the Nyctalope's servant companions, who were on holiday with their "boss" at the Château des Pins, went to recover the corpse from the ditch were Saint-Clair and Mademoiselle d'Olbans had hidden it. They brought it to the château. An interior pocket of the jacket contained a wallet containing identity papers. On the morning of June 20, the domestics were told that Vitto and Soca, in the course of a morning stroll, had found a dead man at the foot of a tree near the entrance gate. In the meantime, Saint-Clair had communicated by telephone with Monsieur Lamurat, Prefect of the Sarthe, who arrived by car at the château at 10 a.m.

There was nothing astonishing about the visit; it was not official. Monsieur Lamurat and Monsieur d'Olbans had known one another for years, and the prefect often visited the chatelain. In his honor, the Maire and the local physician were invited to lunch; that, too, was not happening for the first time.

With the aid of the telephone, it did not take long to ascertain that the deceased, Lucien Demonpel, lived in Le Mans, where he was employed as chief accountant to a manufacturer, that he was a bachelor, whose only living relative was a married sister, the mother of a family. He was on paid leave at Longpré, where there is a very good inn. In the course of a walk in the woods on the d'Olbans estate, he had died of an embolism—that is what Dr. Serres, the official physician of the commune of Longpré, declared. The sister came to collect her dead brother, who had been put in a coffin at the château. He had left a few savings, which she inherited. She seemed only moderately affected by the death her brother, who had been something of a misanthrope and of whom she had seen very little since her marriage, fifteen years before.

The secret of the disappearance of the Z-4 was therefore only known to Maxime d'Olbans, his niece Véronique, the Nyctalope, Vitto and Soca and the Prefect Lamurat.

On June 21, the dead man was taken away by his sister, and everything at the Château des Pins resumed its normal course. The incident of the sudden death of Lucien Demonpel was closed—but a prodigious adventure had just begun.

On the afternoon of June 21, the Prefect, Monsieur Lamurat, came back from Le Mans; he was to dine and stay overnight at the château. Dr. Serres had been invited; he reached Les Pins at 6 p.m.

At 7 p.m. Maxime d'Olbans was to carry out an experiment not only to be witnessed by Véronique and Saint-Clair, but by the Prefect, the physician and the two Corsicans, Vitto and Soca.

Since the production of the phenomenon, the scientist and the Nyctalope had reflected and conversed, formulating certain hypotheses based not only on Monsieur d'Olbans' work but also on a recent astronomical discovery, with which the observatory of the Château des Pins was not unconnected.

Thus, at 6:45 p.m., the young woman and the six men met in the laboratory. Only Monsieur Lamurat and Dr. Serres were unaware of the reason for the gathering. Perhaps they had some prior inkling of it, but no one had told them.

When the seven witnesses had taken their places on seats arranged in a semicircle about two meters from the central table of the laboratory, directly opposite the French windows on the other side of the room, Maxime d'Olbans, the only one still standing, started to speak.

His voice was naturally deep, but clear, and his straightforward elocution was easy on the ear.

"You, Véronique, and you, Messieurs, know what happened here the other day; as soon as it was disengaged from its lead envelope, a mass of grains of my Z-4 flew through the air through the open window. Why?

"For 48 hours, my friend Saint-Clair and I have been studying the problem minutely, analyzing every detail of the various aspects of the phenomenon.

"The circle of hypotheses, vast at first, has gradually narrowed, to the point of only retaining within its circumference a single hypothesis, and we shall be surprised if, in a few minutes, that one has not become a certainty."

On that word, pronounced with calm force, Maxime d'Olbans looked at the large laboratory chronometer.

"6:55 p.m.," he said. "Six minutes to go. For it's at 7:01, at our present altitude and location on the Earth, that the reproduction of the phenomenon will become possible."

At a slow and slightly gliding pace, he went straight to a closed cupboard, opened it, and took a packet off one of its shelves, which he came to set in the exact center of the table, whose thick glass plate was entirely bare.

That flat, rectangular and relatively thin packet, wrapped in a sheet of lead, measured about 25 centimeters by ten.

Having set down the object, he did not resume the place where he had stood, facing one of the short sides of the table. Instead, he went to the French windows opening on to the balcony, which were wide open to the beautifully pure sky, bright blue tinted with pink, of that splendid late-spring day, and resumed speaking:

"For all useful purposes, I have here at the château a small stock of plates and sheets of glass of various dimensions and thickness. Yesterday, the cabinet-maker from Longpré, used to working for me, mounted in a frame set on castors a plate of glass five millimeters thick, of such a size that I can fit it exactly, with its frame, within the frame of this open window. Open, Messieurs, because I did not wish to expose the wooden frames of its small panes to a damaging perforation."

While speaking he had, in fact, carefully pushed the large single pane, which fitted perfectly, into the empty space of the window between the laboratory and the balcony.

"6:59!" he pronounced. "Two more minutes. You'll all be able to see clearly, on the unfolded sheet of lead, the heaped-up mass of half a pound of Z-4 granules."

Returning to the table, he rapidly and adroitly unfolded the packet, flattening the four corners of the lead sheet, thus laying bare, displayed on the flat rectangle, the granules of the mysterious metal of which he was the secret inventor and the sole manufacturer.

The emotion of the spectators was, at that moment, composed of the keenest curiosity. They all looked at those granules, consisting of minuscule cubes, visible equilateral; rifle-pellets that, instead of being gray-black, was silvery white, and, instead of being round, were cubic.

All of a sudden, Maxime d'Olbans, standing to the right about two meters from the table, raised his right hand and said, excitedly:

"Pay attention! Two more seconds..."

An instant afterwards, 100 tiny lightning bolts shot through the relatively dim light of the laboratory, at the same time as the glass screen in the window-frame was pierced almost at its center with a crystalline tinkle.

On the table, the lead sheet no longer supported anything; the Z-4 particles were no longer there.

There was a brief silence; then the scientist's grave and tranquil voice resumed:

"Don't worry. This time, there's no one out there on the ridge of the road. Without knowing why—without knowing anything—my gamekeepers, positioned outside the trajectory of the Z-4, are on sentry duty there, in accordance with the unexplained orders I gave them a little while ago.

The most excited of them were Monsieur Lamurat and Dr. Serres, for Véronique, Saint-Clair, Soca and Vitto, forewarned, had expected the phenomenon that had just occurred. The Prefect and the doctor had only had, the day before, vaguely hypothetical explanations regarding the death of Monsieur Demonpel. What they had now just seen told them more, enlightening their minds—but not completely. The perplexed face that each of them turned to Monsieur d'Olbans was not merely interrogative but passionately interrogative and profoundly emotional.

Fortunately for the satisfaction of that legitimate curiosity, Maxime d'Olbans was not one of those loquacious scientists who envelop demonstrative explanations in needless prefatory remarks and commentaries. He spoke clearly and briefly.

"Messieurs, you could have read in any newspaper that, exactly three months and six days ago, astronomers discovered a new planetoid. Do you recall?"

The six listeners answered in the affirmative by saying "yes" or nodding their heads.

"Since that discovery," Monsieur d'Olbans continued, "I have maintained that celestial body, which I christened Rhea, in the field of my telescope—which, moved by a system of clockwork and equipped with an automatic camera, is continuously observing and recording what it can recover from the planet Rhea. Now, for ten days, and for a further 295 days, that planet has been and will be visible from our hemisphere, twice a day, at varying times but for an equal lapse of time measuring about three hours and 48 minutes. But not entirely visible—only partly, and fractionally, 80% of its mass being hidden from us by the Moon."

Monsieur d'Olbans smiled during a short pause, and then went on:

"I'll spare you the studies, observations and calculations by virtue of which I arrived, yesterday, at the conviction that the phenomenon—which is to say, the departure of the Z-4 granules—is simply a phenomenon of attraction. Yes, the attraction of the planet Rhea with regard to the entirely new metal—new to the Earth, at least—constituted by my Z-4. The experiment you have just witnessed has made that conviction a certainty. Moreover, we ought to consider as demonstrated, firstly, that lead is, for Z-4, an insulator that annuls the power of attraction; secondly, that glass is not an insulator, any more than the various materials making up the human body, since the Z-4 went through a man the other day and that pane of glass today... and that's all! I mean, that's all we know."

Silence—but soon, within that silence, the wonderstruck voice of Monsieur Lamurat said:

"But that's prodigious!"

Maxime d'Olbans was quick to reply, slightly ironically, as he often did when his mind had good reason for self-satisfaction:

"Nothing is prodigious about a fact of nature. It's simply natural. But what humans do with it... oh yes, that's sometimes prodigious. With your permission, though, I'll hand the floor to the Nyctalope, for, even before the demonstration that has just been made and the certainty we're just acquired, my

23

friend Saint-Clair had an idea. He'll explain it to you. And then, if we can succeed in making that idea a reality, we shall see something truly prodigious!"

The Prefect, Monsieur Lamurat, and Dr. Serres did not only know LeoSaint-Clair, a.k.a. the Nyctalope, by virtue of having met him two days earlier and today at the Château des Pins. They knew what every educated man in the civilized world knew about him. By virtue of multiple exploits of the most various character, LeoSaint-Clair had become famous. Explorer, diplomat, strategist, detective, physiopsychologist, knowledgeable in natural sciences and occult sciences, politician, economist, memoir-writer and author of numerous works published first in French and then translated into many other languages, LeoSaint-Clair was also the Nyctalope—which is to say that, by one of the rare caprices of nature, he possessed the physical faculty, like certain animals, of being able to see as clearly in darkness as in broad daylight. And that, as one can imagine, had been an enormous advantage in his astonishing career as an encyclopedic mind and a man of adventure.

Thus, an idea of Saint-Clair's inspired by the phenomenon of Z-4, was even more likely to excite the body and the soul than the phenomenon itself!

Maxime d'Olbans was, at present, the only one who knew what he idea was; so, the faces of Véronique, Monsieur Lamurat, Dr. Serres, Vitto and Soca all turned avidly toward Saint-Clair.

Even less than Monsieur d'Olbans, when the Nyctalope had something to say, he did not bother with superfluous words. To his friend's gestured invitation, Saint-Clair acquiesced with a smile, and said quite simply, in his clear and ever-incisive voice:

"If we use metal Z-4 to construct a kind of new craft, and use the attraction of the planet Rhea, subjecting it to a measure of discipline, it's not out of the question that humans might get close—very close—and even set foot on the planet newly appeared in our region of the Solar System."

"There! That's perfectly simple!" interjected Véronique d'Olbans, spasmodically.

The young woman had stood up abruptly; everyone looked at her. Her eyes were full of tears. Distressed by the sudden awareness of her emotion, she took two steps backwards and put her hands over her face, stammering:

"Excuse me—I'm being silly..."

Dr. Serres, however, who had seen her born 20 years earlier, and who had almost as much quasi-paternal affection for her as her uncle, Maxime d'Olbans, got up and went to her, took her hands and gripped them, saying gently:

"Calm down, Véronique, my dear. We're containing ourselves better, but we're all as emotional as you are. What we've just seen... what Saint-Clair has just thrown into out minds... you aren't being silly... or we're all as silly as you."

He turned to the Nyctalope, without letting go of Véronique's hands. "Really, my dear chap, is that possible?"

Saint-Clair did not reply immediately. He looked hard at the young woman, who was also looking at him. What could he see in her that he had not yet noticed? He went pale. For a brief moment, a quiver ran through is features. His eyes closed—but he opened them again immediately, and he stood up. He walked rapidly to the far end of the large room, came back, and without any apparent emotion, he spoke, only looking at Dr. Serres, who let go of Véronique's hands then and took a step away from her.

"Yes, I firmly believe that it's possible. It even seems easy to me. But listen: to depart aboard an aircraft made of Z-4, to leap like lightning outside the terrestrial atmosphere... Yes, really, quite straightforward and practically imaginable in many details. But what will happen afterwards? It's necessary to do it in order to find out, as the popular saying has it—but I'm convinced, I repeat, that if we want too, it will be possible, even easy, to do it. Won't it, Maxime?"

"Of course," said Monsieur d'Olbans.

Chapter II
The Question of Gno Mitang

So, on that June 21, the Prefect, Monsieur Lamurat, and Dr. Serres dined at the château. After the meal, the five guests gathered once again in the laboratory in the tower. There they found Vitto and Soca.

Companions-in-arms and often collaborators in the adventures of their boss, the Nyctalope, the two Corsicans were also perfect servants. Certainly, they would take part in the conversations, scientifically experimental or hypothetical, that would animate the evening—but first, they would serve coffee, liqueurs and vintage port, and open boxes of cigars and cigarettes, for neither Maxime d'Olbans not LeoSaint-Clair were opposed to coffee, tobacco and alcohol—"poisons" that, if they are of good quality and taken in reasonable doses, have never prevented a human being from living to be 100 while remaining healthy.

Comfortably installed in leather armchairs, with which a part of the laboratory was as judiciously furnished as it was intelligently garnished with bookshelves, the young woman and the six men relaxed, with the greatest of individual liberty, into a conversation that soon became very animated, concerning the metal Z-4, the planet Rhea, the craft that would be constructed with that metal, the voyage which, thanks to that metal, might practically be made to the planet, and, finally, the hypotheses whose construction the present state of astronomical science permitted regarding the consequences of such a voyage—the first of its kind that earthly human beings might actually attempt to accomplish.

They did not part until midnight, after they had all sworn to maintain absolute secrecy regarding everything that had been done, said and decided that day.

Dr. Serres went home on foot; the night was serene and the village of Longpré, where he lived, was no more than three kilometers from the Château des Pins.

The next morning, after breakfast, Monsieur Lamurat left in his car for the prefecture, and Monsieur d'Olbans telephoned Monsieur Fageat, his steward, asking him to come to his study immediately. The detached house in the forest where Monsieur Fageat lived was 500 meters from the château, linked to it by a private telephone line.

Nine o'clock was chiming on that June 22 when Monsieur Fageat arrived at Monsieur d'Olbans' study. The room, furnished with a large stable and several chairs, fitted out with filing-cabinets, ornamented with plans and a map of the vast estate of Les Pins, was situated on the ground floor of the château. On one side it opened on the large entrance-hall, on the other to the flower-garden, which two gardeners maintained under the benevolent dictatorship of Mademoiselle Véronique.

The weather had changed at daybreak. A storm was rising in the south-west. Before being introduced, the steward put his iron-tipped cane, his large leather gloves and his waterproof hooded cape into the hands of the valet who welcomed him.

"Ah, you've anticipated the rain, Monsieur," said the old domestic, with customary familiarity.

"Not difficult!" muttered Monsieur Fageat, unceremoniously.

"That means," Alfred went on, naively proud to demonstrate that he knew a great deal about the locality even though he was a Parisian, "that the vale of the Pas-de-Loup, which you can see from your windows was full of mist yesterday evening."

"If you wish," said the steward, shrugging his shoulders—and as Alfred opened the study door, he went through it.

If he was astonished to see Maxime d'Olbans and LeoSaint-Clair sitting face to face, leaning over land-registry plans spread out on the table, his expression gave no sign of it.

His face was coarse and square, with a short-cropped back beard, an aquiline nose and sharp, hard eyes deep-set beneath protruding and hairy brows.

"Bonjour, Messieurs," he pronounced, in a voice that was always a trifle grating.

Saint-Clair only replied with a nod of the head; he did not like Monsieur Fageat, and had good reasons for that, although he kept them secret. The antipathy was only translated into a strict and dry politeness in the occasional relations that Monsieur d'Olbans' illustrious guest had with the steward. The steward, who doubtless saw clearly, had never departed from the profound deference that a man like him owed to a man like the Nyctalope, but in the latter's presence he always put as much distance as possible between them, or hung back in such a fashion that appeared, in sum, to be nothing but a respectful reserve.

"Bonjour Monsieur Fageat," said Monsieur d'Olbans, half rising to his feet and holding out a cordial hand, adding, as he sat down again: "Bring up a chair and sit down there... Good! Listen to me."

The proprietor of the Les Pins domain had a good deal of consideration for is steward. That was because Ariste Fageat was not, in his employ, an ordinary man. Only about 35 years of age, he had very extensive theoretical and practical knowledge. A graduate of the École Centrale, he was an agronomic engineer and forester, an architect and master mason. He had amended and augmented the diverse and profound knowledge he had acquired at university by applying himself for several years before being employed—on the recommendation of the Minister of Agriculture, who held him in high esteem—as the general steward of the immense estate of Les Pins, which included large forests of exploitation and hunting, twelve farms growing cereals and raising cattle, a small private generating-plant powered by the waters of the fast-flowing stream of the Miambe, which furnished electricity, heat and light to the château and its immediate dependencies, the farms and the dairy.

Since he had started work at Les Pins, Ariste Fageat had merited nothing but praise; nevertheless, although Monsieur d'Olbans treated him with cordiality, no intimacy had been established between them, and it is must be admitted that the steward, although perfectly honest, correct, precise and very moderate in his speech, was not well-liked by anyone in the entire property. He did not have a single friend in the village. In his cottage in the grounds, he was served by an old maid-of-all-work, unsociable and steeped in piety, whom he had obtained from an employment agency in Le Mans; her name was Sidonie. She had no contact with anyone, save for the serving-woman of the curé of Longpré.

"Listen to me," Monsieur d'Olbans had said. After a brief habitual pause he issued his instructions, while indicating the places to which he referred on the land-registry plans with the point of a pencil.

"This is the summit of Gorse Hill, in the northern sector of the Forest of Dales. You have to flatten that summit in such a way as to obtain a rigorously horizontal area a thousand meters square. On that you'll construct, first of all, a principal edifice 20 meters high, as large as possible, which will be a kind of big workshop. In a few days' time I'll give you the list of machine-tools, forges and furnaces to be installed there, on a concrete platform 20 meters square. That central building will be flanked by a foundry and various other less important workshops, of which you'll have the rough plans tomorrow, which Monsieur Saint-Clair and I will draw up today. That factory complex you'll link to the highway between Angers and Le Mans, here, by a road that you'll open through the middle of the forest, which needs to be broad enough to give easy passage, in one direction, to five-tonne trucks. As the road will be more than three kilometers long, though, you'll incorporate a few crossing areas. Do you understand?"

"Perfectly, Monsieur le Comte," said the impassive steward.

Monsieur d'Olbans smiled as he said:

"But you can't see the reason for all this upheaval—these earthworks and constructions?"

"No, Monsieur le Comte."

"I'll reveal that to you in due course. What I've just told you is sufficient, I think, for you to begin to make your initial arrangements today with regard to the manual labor of clearance and ground-leveling, and felling trees for the opening of the new road."

"It is, indeed, sufficient."

"It needs to be done quickly," Monsieur d'Olbans went on, with a contained feverishness. "The buildings need to be light, but capable of resisting all weathers. We'll draw up the architectural plans together, in a few days' time. What I'm trying to do will raise a particular series of questions. The first to be resolved, and the easiest, are the leveling of the hill and the piercing of the rod. When do you think you'll be able to start work?

Ariste Fageat reflected for a quarter of a minute and then replied:

"I'll go to Le Mans today. After a few preliminary steps, I think I'll be able to hire sufficient crews of woodcutters and earth-movers tomorrow. I'll lodge and feed them in the commons of the Lancelot farm, which will be furnished with the personnel necessary for that purpose; it's less than a kilometer from Gorse Hill. In sum, the work can begin next Monday."

"Listen, Fageat," Monsieur d'Olbans pronounced firmly. "I want the ground and the road to be ready by the end of July, in order that the factory and its annexes can receive all the machinery that will be ordered tomorrow from various manufacturers. Do you think that's possible?"

"Quite possible, Monsieur le Comte—but it will require a lot of men and will be very expensive."

"Submit your first estimates to me on Sunday, along with your first demand for credit. The new work is dear to my heart; I'll devote the necessary millions to it."

Monsieur d'Olbans got to his feet. The steward got up too, took the proffered had, shook it, nodded his head to Saint-

Clair, who returned the gesture, and went out at his usual pace, supple and heavy at the same time.

A moment later, the Nyctalope said:

"A singular fellow who seems not to be interested in anything, isn't astonished by anything, and never asks questions."

"Yes," said Monsieur d'Olbans, shrugging his shoulders, "Fageat is taciturn—but he's a first-rate engineer, a competent steward and a zealous servant. You really don't like him, do you, my friend?"

"No."

"Me neither, deep down—but he keeps to his place, serves me well and doesn't steal from me. The last certification I only advance on behalf of my notary, who does me the favor of scrutinizing all the estate's accounts minutely, and knows what he's doing."

"I know. Maître Blanquer is an exceptional notary. Him, I like a great deal."

"You'll see him on August 26. I've invited him to lunch. There! Now, let's get on with our work." He sat down, picked up the pencil and placed a blank sheet of paper in front of him. "The form of the apparatus, my dear friend," he said. "Is it like is this that you see it?" And before Saint-Clair's attentive eyes, Monsieur d'Olbans started drawing.

The knowledge, will-power and fortune of Monsieur d'Olbans, the organizational genius of Saint-Clair, the intelligence, technical knowledge and zealous obedience of the steward Fageat: those combined forces accomplished in a few weeks an endeavor that won the admiration of a few people initiated into the reasons and informed as to the goal of the work.

To begin with, Gorse Hill, in the northern sector of the Forest of Dales, was razed, flattened and rigorously leveled within a perimeter a kilometer square; through the woods the truck-road opened up connecting to the Le Mans/Angers road. Then the immense factory, the small workshop and their numerous annexes were rapidly constructed, thanks to the rational organization of the work and the active multitude of manual workers judiciously chosen from among the best specialists in every trade.

At the end of July, the machinery ordered from Creusot and Essen was in place, ready to function.

Then began the massive production of Z-4 necessary for the construction of the first interplanetary ship, baptized in advance the *Olb-I*. The effective baptism, with a bottle of Champagne, was celebrated on August 25; Véronique d'Olbans was the ship's godmother.

That same evening, Monsieur d'Olbans and Saint-Clair decided that the departure would take place on August 30, at the first solar hour, exactly 37 minutes before sunset on the Paris meridian. The day and time were fixed by Monsieur d'Olbans after long and minute calculations, after which he had determined: firstly, that the planet Rhea would then be at the closest point of its orbit to the Earth, due east, visible in a telescope on a rigorously horizontal line; secondly, that the attractive force of the planet Rhea on the Z-4, and thus on the *Olb.-I*, would then begin to enter its period of maximum intensity, a period that would last 24 hours with a slight increase from minute to minute, to decrease thereafter to virtually nothing at the end of six months; after that the Earth's power of attraction, itself increasing from minute to minute, would regain the upper hand, increasing for three months, diminishing during the second semester, and then beginning to decline, at least with regard to Z-4, by virtue of the attraction of the planet Rhea, which would become visible again, this time to the west of Earth.

On August 26, at 3 p.m., a meeting took place at the Château des Pins, the most importance, and also most emotional of all those held since the day when the attractive power of the new planet Rhea on the Z-4 had become manifest.

Those present at the supreme meeting were Messieurs d'Olbans and Saint-Clair, the Prefect Lamurat, Dr. Serres, the notary Blanquer, the steward Ariste Fageat, the two Corsicans Vitto and Soca, and, in addition, an individual of the highest rank: His Excellency Gno Mitang, diplomat and minister, privy councilor to His Majesty the Emperor of Japan.

For several years, Gno Mitang had been Saint-Clair's best and most intimate friend. He had often been his companion in adventure—and what adventures! Finding himself in Paris that August, Gno Mitang had been called on the telephone by the Nyctalope, who, with the agreement of Monsieur d'Olbans, had invited him to come, not without a few mysterious hints—and the illustrious Japanese had come running. Having arrived just in time to sit down at the lunch table, with his customary discretion, he had not asked any questions. At table, nothing had been said about what motivated the meeting of such guests, except that a council would be held at 3 p.m. and that everything would be explained then.

Gno Mitang was, in any case, the only one who did not know what it was about, because several days before, with Saint-Clair's assent, Monsieur d'Olbans had put his steward Fageat completely in the picture. The latter had previously only had the conjectural ideas he had formed in the course of certain constructions to inform him as to the great reality of things—ideas that lacked the principal element of information and certainty: the properties of Z-4 in relation to the planet Rhea.

It was, therefore, for the sole benefit of Gno Mitang that Maxime d'Olbans spoke at the opening of the council, and to him that he addressed himself directly

"Excellency," he began, "a few words will suffice to make you party to the grave and capital discussion that is about to begin, and which, I hope, will allow us to make, today, the most extraordinary decisions that humans have ever been able to take."

Gno Mitang, short, neat and broad-backed in his perfectly-tailored gray jacket, had an almost-imperceptible smile and a serious expression' he made a slight bow.

Then Maxime d'Olbans explained the entire history of his discovery of Z-4, the phenomenon of June 19, and the multiple endeavors that had been the consequence of the Nyctalope's idea, inspired by that phenomenon.

Gno Mitang was a difficult man to astonish; he knew the audacious genius of the Nyctalope better than anyone; even so, his impassive face quivered and he looked at his friend with his eyes opened wide when Monsieur d'Olbans concluded, with the simplicity of great scientists:

"Everything is therefore ready for the voyage from Earth to Rhea."

Then there was silence for thirty seconds, during which all gazes were fixed on the illustrious Japanese.

Softly, Gno said: "The life of the astronomical universe had always interested me greatly. I keep myself up to date almost day by day, with the studies that the principal observatories have made and are still making with regard to the newly-discovered planetoid. We know that on August 30, Rhea will be at the nearest point of its orbit to the Earth, and six months later move away from our planet, never to be seen again."

"Yes," said Monsieur d'Olbans."

"We also know," Gno continued, "that the shortest distance between the Earth and Rhea will be 95,000 leagues, a little less than the distance from the Earth to the Moon. We know, too, that the size and mass of Rhea are about a sixth of those of Earth. Finally, we have solid scientific reasons to think that Rhea bathes in an atmosphere that is not without analogies with the terrestrial atmosphere, and that, in consequence, life ,such as we know and conceive it, might exist on Rhea's surface."

"Yes!" said Monsieur d'Olbans, again.

"Very good!" Gno concluded. And with the little evasive gesture just mentioned, the Japanese passed on immediately to another order of ideas. Clearly, and just as emphatically, he asked in the same discreet voice: "Which men will go in the first interplanetary vehicle, the *Olb.-I*?"

"Bravo, Gno!" said Sant-Clair. I expected that conclusion from you, which will open the debate for which we've assembled today. Until now, my friend d'Olbans and myself have, by tacit agreement, left that question unasked. Personally, I didn't want it to be raised in your absence, Gno, since you were in Paris, but free to be here at my first appeal. You've posed it yourself; that's what I wanted. But don't you think, all of you, that it is up to me to answer it?"

Saint-Clair, slowly turning his head from left to right, interrogated with his penetrating gaze, first Gno, then Maxime d'Olbans, then the Prefect Lamurat, Dr. Serres, the steward Fageat, the notary Blanquer, Vitto, Soca and, finally, Véronique d'Olbans.

The young woman, who was very emotional, was extremely pale. Saint-Clair understood that she wanted to speak, while the other participants, perhaps equally emotional, were content to wait. He encouraged her by softening his gaze, and with a smiling. Then, blushing by virtue of an abrupt rush of blood that a sudden determination caused to circulate violently, Véronique said, in a tremulous voice:

"Don't you think that, before the interplanetary voyagers volunteer themselves, it would be appropriate to think about the return journey? I mean that everything is ready to go from the Earth to Rhea, but how do you anticipate coming back from Rhea to the Earth?"

Under Véronique's passionate gaze, it was the Nyctalope's turn to go pale. Immediately, however, he suppressed his emotion, and replied without hesitation, softly, with a gesture that designated Monsieur d'Olbans:

"Great scientists have these distractions! I confess that I, working as hard as your uncle on the preparations for the voyage, have not once thought about the voyagers' return."

"The fact is..." Monsieur d'Olbans murmured, put out.

These two replies rendered a situation that the young woman's perfectly natural question had momentarily made tragic irresistibly comic. Everyone present burst out laughing, except for Véronique, who went very pale again and remained serious. To tell the truth, the laughter was nervous, particularly that of Ariste Fageat, which was sharp and convulsive. With an authoritative, perhaps unreflective gesture, the reasonable and passionate young woman uttered the laugh of someone with taut nerves, and in the same tremulous voice, but in a clear tone, said:

"To go to the planet Rhea without being assured of a means of return is suicide—and a futile suicide, since no one on Earth would ever know..."

"Forgive me, my child forgive me!" Monsieur d'Olbans cut in, swiftly. "I'll stop you there."

With everyone looking at him and listening to him, except for Saint-Clair, who was avidly studying Véronique's face, the scientist explained himself immediately, in a casual manner:

"Neither Monsieur Gno Mitang nor I have mentioned everything that astronomers have established scientifically with regard to the planet Rhea—in particular, that which myself and Saint-Clair have determined with regard to possible analogies between that planet and the Earth. For another month, and then for eight months during the following trimester, the four most powerful telescopes in the world, including mine, will permit a precise and detailed close-range analysis of Rhea—so detailed, so precise and so close-range that we have been able to foresee the eventuality of powerful luminous signals, effected on Rhea, being visible to terrestrial astronomers at certain times, which we have calculated minutely and delimited very exactly. Behind a movable leaden carapace at the dome-shaped rear of the *Olb.-I* is an enormous projectile lens. To explain everything to you in detail would take too long; let it suffice for you to know that the travelers will take what is necessary to transform the *Olb.-I* into a light-projector of enormous power, as long as there is running water on Rhea. And there must be running water out there, since there is air, mountains and snow! Thus, the eventual suicide—admitting that the word has any propriety here, which is highly debatable—would not be futile, since the Terrans who have reached

36

Rhea will be able to send messages to the Earth, and probably receive them too."

"So be it!" said Véronique, resolutely bent on combat. "it remains no less true that the Terrans who have reached Rhea, as you put it, would probably not be able to get back—and, therefore, that those of us who remain here will never see them again."

"Perhaps! For every problem is soluble. If they..."

Then Saint-Clair, cutting short the manifestation of any emotion, turned his gaze to Véronique's face, and in his incisive voice, said:

"Let us admit as simply possible that neither the voyagers on Rhea nor the scientists on Earth will find the means of making the interplanetary voice two-way, although I estimate myself that anything is now realizable in that order of scientific and practical activity. Yes, in spite of my contrary hopes, let's admit that the voyagers of the *Olb.-1* will never come back. That only makes the choice of voyagers easier."

"Easier!" exclaimed Véronique, simultaneously indignant and amazed.

But yes, my dear friend!" said Saint-Clair, earnestly. "As you shall see. Let's proceed by elimination."

He closed his eyes in order to focus his thoughts and only pronounce the essential words. Breathless now, everyone was looking at him—everyone except Ariste Fageat, who was observing Véronique with a somber expression, which no one noticed, except perhaps Gno Mitang, who was discreetly observing everyone. There was a brief moment of expectation, in which there was still more curiosity than anxiety. Raising his eyelids, looking at his friend Maxime d'Olbans first, and then the other men, whose names he pronounced, the Nyctalope spoke:

"It's quite evident that Monsieur d'Olbans must remain here. The new inventions and discoveries that he is in the process of making might well answer all the questions that have been or will be posed. Prefect Lamurat is needed in his Prefecture, Dr. Serres by the invalids of the canton; besides which, they each have a wife and children. Maître Blanquer is a bachelor, and, strictly speaking, his nephew and chief clerk could replace him, but our dear notary is 70 years-old, although young at heart. Monsieur Ariste Fageat in the excellent steward of the estate and the competent director of Monsieur d'Olbans works; he must therefore stay here. No reasonable protest can be raised against these eliminations, isn't that so?"

Not one mouth opened, but it was evident that all the expressions expressed acquiescence.

"Good!" said Saint-Clair—and went on, in an almost-cheerful tone: "My dear Gno, I believe that if I were to offer to let you leave with me in the *Olb.-I*, you'd accept immediately?"

"Without a doubt!" pronounced the Japanese, with a smile that lit up and rejuvenated his entire face—the taut and angular face of a quinquagenarian Asian.

"In that case, I offer it to you, my friend—for I shall be leaving in four days for Rhea. Naturally, I shall take Soca and Vitto, with whom I can't do without, and who would die of boredom on Earth without me. Eh, Vitto, Soca?"

"Yes, Monsieur!" said the two Corsicans, in unison, quite simply.

"Well, then," said Saint-Clair, "it seems to me..."

But Véronique's voice cut in, sharply and firmly.

"What about me?" she asked.

"You?" exclaimed Monsieur d'Olbans.

All eyes were suddenly fixed on the young woman—but she was only looking at the Nyctalope, and she continued in the same resolute tone:

"Yes, me. Here, I'm useless; I don't participate in any of my uncle's endeavors. On the estate, I've only ever occupied myself with the garden, and only to grow flowers and fruits. Now, the head gardener can do that better than me. On the other hand, on the *Olb.-I* and on Rhea, a woman might be necessary. I'm a qualified Red Cross nurse; I can sew; I..."

Blushing suddenly, she interrupted herself. She felt that the Nyctalope's eyes and mind were penetrating her, all the way to the utmost depths of her soul. For a brief instant, she was infinitely troubled, but with the consciousness of a happiness so great that she immediately regained her usual self-control and, sweeping away the possible explanations with a gesture, she concluded:

"The *Olb.-I* can carry eight people. Including me, there are presently only five of us. Three places are still available. Who will you chose, Monsieur Saint-Clair, among the people you know and are not here?"

"Pardon me," said the Nyctalope, with the utmost calm. "Even supposing that I were to agree to your participation in a voyage that you described just now as perhaps no more than a new kind of suicide, the authorization of your uncle and guardian is indispensable in any matter concerning you, for not only are you a minor, being only 20. In any case, Maxime d'Olbans is the sole master of everything here; nothing can be done without his approval."

"Well, Uncle?" said the young woman, immediately.

All the evidence suggested that the scientist had not expected the question of the choice of the interplanetary voyagers to be posed in such a way that his daughter would be involved in it. Focused on the planning of his endeavors, he had not taken much notice—or any notice at all—of the lives of those around him. For him, Véronique was still the little girl that he had taken in after the death of her parents. And now she was demanding to depart for the planet Rhea! He was dumbfounded. Wide-eyed and open-mouthed, he stared at his niece without being able to reply.

To a certain extent, Dr. Serres, Monsieur Lamurat and the notary shared his astonishment, and their facial expressions did not hide the fact. Outside the debate, since he had only been acquainted with Mademoiselle d'Olbans for a few hours, Gno Mitang remained impassive and observed the scene attentively. Quite calm and with a slight smile, Saint-Clair waited. And, as all eyes were on the young woman and her uncle, no one noticed the rapid, brutal and singularly expressive play of the features of the steward Fageat.

No one? Perhaps Gno Mitang...

From the moment when Véronique had manifested her desire and determination to take part in the voyage until she had pronounced in a firmly interrogative tone: "Well, Uncle?" Fageat's somber and coarse had become coarser and darker, but without any expression of surprise; then a violent anger, poorly restrained, rendered the steward's eyes, fixed on Saint-Clair but immediately turned away from him, full of hatred. On his knees, his large, strong hands clenched into solid fists. Long habituated to dissimulation and deception, however, the steward mastered his sentiments, and finally appeared, like all the others, to be possessed by nothing more than curious expectation as to what reply Monsieur d'Olbans would make.

In a silence untroubled by the slightest noise, that response was delayed for a full minute. It was as Saint-Clair, at least—who knew his old friend well—had anticipated.

"But you're insane, little girl!"

Véronique must also have anticipated that response, for she was not upset by it; she even uttered a brief laugh of affectionate indulgence, and immediately, replied, addressing Monsieur d'Olbans as "*tu*," as she sometimes did:

"But why, Uncle? Realize that I'm no longer a little girl, and you'll understand that my mind has learned from yours to be audacious. Given that you've conceived an interplanetary voyage and done everything possible to realize it, what's exorbitant about me, your brother's daughter, and thus of your own blood, finding it entirely natural to represent our family and our name in the voyage?

"Would you like an argument of a sentimental kind? Well, here it is: I know with total certainty that you love Monsieur Saint-Clair as much as me..."

"Oh!" exclaimed the scientist and the Nyctalope, simultaneously.

"Yes!" insisted the young woman, smiling. "You love each of us in a different manner, to be sure, but him as much as me. How, then, can you find it normal that Monsieur Saint-Clair should go, but abnormal that I should accompany him?

You're being illogical. And to conclude on another plane, by means of a final argument whose verity, force and irrefutability you can't deny: I'm less useful here than your housekeeper, Madame Gervais, or your steward, Monsieur Fageat, or your laboratory assistant, Monsieur Louze."

"Oh!" said Monsieur d'Olbans again, raising his open hands.

"Yes, Uncle, yes! And that's natural. You've always lived with your brain more than your heart. The excellent maintenance of your house, the perfect regulation of your estate, your physics and chemistry laboratories and your astronomical observatory: all of that is more important in your life than my existence and my boudoir-cum-library. I find that perfectly natural, and love you no less for it. But if you love me, you must understand me when I speak in accordance with my most ardent and most profound thoughts. And you must give my departure the approval that the scrupulous Nyctalope deems, rightly, to be absolutely indispensable."

Having said that, with emotional inflections in her voice, Véronique stood up, marched rapidly up to her uncle, put her hands on his shoulders, kissed him on both cheeks and, simultaneously calm and fervent, in a tone scarcely above a whisper, this time only speaking for him alone, said:

"Uncle, my dear Uncle, I beg you!"

The young woman's eyes, which only he could see, very close to his own spoke more eloquently than her lips. Maxime d'Olbans had been young; he had been loved; he had loved; he understood. Immediately disengaging Véronique's hands by grasping them in his own, and drawing her whole body toward him, he kissed her cheeks in his turn, and said, simply:

"All right, child; you can go."

Only then were the prefect Lamuarat, the physician Serres and the notary Blanquer able to express their tumultuous thoughts to one another and to Monsieur and Mademoiselle d'Olbans.

Vitto and Soca formed a group with the steward Fageat, who had not become their friend but whose vast technical knowledge gave rise to conversations as interesting as they were useful. Besides, in the course of the works that Fageat had directed, the two Corsicans had been very precious aides, by virtue of their qualities and because a certain authority devolved naturally upon them by virtue of their continual frequentation with their master, the Nyctalope.

It was soon evident to Soca and Vitto, however, that the engineer-steward did not pay a great deal of attention to the conversation that they struck up with him. His gaze went far less to his interlocutors than to Saint-Clair, who, with Gno Mitang, was leaning over a celestial map of large dimensions, spread out in the middle of a table.

Suddenly, his patience having evidently run out, Fageat said to the two Corsicans:

"Excuse me—it's absolutely necessary that I speak to Monsieur Saint-Clair, about a detail of the equipment of the *Olb.-1*... A very important detail..."

With no further politeness, he left them, went straight to Saint-Clair with his supple tread—which, whether fast or slow, had something feline about it. Artfully taking advantage of the fact that the Nyctalope and the Japanese were not talking at that moment, the steward immediately ventured, in a low voice:

"Monsieur..."

He was close beside Saint-Clair—who, having heard him, straightened up and turned his head. Immediately, Fageat, in a respectful attitude and with a matching expression, containing his voice but speaking but in a firm and deliberate tone, said:

"Monsieur, I'd like to talk to you in private."

Saint-Clair showed no surprise, although he was astonished by the unexpected request.

"Now?" he said, with a courteous half-smile.

"Yes, please."

"Shall we go into the smoking-room?"

"Yes, Monsieur—thank you."

From the beginning of that rapid and brief exchange, Gno Mitang had appeared still to be more interested in the map spread out before his eyes. With a rapid glance, however, he had first studied the steward's face and had then listened to the sound of his voice and the highly characteristic inflection of his elocution. And he said to himself: *A strange individual! Doubtless prey to a violent and profound passion, he forces himself to be calm and impassive; he won't always succeed— but his rude appearance and his voice, guttural and muffled at the same time, easily deceive. A valuable man, moreover, who would be, if he wished, a first-rate adviser and lieutenant, a perfect second in command...*

At that moment, Gno Mitang heard Saint-Clair say:

"Excuse me for a few moments, my friend..."

The Japanese merely made an acquiescent gesture with his right hand.

Between the large book-lined drawing-room where the meeting was taking place and the dining room of the Château des Pins, there was a relatively small smoking-room, fitted with low-set bookshelves freely offering their volumes to the hands of people sitting in the leather-upholstered armchairs with velvet cushions that were spread around the room. In the middle part of the room four low tables were aligned, but their feet were fitted with castors so that they could be moved around; they were laden with boxes of cigars and cigarettes, pots of tobacco, electric lighters and even, in amusing little racks, new pipes of every caliber and form, from which a guest might choose—for Monsieur d'Olbans gladly expended the laws and customs of hospitality.

Having entered the room, followed by Ariste Fageat, Saint-Clair headed for one of the two corners most distant from the doors of the drawing-room-cum-library and the dining room, which were facing one another. With a mechanical gesture he was already indicating an armchair prior to proffering the banal phrase: "Would you care to sit down?" but his gesture was interrupted and the ritual words were never pronounced. Remaining standing, facing the steward, Saint-Clair said, courteously but without any particular amiability:

"I'm listening, my dear Monsieur."

Fageat did not hesitate for a second. His hard eyes met Saint-Clair's incisive stare while he spoke—without interruption, for Saint-Clair, as a matter of rule and habit, always let his interlocutors spell out the whole of their thought.

"Monsieur, I did not permit myself to protest when you declared that I was not to take part in the interplanetary voyage for the reason that I am indispensable to Monsieur d'Olbans with regard to the estate of Les Pins. I though that it would be lacking in respect for you, and doubtless also for Monsieur d'Olbans, to begin a discussion that was, apparently at least, solely concerned with my person and my functions as a steward. First, I thank you for granting me this private interview—and I ask you to listen to the reasons why I believe I can solicit the honor of going with you in the *Olb.-I* to Rhea."

He paused, inclined his head slightly, straightened up again, and waited, his features very calm.

Again, Saint-Clair did not manifest any surprise—and again he simply said:

"I'm listening."

A trifle stiffly, with his head held high, his expressive eyes calm and coldly resolute, Fageat went on:

"Monsieur, it is not true—or, rather, it is no longer true—that I am indispensable to Monsieur d'Olbans to run the estate. The tenant of one of the largest farms, La Charmette, is an old farmer, still robust, named Père Martet; he has a son of thirty-two named Ludovic, married, intelligent and serious, who has studied at the École d'Agronomie. I have often recruited him as a deputy in the last two years, particularly in the last three months: I have educated him fully in my duties as steward of the Les Pins estate. Ludovic Martet is capable of replacing me. I can assure you that Monsieur d'Olbans would not lose by the substitution."

As Fageat paused, Saint-Clair made a gesture of acceptance and said:

"Fair enough; I have no reason to doubt your affirmation. So?"

"Well, Monsieur, although I am no longer indispensable to Monsieur d'Olbans, I believe I could be useful to you during the entire duration of the interplanetary voyage. I dare say, and I don't think that anyone would tell you otherwise, that my technical knowledge is various and profound; that I have courage, energy and character; that my health and physical vigor are intact; and finally, that I lack neither imagination nor ingenuity. On the other hand, by virtue of having collaborated on a daily basis, in a thousand ways, with the construction, equipment and provisioning of the *Olb.-I*, I know our interplanetary vehicle better than anyone, and the manipulation of all its mechanisms has no more secrets from me than from you. Excuse me, Monsieur, for seeming to be composing my eulogy in this manner: I have no misplaced pride, I assure you, much less imbecilic vanity—but I know myself. I know what I am worth, in spite of certain faults of my nature, which are not injurious in any way to the notion of my duty and the accomplishment of my work. Such as I am, I am therefore certain that I do not deserve to be excluded from the most extraordinary scientific and biological adventurer that humans have ever undertaken. Take me with you, Monsieur. I will be an associate whose services you will appreciate…and, I dare add, a man with whom Vitto and Soca will be happy to work."

Fageat fell silent, this time because he had nothing more to say. At that moment the Nyctalope was thinking: *The fellow certainly isn't stupid, to have concluded with that allusion to his good working relationship with my two faithful followers!* And he smiled.

At the sight of that smile, Ariste Fageat thought that his cause was won. His face relaxed, and his entire body appeared to lose its tension.

Saint-Clair's smile was brief however. To be sure, he had no precise prejudice against the man. He subscribed without hesitation to all the eulogies that Fageat had made of himself technically, so to speak; he held him in great esteem and judged him very valuable—but still he felt within himself, in Fageat's regard, a kind of indefinable repulsion, which was more than mere antipathy. What was it, then? Saint-Clair had never analyzed the sentiment—or only, perhaps, the impression—that had always, in confrontation with Monsieur d'Olbans' steward, put him in a state of mind that was translated as a slightly cold and distant attitude.

At that moment, head bowed, Saint-Clair analyzed himself—but saw nothing therein that really argued, in a serious manner, against Monsieur Fageat's unexpected request. On the other hand, it was evident to him that, in the course of the interplanetary voyage, the man might have a multiple and precious utility. The *Olb.-I* could carry eight passengers. Thus far only five had been designated, including Véronique. For such an adventure, four men was very few—not that it was necessary to have eight. Fageat would make a fifth of rare quality; why not recruit him? Why not?

Suddenly raising his head, Saint-Clair said:

"I admit that you can be replaced in the administration of the estate, but Monsieur d'Olbans special endeavor will not cease; you have been the technical director and the veritable lynch-pin of the work; there, Monsieur d'Olbans would miss you."

"No, Monsieur, no!" Fageat retorted, visibly satisfied that Saint-Clair was raising such an objection instead of replying with a definitive refusal.

"Why not?"

In a tone that was almost light, the steward replied:

"You know the engineer Desclosi, whom I took on as an assistant when the work began. You've seen him at work and you praised him to me one day yourself—a eulogy more merited than you thought, Monsieur. Well, Desclosi can replace me in the factory and the workshops. I have, moreover, prepared him, in the hope..."

"That's enough!" Saint-Clair interjected, swiftly.

He took a step forward, and offered his open hand, sincerely—which Ariste Fageat took in his own hard hand. There was a brief grip, and then, moving back slightly, Saint-Clair continued:

"I can admit to you now that I've often thought of taking you. I didn't decide in the affirmative for the reasons that I spelled out just now in the meeting and which I've just repeated to you—and which you have refuted pertinently. But there's one other thing..."

Again Saint-Clair moved back slightly, as if to get a better view of the man in his entirety, from his stout shoes to his short-cropped hair, and he went on gravely, almost severely:

"I don't like you, Monsieur."

The steward-engineer went white, started abruptly, and exclaimed:

"Oh! Monsieur!"

But the Nyctalope, not without an imperceptible smile of indulgent irony, continued:

"Monsieur Fageat, if I had not consented to work, throughout my life, with people who did not seem spontaneously sympathetic to me at first, I would not have done very much and I would have lived, I think, almost as an anachorite. In your case, moreover, it would be quite impossible for me to give you reasons for my antipathy in your regard: it's muted and vague, indeterminate not amenable to complete analysis— and credit me with the justice that I have never shown you anything but benevolent courtesy, and that I have always rendered justice, in private as in public, to your real and evident merits..."

"That's true, Monsieur," said Fageat, dully, with a sort of confusion, lowering his head slightly.

Serious again, Saint-Clair continued:

"Perhaps there's nothing between us but an opposition of physical nature, entirely material. The mind must overcome that, especially in such exceptional circumstances—for I have taken account in the last two months, and I admit it without hesitation, of the fact that you might indeed be extremely useful in the interplanetary voyage. I shall therefore take you, Monsieur... and I hope that the collaborator you will be will

47

make me forget that there is something vague and inexplicable within me that, in the ordinary circumstances of existence, would have prevented me from being your friend."

There was such grandeur in these words that Ariste Fageat, whatever his hidden agenda might be, could not help being moved by admiration and respect. Human beings are not as simple as certain philosophers claim, and Fageat was doubtless sincere in pronouncing, with his head held high, his gaze direct and his voice firm:

"Monsieur, with the full measure of my knowledge and strength, I swear to you that I will be the technical collaborator that you hope for in me."

With a flash of intuition, Saint-Clair thought: *Why did he add the word* technical? *Thus placed, the word seems to me to be restrictive.*

But the Nyctalope had always enjoyed playing with obscurely dangerous men and the most indeterminate perils, sure as he was of his own capacity eventually to dissipate the darkness and emerging into the light victorious. He therefore concluded, simply:

"Let's go back to the drawing room, Monsieur. I'll announce myself that I've changed my opinion in your regard, and I'll explain why."

Half an hour later, finding himself alone with his friend in the room that Mademoiselle d'Olbans had prepared for the eminent Japanese, Gno Mitang said to Saint-Clair with the affectionate familiarity that they manifested in private:

"Leo, perhaps you're right, in practical terms—you're certainly right, for your judgment is infallible—to take Ariste Fageat on the *Olb.-I*, but I have the impression that the man needs to be closely watched."

"I have that impression too," said the Nyctsalope, simply. "But do you know why?"

"No; in truth, no..."

"Me neither."

"Not yet, at least," added Gno.

"Agreed!"

And the two friends smiled, glad to establish that in confrontation with people and facts, even in indefinite matters, they had, as they had always had had, the same sagacious, audacious and prudent conception of the manner in which they needed to act.

Chapter III
The Departure

With regard to the essence of the extraordinary endeavors suddenly undertaken and rapidly completed in the wildest and most isolated part of Maxime d'Olbans' vast estate, secrecy had been carefully maintained.

To be sure, the regional newspapers had been actively curious; the Parisian press had been immediately alerted by its local correspondents, and had sent reporters—but the principal workshops had been strictly watched and the people who were party to the secret were not numerous. The journalists and the public, in consequence, new no more than the workers and manual laborers did. That could, in the final analysis, be summarized thus:

Monsieur d'Olbans is constructing a machine to venture into the stratosphere, as many scientists have done before him. He has an illustrious collaborator in the person of Monsieur Saint-Clair, a.k.a. the Nyctalope, who will be the pilot of the apparatus when it takes off from the ground toward the zenith.

The newspapers of France and the world, of course, wrote about it at much greater length, but they did not say any more than that.

Nevertheless, Messieurs d'Olbans and Saint-Clair had no intention of keeping the secret forever. On the contrary, they wanted the scientific community first, and then the general public, to be fully and accurately informed.

That is why, on August 27, 20 scientists and journalists, almost all resident in Paris, received by registered mail an invitation to go to the Château des Pins on August 29. Hospitality was assured until August 31. On the 29th, an "informative lecture" would be given to them by Monsieur d'Olbans; the bext day, they would witness "the departure of Monsieur Saint-Clair and others for an unprecedented voyage." The letter of invitation gave no further details, but it contained all the necessary directions for the guests to get to the Château des Pins easily, without error or delay, via Le Mans and Longpré (Sarthe).

There was, therefore, an influx of guests at the château on the afternoon of August 29. All the friends who had attended the final council meeting on August 30 were there, of course. Madame Gervais, the housekeeper, had a great deal to do, all the more so because the domestic staff of the château had had to be augmented by the recruitment of two head waiters, four valets and four chambermaids, hired in Le Mans, Tours and even Paris. The Prefect of Le Mans had lent them his own cook.

Véronique, of course, had nothing to do with all that. On her uncle's orders, she was resting, having nothing else to do except to pack, with the aid of her own chambermaid, the garments and other small objects that, in accordance with Saint-Clair's advice, she would take to Rhea. It was light luggage, for the interplanetary voyagers could not clutter up the *Olb.-I* with their personal baggage.

Specially-designed and expertly-fabricated clothing, uniform although not all of the same height and girth, formed part of what Monsieur Fageat had loaded into the "vehicle" under the accounting denomination of "general provisions." Included therein was enough to eat and drink for a long time; clothing for the most various temperatures; gifts to offer as gestures of peace; and weapons in case of armed hostility. Saint-Clair had drawn up the list of al that, all of which had to be bought or manufactured to order, and the list had been the subject of much examination, calculation and discussion between the Nyctalope, Monsieur d'Olbans, Soca and Vitto.

The August 29 lecture filled the entire audience with admiring astonishment. Monsieur d'Olbans simply told the story of the discovery and fabrication of the new metal Z-4, performed a demonstration of the attraction of the planet Rhea upon that metal, listed the decisions made and the works accomplished, and, finally, gave a clear explanation of the logical hypotheses whose formulation science permitted regarding the possibilities of the interplanetary voyage and a sojourn on Rhea by human beings.

Hardly anyone at the château and in the workshops got any sleep on the night of August 29.

On the final day, the morning was devoted to visits by small groups to the interplanetary vehicle, the *Olb.-I*, and the admiring astonishment of all the visitors only increased. What commentaries! What doubts! What certainties! What apprehensions and hopes!

Finally, at 4 p.m.on August 30, it was the moment for farewells—intimate to begin with, between family and friends, in Monsieur d'Olbans; book-lined drawing room. Véronique, who was inwardly exultant with joy, had the strength to discipline her emotion, holding back the tears that sprang up in her eyes. The Nyctalope and the scientist embraced one another. On the part of His Excellency Gno Mitang the farewells were a trifle more ceremonious; Ariste Fageat's were cordial; those of the exuberant Soca and Vitto warm, and even cheerful.

Afterwards, in the main courtyard of the château, the seven interplanetary voyagers—for, with Saint-Clair's permission, the two Corsicans had recruited Jean Margot a highly-experienced, skillful, ingenious and a trifle mischievous young mechanic, also endowed with courage and a cool head, who had come from Paris when the work began and whose work all the bosses had been able to judge—shook hundreds of hands, responding with as many emotional smiles.

Then a kind of procession formed, which set off on that beautiful summer afternoon through the shady woods, toward the henceforth-famous Gorse Hill, where a huge crowd had assembled, kept in order and at an adequate distance by several brigades of gendarmes mobilized for that purpose by the prefect of Le Mans.

The *Olb.-I* was a parallelepiped 20 meters long by five broad, with double walls of aluminum. Its front, or anterior face, had a third lining made entirely of Z-4; 40 exterior panels formed of lead sheets wedged between two asbestos plates, movable electronically and also by means of a system of manual controls, covered that front and were able to uncover it in proportion to the quantity of attractive Rhean force that he interplanetary voyagers judged it appropriate to utilize.

The rear, or posterior face, was entirely given over to a projector of unprecedented power. As for the interior of the *Olb.-I*, between the foe and aft machine-rooms there was a living-space 15 meters in length, with four private cabins, crew-quarters with four bunks, a watch- and work-room that was also a dining-room, a kitchen-cum-parlor, and, finally, the indispensable commodities. From one end to the other, under a floor with six trap-doors, ran a succession of eight storage compartments, containing clothing, provisions, various tools, items of exchange, useful materials, weapons and ammunition: everything that seven human beings would need to live for a year, subject to rationing—on condition, of course, that Rhea furnished the liquid element: drinkable water. The astronomers had been unanimous in affirming that there were rain-clouds in the atmospheric layer surrounding the newly-discovered planet.

Thus, even if the pessimistic hypothesis of the total absence on Rhea of matter comestible by humans were to be realized, the Terrans were certain of having sufficient nourishment until the date, scientifically calculated and determined, of their possible return to Earth.

It was at 5:30 p.m. on that August 30, that—all the farewells having been concluded, in the midst of immense general emotion—the interplanetary voyagers sealed themselves into the *Olb.-I*.

Véronique d'Olbans was the first to climb the mobile staircase; Gno Mitang followed her; then Vitto, Soca and Jean Margot, and finally Ariste Fageat and LeoSaint-Clair.

After a final salute with his right hand, the Nyctalope drew the double aluminum door toward him and the lock immediately sealed it hermetically. The mobile staircase folded up automatically and was enclosed underneath the doorway in the rectangular compartment designed to accommodate it.

Henceforth, the seven Terrans would be separated from the terrestrial world for at least a year.

For several days they had been so thoroughly prepared for that separation, and had lived that supreme moment in advance so often, that all the emotion of the farewells had died away in each of them at the moment when the passed from the last step into the vehicle that was about to transport them through the thousands of leagues of the stratosphere—which is to say, the empty space that separated the terrestrial atmosphere from the Rhean atmosphere.

In the vehicle, each of them had an allotted place for the departure: Véronique and Vitto in the kitchen and the watch-and work-room that was also the dining room; Saint-Clair and Gno Mitang in the forward machine-room, Soca being their assistant mechanic; Fageat and Margot in the compartmentalized store-rooms, whose trap-doors were open—for it was important to observe the comportment of everything, everywhere within the vehicle, for at least the first half-hour of the voyage—which, according to Maxime d'Olbans' calculations, ought to have a duration of approximately five hundred hours at a mean velocity of 60 kilometers a minute.

The first word pronounced aboard the *Olb.-I* was uttered by Saint-Clair:

"Ready?"

He had his hand on the lever controlling the electrical mechanism of the obstructive panels. The lever turned through the graduated 40-degree arc of a circle; every degree corresponded to one of the 40 panels that covered, then would uncover and eventually recover the forward sections of the *Olb.-I*, each composed of a continuous surface of Z-4. The Nyctalope and the astronomer had calculated that, for the take-off of the heavy vehicle and its departure into space, it would be sufficient to open 20 of the 40 panels.

A short distance away from Saint-Clair, Gno Mitang was monitoring the control apparatus; the latter would reveal either the efficient operation of the various mechanisms activated or any possible perturbation. In reply to Saint-Clair's query, the Japanese replied:

"Ready."

It was a violently emotional moment! There was a silence, during which everyone was attentive. Hearts beat rapidly; faces were pale. On the threshold of the partition separating the machine-room from the central compartment, Véronique and Vitto were standing; in the cabin itself, Fageat and Margot were only showing the upper parts of their body, for they were half-hidden in the depths of the hold. As for Soca, the mechanic, he was standing two paces behind his two bosses, ready to leap into action in the event of receiving a necessarily-brief order that would have to be carried out instantly.

Suddenly, the Nyctalope said:

"We're off."

And his right hand rapidly pulled the lever, in such a way as to bring the odd-numbered obstructive panels—one to 39—into play.

There was no perceptible sound, and scarcely any shock, for the *Olb.-I* had been placed on a long 100-meter slipway, carefully greased, in such a way that no friction, however brutal it might be, could produce any. They could not see anything outside because, for the sake of prudence—no one knew what reaction might take place with matter in such novel conjectures—the portholes, numbering 20, that had been set at intervals along the vehicle, to the right and left, were closed.

Convinced that the departure had taken place, Saint-Clair said then:

"Going to maximum velocity."

With the same gesture as before, he moved the lever, this time applying the heel to the electrical contacts bearing the even numbers, from two to 40.

While the seven voyagers remained silent and motionless, one, two, three and the four minutes went by, marked by the large chronometer visible from everywhere in the control-room.

Then, in his delicate and extraordinarily calm voice, Gno Mitang said, with a slight smile primarily perceptible in his eyes:

"If all's going well, we're 300 kilometers from Gorse Hill."

"Yes," said Saint-Clair. Turning to Soca, he added, with a slight smile: "Open the portholes."

"On both sides?" the Corsican queried.

"Yes."

Soca started on the right, unscrewing the locking system of the aluminum portholes; soon, six crystal lenses, three to the right and three to the left, were uncovered. Those lenses, immensely thick, could support enormous pressures and the most violent shocks.

Moved by the same impulse, Saint-Clair, Gno Mitang, Soca, Véronique, Vitto, Fageat and Margot ran to the portholes. Avidly, they looked outside. They saw nothing but darkness, peppered with stars; that was perfectly natural, for the terrestrial atmosphere in only 64 kilometers thick, and the *Olb.-I* had already emerged from it.

On the other hand, they had neither the sensation nor the impression of any movement; they could have believed—and it required an effort of thought not to believe it—that they were in a vehicle that was completely motionless; no movement betrayed its progress through space. The displacement, rapid as it was, could not produce any sensible effect on the organism while the mass of air in which the human body is located was displaced with it. No inhabitant of the Earth perceives the velocity of the globe, which is traveling through space, with its layer of air, at 90,000 kilometers an hour. Movement in those conditions still seems to be immobility.

All the voyagers knew that, for they had been well instructed as to the special conditions in which their voyage would be accomplished. Nevertheless, they could not help feeling a certain astonishment. One does not realize immediately that one is traveling at a fantastic speed when ne feels that one is motionless and sees everything motionless around one.

Finally, the silence and stillness were broken. Saint-Clair said:

"Open the forward portholes, Soca."

In fact, accommodated within the mass of the Z-4 that formed the front of the *Olb.-I* were two portholes. They were not covered by movable lead panels but strong aluminum shields. By means of an admirably-designed mechanism, the external shield opened when the internal shield as opened. The crystal windows of these portholes were even thicker than those of the lateral portholes. One of them—the one on the right—was a magnifying lens analogous to the lenses of he most powerful telescopes, with the consequence that, because the *Olb.-I* was flying directly toward Rhea, the travelers could see the planet as it appeared to the naked eye through the porthole on the left without any diminution of distance, but through the porthole on the right they could see the planet greatly magnified, enabling them to determine the details of its structure in advance.

Then the seven voyagers, grouped at the forward porthole on the left, had the impression that they were traveling through space—and impression produced by the sight of Rhea, visibly increasing in size from one second to the next.

And after that, nothing happened—nothing at all.

It might be difficult to imagine that the most extraordinary voyage that humans had ever undertaken would be devoid of any incident, and even, strictly speaking, anything picturesque.

Launched further and further way from the Earth toward Rhea by virtue of the attraction exerted by that planet on the *Olb.-I*, the enormous vehicle progressed through space in a straight line, without any noise or shock. The woman and the men that it was transporting could not see anything through the lateral portholes any other scenery than the infinity of starry space. Moreover, the displacement was so rapid that the stars always seemed to be the same. Through the porthole, however, one could see Rhea gradually increasing in size, with the consequence that it was the only spectacle to which the seven occupants of the *Olb.-I* sought out with a passionate avidity. They all assembled in the control room, and they passed alternately from the porthole on the left to the one on the right, the first normal, the second magnifying. In the latter, the planet appeared increasingly similar to what one might imagine that the Earth would be if it were seen from hundreds of leagues away: mountains, plains, seas—or, rather, extents that must be liquid mass similar to our seas and oceans.

"What's curious," Véronique said, suddenly, "is the color. Everything on Rhea is yellow, an increasingly bright yellow—the color of buttercups, for example."

"Indeed," said Gno Mitang.

For the next quarter of an hour, no words were pronounced. Everyone's thoughts were simultaneously perplexed and tumultuous. They did not know what to say because there was too much to say. A thousand hypotheses were seething in their minds. Saint-Clair, however, whose practicality was never abolished no matter how extravagant the circumstances were, turned his back on the forward portholes, looking from left to right at Véronique and his companions and said, with a smile:

"I believe, Véronique, that it would be a good idea to have a meal; I'm hungry."

"That's true," said the young woman, laughing. "I wasn't thinking about that any longer."

She ran toward the central compartment, which served simultaneously as a work-room, a meeting-room and a dining-room. She and Vitto had already laid the table immediately after departure; food brought from Monsieur d'Olbans château made up a cold meal. That evening, they drank the champagne that Saint-Clair, a connoisseur of good wines, had selected specially. The seats were stools, both light and solid. They each took their places, three on one side, three on the other and Véronique at the end of the table. Vitto and Soca got up from time to time to serve. And that was the first meal that he voyagers had in the spacious and comfortable vehicle, which was carrying them through the stratosphere at a velocity of a kilometer a second, 60 kilometers a minute, 3600 kilometers an hour.

The atmosphere in the vehicle was maintained by an apparatus that produced oxygen and absorbed carbon dioxide; another electrical apparatus maintained a constant temperature of eighteen degrees. If the voyage had to be prolonged for several days more, the air apparatus would not be sufficient to regenerate the atmosphere constantly; it would be necessary to bring another apparatus into play, more powerful, more productive and more absorptive, which was being kept in reserve in case the atmosphere of Rhea was not completely suited to human lungs and it proved quite impossible to adapt themselves to it.

The diners had a keen appetite, although they had lunched well at the Château d'Olbans, because their vital machinery had been singularly excited, without their being conscious of it. They were exceptionally cheerful; the most innocent words made them laugh, and even Fageat, the somber and taciturn Ariste Fageat, became a merry companion. Gno Mitang, who was watching him carefully, did not catch a glimpse of the slightest expression that was in any way suspicious.

Thus they arrived sat the moment when 12 silvery chimes were sounded by the large chronometer in the control-room.

"Midnight!" exclaimed Véronique. And without any other motive she burst out laughing. She got up, went into the control-room and went to stand before the magnifying lens.

"Oh!" she exclaimed. "We're going to crash."

But Saint-Clair, who had immediately followed her, placed his hand gently on her shoulder and said:

"No—that's the effect of the telescopic lens. Come to the other porthole."

Gno Mitang, Fageat, Vitto, Soca and Margot were behind them, and they all contemplated Rhea, sometimes with the naked eyes and sometimes through the magnifying lens.

Gradually, however, fatigue crept up on them, and in the end, they could not resist it. Saint-Clair declared that he would remain on watch for two hours, and would then wake up Gno Mitang, who, in his turn, would wake Soca, who would be replaced by Vitto. The watch rota having thus been established for the next eight hours, everyone went either to their cabin or their couchette. And with the Nyctalope alone staying up, the *Olb.-I* continued to hurtle toward the planet, which was now dark, almost invisible, for it was no longer receiving the direct rays of the Sun, hidden from it behind the Earth.

Chapter IV
The Arrival

LeoSaint-Clair was endowed with a powerful and vivid imagination, but he knew how to discipline it. He did not repress its leaps—no, he waited for each one to complete its entire trajectory and extend all its ramifications. Then he submitted it to cold, lucid and severe criticism. That gave him the advantage of not living in his illusions, while conjecturing logically with regard to the future. Thus he was generally able to regulate his conduct in advance, while being ready to adapt, in matters of detail, to actual events as they unfolded.

During the two hours of his watch, while Rhea grew in size before him by the minute, bathed in a sort of nebulous obscurity, but nevertheless sufficiently visible for him to observe it—for the Nyctalope, of course, darkness did not exist, and he had taken care to put out all the electric lamps in the control room—Saint-Clair amused himself by imagining rationally what conditions might be like for Earthly humans on the alien world.

Like the body, the mind has its sensualities, perhaps more intense and certainly more durable. It is no exaggeration to say that, during those two hours, LeoSaint-Clair experienced the most intense mental sensualities of his life.

And it was as if he were gripped by vertigo when, the hour having chimed that brought him back to immediate contingencies, he went to wake Gno Mitang.

"Nothing to declare," he told him. "Everything is normal; everything is as Maxime d'Olbans and I anticipated."

"Very good," said the Japanese.

Arranged on both sides of the corridor that linked the central chamber to the crew quarters, placed in front of the parlor and kitchen, the four cabins resembled the compartments of a railways sleeping-car, each having only one bunk. The strict necessities were provided there to dress and wash, and also to create a personal ambiance with sections on the wall to which photographs or small pictures could be attached, bookshelves, a small table, a linen-cupboard and a minuscule but adequate wardrobe.

On the starboard side of the *Olb.-I* were Saint-Clair's cabin and that of Véronique d'Olbans; on the port side, those of Gno Mitang and Ariste Fageat. As for the crew-quarters, it contained, with their accessories, four comfortable hammocks, three of which were employed by Vitto, Soca and Jean Margot, the fourth remaining rolled up and suspended from a stout iron ring in the ceiling.

Like his companions, Saint-Clair was tired, for no one in Monsieur d'Olbans' château had got much sleep in the last few days. Scarcely had he lain down on his bunk in his pajamas than he fell into a calm and profound sleep—and a long one! When every voyager except Véronique had taken a turn on watch, Saint-Clair was only woken up, by Vitto, ten hours after going to sleep. It was the kind of child-like sleep, perfectly restful and reparative, on emergence from which a healthy man, whatever his age, feels 20 years younger.

"August 31, noon," he pronounced, looking at his wrist-watch as soon as his eyes were open.

Formally, Vitto announced:

"Monsieur, Mademoiselle d'Olbans reminds you that lunch will be served at 12:30 a.m."

"Very good. Anything new?"

"Nothing, Monsieur. The voyage is continuing without any shock. We're beginning to see the relief of the hemisphere that Rhea is presenting to us. It's like the Earth, except that there are enormous vapors in the depths."

"You're unusually loquacious today, Vitto!" said Saint-Clair, smiling.

"Excuse me, Monsieur," said the Corsican, humbly—who was, indeed, ordinarily taciturn and given to monosyllabic speech. "I believe it results from the air apparatus giving off too much oxygen. It's intoxicating. Monsieur Fageat agrees with me; he's in the process of regulating the apparatus."

"Good. Let me get dressed—I'll be there in a quarter of an hour."

Fifteen minutes later, Saint-Clair came into the central compartment.

"Bonjour, Véronique!" he said, softly.

The young woman, alone for the moment, was arranging some magnificent roses in a vase on the table, still damp as if from morning dew, which seemed only to have been picked a few minutes before. Swiftly, she turned round, dropping the flowers, smiling and blushing, so visibly happy that LeoSaint-Clair immediately felt a pang of joy.

With a simultaneous movement, they extended their hands, and, Saint-Clair retaining Véronique's in his, they looked at one another, at first without speaking, for a moment, during which their fluids interpenetrated, revealing to each of them their own thoughts and the other's. Then the man, opening his hand nervously, said:

"Did you sleep well during that first interplanetary night, Véronique?"

The young woman withdrew her tremulous fingers.

"Very well—but that's not surprising. So much emotion before and after the departure from Earth! I couldn't do any more. I slept like a stone. What about you?"

"Like a rock."

After these banal words they no longer dared look at one another. They were afraid of pronouncing other words; they felt confusedly that neither the time nor the place was appropriate.

Turning away slightly, Véronique said:

"Do you like my flowers? They have a dawn-like freshness, don't they? That's thanks to Vitto; he had the idea of putting the freshest of the hundred roses I brought in buckets full of water at the back of the rearmost store-room. By the way, will we find flowers on Rhea? That's a question I should have asked my uncle."

63

She burst out laughing.

Excess oxygen, thought Saint-Clair—and he laughed too, before replying:

"Your uncle would have told you that it's possible."

"Is that all?" said Véronique, shrugging her shoulders. "That wouldn't have been a reply, for everything's possible."

Again the man looked directly at the young woman, and said, gravely:

"Yes, everything's possible... everything... since you're here with me."

"And for you, Leo," she said simply.

Radiant, he opened his arms. Smiling and suddenly pale, she was already launching herself into them—but a door opened and Fageat appeared, saying, immediately:

"Monsieur! His Excellency is asking for you. The planet..."

"I'm coming," Saint-Clair cut in.

He walked rapidly. The engineer stood aside to let him pass, and followed him immediately, after enveloping Mademoiselle d'Olbans with a strange gaze. She had immediately got a grip on herself, and was leaning toward the roses, reaching out her hands as if to rearrange them.

"Bonjour, Saint-Clair!" said Gno Mitang. "Are you well?"

"Entirely. You too, from what I can see."

"Yes."

Addressing the engineer, however, who was standing two paces behind the Nyctalope, the Japanese added, smiling:

"Monsieur Fageat, I heard you say 'His Excellency' in referring to me. You ought, in future, to say simply 'Monsieur Mitang.' Only one of us, henceforth, has any right to a title, and that is Monsieur Saint-Clair. That title is 'Captain' or 'Boss,' as you please."

Everyone was there to hear: Vitto, Soca, Margot and also Véronique, who was coming into the control room from the central chamber at that moment.

Immediately, Gno Mitang continued:

"Saint-Clair, look at the planet through the telescopic porthole. Something's happening there. I've been wondering for a quarter of an hour what it might signify."

Because of the magnifying power of the enormous telescopic lens, only a small part of Rhea could be seen through the porthole. That region appeared to be wooded, with numerous valleys, at least so far as it was possible to form an idea of the new world based on the terrestrial knowledge to which human are accustomed. To the eyes of Saint-Clair and his companions, those valleys and woods were appearing and disappearing alternately, as perfectly opaque white vapors formed and quickly dissipated again.

"The strangest thing," said the Nyctalope, "is that the vapors seem to be springing from the ground of the planet, sometimes here, sometimes there, as if by some unknown hazard."

"Yes," said Gno Mitang. "And what is striking is that they're stirred up, dissipated and annihilated immediately after their eruption and their cloudy expansion in the atmosphere; there must be a wind—a regular and violent wind, which only blows at a certain height above the ground of Rhea."

"It puts one in mind of geysers," said Fageat, in a timidly reserved tone.

"Exactly!" Saint-Clair approved. "But geysers of which one can't see the source—the orifice—and which erupt here and there, I repeat, according to some unknown hazard... or law?"

There was a pause.

Suddenly, Véroniqe said:

"How far away are we from the planet?"

It was Gno Mitang who replied, with an affectionate smile:

"We've been flying toward Rhea since 6 p.m. yesterday at a speed of 3600 kilometers per second. It's 12:30 a.m. We're therefore in the 19th hour of our journey; we have about 68,400 kilometers behind us. Rhea being 380,000 kilo-

65

meters from the Earth, 311,600 kilometers therefore remain for us to travel. In consequence, if nothing unexpected occurs, our voyage will last about another 86 hours."

A few minutes after these words, at 12:36 a.m. exactly, while they were observing the vaporous phenomena of Rhea, silently and meditatively, the interplanetary voyagers began to feel the effects of their progressive entry into a world that was not that of their native Earth. Was that because the air-purification apparatus aboard the *Olb.-I* was poorly regulated?

First the propensity to hilarity, already observed, increased to the point at which they burst out laughing for no apparent reason. At the same time they entered into a sort of unconsciousness that soon rendered them inapt for observation, reflection and the logical extrapolation of their actions. Then their bodies became light, to the point that they seemed to be floating in the air, while, the center of gravity being displaced, they and all the objects around them—all the mobile objects, at least—were on the point of falling and making contact, no longer with the floor of their vehicle but with the forward partition-wall. That caused a material disorder that increased the confusion of their minds.

They ate and drank that day while laughing and catching dishes and bottle in mind-air that flew from the table as if by some marvelous conjuring trick. That was their last meal, and also their final moments of consciousness. Perhaps they had fallen into a kind of slumber?

Slumber or something else, that state lasted for a number of hours that they did not think of calculating when they "awoke."

Véronique was the first to benefit from that return to life and mobility—perhaps because she was the youngest, because she had an entire physical organism that was newer, healthier and more intact than that of each of her traveling companions.

Shortly after she acquired that new consciousness of existence, the young woman had the sensation of a heavy weight on her legs and her left shoulder. She opened her eyes. To begin with, she saw that everything around her was bathed by a white, limpid but slightly nebulous light, and that everything was in a fantastic state of disorder.

She was lying on her back across the bodies of Vitto and Soca, which were lying side by side. To her left, Saint-Clair was stretched out, his head weighing on her shoulder. The weight she had on her legs was Gno Mitang's torso. Finally, to her right, their arms and legs entangled, were Monsieur Fageat and Jean Margot.

All seven had for a "bed" one of the forward portholes of the *Olb.-I*: the telescopic porthole.

Mademoiselle d'Olbans required a few minutes to take account of all that. Her amazement was great—but at the same time, her intelligence was reassured, for she experienced, by virtue of her observations themselves, an increasing mental lucidity.

The first movement she attempted was to free her legs, which she disengaged easily. By means of the second she wanted to liberate her left shoulder, but first she turned her head in order to look at Saint-Clair again. She had never seen the man's face asleep: a fine and energetic visage, which age had not yet begun to wither, and to which the state of sleep gave a juvenile serenity.

Véronique had a womanly thought then; with a swift glance around she reassured herself that she really was awake. Then, leaning sideways, she placed her lips gently on Saint-Clair's. In the first loving kiss that she had ever given to a man, the young woman experienced a great disturbance. She indulged herself, eyes closed. She savored the warm softness, the fleshy firmness of the man's immobile lips. She thought about the kiss that she would one day—she was convinced of it!—receive from those lips. And she drew away, shivering, slid sideways so as no longer to be on top of the bodies of Soca and Vitto, and finally rose to her feet

She was standing with her feet on the crystal of the porthole. Around the six men felled, in strange positions, by the enigmatic sleep were all the mobile objects contained in the vehicle, whose doors were open, spread out and heaped up pell-mell, including broken plates and glasses. The left-hand porthole was completely covered by them, obstructed...

Surprised and striving to understand, Véronique said to herself: *Everything here is subject to the attraction of Rhea. Everything is "falling" toward it, by virtue of what we call on Earth "The law of gravity."*

Thinking about Rhea in this fashion, she lowered her head toward the porthole.

"My God!" she cried. "We're falling!"

Her blood froze. All she could see was the ground—that of the planet Rhea, no doubt—approaching with vertiginous rapidity. The sensation of falling was given to hr be that vision, that perception. She was afraid.

"Leo! Leo!" she shouted.

It was not Saint-Clair who responded, but Jean Margot. The young man had woken up at the moment when Mademoiselle d'Olbans had gotten to her feet. His mind being both keen and cool, he had recovered consciousness quickly. Knowledgeable, he understood immediately the significance of what he was seeing. On all fours, he disengaged the handles and wheels controlling the Z-4 panels and the system for deadening the landing from human bodies and various objects. He heard the young woman's "My God! We're falling!" and then the appeal "Leo! Leo!" With a firm voice that was also joyful, he said:

"Don't be afraid, Mademoiselle! The voyage is over. We're arriving. We'll land softly."

Seven, eight, ten and fifteen minutes later, when Saint-Clair, Soca and Vitto, Gno Mitang and, finally, Ariste Fageat came round, the *Olb.-I* was immobile, positioned the right way up without any apparent damage on bright gray ground bristling with pale yellow bushes. All the portholes were sealed, had their shutters open; they could see outside, but the exterior air was not coming in. The internal atmosphere was breathable, although heavy, with a faint reek of spoiled fruits and spilled wine.

The gilded rays of the sun, full of dancing dust-particles, entering through the starboard portholes, were traversing the vehicle.

Then the profound silence was broken by Saint-Clair.

"September 4, 9 a.m. Five hours later than the time anticipated by Maxime d'Olbans, we've arrived on Rhea."

Chapter V
The First Day

To see, first of all, to see the new world on which, it was true—really, incontestably true—that they had landed, as easily, in sum, as an airplane departed from Lille lands at Bordeaux…!

To see, first of all, to see…!

To the right and the left in the vehicle, in front of the portholes, the seven Terrans stood still. Here, Véronique between Saint-Clair and Gno Mitang; there, Vitto and Soca; on the other side, each alone at a porthole, Ariste Fageat and Jean Margot.

The *Olb.-1* was correctly posed on its take-off and landing frame, almost in the center of a clearing which was about the size of the Place de la Concorde in Paris.

Where the ground was bare, it seemed to be composed of fine sand, bright gray in color. In places it was covered with bushes of uniform height—about a meter—which were reminiscent of holly in their nature and form, but whose branches and foliage were pale yellow. Around its entire perimeter the clearing was enclosed by a forest whose trees, all similar, must have been about 20 meters high, reminiscent of terrestrial poplars but more liberally furnished with branches, also pale yellow in color. They were widely spaced and it was possible to see a long way beneath their crowns. Between the rounded trunks were bushes similar to those in the clearing.

Animal life was manifest in the form of birds—bizarre birds, with long cigar-shaped bodies, with long beaks like sword-blades and short square wings, entirely snow-white. They were flying from tree to tree with single gliding leaps, which gave an impression of extraordinary lightness.

Again, Saint-Clair was the first of the Terrans to speak.

"With regard to the possibility of the existence of life on Rhea," he said, "Monsieur d'Olbans' principal hypothesis is verified: there is an atmosphere here sufficiently analogous to that of the Earth, since there are plants, trees and animals. But are there beings more or les analogous to humans?"

"We'll soon find out," said Gno Mitang. "We only have to go out."

"Yes, but not without taking certain precautions."

"Naturally."

The precautions had been anticipated. Saint-Clair gave instructions:

"Fageat, Margot—open the atmospheric intercommunication valves."

Monsieur d'Olbans had anticipated that Rhean air, even if it were respirable by Terrans, might not have the same composition and density as Terran air. According to his observations and calculations, Rhean air ought to be much lighter and subtle—like that, for instance, found on Earth in the highest mountain regions. By opening in a progressive manner the valves constructed for that purpose and fitted at various places in the *Olb.-1*, the interior air could be expelled and the external air let into the vehicle. That aeration would be carried out slowly and prudently, easily increased or diminished, in such a way that the Terrans' lungs could become accustomed to Rhean air without any mishap.

Obedient to Saint-Clair, Fageat on one side and Margot on the other operated the clockwork mechanisms controlling the graduated opening of the valves—and they waited in silence, while continuing to stare, with a kind of wonder, at the bright gray ground, the pale yellow trees and the long white birds perched here and there or flying from branch to branch.

It was soon evident that the air in the vehicle was being purified, becoming lighter and refreshed, and also—the first strange sensation given by the unknown world—perfumed. That, in particular, was so sensible that Véronique, cheerful and emotional at the same time, exclaimed:

"It smells like jasmine!" Shortly afterwards she added: "Very strong jasmine, as in the gardens of Cannes, Nice and Menton. It's delicious!"

It was, indeed, delicious, but more because of the lightness of the air than its perfume.

"Pay attention to our movements!" said Gno Mitang, suddenly.

"Why?" asked Véronique, astonished because she could not remember any of what her uncle, on Earth, had conjectured with regard to the possible conditions of human life on Rhea.

Smiling, the Japanese replied:

"Because on Rhea, whose mass is only a sixth of Earthly mass, its diameter being five times smaller, our weight is only a sixth of what it is on Earth."

"So I only weigh 11 kilos instead of 66?" said Soca.

"Yes, and I repeat: pay attention! As our muscles and limbs are used to making efforts in accordance with our terrestrial weight, the result of that effort on Rhea will be six times greater. One stride will therefore launch us the distance of six; a three-meter jump will be a leap of 18. And the rapidity of our transit will, in the same way, be six times greater than what it was on Earth."

"That will be amusing!" said Véronique.

"But it might be dangerous. We need to think about our slightest movements, until we've adapted our efforts to our intentions—for a badly-calculated bound might send the imprudent jumper to fracture his skull against a tree-trunk."

Everyone laughed—and at the same time, everyone took account of the fact that Rhean air, undoubtedly richer in oxygen than terrestrial air, rendered human beings hilarious.

"That also we must remedy by an effort of will," said Saint-Clair. "For if, as is probable, Rhea is populated by intelligent beings, more or less analogous to the human species, can you imagine us bursting into laughter in front of them, continually and inappropriately?"

"Unless they…" objected Gno Mitang.

"Yes, unless they…" repeated Véronique. She laughed—and everyone laughed again, irresistibly.

It was then that they experienced for the first time the disequilibrium between the forceful effect of bringing their muscles into play and the relative weight of their bodies.

Abruptly, the light coming in from outside changed its hue; it was slightly milky and sunlit, but suddenly became nebulous and devoid of radiance, as went one finds oneself on an Earthly mountain, in morning mist. A few minutes before, while Gno, Saint-Clair and Véronique were talking, everyone had turned away from the portholes and mechanically gathered in the middle of the vehicle. At the abrupt change in the tone of the light, they turned round, and, still mechanically, moved toward the portholes—but the movements they made, to the right or the left, threw them violently against the portholes, into which they bumped, either a forehead, a breast or a shoulder, with such brutality that they cried out in pain.

There were a few second of amazement; then Gno Mitang said:

"You see? My warning was reasonable."

"Indeed," said Véronique, rubbing her breasts, which had collided with the hard crystal.

Then, prudently immobile, they looked out again. Above the forest trees, the swollen mass of a vast cloud was passing, which absorbed the rays of sunlight and only diffused them as a dull and uniform light. A furious wind was stirring the cloud, but did not affect the leafy crowns of the trees, which remained perfectly still. But it was only temporary. The strange cloud suddenly presented its last enormous swirls, and then, as before, there was blue sky, rays of sunlight and bright light, slightly milky, between the trees, on the ground and inside the *Olb.-I.*

Almost immediately, Ariste Fageat's voice was heard. The engineer said:

"The external air has completely replaced the air we were breathing before the valves were opened."

There was obviously nothing comical about that; even so, the somber Fageat burst out laughing. Conscious and determined, however, he suppressed the hilarity and cut off the laughter abruptly. Like him, everyone else restrained them-selves—and it was thus that the seven Terrans began to adapt to Rhean conditions of life.

Saint-Clair decided then that they should not wait any longer before going out of the *Olb-I*. They were breathing very well, save for a slight constant oppression, which became more sensible from time to time, inciting deeper, longer and more profound aspirations. And they felt light: as light as in dreams in which one has wings and can fly from hill to hill.

All seven were impatient to get out; none of them was hiding that impatience—but they were all reasonable, includ-ing Véronique, who realized no less than the six men how prodigiously solemn the moment was: the moment when, for the first time since the birth of the human species on Earth, within the infinite system of the cosmos, human beings, hav-ing escaped the atmosphere of their native planet, were about to try to live on the surface and in the air of another.[3]

Briefly, Saint-Clair gave his orders. They had, in case, been anticipated, for the present eventuality had often been envisaged in all its details in the course of conversations held in Monsieur d'Olbans' laboratory and smoking-room.

Each of the seven voyagers, having reached their goal, was comfortably dressed according to hypothetical expecta-tions, whose realization nothing so far seen on Rhea gave any reason to doubt. The vestments were made of sturdy fabric, with short trousers, collars that freed the neck, sufficiently ample to give the body and the limbs the greatest possible lib-erty of movement. Gaiters in strong fabric guaranteed against thorny bushes; gloves of solid and supple hide and colonial helmets with neck-flaps completed the costume. For weapons, they had short-barreled rifles, revolvers, hatchets and daggers, plus canes with curved handles and iron tips. For that first sor-

---

[3] Obviously, memories of the defunct Mars colony have now faded.

tie, they did not take provisions of food, because they were not going far from the *Olb.-I*.

"Are you ready?" Saint-Clair asked.

"Yes, yes," came the reply from every side.

"Good. Soca, open the right-hand door."

The Corsican lowered the lever that controlled the hermetic seal, pulled back the bolts, turned the key, took out the key, put it in one of his pouches and, with a slow gesture, opened the door. Each of them had a similar key, in order that, in case of danger or separation, each of them could get back in without waiting for the others.

Then Saint-Clair, bowing and smiling, said:

"Véronique d'Olbans, in tribute to your uncle, thanks to whom we are here, the honor of being the first to set foot on the soil of Rhea is yours. But be careful of your movements!"

Pale with emotion, the young woman obeyed. With a certain apprehension, she leapt down from the threshold of the *Olb.-I* on to Rhean soil. Although restrained, the jump brought her to earth three meters away.

"Oh!" she said, unable to help laughing.

With an approximately calculated leap, Gno Mitang followed her, then Ariste Fageat, then Jean Margot, then Soca then Vitto, and finally Saint-Clair—who having not gone as far as he could, turned round to lock the door of the interplanetary vehicle with a key.

Three meters further on, the seven were reunited as a group, and Saint-Clair said to Vitto and Soca:

"You'll bring up the rear. Every 20 meters or so, you'll mark a tree to the right and the left with hatchet-blows. That will mark out our return route. It's a matter of not getting lost. The pocket compass that each of us carries should be sufficient to put us on the right track."

"Yes, Monsieur," said the two Corsicans in unison.

And they started walking, Saint-Clair at the head, immediately followed by Gno Mitang, side by side, and behind them, Fageat and Margot.

With their backs turned to the right flank of the *Olb.-1*, they crossed the clearing in a few strides that were bounds of three or four meters. Their lightness delighted them. In the woods, they had to calculate their first strides precisely, in order not to bump into a tree. They observed with satisfaction that they rapidly became accustomed to walking, and they soon had no further need to discipline he movements of their limbs.

For a quarter of an hour that wood did not offer them any new aspect. The trees succeeded one another, all similar, all very nearly the same distance apart.

"It's interesting to observe," said Gno Mitang, "That we aren't frightening the birds. Might they be accustomed to seeing bipeds of our kind, or very nearly, which never do them any harm?"

"Probably," said Saint-Clair, without turning round. Immediately afterwards, he added: "Ah! The terrain's becoming uneven. Here's a hill."

The hill appeared abruptly, as the walkers emerged into a new clearing after traversing a forest enclave in which the trees, more numerous and more densely packed hand interrupted their view for a few minutes.

The new clearing was much more spacious than the one in which the *Olb.-1* had landed. Immediately, it offered new experiences to the ears as well as the eyes of the Terrans.

Thus far they had only heard the slight sound of their footsteps on the dead leaves that littered the soil, and the occasional hatchet-blows inflicted by Vitto and Soca on the tree-trunks. The only living things they had seen were the white birds with the long mute beaks, silent in their flight.

As soon as they emerged from the covert in which they had come to a halt, grouped on the edge of the clearing, however, they saw animals in a tightly-grouped herd running away from them, uttering shrill cries with a metallic ring. Having reached the trees on the far side of the clearing in a mater of seconds—widely-spaced trees that scaled a rocky slope, the animals hurled themselves at the tree-trunks and climbed up with extreme rapidity, disappearing into the bushy foliage. After that disappearance the silence was almost total.

"Monkeys!" Véronique exclaimed.

"Quadrumanes, at any rate," said Gno.

"Which are afraid of us," added Saint-Clair. "Thus, there are bipeds on Rhea that hunt those animals, even if they leave the white birds alone—but are these hypothetical biped hunters savage animals themselves, or beings analogous to our human species?"

For a few minutes the Terrans reflected, in the absolute silence of Rhean nature.

Suddenly, Saint-Clair said:

"Forward march! Let's climb the hill."

Between trees similar to those on the plain, but stouter and taller, thorny bushes and protruding rocks abounded. The rocks were of all shapes, from squat boulders to long monoliths, all uniformly iron-gray in color, with shiny micacious streaks. It was necessary to jump over obstacles or go around them, but the adaptation of the Terrans' muscular strength to the lightness of their bodies was already complete, and no accident interrupted the raid climb.

The hill became quite steep, the trees less and less numerous. Finally, there was nothing but a tumultuous heap of rocks beneath an empty sky in which the sun, still high above a nebulous horizon, was just as the Terrans had seen it from their naïve world on thousands of spring or summer mornings.

Suddenly, they felt the wind—which is to say that they entered without transition into the region of the wind by which the clouds had been furiously stirred, dragged away and carried off.

Bounding from rock to rock, Saint-Clair had drawn a hundred meters ahead of the tightly-knit little group formed by Véronique, Gno Mitang, Fageat, Margot, Vito and Soca, who were similarly bounding along. It was, therefore, him that the wind struck first—for he did feel that he had been struck, in the face and his whole body, as if by an enormous slap: struck and immediately lifted up, carried away as if he were no more than an impalpable fragment of cloud. He shouted, but could anyone hear him?

Gno Mitang saw him, though, and understood immediately.

Where Saint-Clair had just been lifted up, the fixed tumult of rocks stopped dead, and a bare plateau extended, an immense arena, offering no projection to the invisible, silent and mighty surge of the wind.

"Stop! Stop!" cried the Japanese, breaking his own stride and putting his arm around Véronique's waist, flattening himself with her against the last upright rock.

For Saint-Clair, borne away like a wisp of straw, passed above his companions' heads, 20 meters up in the air.

It was rapid and brief, however, for the Nyctalope had the necessary reflexes.

The wind's carrying me away, he thought, *as a current of water carries away a swimmer, or a diver even more so. I have to maneuver my way out of the current.*

With his arms and legs he mimicked the movements of a diver, but instead of reaching upwards—which, for the diver, is the surface of the water and respirable air, Saint-Clair headed downwards, which was for him the solid surface of he planet. The wind supported him and transported him, but like a large leaf that maintains a floating equilibrium as it travels. Vigorously effected and methodically repeated, this movements had the desired and anticipated effect—which is to say that, in less than a minute, the "aerial swimmer" slid toward the layers beneath the air current in which he was bathed, emerged from it abruptly, and, his body no longer obedient to anything except the law of gravity, fell. Fortunately, his relative lightness prevented the fall from being dangerous. Flexing his hamstrings, the man landed lithely on his feet, folding his body smoothly, and stood up straight again.

He found himself half way up the hill, where the trees stopped and the chaos of rocks was heaped up to the level of the upper plateau.

"Good!" he said. "I just need to climb up again."

He was breathing awkwardly, though. He forced himself to keep still, and to adopt a pulmonary exercise that gradually restored the necessary regularity to his respiration. Then he started scaling the hill with long, light bounds.

Five minutes later he saw Véronique and his companions, who were grouped together beneath the invisible aerial current, well-sheltered at the foot of an enormous rock whose truncated summit was like a final step before the smooth extent of the plateau. He rejoined them with a single bound. Relaxed and happy, they all burst out laughing.

The first to calm down, Gno Mitang expressed their common thought briefly and clearly.

"In accordance with what we've been able to observe through the *Olb.-I*'s telescopic porthole, and your transformation into an aerial swimmer, my dear Leo, it's evident that this region of the plant Rhea is swept in a continuous manner , at a certain altitude, by an aerial current of great power."

"Yes," said Saint-Clair, animatedly. "Yes—but I've seen the plateau that extends a long way to the west above this rock on which we're supported, and I believe that the wind is continuous and permanent, always blowing at the same altitude, century after century! It has leveled the summit of the mountainous hill and made it an arid, bare, absolutely horizontal plateau. Above that line of demarcation between the calm air and the aerial current, all vegetal or animal life is impossible: the wind flattens or carries away everything."

With the same reflexive movement, the seven Terrans raised their heads and gazed at the sky. It was pale blue at the zenith, pink-tinted in the west, silvery to the east, where the sun had risen. The wind was invisible, like any wind, but strangely silent.

On the Earth, when the wind blows, there are murmurs and whistling sounds in the streets of towns and villages, among the trees and rocks of the countryside, and the waves of the sea—thin noises or enormous dins, infinitely various. The wind sings and plays, moaning and whistling through obstacles. Here on Rhea, though, over the centuries, the wind had destroyed all the obstacles that had opposed its powerful, inde-fatigable current after the solidification of the planet. But the strangest thing of all for the Terrans, at that moment, was the evident immutability of its "underside." Beneath the horizon-tal line ideally prolonged along the plane of the bare plateau, the air was light, as if alive, but immobile and calm to a point that seemed absolute to Terran senses.

"In sum," said the taciturn Fageat, suddenly, "there's a means of traveling at great speed on Rhea—a natural means. To climb into the region of wind is to allow oneself to be car-ried away. Perhaps there's no danger if one succeeds in main-taining oneself at the lowest level, in such a way as to be able to get out of it by means of a series of swimming movements, as you've just done, Monsieur!"

"Make no mistake, Fageat," said Saint-Clair, simply. "The force of the wind prevents respiration. The lungs con-tract and no longer function. If I hadn't been able to get out of the aerial current at the moment when I realized that, I would have been asphyxiated, and my unreactive body would have been borne away to God knows where."

"My God!" exclaimed Véronique, in a sigh.

Immediately, however, Saint-Clair said:

"Let's go. Let's continue our exploration. Here we can only see before and beneath us the immense forest, in a clear-ing of which we landed and of which we've traversed a small part from east to west. We need to go around the hill, keeping as high as possible on its flank, almost touching the edge of the upper plateau."

"We're certainly the first beings to walk on this ground," said Jean Margot. "The soil's sandy between the rocks, but I haven't seen any trace of foot- or hand-prints."

"Very good, Monsieur Margot," said Gno, with an ap-proving nod of the head. "But I've just thought of something else. Look at your watches."

Everyone, including Véronique, bent their left arms, rais-ing the wrists slightly.

"Noon!" pronounced the young woman.

"Noon!" repeated everyone else.

"Yes," said the Japanese, "noon. When we opened the portholes of the *Olb.-I*, the Sun's rays were arriving obliquely. It was then 9 a.m. The Sun had risen three hours earlier on this September 4. Our watches are working normally since they're all showing noon, having been set by the *Olb.-I*'s chronometer when we left. Now, at noon on September 4, the Sun ought to be nearly at the zenith. Far from it! It's scarcely climbed half way up the celestial cupola. Conclusion?"

He turned to Mademoiselle d'Olbans, and with his habitual ceremonious and affectionate gallantry with regard to the young woman, he said:

"You're not the niece of that savant astronomer Monsieur d'Olbans, Mademoiselle, if you can't formulate that conclusion."

Véronique smiled, glanced at Saint-Clair, blushed and said:

"I'd like to—but I'm not a scientist, and if I'm mistaken, you'll make fun of me."

The Japanese protested with a gesture and a grimace of his grave and intelligent face."

"Well," said Véronique, "the conclusion appears to me to be that the rotational movement of Rhea on its axis is slower than that of Earth; in consequence, the Rhean day is longer than the terrestrial day."

"Very good, Véronique!" said Saint-Clair, laughing, while Gno bowed to the young woman. Immediately, though, he added: "Having ascertained that fact, let's try to ascertain others. Forward march, then!"

They were obliged to form up in Indian file and to describe numerous detours and zigzags, for the entire summit of the hill immediately beneath the plateau, was heaped with numerous tightly-packed rocks that only left narrow intervals between them. Often, there were no intervals at all and they had either to go around an insurmountable chaotic mass or to climb over its lowest and most accessible parts. Sometimes, in the course of these climbs, the Terrans overstepped the invisi-

81

ble boundary of the calm air—a boundary that was invisible, but was, so to speak, tangible, for one was slapped by such a brutal gust that the wind acquired a sort of materiality, like an avid, clutching hand attempting to remove clothing in total darkness.

No other incident saved for these rare collisions with the Rhean wind marked the march, which lasted a good half-hour, while the Terrans followed the arc of a circle around the hilltop for approximately three kilometers, which gradually took them from the forest landscape to a view of a very different landscape replete with alternative suggestions. Their route through the rocks rendered the view of the country overlooked by the hill fragmentary and incoherent, but in progressing gradually from north to south in describing an arc that bulged eastwards, the explorers were increasingly exposed to the sun and felt considerable benefit therefrom.

So, they all uttered an enormous cry of joy, followed by outbursts of laughter, when—chancing to be tightly bunched at that moment—they emerged on to a broad ledge, which, like a balcony, overlooked the entire landscape to the south and south-east from a great height.

There was good reason to be astonished, and the Terrans were, to the extent that after a few bursts of laughter they stood there for several minutes, mute, motionless and uniquely contemplative.

Before and below them extended a large plain, bordered on all sides for league after league by a semi-circular chain of hills. The extreme purity of the air permitted the Terrans to observe with the naked eye that those hills were of the same nature and, undoubtedly, of the same height as the one on which they were standing. The mountainous chain did not hold their attention for long, however, because what they could see on the plain as much more exciting.

"A city!" exclaimed Véronique.

"A small city," said Saint-Clair, more precisely.

"And very strange," added Gno Mitang.

Coming from the west of the chain of hills, a broad river snaked across the plain to vanish in the east. Approximately half way through its sinuous course, it divided into two arms, which came together again further on. The islet thus formed was oval, much longer than broad, and it was entirely occupied by the "city."

Imagine an extraordinary continuous wall at least 100 meters high, a bare, smooth wall with no door or window. From the elevated observation-point where they were standing, the Terrans could not see any bridge across the wide river anywhere. No practicable communication existed, therefore, between the island and the outer banks of the watercourse.

Obedient to the same thought, each of the seven took out a pair of binoculars, which formed part of their equipment. They aimed them and focused them—and what they saw distinctly was this:

Inside the enormous and long encircling wall, from which they were separated by a broad round road, stood buildings, various in their form, height, volume and surface. Extremely sinuous and mazy streets wove through the architectural mass. Everything, including the enclosing wall, was a uniform silver-gray in color. Nowhere could doors or lateral windows be seen, but every edifice, larger or small, round, oblong, triangular or square, had an indented pyramidal roof, and on the summit of the pyramid there was, instead of the tip of the final stone, a hole: an entrance and exit "door," whose convex panels and lock the Terrans could make out quite clearly.

"My God!" exclaimed Véronique. "Are they humans or birds?"

"Flying humans, at any rate!" murmured Saint-Clair.

For the city was inhabited, and densely populated. There were numerous living beings entering or emerging from the edifices and flying between them, or descending into the streets and circulating there on foot, or moving on the round road—or, finally, launching themselves into the air from the top of some formidable rampart, crossing the river in a sort of descending glide and landing on the ground of the plain.

The plain itself, for an extent of approximately three kilometers to the south and north of the island, was strew with numerous small forests, and it was beneath the bright red foliage of these woods that the flying beings were disappearing.

By contrast, many of the beings, who had doubtless been early risers, were emerging from the woods, bounding in long trajectories toward the river, and suddenly, with a stronger thrust, rising into the air above the river, reaching the top of the rampart. Then, either immediately or after a pause of varying duration, during which they came together in groups of various sizes, they quit the top of the rampart to descend into a street or to gain access to a pyramid, into the hole of which they entered by letting themselves fall stiffly, feet downwards and arms raised in parallel.

"They're beings of human form," said Gno Mitang placidly. "They have legs, a torso, a head, arms. Between the elbow and the flank is a folding membrane, thanks to which—and also thanks to their lightness—they can effectuate those long bounding glides."

"They seemed to be naked," said Fageat.

"No," said Saint-Clair.

"No," repeated Véronique. "They're uniformly covered in a one-piece garment analogous to our bathing-suits. It's difficult to see, even with binoculars, because the cloth of the garment is the same pale pink color as the body, but it make pleats sometimes during certain movements."

"Yes," said Soca.

There was a long silence. The Terrans did not weary of looking at the city, its inhabitants, the river and the red woods. They were very calm, for they were now ready for anything, no matter how extraordinary. They knew that everything on Rhea would be extraordinary for them, and they believed that nothing could astonish them any longer. Perhaps they were mistaken on that point.

Suddenly, Véronique said in a serene voice:

84

"Different from us as they are, they're beings we can qualify as human. What shall we call them, in general?"

"Well," said Saint-Clair, smiling, "we're Terrans; to us, they're Rheans, derived from Rhea. A grammarian, even one as pedantic as Abel Hermant,[4] would not, I believe, think that incorrect."

Véronique laughed, and so did everyone else. In the first phase of their acclimatization, at least, the Terrans were decidedly full of joy.

The fact is that the color of he sky, the purity, the lightness and even the perfume of the air, the appearance of the vast landscape, the spectacle of the pale pink Rheans flying above and around their strange silver-gray city, the bight green ribbon of the sinuous river, and the gilded tones of the plain were all delicate and pretty, pure, spring-like and cheerful, with a kind of ambience of eternal idyllic youth. That was what Véronique thought, and put it very well.

"Yes," said Saint-Clair, "I can't disagree that these light and roseate beings, so gracious in their founding and flying, who don't seem constrained to any labor, strolling, gathering, chatting… yes, those delightful appearances seem to prove you right, Véronique. But there are other appearances down there, which aren't delightful… isn't that so, Gno?"

"Of course," said Gno Mitang. "That exceedingly high wall, continuous in its circumvolution, with no doors or posterns, no windows or loopholes—and also the buildings: all those buildings with high smooth walls, with no opening except a hole at the summit of the pyramidal roof, so narrow than the Rheans, although slender, can only go in and out one at a time with their legs stiff and their arms upraised. You're right, Leo."

"No, not just me," Saint-Clair replied. "Mademoiselle d'Olbans is right too. It's evident that, in the good hour we've been observing them, the Rheans have been living in a rhythm

---

[4] (1861-1950); French novelist, playwright, essayist and writer, and member of theAcadémie.

of liberty, peace and absolute security. But why that thick wall, at least 100 meters high? Why those habitations, similarly so high, better defended against the outside that the sternest fortresses of our Middle Ages? And the moat with no bridge or walkway, the broad moat formed by that river, whose current, if one observes it through binoculars, seems to be rapid, imparted by the inclination of the plain from west to east—which is to say, from upstream to downstream of the watercourse. Yes, why all that, if not for a permanent defense against some danger?"

"But what danger?" asked Véronique.

"That's the question," said Gno, with almost imperceptible sarcasm.

Again, silence fell among the Terrans. They resumed observation through the binoculars, but did not discover anything new.

A thousand questions were posed in their minds; sensing that they were all posing them, they did not formulate them in speech, although they repeated them internally.

Were those beings, human in form—except for the addition of the bat-wing membrane between the upper arm and the flank—divided, like he inhabitants of the Earth, into two different and complementary sexes, male and female? Nothing that could be distinguished by means of the binoculars suggested answer to that question.

What were they all doing in the woods? For all of them, with greater or lesser haste but without exception, only came out of their habitations to go into the woods, and only reappeared to return to the city, after having disappeared into one or other of the numerous little red forests scattered over the pale yellow and silvery gray plain.

How did they live? What were their industries? Nowhere could a chimney or the smoke of any fire be seen, nor electrical wires, nor any means of street-lighting in the city, nor domestic animals, nor vehicles of any sort, nor, finally, any indication of daily labor.

Why, then, in the vast extent, was there no village, no isolated habitation, no appearance of agriculture? For league after league, in that prodigious elongated circle bounded by forests and rocky hills with high, deserted and bare plateaux, was there nothing but that city, that unique little city on its isolated islet, within the enclosure of its mighty wall?

Suddenly, Véronique said, simply:

"Leo, I'm hungry and thirsty."

He started.

"Damn!" he exclaimed. "Me too!" In a different tone, shaking his head, he added: "But I was thinking..."

"What?" asked Gno.

"That the security of the Rheans seems, indeed, to be absolute—by day. But during the night... is it because of terrible nocturnal dangers that things here are as we se them?"

Véronique d'Olbans, Gno Mitang, Ariste Fageat, Jean Margot, Vitto and Soca all exclaimed:

"Yes of course! That's probable... certain! Night, eh! But what dangers?"

There was another silence.

"In truth, I too am hungry and thirsty," said the Japanese, abruptly. And he added: "Saint-Clair, I propose that we return to the *Olb.-I.* Nourishment, rest, completion of our on-board journal. Then another meal, light but substantial. Afterwards, we can attempt another expedition by night, going straight through the forest and across the plain to the city, whose direction we now know in relation to the clearing where we landed."

"Agreed," said Saint-Clair, putting his binoculars back into their case.

Two minutes later, the seven Terrans, bounding from rock to rock, were descending from the top of the hill toward the great forest of yellow trees, in a clearing of which they had left the *Olb.-I.*

Thanks to the marks made on many trees by Vitto's and Soca's hatchets, they had no need to hesitate over which direction to follow through the undergrowth.

Again they encountered the quadrumane animals similar to terrestrial monkeys, which fled yelping in terror. Then they saw the silent and tranquil birds again. And they found, intact and locked in the solitude of the large clearing, the solid and comfortable vehicle in which they had traveled so bizarrely from Earth to Rhea.

On seeing it, they were relieved of a vague dread, unexpressed by born in each of them as soon as they began the return journey: that the *Olb.-1* might be surrounded by new "human beings" different from those in the city. But no! Nothing lived in the forest but fearful quadrumanes and indifferent birds.

Chapter VI
The First Night

In the *Olb.-I*, thanks to the diligence of Véronique, aided by Vitto and Soca, lunch was soon ready, as abundant, variant and succulent as they could wish. As an exception, after the coffee, there was old Armagnac, fine champagne or liqueurs according to taste, and cigars, cigarettes or pipes. Rest followed for a few hours, consisting of a few general conversations in which, all their observations having already been well coordinated, they allowed themselves to formulate a thousand hypotheses regarding the inhabitants of Rhea and their conditions of life.

Finally, after a long dusk, darkness fell: a clear night with a pure, starry sky, with the particular spectacle of two lunar bodies, one being the Moon itself, the other the Earth.

On Saint-Clair's orders, everyone added a portable electric lamp to their equipment, except for Saint-Clair himself—for he was the Nyctalope, whose eyes had the rare faculty of being as clear-sighted in darkness as in daylight.

And for the second time, the doors and portholes being securely shut, the *Olb.-I* was left alone in the clearing by the Terrans, who, having got their bearings, drew away from it through the woods in a south-south-westerly direction.

It took them two hours of long-striding but prudent marching to emerge from the forest region and discover the vast plain ahead of them. They did not see any birds; doubtless they were sleeping in their nests or on branches, hidden in the foliage. They saw the simian quadrumanes flee, chattering, though.

"It seems to me," said Mademoiselle d'Olbans, "that those animals are even more curious than fearful."

That remark had no echo. She was right, and merited general approval, but the six men were preoccupied with other problems, and hey did not enjoy the serene and astonishing freedom of spirit that was one of the young woman's principal qualities.

On emerging from the undergrowth on to the plain, they all came to a sudden halt, exclaiming in surprise.

"My God!" said Véronique. "What strange enchantment!"

"That was unexpected!" said Saint-Clair.

Because of the wan light spread by the Earth, the Moon and the innumerable stars, the plain was entirely pale gray in color. By virtue of their low altitude, they could only see the upper part of the river to the west, upstream of the city. As for the city itself...

How can it be described? How can one give an idea of its fantastic, magical appearance?

It was not fire and it was not light; only the word *phosphorescence*...

The Terrans could only see, in the far distance, its enormous wall and half a dozen pyramidal roofs whose exceptional height surpassed it.

That wall, and those roofs were all luminous, and that light, seemingly internal, cold, motionless and devoid of radiance, was phosphorescence.

"Astonishing!" said Gno. "That's not produced by projectors or any kind of lamps; it must emanate from the very matter of which the wall and the edifices are constructed."

"But why?" asked Ariste Fageat. "Nothing is phosphorescent, hereabouts at least, in Rhean nature—neither the trees, nor the ground, nor the water in the river, nor the rocks on the hills; we can only see that nature because it's illuminated by the stars. Only the architectural constructions of the city are phosphorescent. How and why?"

"Bah!" said Saint-Clair. "We'll find out. And to discover that, and many other things, let's go!"

He resumed walking. Everyone followed him. Véronique and Gno Mitang placed themselves by his sides with a single bound. Behind them, bounding in equally long trajectories, came the group formed by Margot, Fageat, Vitto and Soca.

What delights and intoxications there were in that strange progression over the even ground, in the pure, light air, almost as delicately warm as during the day! Truly, it was not an excess of imagination on the part of the Terrans to think themselves equipped with wings!

An without encumbrance or delay, without any encounter of any sort, in less than an hour, they came to the bank of the river in front of the city, facing the city's fantastic wall. They were only separated from it by the width of the river.

"A hundred meters," said Fageat, in a low voice.

Véronique leaned over, putting her bare hand into the water that ran alongside the sandy and gently-sloping bank.

"Oh, it's warm—almost hot!" the young woman murmured.

Everyone imitated her. Saint-Clair tasted the water, and Gno Mitang too.

"It seems to be drinkable," he said.

Standing up, ranged along the water's edge, they gazed at the city—or, rather, at it's wall—for they were so close to it, that they could not see anything except that bewildering wall.

It was then that there was a further occurrence—not a static fact like the phosphorescence of the wall or the warmth of the water but a dynamic event. New living beings appeared.

It was Vito who called attention to them, confusedly. He had chanced to turn his head to look toward the hills on which they had found themselves during the morning; and he saw...

"Boss!" he said, in a low voice. "Turn around and look—what's that?"

Pronounced by Vitto or Soca, the word "boss" could only be addressed to Saint-Clair.

The Nyctalope turned round. What the Corsican, Véronique and everyone else only saw confusedly—indecisive and obscure moving masses against the background of blue-grey ground, the Nyctalope saw clearly.

"Aha!" he said. "Take cover, quickly!"

A short way downstream, the edge of the water made an elbow in the shore, the floor of which offered a series of small

91

sand-dunes. Saint-Clair dragged Véronique, whose hand he had grabbed, toward those dunes. The others followed. Soon, they were all lying on the sand, two or three meters from the water, hidden upstream and downstream and from the great plain by the little dunes. Having hollowed out gaps in front of them with their hands, they could see in all directions with the minimum risk of being seen—and they watched avidly.

Almost immediately, the Nyctalope had said:

"They're Rheans of another species. Sometimes resembling humans and sometimes gorillas, according to whether they're advancing by bounds on four feet or two. Many are dragging tree-trunks, or entire trees with their branches. They must have Herculean strength."

Thanks to his nyctalopia, Saint-Clair had been able to discern all that from afar, in the semi-darkness of he depths of the plain in the direction of the woods and the rocky hills. The other six Terrans, however, could not see anything at first but a large somber mass advancing rapidly, increasing in height, width and depth. The noises they heard were those of animal footfalls on had ground and those of violent and continuous friction, as objects were dragged that sometimes fractured with dry snapping sounds.

In the light of the two "moons" and stars on the near extent of the gray-blue plain, however, the moving masses did not take long to be discernible in their distinct parts.

"But they're giants!" Véronique murmured.

"Yes," said Saint-Clair.

"Evidently," said Gno, "it's gorillas they call to mind most of all."

"And there are hundreds of them!" said Fageat.

"Luckily for us," remarked Margot, "they'll arrive at the edge of the river half a kilometer away from us if they don't change direction."

Soca, who was very observant, noticed that the strange galloping host was heading for a point at which, the river being less wide than elsewhere, the bank was closer to the wall.

"Are they going to throw in the trees they're dragging to make a kind of floating bridge?" asked Vitto.

They shut up, all gripped by the fantastic sight of those enormous gorillas, or giant humans, charging toward the river. Not a cry was uttered by that galloping host, but they emitted heavy breathing sounds, hoarse and panting, and savage grunts.

Having reached the water's edge, the first ranks of the horde only paused momentarily. With a sort of frenzy they hurled into the water, or on to the water, a dozen enormous trees, long and branches, which they had been dragging or carrying—and they threw themselves into the midst of those trees and branches, which were partly afloat, dragged into the middle of the river by the violent current of the water, gleaming with reflections of he phosphorescent wall.

Without any discontinuity, however, other "gorillas" were arriving and throwing more trees.

"Within five minutes," whispered Saint-Clair, "the entire width of the river will be covered by an inextricable tangle of branched trunks. The current is only strong in the middle, where the bed of the river must be quite deep. Supported on the sand of the bank and the base of the wall, though, the long woody entanglement will make a kind of bridge, resistant to the current."

"My God!" said Véronique, with passionate interest. "What are those giant ape-men trying to do?"

"Probably striving to climb the wall."

"But how?"

"There are only two means, I believe. Eh, Gno?"

"To tell the truth, I can only imagine one," the Japanese replied, tranquilly. "The human pyramid, as it's called in gymnastics on Earth."

Saint-Clair and Gno had guessed correctly.

Having reached the foot of the wall—where the water was only thigh-deep—in a seething mass, those "nocturnal Rheans," as Margot ingeniously labeled them, set about forming a human pyramid with one row at the base, a solid founda-

93

tion of a hundred individuals coupled back-to-back. On those fifty pedestals, forty-eight more pedestals were formed, those two of two individuals each. Then, above that, the pyramid continued to rise up rapidly, amid the mingled noise of branches stirred by the water and the groans and exhalations of the nocturnal gymnasts.

Then Vitto, who rarely spoke but always to express a pertinent and wise thought, said:

"Aren't the Rheans in the city going to defend themselves, Boss?"

"We'll see!" said Saint-Clair.

And they saw almost immediately. "Diurnals" appeared at the top of the wall.

"Oh!" exclaimed Véronique. "They're phosphorescent too, like the wall!"

It was, however, because of the flying leaps with which they were detaching themselves from the high platform that they were distinguishable. Yes, their entire bodies were phosphorescent, but their torsos, clad in the tight-fitting garments, were more brightly illuminated than their heads or necks.

"They're armed!" Margot exclaimed.

Immediately, the Terrans witnessed a battle between the nocturnal Rhean assailants and the diurnal Rheans prohibiting access to their city.

The only weapon that the defenders appeared to have at their disposal was a sort of hatchet with a long, flexible shaft.

For the Terrans, passionately captivated by the spectacle, it was like some kind of vertiginous nightmare, in which, fortunately, they had a very clear sensation of not being involved.

Over the river, the trees and the tangled bridges across the stream, amid the swarming of the assailants not yet engaged in the monstrous pyramid inscribing itself in black against the phosphorescence of the high wall, and also on all the stages of the pyramid—especially its upper ones ceaselessly under construction—Nocturnals and Diurnals, the former quadrumanes, with no other weapons than their enormous hands, and the latter winged and armed with long-handled hatchets, engaged in a fierce, almost silent battle of extraordinary rapidity and maneuvering skill.

Saint-Clair, Véronique and their companions soon discerned, within the strange battle, that the Nocturnals evidently had only one goal: to grab hold of the Diurnals and carry them off. When one of the black gorillas was able to seize a phosphorescent Rhean, it disarmed the captive. Then, if it was part of the pyramid, it passed the captive down to another Nocturnal, and from one monstrous hand to another, the Diurnal was transmitted to a group of gorillas waiting on the bank. One of the group then took charge of two Diurnals, now without resistance, and carried them off at a gallop toward the hills.

By contrast, the Diurnals had two objectives: firstly, to prevent the pyramid of assailants reaching the top of the wall; and secondly, not to be captured. The tragic necessity of achieving the first aim, however, was detrimental to the attainment of the second. Fighting courageously, wielding their hatchets cleverly, the phosphorescent Rheans, although they were now succeeding in preventing the highest ranks of the growing pyramid from reaching the summit of the wall, they were exposing themselves heroically, by virtue of that very fact, and many of them were unable to avoid being captured. Fortunately, the contingents of the phosphorescent Rhean army must have been sufficiently numerous within the city, for new companies were arriving incessantly on the platform of the encircling wall, and hurling themselves recklessly into the battle.

That fantastic skirmish between the "gorillas" and the "bat-men" was, at any rater, as brief as it was violent.

Gno Mitang, calm and attentive, had counted about a hundred phosphorescent Rheans seized and carried off by the enormous quadrumanes when a savage cry, both ample and piercing, rose above the tumult—and suddenly, the incomplete pyramid came apart, its elements falling back, flooding back across the river.

It was then that Saint-Clair, in his clear and hard voice of command, pronounced aloud, in such a manner as to be heard by all his companions in adventure:

"Véronique, don't move. Gno, please stay here and watch over Mademoiselle d'Olbans. Vitto, Soca, Fageat and Margot, follow me. The mission is to take possession of the last monster carrying one or two Rheans. That one, it's necessary to capture alive. Soca, Vitto, you'll help me with that. Fageat, Margot, you'll shoot with pistols any gorillas that try to oppose my action. Gno, Véronique, when you hear my whistle-blast, come quickly to rejoin us. Understood, everyone?"

"Yes, yes!" came from everywhere around the Nyctalope.

"All together, then—up and away!"

As soon as the pyramid collapsed and the last assailants were in flight toward the bank across the partly-dislocated and partly-immersed bridge of trees, the phosphorescent Rheans arranged themselves along the top of the wall, doubtless to make sure that no further assault was attempted by their enemies. How amazed they must have been by the spectacle— rather confused in the pale starlight but a discernible anomaly nevertheless—presented by the action of unknown beings, by unimaginable means, against the last retreating group of the Nocturnals!

At the rear of that group, galloping in convoy were two "gorillas" each bearing a phosphorescent Rhean under its arm.

Ten paces from the Nocturnals, Saint-Clair commanded:

"Soca, Vitto, it's necessary to catch these last two. Tap them on the head with the blunt ends of your hatchets, hard enough to stun them but not to kill them. Then tie them up immediately."

"Yes, Boss," the two Corsicans replied, in unison.

"Let's get 100 meters ahead of them first, so as first to astonish them by our appearance. Then rush them as we come back."

"Yes, Boss."

Between the last two Nocturnals and the bulk of their fellows, galloping like them toward the hills, there was a gap of about two hundred meters, for the abductors of the final phase of the battle had hung back slightly in order that they might each capture a prey that had come within arm's reach. It was into that gap that the three Terrans, relatively dark in the lunar light because of their clothing, suddenly surged, and then turned around and bounded toward the two Nocturnal Rheans.

The Nyctalope had no been wrong to count on the overwhelming surprise that such an apparition would cause the "gorillas."

Bounding together in a long stride, the latter saw the three unknown forms when the trajectory of their present bound was still incomplete. When their huge feet hit the ground again they remained there as if frozen and rooted to the spot; that was evidently because the appearance of the new beings was totally different from that offered by the Diurnal Rheans, and doubtless all the other animal species living on the planet Rhea.

The stupor of the two Nocturnals was so paralyzing for them that they did not defend themselves, or try to escape, if they were even conscious of the danger facing them. Lifted up by a leap to the height of the colossal stature of the "gorillas," neither Vitto nor Soca had any difficulty in bringing down his reversed hatchet on the right spot. The two iron hammers struck the two naked skulls. Opening their arms and dropping their captives, the Nocturnals tottered—but they were tough; they did not fall. Instinct kept them upright; fear gave them the determination to flee. They took one large stride backwards, turned away, tried to run...

But Vitto and Soca were on them again; the second hammer-blows were completely efficacious. One of the monsters fell to its knees and then prone; the other fell sideways like a dead weight.

At that moment, Fageat and Margot arrived, who, in the capacity of a rear-guard, were ready to use their pistols to stop any offensive return of a more or less numerous group of

Nocturnals at a distance. In all probability, however, none of the others had been aware of the unimaginable drama that was unfolding behind them, for not a single one came back. Already, the dark host, fleeing rapidly, was confused in the darkness with the black shadows of the rocky wooded hills toward which they were running.

With the engineer as his second, Saint-Clair ordered:

"Help Soca and Vitto to tie up the Nocturnals securely. I'll see to the Diurnals."

Before that, however, he raised the powerful whistle with which he was equipped to his lips and launched a strident blast into the night. In the distance, two dark forms stood up in the small dunes: Véronique d'Olbans and Gno Mitang.

Released by the arms of their abductors, the two phosphorescent Rheans—the "Diurnals," or "bat-men," according to the general and distinctive appellation that the Terrans had tacitly agreed to give them—were still stretched out on the ground, motionless. Leaning over one of them, Saint-Clair saw its eyes: very large almond-shaped eyes, heavily wrinkled toward the temples, opening between the brow-ridge and the cheeks in the same plane, devoid of eyebrows, lids or lashes. They were very large—immense by comparison with the dimensions of the whole face—and each composed of a pale pink globular sclerotic, a blue cornea and a pupil that was no more than a golden dot. The blue of the cornea—the color of the eye, in sum—was infinitely pale in hue, clear and transparent. Like a large drop of pure water, beyond which there was nothing but the atmosphere, the air, the sky... a pale sky...

If ever the epithet "unfathomable" could be applied to eyes, the Nyctalope thought, *it's to these eyes...*

For those Rhean eyes, which could not close since they had no eyelids, which were alive, since the pale blue corneas with their golden pupils were moving upon the pale pink sclerotics to follow the movements of Saint-Clair's head, were devoid of expression! Nothing! No sentiment: neither surprise, nor fright, nor pain nor pleasure—nothing! They were looking at him as if they could not see anything—but they could see, since they were moving to the right and the left, toward the forehead or the cheeks, according to whether Saint-Clair's head, moving in order to observe accurately, went one way or the other, was raised or lowered.

"In any case," he whispered to himself, "they're lovely eyes!"

He stood up and looked around.

Véronique and Gno Mitang, kneeling beside the second Diurnal, were leaning over and making a close examination.

With the reels of slender and sturdy cord that formed part of each Terran's equipment, Vitto, Soca, Fageat and Margot were finishing tying up the two Nocturnals, with their legs together and their arms bound to their sides. The latter were docile and resigned, but not unconscious, for they had emerged almost immediately from the daze caused by the second impact, and were breathing and wheezing, but without putting up a fight. Saint-Clair was close enough to one of them to see its face—a face much more similar to that of a large terrestrial gorilla than the faces of the Diurnals were to those of the men or women of Earth. Evidently, the Nocturnal and Diurnal Rheans were two distinct species.

But are these Herculean ape-men like the apes of our world? the Nyctalope wondered—for in the grunts that alternated with the inhalations and exhalations he seemed to distinguish the essential characteristics of a language. Soon, it seemed certain to him that the two Nocturnals were talking to one another—and their eyes were so expressive! Truly "human" eyes!

Thanks to his extraordinary faculty of seeing as clearly in the darkness as in daylight, the Nyctalope cold make out the slightest details of the troubling physiognomy of the Nocturnal lying close to him, whose legs had just been securely tied up by Soca and Margot. Those eyes! With eyebrows, lids and lashes, they really were "human" eyes, in spite of their vivid red color, with dark green pupils and pale green sclerotics: bizarre colors for an eye, by Terrans standards—but human in their expression and gaze.

Strange! Saint-Clair said to himself. *For it's these Nocturnals that appear to be savage animals—brutes—while the Diurnals, with their inexpressive eyes, seem to be civilized beings, thinkers...*

He would have let himself drift into a long meditation had the not abruptly become aware of the fact that, now that the two "gorillas" were tied up, while the two phosphorescent Rheans were still lying motionless on the ground, Véronique, Gno Mitang, Fageat, Margot, Vitto and Soca were all standing up, awaiting his decision and his orders.

Immediately, he said:

"There are still some branches trees on the bank; the current of the river hasn't carried away all those the Nocurnals brought to make a bridge. Go and cut a few branches of the right length to make two stretchers, on to which we'll load our four captives... or two, if the Diurnals, taken by the hand, understand that we want them to come with us and consent to do so."

Rapidly, Vitto, Soca, Fageat and Margot went to cut the necessary branches with their hatchets from the uprooted trees dragged by the Nocturnals from the forested hills to the edge of the river encircling the city.

Véronique, Gno and Saint-Clair remained alone for almost a quarter of an hour with the two Diurnal Rheans, now lying side by side, but not budging, even though all four of their limbs were free. Their immense, magnificent, unfathomable and inexpressive eyes were still following, with a gaze that was evidently sighted even though it appeared blind, the slightest movements and displacements of the new beings that had saved them from their abductors.

"Leo, Gno, look!" said Véronique suddenly.

The top of the wall, from one end to the other of that side of the city, was now swarming with phosphorescent Rheans.

"Yes," said Gno. "The entire population of the city is assembling to observe or contemplate the unexpected spectacle that we're presenting to them."

Saint-Clair added:

"I still don't know whether they understand anything, or what ideas they have. I hope to find out soon from these two, whom we'll take back to the *Olb.-1* with us, voluntarily or by force. They have an architecture, so they must have a geometry, writing and probably a language, since they have a mouth, teeth and a tongue like ours. Fundamentally, though, their eyes are disconcerting. The wings under the arms are trivial—but those eyes!"

"That's true," said Véronique. "They're much less human than those of the Nocturnals."

"The Nocturnals also have a language," said Gno. "These two were talking to one another just now—there's no doubt about it."

"Well, we'll soon know that and other things," the Nyctalope concluded.

Then, however, a phenomenon occurred with which the Terrans were already familiar, but which was nevertheless far from their minds at that moment.

Above the dark background of the western horizon, clouds suddenly rose, spreading so rapidly that they ran from one extreme of the sky to the other like a violently-tugged veil; and they were so thick, so opaque, that they completely blocked the light of the two "moons" and the stars, so effectively that in less than a minute, Rhea was plunged into the blackest darkness.

Only the Nyctalope could see that the clouds, rolling up above in enormous agglomerated masses, were racing eastwards at high speed. He assumed that the phenomenon would be of short duration, as the others of the same essence had been. Nevertheless, he was impatient to get back to the *Olb.-1*, so he ordered:

"Light the electric lamps—we're leaving."

Véronique, Gno Mitang and the others obeyed immediately—but there was a further surprise. Several luminous beams hit the faces of the two bound Nocturnals, who immediately howled in pain, closing their eyes, and rolled over in order to press their faces to the ground.

"Aha!" said Saint-Clair, who had seen everything. "The Nocturnals can't stand light! Are they Nocturnal through and through? Might the evidently artificial phosphorescence of the city's walls and buildings, the phosphorescence of the garment, and the less vivid phosphorescence of the Diurnals' faces, be a means of defense against the Nocturnals? A means of diminishing the visual power of the Nocturnals in the Rhean night?"

"That's interesting!" exclaimed Véronique.

"Yes." And Saint-Clair went on, with evident impatience: "Let's go! Avoid directing the beams of the electric lamps at the captives. Fageat, Margot, Vitto and Soca, load the two Nocturnals on to the stretchers; you carry them. Véronique!"

"Leo!"

"An experiment. Gno, illuminate her clearly, so that the Diurnals can see her; the light won't harm them, and even interests them, to judge by the movements of their heads and eyes. Good. Véronique, lie down on your back on the ground, there, as the Diurnals are lying."

The young woman obeyed.

"Perfect," said Saint-Clair. He leaned toward her. "Give me your right hand. There! And now, as if obedient to the pull of my hand, get up."

That was done.

Gno, Véronique and Saint-Clair saw that the two phosphorescent Rheans had missed nothing of the little pantomime.

When Véronique was upright, Saint-Clair said to her:

"Now lean over and take the right hand of that Rhean— and pull! Is it getting up?"

It was an emotional moment. If the solicited Rhean stood up, it would reveal by that action that it was in possession of a truly "human" intelligence and faculty of obedience.

The Rhean allowed itself to be taken by the hand without resistance, and in response to Véronique's muscular solicitation, it obeyed! It rose up, with a supple surge of its entire body, to a standing position.

"Now the other, Véronique!" said Saint-Clair, swiftly.

"Yes."

And without letting go of the first Rhean's hand, the young woman leaned toward the second and tried to grasp its left hand—and that one raised its own hand and grasping the fingers, illuminate by Gno's electric torch, that were offered to it. It too stood up.

"That first experiment opens up immense and fortunate prospects," said Gno Mitang. "The Rheans have an intelligence analogous to ours."

Pointing to the Rhea standing to the right of the delighted Véronique, Saint-Clair said:

"That one's a male." Then he pointed to the other. "That one's a female."

There was, in fact, no possible doubt. Each of them molded by the one-piece garment, the two phosphorescent Diurnals presented, in the forms and contours of their bodies, especially at the breast and the hips, differences as distinct as they were evident. Their hair could not be seen, for they were each coiffed in a kind of tight bonnet made of the same material as the body-stocking, which encircled the forehead and cheeks, leaving the ears free, and the neck immediately beneath the chin. Their faces were different too, the female's being more oval and apparently less bony than the male's.

"We're ready, Monsieur," said a coarse voice.

It was Fageat's. He and Margot had an improvised stretcher on their shoulders, holding it with both hands. Beside them, Vitto and Soca were carrying the other; the Nocturnals were solidly attached to them.

"Good!" said Saint-Clair.

The clouds were still covering the sky. The night was so dark that without the electric lamps the Terrans would have been unable to see one another—except for the Nyctalope, who could see everything. Beyond the river, which was reflecting the phosphorescence of the high city wall, the latter was like a scene of enchantment. At the very top, there was still the phosphorescent crowd of Rheans, doubtless passionately interested by the spectacle, incomprehensible to them, of the two isolated Rheans and the beams of light that were bobbing around them. To the Terrans, it was obvious that the Rheans could not see in the darkness of the night, while the "gorillas," or Nocturnal Rheans, nyctalopes like Saint-Clair, could not bear any light brighter than the enigmatic phosphorescence of the city and its inhabitants.

"Gno, my friend," said Saint-Clair, "I'll lead the way. Follow me while illuminating Véronique and her companions. Fageat, Margot, Vitto and Soca—forward mach! We're going back to the *Olb.-I.*"

The four stretcher-bearers had each attached an electric lamp to one of the buttons of their jackets.

"Will they want to come with me?" Véronique asked.

"I don't doubt it," said Saint-Clair. "They seem to me to be simultaneously docile and prodigiously curious. They understand that we don't mean them any harm, since we've saved them and made certain that their aggressors can do them no harm. They're wondering what we are and where we come from, as we'd be wondering on Earth if… but enough talking. Véronique, make the necessary movements to tell them what you want."

And, having orientated himself with respect to the position of the distant hills to the left, and the river and the city to the right, the Nyctalope took the first bound of the return journey to the *Olb.-I.*

Well-illuminated from the side by Gno Mitang, Véronique moved her arms while gripping the Rheans' hands, sketching out a first step. She perceived no resistance in the warm and slender fingers of her two voluntary captives, but a significant acquiescence. Then she launched herself forwards, toward Saint-Clair, who the beam of Gno's torch immediately sought out and found, fifty meters ahead. And like her, the Rheans leapt forward. Lighter than Véronique, however and equipped with wings of which she was deprived, and also endowed of a muscular strength that astonished her when she perceived it. The Rheans supported the Terran woman in the air, in a bound much higher and longer than she could have contrived alone.

That appeared to her to be so amusing and s comical that she laughed with pleasure. To her right and left, a cascade of silvery sounds burst forth; like the Terran, the Rheans were laughing!

Chapter VII
A World Without Fire

There were no more clouds gliding in the pure sky, and the eastern horizon was tinted with a rosy mauve when the strange troop of the Terrans, the Diurnal Rheans with Véronique and the Nocturnal Rheans carried on stretchers reached the edge of the forest in a clearing of which the *Olb.-I* was located.

Within the woods their progress was less free because of the trees, and thus slower; it was almost daylight when the Terrans stopped in front of their vehicle.

The solitude of the clearing had not been violated; everything was intact.

"Put the Nocturnals in the crew quarters with the portholes closed, in the dark," Saint-Clair ordered, "for their eyes suffer a great deal in any light brighter than the cold and pale Rhean phosphorescence. We'll deal with them later. The first essential thing is to create a rapport of intelligence and comprehension between the Diurnal Rheans and ourselves. Véronique, I'll leave it to you to introduce them and accommodate them in the central compartment, our living-room."

"Yes," said the young woman, "but I also want to put on my light pajamas right away. I'm stifling in all this equipment. Even at night it's warm on Rhea. A mild and pleasant warmth, but in which one doesn't require overmuch clothing. I can understand the simple body-stockings of these Diurnals and the near-total nudity of the Nocturnals."

Saint-Clair, Gno Mitang and the other Terrans, who had overheard, exclaimed:

"Oh yes! To the wardrobes—new clothes! We'll live in pajamas or short trousers and shirts without sleeves or collars! The experiment of the first day and night was conclusive with regard to the question of costume, at least in the present sea-son—if there's a seasonal regime on Rhea analogous to that on Earth."

An hour later—the Nocturnals, still bound, having been sheltered from any light—the seven Terrans ate a rapid but substantial meal in the central compartment, before the two seated, immobile and attentive Diurnals, visibly interested observers. And then—for they were so excited that no one thought of going to sleep, in spite of the long and active night they had spent—the Terrans began the exciting work of entering into a reciprocal intelligence and comprehension with the two Diurnal Rheans.

It was much easier and more rapid than they had dared to hope.

Immediately, several certainties imposed themselves, which the Terrans' minds took to be conclusively acquired notions.

The Diurnal Rheans were endowed with extremely musical and nuanced voices; their language included all the vowels of human languages, but fewer consonants. In their species, the ear, the nose, the tongue, the conformation of the mouth and the dentition were very similar to those of the human species, except that they had no incisors or canines, but only twenty-four molars in two rows of twelve, similar to the most beautiful ivory. Their eyes had an entirely Rhean, but uniquely Diurnal, originality, like the almost total generality of human eyes. Their bodies, male and female, functioned like the bodies of terrestrial males and females, but with a more summary gastric and digestive apparatus. The hands each had five fingers arranged like human digits, but longer and proportionately more muscular. The feet had six toes, also long, and prehensile, like those of the majority of terrestrial monkeys. The natural suppleness of the Diurnals' bodies was comparable to that acquired by the best acrobatic dancers of the human species.

As for the Diurnals' intelligence, comprehension, and faculties of adaptation and assimilation, they were revealed in a matter of minutes to be extremely keen, profound, highly-developed and immediate in their application.

For example, constructive beings, making continual progress in the art of construction, and hence intelligent and reflective architects, incessantly improving their constructions, cannot be ignorant of geometry. Now, geometry is the same throughout the universe; on no matter what planet inhabited by beings thinking and acting in a human manner, or very nearly, a triangle is a triangle, a circumference a circumference, etc., etc.—and it was by means of a few simple geometric diagrams that Saint-Clair and Gno Mitang established a primary intellectual rapport with the male Diurnal.

Fageat, Margot, Vitto and Soca were wonderstruck spectators, as were Véronique and her Rhean companion, for the female Diurnal had spontaneously sat down beside the young woman on the divan, and had extended a hand to her, which she held and caressed.

The first dialogue—for that expression can be authentically applied—between the world of the Earth and the world of Rhea only took place at first, between the male Diurnal on the one hand and LeoSaint-Clair and Gno Mitang on the other. After three hours, which passed with a rapidity that surprised the Terrans, Saint-Clair and Gno were able to exchange with their prodigious interlocutor a few of the simplest words, as two knowledgeable linguists of different nationalities, who had been totally unfamiliar with one another's languages until then, could have done on Earth.

The endurance of the Diurnals was exhausted, though. Véronique was the only one who noticed it, for she was looking as keenly as she was listening. Being devoid of eyelids, the Rheans' eyes could not betray fatigue by their gradual closure and struggling against sleep in an evident manner by striving to keep them apart, as human eyes would have done—but their limpidity, so astonishing in the state of normal wakefulness, became dull, like a sky veiled by mist, or transparent water in which a gray powder had just been dissolved. Devoid of human expression, but alive, the Rheans' eyes visibly lost even the appearance of life. Moreover, Véronique felt the hand of her Rhean friend become limp within her own, losing all its nervous tension and muscular strength. And on the cushions of the divan, the seated body sagged.

"Leo!" called Véronique, when she was certain of the reality of her observations and their consequences. "Leo, the Rheans can't do any more; they're falling asleep—my neighbor as well as your interlocutor."

A few moments later, their eyes totally deprived of all life, as if made of tarnished colored porcelain, their supple bodies, utterly abandoned and devoid of force, the two Rheans were asleep—or, at least, they were in a state equivalent to that of human sleep, calm and profound, with a silent respiration and scarcely-apparent rhythmic movements of the throat and neck.

There was a momentary silence, while al the Terrans looked at the sleeping Rheans. Suddenly, Gno Mitang said:

"Why have Terran novelists who have imagined voyagers to other planets only populated them with monsters? It's simpler and more logical to assume, as we can observe today, that the majority of inhabited worlds include inhabitants of a species closely analogous to the human species, whatever physical, intellectual and moral difference there might be. There's truly too much pride in thinking that humans are the only ones of that nature living in the infinite universe, of which the Earth is only an infinitesimal part."

"Indeed," said Saint-Clair.

Again, silence fell. Then Véronique, in a restrained voice that was hesitant at first, said:

"The enigmas that Rhea presents to us so numerously will, I think, be all the more exciting to elucidate—and I also think that we shall be able to elucidate them all, since the Rheans are endowed with an intelligence and a language open to our own intelligence and language. It's merely a matter of being patient."

Ariste Fageat, however, grumbled:

"Our patience won't sustain such a long ordeal!"

"Very true," Saint-Clair agreed. "We too need rest and sleep. Afterwards, Véronique, you'll prepare a meal that the awakened Rheans will witness. A great diversity of foodstuffs will allow them to share it. By means of brief syllables, onomatopoeia and gestures we'll apply ourselves to conversing with them. In a matter of hours we'll know a great deal, I'm convinced of it—and I admit to you that I'm in a particular hurry to find out about the great drama of Rhean life—the antagonism of the Diurnals and Nocturnals. I think that it's that antagonism which shapes the entirety of Rhean civilization. But enough talk. Let's close the *Olb.-I*'s doors and portholes and go to sleep, in the complete safety of our inviolable fortress..."

When they awoke, it was with giant strides that the Terrans and the Diurnal Rheans entered into and progressed rapidly through the vast field—seemingly unlimited for a long time—of reciprocal knowledge and comprehension.

To record the details of the progress would require many thousands of lines, but intelligent readers may amuse themselves by imagining those details in following its various consequences.

To begin with, only one of the foodstuffs served at the Terrans' table was comestible by the Rheans: roasted hazelnuts, which Véronique served among the desserts. The two Diurnals, smiling, succeeded in making it understood that their nourishment consisted entirely of fruits analogous to those nuts, but devoid of shells. The woods and forests of Rhea, comprising millions of trees, were primarily formed by those "hazels." The germination and maturation of the fruit, which the Rheans called *doa* in their own language, were not seasonal but constant and continuous: flowers, ripening fruits and ripe fruits succeeded one another on a daily basis, with the result that the Diurnal population of Rhea was nourished at its leisure, without any other labor than gathering, which was not subject to any timetable; the nourishment of the body was thus ensured by nature, without labor, by a single superabundant aliment, whose productive trees belonged to everyone.

It was almost the same for the fabric from which the garments and bonnets that formed the Diurnal Rheans unvarying costume were made; every individual, male or female, wove it with extreme ease, from childhood onwards, by means of a fiber produced in inexhaustible abundance by the trunks of the "hazels"—which is to say, the *doas*. Because the problem of clothing did not exist on Rhea, any more than the problem of nourishment, there was no "social problem" or "class struggle" there, nor any kind of monetary system whatsoever, and hence no "economic law," so harsh for terrestrial humanity.

In sum, the only legally obligatory work was the construction and maintenance of the edifices and encircling walls of cities, and that was such vital defensive work that all Rheans—children, adolescents, adults and even old people of both sexes—devoted themselves to it with a great and joyful ardor, in accordance with rules handed down from the remotest Rhean eras, which were so perfect that no Rhean, even those of genius—which did exist—ever tried to modify them.

With reference to that subject, however—the vital work of defense on the one hand and their joy of living on the other—the Terrans were soon enlightened as to the general and individual conditions of the lives of the Diurnal Rheans in the cities; that process had been hastened by the determination of Saint-Clair the Nyctalope, who was impatient to arrive at what seemed to him to be the most essential condition of all: the mortal antagonism between the Diurnals and the Nocturnals.

Rhean days last about 36 hours from sunrise to sunset, all through the year, for there are no seasons on Rhea. The temperature there is always the same, about 25° Réaumur,[5] and thus pleasantly warm. The Terrans were unable to explain why, for their exchanges of words and signs with the Diurnals

---

[5] 88 degrees Farenheit / 31 degrees Celsius.

111

were still too summary. They had no doubt, however, that they would soon be fully informed about that, for the astronomical conditions of the planet Rhea were insufficient to explain the absence of different seasons and the almost-immutable temperature.

After a meal, at 4 p.m. on September 5—adapting the terrestrial calendar to Rhea—the Terrans emerged from the *Olb.-1* again. They were not seven but six, for one of them remained on board.

They left the two Nocturnal Rheans behind, still tied up and lying in the darkness of the crew quarters, reserving them for particular study the following day—for the two Diurnals had refused, with abundant gestures, signs and words of fear and horror, to speak to those "monsters."

Ariste Fageat stayed to guard the Nocturnals.

Saint-Clair had said, during the meal:

"One of us has to make the sacrifice today of keeping watch on our two captives. Vitto? Soca?"

The engineer had said, however:

"With your permission, Monsieur, that ought to be me. Last night, coming back from the city with the front shafts of the stretcher on my shoulders, I touched down after one of my leaps in such a way that my left foot landed awkwardly on a stone, and I think I have a sprain or a pulled muscle, or at least a bruise. When I put my weight on that foot, I feel a sharp pain and my leg buckles."

No one doubted him. In its habitual gravity, Fageat's coarse, emaciated face, with its short black beard, always seemed to be suffering.

"In that case," Saint-Clair said, "you can stay here, Fageat. Look after yourself. The *Olb.-1*'s pharmacy contains ointments and liniments appropriate to beneficial applications and frictions. I hope that you don't have a sprain or a pulled muscle that will immobilize you for days. A bruised foot is, indeed, painful, but might ease in 24 hours."

"I hope so!" Fageat concluded, with the shadow of a smile.

Thus, the Diurnal male and female went out with the six Terrans whom they wanted to take to their city.

In daylight the Diurnals were not phosphorescent either in their skin or their clothing and headgear, but a pretty bright pink color that was common to the vestments as well as their bodies—by virtue of which they could seem to be naked when seen from a distance.

Saint-Clair, Véronique and their companions had made a close examination of the membranes that folded and unfolded between the upper arm and the flank, constituting, in sum, a pair of wings. They were made of smooth, relatively thick and very sturdy skin, with a framework of powerful tendons.

As for the eyes—the most astonishing part of the Diurnal body—they were not protected by eyelids but they were unbreakable, make of a substance so hard, in its limpid transparency, that nothing could pierce or breach it.

"Yes, truly," Véronique had said, "out of everything in the physical constitution of the Diurnals, those eyes are the only substance, the only incomprehensible organ completely unknown to us and with no analogy anything familiar to all Terrans."

Those inexpressive eyes, however—the materially and physically inviolable eyes of the Diurnal Rheans—were nevertheless alive and clear-sighted, able to see at distances that were practically unlimited.

"Living telescopes!" said Soca.

That was accurate, but so preposterous that everyone started laughing, including the two Diurnals, for they were naturally joyful and their laughter—a kind of pearly musical cascade—was very frequent.

The journey from the *Olb.-I* to the city was completed in less than an hour, and therefore very rapidly, because the Terrans were now habituated to their lightness in proportion to their muscular strength, and, although they made shallower and sorter leaps than those of the Diurnals, they repeated those leaps forcefully and without pause, so effectively that the Di-

113

urnals, lifting the delighted Véronique, only kept slightly ahead of them.

Left alone in the *Olb.-I*, Fageat decided to wait patiently for half an hour, in order to be sure that no one was coming back in order to pick up some implement whose utility had been perceived a trifle belatedly.

The engineer put a good portion of that 30 minutes to good use, plastering his left ankle with arnica and wrapping a carefully-contrived bandage around it. And while amusing himself thus he sniggered:

"That's very good! A Saint-Clair, a Gno Mitang, those great minds, and a Véronique d'Olbans, that delicate creature, are easier to fool than the meekest of imbeciles and the dullest of swineherds."

Then—walking, of course, without the slightest difficulty or the slightest pain—he went into the crew quarters, transformed into a dark prison for the two Nocturnals.

Immediately, he spoke in a loud voice, not in the hope of being understood, but to make his voice heard, to make it clear—for he was sure that the two captives would understand—that his voice was calm and devoid of animosity. He spoke, therefore, in a soft tone, albeit with a firm and forceful register.

"I have all the time I need! Saint-Clair, Véronique and the others will be away a long time visiting he city and talking to the various clan-leaders, as they put it, of the Diurnals. Perhaps they'll even take a trip to the 'region of vapors,' as they also put it. I have at least 24 hours ahead of me. I hope that in such a span of time, I'll be able to reach a good enough understanding with the Nocturnals to prepare the future… the future as I've been envisaging it for some time. A life that will no longer have anything terrestrial about it, but will be entirely Rhean, but which will be full of delicate charm and strong emotion, the amalgam of which will be a very happy existence for me."

While speaking thus, Ariste Fageat had closed the door communicating with the central compartment. Then, feeling his way, he had gone to the nearest pothole and had opened it slightly—just enough for a thread of daylight to penetrate the room.

"No, that won't do!" said the engineer, still speaking aloud, slowly and softly. "Not enough light for me to be able to see the Nocturnals' eyes clearly—but if I open it any wider, those eyes might not be able to bear the light, and they'll close their eyelids obstinately."

He reflected momentarily in silence.

"Let's see," he said, suddenly, "the problem poses itself as follows: to create lighting here as closely similar as possible to that of the Rhean light, in which its two 'moons' and the stars shed that 'obscure clarity' of which, it's said, the poet talks—which is exactly the circumstance necessary for an ordinary Terran and Rhean Nocturnals to be able to see sufficiently clearly. That's the problem—what's the solution?"

He reflected further, and suddenly slapped his forehead.

"Oh! I've got it! Véronique's big blue veil."

He left the room, went straight to Mademoiselle d'Olbans' cabin and immediately located a large blue silken veil in a drawer under the bunk, with which the young woman sometimes liked to cover her head, fashioning it in the various fashions that a milliner of taste and talent would have admired equally.

Then, furnished with the veil, Ariste Fageat went back into the crew quarters and went to open another porthole in addition to the one he had left ajar. This one was placed in such a way that its light shone directly upon the two parallel hammocks in which the Nocturnals were lying, still bound.

When the porthole was open, however, Fageat began talking while he acted.

"There! Now, thanks to the rail supporting the little curtain of coarse cloth, leaving that curtain extended over the crystal, I suspend the blue veil. Good—and quite simple... no, it won't do; the light's still too bright. Fortunately, it's a large veil. Let's fold it in two... aha! That's better, but what if it were tripled? Is it broad enough, long enough? Yes. Bravo! That's exactly the degree, the tonality, the nuance and the lack of intensity required. For myself, I can only just see, but well enough. As for the Nocturnals, it'll be exactly like the Rhean night. Perfect! But are the swine asleep or awake?"

First, Fageat went to close the first porthole. Then he came back to place himself between the two hammocks in which the giant Nocturnals were lying, their heads sticking out, supported on the beam to which the hook was attached.

Immediately, the engineer saw, to his delight, that neither of the two captives was asleep. Their eyes were wide open.

"Ah!" Fageat exclaimed, immediately. "You're still looking at me with the same avid and violent curiosity, eh? Just like the Diurnals, until they got their summary explanation, you're wondering what sort of animal I am and where I come from. Well, my fine gorillas, we'll try to reach an understanding, you and I. To begin with, that will be thanks to the prodigious faculty of expression your eyes have. I'll find out right away whether your real intelligence is proportionate to the intense life of your gaze. For that, I'll be content to appeal to the primordial need of every living creature—the need for nourishment."

Then, before the two Nocturnals, evidently very attentive and curious, sometimes leaning over one and sometimes over the other but always clearly in view of both at the same time, he opened and closed his mouth, showed his teeth, clicked them and, touching the thick protruding lips of the Rheans, made them understand that he wanted to see their own teeth.

Fageat was not obliged to prolong the mime. At the fourth repetition, he was understood, and with a sort of broad rictus, the Nocturnals parted their lips in such a way as to uncover their teeth, with their jaws clamped.

"Damn!" the engineer swore. "What fine carnivorous teeth! Let's count them. One, two..." And he concluded, at the end of the second row: "Forty-six! And all there: molars, canines, incisors. I understand the terror, when they saw that we

116

were bipeds, of the little simian quadrumanes in the forest. They must often have been chased by the big Nocturnals, and devoured when captured. So you're carnivores, gentlemen, although the Diurnals are specialist fructivores of a sort. Good! I'll try to make you understand, now, that I'll be a friend to you. Wait a minute!"

He went to the storage-locker, opened a refrigerator, and took out a quarter of beef, which he divided in two with a slash of his knife, and, putting them on a plate, he went back to the other room.

At the sight of the meat, the Nocturnals' red eyes sparkled, and they exchanged words—they were definitely words, the brief, articulate sounds that emerged from the Nocturnals' mouths; Fageat had no doubt about it—in their strange guttural voices.

Knowing what he knew, the engineer deemed that the electric light would, in case of danger, be an immediately effective and victorious weapon.

I only have to flick a switch, he told himself.

And after having put the plate on the table, he did not hesitate to untie and unravel the rope that attached the arms of one of the Nocturnals to its sides—but he did not touch the one that bound its legs together.

Being stiff, the Herculean Rhean had some difficulty, at first, in moving its arms and its hands. That was brief, though; the blood circulation and the play of the muscles was rapidly reestablished. Then Fageat handed it the plate.

With one hand, the Nocturnal took a piece of meat and voraciously set about eating it, with grunts of pleasure and joyful gleams in its red eyes.

Immediately, the engineer did the same for the other captive.

Five minutes later, an exchange of ideas began, by means of gestures, signs and vocal sounds.

It required Ariste Fageat to employ all the ingenuity, patience and persistence of which he was capable. That capacity was great; it could only be limited by time—and Fageat was expecting to have at least 24 hours ahead of him, if not 36. He did not hurry feverishly—he had never been so calm and so self-controlled—but he did not waste a minute. Not one glance, not one change of expression, nor a movement or gesture or sound emitted by him was unnecessary. Everything was aimed toward his objective and nothing but his objective—which was to make himself understood to the Nocturnals and to understand them, to seduce them, to subjugate them, to dominate them, to make allies of them while remaining their master, their only master, even when he set them free—for his cunning and terrible plan of action included, of course, the Nocturnals returning home, to their native habit, their natural Rhean environment.

After an hour's work, he was able to take as exact and certain a certain quantity of data, which he formulated himself in a loud voice, while going to put together in the store-room the elements of a meal that the Nocturnals would share with him.

"Their language is extremely simple—much simpler even than that of the Diurnals, the vocabulary of which isn't very extensive nor the syntax very complicated. The language of the Nocturnals corresponds to the primordial needs that were doubtless those of terrestrial humans in the Stone Age, in the prehistoric eras of Earth. It won't take me long to get a thorough knowledge of it and to make use of it easily. That will suffice, broadly, for what I want these Nocturnal people to do.

"The most astonishing thing is that they can't bear daylight, and know nothing whatsoever of any artificial light, except for the inexplicable phosphorescence that the Diurnals use. In particular, above all, they're unacquainted with fire..."

On that, Ariste Fageat stopped speaking and moving. Then he repeated:

"They're unacquainted with fire! For if the Diurnals knew about fire, they'd use it as a sovereign weapon against the Nocturnals. Thus, the planet Rhea knows nothing of fire. That's truly amazing! For if that's so, everything that is provided and produced on Earth by fire, and by means of fire, must be unknown, ad even impossible, on Rhea. A world, a civilization, from which the element of fire is totally excluded! All human civilization, on Earth, depends on fire, the knowledge and usage of fire. But here... yes, yes... that's amazing! All the rest is trivial!"

A few minutes after his brief meditation, Fageat resumed moving.

From the crew quarters he brought a large tray laden with various foodstuffs, a carafe of water, a bottle of wine, three glasses and the customary cutlery. He had included a large quantity of raw meat, but he also brought a jellied chicken, a potato salad, various game conserves, vegetables and fruits—and a large loaf of bread.

The Nocturnals ate it all, with a sensual voracity. Only the raw meat was familiar to them, and also, albeit by analogy, the hazelnuts.

"So they're omnivores," the Terran engineer concluded, "although the Diurnals only east one single aliment: the kind of hard shell-less nuts produced by the countless trees of the Rhean forests and woods."

Immediately, by a natural association of ideas that had already occurred to the Terrans, he added:

"But what do these Herculean carnivorous Nocturnals, voracious and with a frightful appetite, do with the Diurnals that they capture with such difficulty, at the risk of their lives?"

Fageat did not yet know enough of the vocabulary of the Rheans to ask that question intelligibly, especially in the absence of any Diurnal that could have served as a "subject of demonstration" and would have made the explanation easy.

All right! Fageat said to himself. *I'll find out later.* Laughing, he added, aloud:

"But great gods, what an appetite! If I let those fellows into the stores, they'd devour a month's provisions in a month."

He got them to taste the wine, not by means of a glass but by pouring a few centiliters of the "juice of the vine" into the palm of their enormous left hand.

At first the Nocturnals pulled a face, but they immediately exchanged, in their strangely guttural voices—"Moorishly guttural," as Fageat put it—a few words that were doubtless appreciative. And with the same movement, they held out their cupped hands again.

"Aha!" the engineer exclaimed, enormously amused. "You want some more, in order to have a better-informed opinion? Bravo! But be careful! I don't want to get you drunk, and I want to make you understand that wine, in case of need, will be the recompense for your good conduct—which is to say, your docility toward me, and me alone."

And with untiring patience, an ingenuity that incessantly had recourse to new means, in the wan half-light that did not hurt the Nocturnals' eyes while permitting Fageat to see adequately, the Terran worked for hours to make himself understood to the Rheans, to understand them, and to initiate himself into the essential principles of their language.

Finally, however, he could do no more, and also took account of the fatigue that was rendering the thoughts of his two strange interlocutors slower, more leaden and more obtuse. Ariste Fageat then applied himself very intelligently to the task of terminating he extravagant conversation and obtaining from them gazes, gestures and brief words that gave him the certainty on which, for the moment, he wanted to be able to rely: that the two Nocturnals regarded him as a friend, all-powerful and benevolent, and, by contrast, would remain closed to any attempted seduction by the other Terrans, who were to be considered as perfidious enemies.

To be sure, that was conceived, understood and agreed in a very rudimentary manner, without any explanation of reasons—but Ariste Fageat had no doubt that in the relatively obtuse but instinctive minds of the two Nocturnals, it was conceived, understood and agreed.

"Very good!" concluded the engineer, aloud, rubbing his hands together. "I have only to wait for, or, if necessary, give rise to, an opportunity to act." He laughed nervously, and sniggered: "Ah, Véronique, you're going to find on the planet Rhea a destiny that neither you nor the Nyctalope has foreseen!"

Then, carefully, he returned to their original condition the ropes that attached the Nocturnals tightly to the hammocks—and the monsters let him do it without the slightest resistance. They knew, thanks to the *Woo*—the word that signified "Master" in their language—that their captivity would henceforth be temporary and free of peril.

Chapter VIII
Fageat and Veronique

Ariste Fageat had, in any case, a great deal more time to advance his knowledge of the Nocturnals and to make himself appreciated by them, as much as a benefactor as an all-powerful and redoubtable master. To terrorize them, it was sufficient for him to play intelligently with a simple electric pocket torch, the luminous beam of which their eyes could not support even for a fraction of a second.

Yes, Ariste Fageat had the time to place 100 measuring-posts to ensure the smooth imminent execution of his diabolical plan—for the six Terrans who had left with the two Diurnals remained absent for two Rhean days—which is to say, for 72 hours.

He was asleep, and was woken up by the arrival of Saint-Clair, Véronique and their companions.

They had agreed that the terrestrial calendar would be applied to life on Rhea, and they counted the hours in slices of 24 without taking account of the Rhean day and night. In consequence, terrestrial "midnight" sometimes fell in the middle of the Rhean day, and that was only a simple example of the regular disconnection that was contiually produced and reproduced.

It was, therefore, at 8 p.m. on September 8, corresponding on that day to the 18th hour of the Rhean day, that Ariste Fageat was woken up by the cheerful voice of Soca.

"Hey, Monsieur Fageat! Are you asleep? We're back!"

The engineer was lying on his bunk, fully dressed. He had only to stand up, rub his eyes, put his short hair in order and go into the central compartment, where everyone was assembled.

He saw immediately that there was no Diurnal there. He was glad of that. Immediately, Saint-Clair spoke to him:

"Bonjour, Monsieur Fageat. We're delighted with out sojourn in the Diurnals' city. We'll tell you everything that we've learned. But first, how's your ankle?"

"Thank you, Monsieur," Fageat replied. "A simple bruise. Arnica lotion and a bandage put it right in a matter of hours."

"Good! I hope you've taken advantage of the time to study our Nocturnals?"

Fageat expected that question and several others. His response were ready. He also expected that a great importance would be attributed to what he had been able to achieve with regard to the Nocturnals; he was not mistaken. All faces turned toward him, all eyes interrogating him with the same intense curiosity.

He therefore replied, casually:

"Certainly, Monsieur. I've devoted myself to that, and I've acquired certain notions that I believe to be in conformity with the true reality."

"Well, let's all sit down," said Saint-Clair, smiling. "We can't help being a little fatigued. Sit down, Fageat. Let's talk, to establish the essentials of what we know. Then we'll eat. After dinner, we'll get some rest until tomorrow morning. Then we'll act, for we have a great many important things to do, first of all with respect to the *Olb.-I* and the Earth, then with regard to Rhea and its inhabitants, Diurnal and Nocturnal."

He sat down. They all copied him. Without any pre-planning, they placed themselves in such a way that Saint-Clair, Véronique and Gno Mitsang in the front rank, and Margot, Soca and Vitto a little behind, were all facing Ariste Fageat, in an irregular semicircle.

"Well, what are the notions you've acquired?" asked the Nyctalope, good-humoredly.

Not without rancor, Fageat thought: *They're content! They're happy! And Véronique, what joyful serenity in her eyes, on her lips!* Immediately, however, he replied in a deliberate tone:

123

"Oh, they're not very numerous, for the Nocturnals are very primitive beings. Firstly, they're omnivores, and carnivores for preference. Secondly, they have a summary language, but which has a definite syntax. Thirdly, they're nyctalopes, clearly and exclusively—which is to say that they can see in the dark, but can't bear any light that's brighter than the phosphorescence of the Diurnals and their city. Fourth, they're extremely savage, taciturn and mistrustful. I was only doing good in giving them something to eat and drink, but I was careful only to free their hands and forearms. To be sure, if I'd had to engage them in a struggle, a few beams of electric light would have sufficed to render their brute strength ineffective, but I didn't risk that, thinking that the light might render them definitively blind—that would have been needless cruelty on my part. And that's all, Monsieur."

Fageat was lying, and lying enormously! But he was quite tranquil, for he was certain that the Nocturnals would not do anything that might reveal that he had lied. The engineer was internally jubilant, with an ironic ferocity, when he heard Saint-Clair say, simply:

"What you say doesn't surprise us. It fits in perfectly with everything that the Diurnals have been able to tell us about the Nocturnals."

But Fageat thought: *Of course! So far as the Diurnals are concerned, the Nocturnals are nothing but savage brutes!*

Saint-Clair continued:

"We don't know what the Nocturnals do in their mysterious unexplored lairs with the Diurnals they capture in the course of their attacks on the cities. I say 'cities' because the one we know is reproduced in tens of thousands of exemplars spread all over the planet Rhea, where there are no oceans, but only streams, rivers and great lakes." The Nyctalope made a gesture, and said in a firmer tone: "But let's leave these details. For Rhea, for Rhean society, there is one essential characteristic." He emphasized his words: "This planet is a world without fire."

By virtue of what the engineer had been able to learn from the Nocturnals, Fageat was already aware of the near-certainty of that "characteristic." Nevertheless, he manifested considerable surprise by means of gesture and speech at the Nyctalope's clear affirmation.

"Oh!" he said. "Without fire?"

"Yes, without fire. And much more devoid of fire than a certain prehistoric humankind whose existence it is easy for us to imagine, before humans had begun to make use of the fire originating from volcanoes, lightning and spontaneous combustion due to the sun's rays. Yes, much more, for on Rhea there are no volcanoes, lightning does not strike, and no spark produced by the combined action of the sun's rays and the splintering of a rock, for instance, has every set fire to a tuft of dry grass, because the sun is always muted here by the atmosphere, in a manner unknown to Terrans."

After a pause, he added:

"Thus, Rhean civilization, which is in certain respects highly developed, thanks to the intelligence of the Diurnals, and Rhean savagery, constituted and maintained by the Nocturnals, is incapable of any progress. In brief, the entire Rhean world, in its entirety and in its details, is a world in which the element of fire is not only unknown but unimaginable—even impossible, for all Rhean substance, including dry wood, is uninflammable."

Saint-Clair fell silent. Softly, as if to himself, Gno said: "Whereas on Earth, all human life has been conditioned, for thousands of centuries, by the knowledge, usage and multiple adaptations of fire."

Ariste Fageat was utterly indifferent to these facts and reflections. He was thinking about Véronique d'Olbans, at whom he nevertheless avoided looking. Apparently, he only had eyes and ears for Gno Mitang and Saint-Clair

The latter went on:

"I'll be brief, Fageat, in telling you the essentials. On Rhea there are only two industries. One is national, all the Diurnals on the planet only forming a single nation; that's the

125

industry of architectural construction. It has three successive phases: firstly, the accumulation and modeling of the building-earth; secondly, the transportation of blocks of earth to the place of employment, and thirdly, the construction and repair of the high encircling walls and urban edifices."

Then Fageat, in order to seem interested in these things—in which, but for his obsessive passion, he really would have been interested—said, excitedly:

"As to the transport and utilization of the blocks, I can form an idea of that—but what do the Rheans do with regard to the collection and modeling of the earth, without iron tools fashioned by fire?"

"Iron ore does not exist on Rhea," Saint-Clair replied, "Or, if it exists beneath the planet's surface, the Rheans are unaware of it. The building-earth is found in numerous deposits, on the surface and at various depths, in humid hollows; it's quite similar to our terrestrial clay. The Diurnals cut it roughly by means of long rigid rods made from the single stem of a plant—a kind of solid reed, or bulrush, which grows in abundance around the deposits. The blocks, cut and removed by hand, are shaped by the Diurnals, still by hand, into perfect cubes. These cubes are immediately transported, each by a Rhean, for whom it is a normal load. At the site of utilization, the encircling wall or urban edifice, the blocks arrive continually, as in a chain, and are positioned immediately. They dry out in a few hours, linking themselves together indissolubly, and only crumble gradually after a time we estimate at 100 terrestrial years—a time longer than the average lifespan of a Diurnal Rhean."

He fell silent, smiling, more at his own thoughts than at Fageat. The latter was about to formulate another question when Véronique, touching Saint-Clair's elbow, said to him:

"Shall we eat? I confess that I'm very hungry. The Diurnals nuts are not, after all, a substantial nourishment for us. In any case, I ate very few of them. I don't like them; their insipid softness nauseates me."

"That's true, Véronique!" said Saint-Clair, getting to his feet. "And we'll all help you. While doing that, we'll continue to bring Fageat up to date with our own discoveries."

But Fageat thought: *Bah! I'll have plenty of time to learn everything for myself about the existence of the Diurnal and Nocturnal Rheans—such petty matters—and also to modify it!* He continued nevertheless to listen in a desultory fashion to what Saint-Clair, Margot, Vitto, Secco and Véronique herself were telling him while they were all coming and going between the dining-room, the store-rooms and the kitchen.

Only Gno Mitang, after offering a smiling apology to Véronique, remained apart, sitting meditatively in an arm-chair, with his eyes seemingly closed and his arms folded.

The *Olb.-I*'s pharmacy had been composed with a great deal of care by Dr. Serres, not only so as to provide an adequate pharmacopeia for the great voyage of exploration, but also in accordance with the imaginative and scientific suggestions of Maxime d'Olbans and Saint-Clair. One "shelf" of the pharmacy was rich in anesthetics, sedatives and narcotics, some for administration by subcutaneous, intravenous or intramuscular injection, others to be respired and yet others to be swallowed. Among the latter, several were colorless, odorless and tasteless.

"You understand," Maxime d'Olbans had said to Dr. Serres, "that our Terrans might be exposed, on Rhea, to the most bizarre combinations of circumstances; we need to anticipate everything, especially the possibility, much less fantastic than is believed, that the might have to render unconscious a being endowed with intelligence and reason without arousing the suspicions of the being."

Thus, on the evening of September 8, on Rhea, Ariste Fageat, while uncorking in the pantry three bottles of a light Vouvray wine—an evening wine—which Vitto then put on the table, was able without any difficulty to charge the wine with a strong dose of a narcotic. The latter had the quadruple property of neither disturbing nor modifying the color of the wine, nor altering its taste, of being undetectable by the sense of smell and, finally, of not producing its effect until two or three hours after ingestion. However, the effect was then massive, and, even in small doses, lasted at least 15 to 20 hours according to temperament.

When that was done, nothing thereafter was of any importance, or even interest, for Ariste Fageat.

Oh, they can talk at length about Rhea and Rheans—my role, fortunately, is merely to listen.

But he did not even listen. He replied from time to time, when a reply was obligatory, with a movement of the head or a monosyllable. He ate a great deal and chewed slowly, as was his habit. And as it was known that he only drank water with the evening meal, with a constancy and severe regularity, no one—not even the observant Gno Mitang—was astonished, or even took any particular note, of the fact that the engineer did not touch a drop of the wine.

Finally, when the meal was over, it seemed perfectly natural for Fageat to say to the Nyctalope:

"Monsieur, I request the first watch, for a period of six hours. I slept for a long time, and profoundly, during your absence; I'm fully alert, while your own great fatigue, and everyone else's, is obvious. After my six hours of guard duty, I'll wake Margot..."

"Yes," Saint-Clair replied. "But tomorrow, we'll devote the morning to our two Nocturnals—all right, Gno?"

"Agreed," said the Japanese, laconically.

Half an hour later, aboard the *Olb.-I*, six Terrans were sleep, either in the bunks in their cabins or in their hammocks.

Three hours passed, and that sleep was no longer a natural phenomenon but a sort of general anesthesia.

Electric torch in hand, Fageat went from cabin to cabin, and then inspected the hammocks.

"Bravo!" he said—aloud, so sure was he of the facts and of himself. "Bravo! I can act now. Now for my Nocturnals!"

Although they resembled one another more closely than humans generally resemble one another, the two captive

128

Nocturnals presented dissimilarities that made them easily distinguishable fro one another. He named them—pronouncing the names in an exceedingly guttural manner—Ggo and Rrou. Ggo was the taller and stouter of the two, with a more prognathous face, smaller dark red eyes and very pale eyebrows, bead and hair, like a terrestrial albino, Rrou was shorter and thinner, with bright red eyes and hair of a bizarre green-tinted color.

Ariste Fageat's first concern was to establish throughout the *Olb.-I*, by means of a few carefully-veiled electric lamps, a pale, lunar light that the Nocturnals could tolerate and which was sufficient for him to do what he wanted to do without having one hand impeded by a portable electric torch—which, even camouflaged like a night-light, would have been less convenient in every way than the moderated but general illumination of the entire vehicle.

Having done that, the engineer equipped himself.

"Let's not forget anything," he said, with that mania for whispered monologue that many taciturn people have when they are alone, especially when they know that people within range cannot hear them. "Weapons, ammunition, the knapsack that I've judiciously equipped, binoculars, electric lamp fastened to shoulder-strap, lasso..."

He had, of course, dressed himself first, lightly but comfortably; he had a Basque beret on his head and was shod in tight knee-length boots.

"Yes, I know!" he continued, without slowing down or disturbing his lucid, reasoned, methodical and precise activity. "I know! I'm burning all my bridges behind me. I'm condemning myself to live, separated from the Earth and the human species, on a planet about which, fundamentally, I don't know very much, and only incoherently.

"On the other hand, I'm abducting a young woman who will hate me all the more because I'm sealing her from the Nyctalope, with whom she's in love. And with her, I'll live in conditions about which I'm almost totally ignorant."

He uttered a scornful snigger, as if he were mocking himself, and went on:

"Bah! As for the second point, given that Véronique, probably by force rather than her own desire, will become my wife; and given that a wife often rapidly becomes a very different person from the young woman she was before; and given, too, that a wife is endowed with faculties of resignation, transformation, adaptation, forgetfulness and renewal, which are mathematically incalculable because they're practically infinite…oh yes, given all that, it's quite possible that Mademoiselle Véronique d'Olbans will one day be in love with Ariste Fageat!"

Again he sniggered, this time more emotionally than mockingly.

"As for the first point," he continued, "the hypothesis isn't excluded that I shall take possession of the *Olb.-I* and return to Earth, especially if Véronique the wife becomes an element of action unlike Véronique the young woman. And that really would be enormous!

"Enormous, yes, but possible! For deep down, I'm a great adventurer. Before the construction of the *Olb.-I*, I dreamed of adventure—of *the* great adventure. A taciturn steward, solitary and home-loving—of a vast domain—I only committed my intelligence and body to that; but my soul, my imagination, my innate passion…to what prodigies of adventure did they not reach out? Deep down, my true life was the one I lived in my voyaging, adventurous, untamable, rebellious thought…

"And then, all of a sudden, the adventure arrived: the unimaginable opportunity that I immediately seized. I would have killed Saint-Clair and Véronique, and been killed over their cadavers, if the Nyctalope had refused to take me with him. Now… well, now, I'm following the logic of my soul, my character, my temperament—in sum, my destiny—in doing what I'm doing, which will seem to everyone else to be a foot of madness, but which is for me, I know full well, an act of pure reason.

"Let's go—giddy up! I'm ready. Now for the Nocturnals..."

From then on, Ariste Fageat abandoned his monologue.

In a few minutes, Ggo and Rrou were unbound, standing up, ready to obey the glances and gestures of the Woo, their Master.

First, he led them to Véronique's bunk. He picked up the profoundly unconscious young woman in his arms, and immediately confided her to Ggo—who, comprehending, disposed his right arm as a chair of which the enormous open hand was the seat; with his left hand, he supported the light limp body delicately against his torso.

Then Ariste Fageat headed toward one of the *Olb.-I*'s doors, followed by Ggo, who was followed by Rrou. The automatic opening-mechanism functioned.

With the same elastic stride, the three made their exit, and Fageat carefully closed the door again.

The Nocturnals' gait did not consist of long bounds, like that of the winged Diurnals. They took steps like Terrans, but each step, of course, took them at least three meters forward, and they did not want to shorten that stride. Fageat had no difficulty in adjusting his speed to their normal speed, and the three fugitives marched abreast, the Terran between the two Nocturnals.

Moonlit and starry, cloudless for the moment, the night was bright, but it was a brightness that the Rhean nyctalopes could tolerate. And that caused an idea to occur to Fageat that was very disagreeable, an apprehension of a dangerous future: *On that particular phenomenal point, the Nocturnals are inferior to Saint-Clair, since his nyctalopia doesn't diminish his normal human clear-sightedness at all...*

But that was a rapid, fugitive thought, for the Terran had to pay much closer attention to the contingencies of the present.

With regard to the direction of the march, he left the initiative to his two simian companions. His intention, which they had understood, was to reach, in the shortest possible time, the profound caverns in which the local tribe of Nocturnals lived.

Soon, Fageat observed that they were heading westwards across the wooded plain, in the direction of the rocky hills, from the summit of one of which the Terrans, during their first excursion, had first made the acquaintance of the Rhean wind and then discovered, after a partial circuit, the Diurnal city.

When they arrived at the edge of the dense forest, however, at a clearing beyond which a hill rose up, with sparser trees and numerous outcrops of rock, a brutal incident occurred that the Terran had not foreseen.

The Nocturnal carrying the unconscious Véronique was to his left, the other to his right. The latter, Rrou, struck the Woo's arm with his hand, proffering the word "Ma!" which signifies, all on it's own: "Halt; stay here, go no further; wait for me; don't move; don't speak; and don't make any noise"—at least insofar as the Terra Fageat understood the multiple and concordant meanings of the word.

"Ma!"

As Fageat and Ggo stopped dead, Rrou made a furious leap forward, which carried him ten meters further on, and immediately leapt back again.

Yelps burst forth, in which Fageat recognized the cries of the simian quadrumanes that the Terrans had seen during their first sortie after passing through the forested region of the large white birds.

At the same time, there were sounds of flight and climbing—and Fageat saw several small animals emerge from the undergrowth and hurl themselves on to the trunk of a tree, which they set about climbing rapidly. The Nocturnal, however, came within range of that tree before all the yelping fugitives was far enough up to defy the Nocturnal's leaps.

Well, Fageat said to himself, *my big fellows aren't climbers—but the little monkeys are.*

Even so, Rrou had jumped as high as he could, and had snatched two clambering quadrumanes from at least six meters up the trunk—and the carnivore reckoned that a great success, for he laughed like a huge rusty corncrake as he returned to the Woo and Ggo. He was holding the two monkeys at arms length, which were struggling and yelping in vain.

Then Ggo, in a tone that was ardently and avidly supplicatory, said: "Woo! Woo!"

"What? What do you want?" said Fageat, mechanically.

From Ggo's attitude he understood that the Nocturnal was asking permission to set down his burden on the grass.

"Yes, yes!" said the Terran, nodding his head and pointing at the ground.

With infinite gentleness, the Nocturnal laid Véronique on the grass at the Master's feet. As soon as he was upright again he bounded toward Rrou, who threw him one of his captives.

"Damn, what carnivores!" Fageat soon exclaimed.

A few paces away from him, each of the Nocturnals had acted in the same manner. Their stout hands took hold of the monkeys' thighs and drew violently apart, which had the effect of tearing each animal in two. Then the Nocturnals set about devouring the quivering prey, spurting warm blood. They ate as a Terran peasant might eat an apple, taking large bites and occasionally spitting out a shred of skin that was too thick.

That feast—hideous to any other eyes but Fageat's, which were curious and deliberately insensitive—only lasted five minutes. Having spat out the last morsels of excessively tough skin and excessively thick bone, Ggo and Rrou wiped their cheeks with tufts of grass, rubbed their hands on moss with a care that Fageat had not expected, and, satisfied, came over to the Woo, before whom they laughed, showing al their teeth.

"Very good!" said Fageat. "But I have an idea, chaps! I'll show you that my power is more rapid and far-ranging than yours! That will increase the enormous respect that you already have for me even more enormously."

Having said that aloud, although he knew full well that such statements could not be understood, the engineer made a gesture and pronounced, firmly: "Ma!"

Rooted to the spot, to the left and right of the recumbent Véronique, by that imperious "Stay there!" Ggo and Rrou watched the Woo's movement carefully.

Fageat took the repeating rifle that he had been wearing over his shoulder in his hands, showed it to the two Nocturnals, and repeated "Ma!" in a rude fashion, touching each of them with the tip of his extended index finger and then pointing at the ground at their feet. The red eyes and entire attitude of the monsters were acquiescent, making the promise. Then, sure that they would not run away and that the terror they would experience would nail them even more firmly to the spot, Ariste Fageat went to put his idea into action.

He headed toward a nearby tree that was more isolated than the others; he had noticed that a good dozen of the quadrumane climbers had taken refuge in its branches.

The animals must not have lacked intelligence, and their curiosity must have been as keen as that of terrestrial monkeys, for when he arrived a few paces from the tree, Fageat saw the quadrumanes sitting on the lower branches, in the open, clearly in sight, leaning over as if to observe what was happening beneath them. At that height, the most furious leaps of the Nocturnals could not reach them—but for a rifle, the perching animals were almost at point-blank range.

The weapon was a repeater; Fageat could have fired a dozen bullets without reloading, but he wanted to conserve his ammunition.

For the demonstration I want to make, he thought, *four shots will suffice*.

The lunar and stellar light coming through the foliage, which was not very dense, gave the sniper a clear sight of his living targets, lined up side by side.

Fageat was a first-class hunter. He raised his weapon and fired four times in as many seconds; four monkeys fell.

Quickly, Fageat went back to the Nocturnals, while suspending his weapon over his right shoulder by means of its strap. Grabbing hold of them, he dragged them, incapable as they were of obeying him by virtue of their total confusion, and showed them the four dead beasts on the ground.

Then he took hold of his carbine again with his left hand, and with the right he took the 7.65 caliber automatic pistol from its holster—which was sufficient in size for an intelligent eye, on seeing the object beside the longer-barreled rifle, to establish a certain correlation between the two weapons with regard to the effects of their utilization.

But Ariste Fageat did not limit himself to showing the Nocturnals, in a parallel fashion, the character of the rifle and the pistol; he wanted to demonstrate to the that with the smaller, more easily manipulable object he could, just as easily and just as mysteriously, achieve results that were just as marvelous.

He was as good a shot with a pistol as with a rifle, and on the lower braches of the tree, other quadrumanes were still sitting motionless, uncomprehending or paralyzed with terror.

"Ggo! Rrou!" said Fageat. W

ith the hand holding the pistol, he pointed to the tree and to a branch—an isolated branch on which a single animal was sitting. Then, extending his arm and taking aim, he squeezed the trigger. The detonation made the two Nocturnals jump, that being their only corporeal manifestation of emotion—and they saw a fifth victim fall to the ground, evidently dead.

Fageat wanted to recommence the demonstration of his two weapons, so terribly and strangely mortal, but he realized immediately that he had no need to weary himself with mime and explanatory onomatopoeia. The Nocturnals had understood that, by means of the objects he was handling, the mysterious Woo had killed living beings at a distance. They did not seem frightened, and Fageat thought: *Is that because mental fear is unknown to them? Do they only know physical pain?*

No, truly, they were not afraid, but, after their initial confusion, they revealed an infinite admiration, respectful and worshipful—if one may employ the latter word to character

135

the attitude of thinking beings of whom one does not know whether they have any kind of religion, or sense of adoration.

Immobile at first, Ggo and Rrou manifested their sentiments by a movement and attitude that was quite unexpected to Fageat, who had anticipated kneeling or prostration. Simply, in unison, both Nocturnals bent down, each uprooting from the soil a trailing creeper, straightened up, attached their wrists summarily together, skillfully formed knots with their fingers and the teeth, and, self-bound, so to speak, they closed their eyes and held out their tied hands to Fageat, their arms bent.

Satisfied, the Terran had to suppress a burst of laughter.

"Good!" he said. "That's clear. It means: 'More than before, you're our Master; eyes closed and hands at your mercy, we're yours. You can kill us if you wish, as you've killed these animals; we won't resist in any fashion.' Well, my word, that's perfect. I couldn't have asked for any more. Let's reward these understanding fellows."

First he untied the lianas and freed their hands. Then he said, firmly: "Ggo! Rrou!"

The Nocturnals opened their eyes. Fageat pointed at the cadavers and used all his fingers to make the gesture of putting nourishment into his mouth.

Ah! They understood him. The two Rhean monsters hurled themselves on the monkeys. It only took them ten minutes to devour them, as they had devoured those they had captured themselves a quarter of an hour earlier. With as much care as before, they rubbed their jaws, teeth and hands with tufts of grass and moss.

"Bravo!" concluded Fageat.

Moments later, the march resumed, but this time it was Rrou and not Ggo who carried the unconscious Véronique.

The Nocturnals still had the initiative in determining their direction. Fageat limited himself to getting his own bearings, making use of easily-discernible reference points in such a manner as to have a good enough grasp of the topography of the places between the *Olb.-I*'s clearing and the entrance to the Rhean caverns.

They did not start to climb the hill but to go around it, at least in part, for, after half an hour, they went through the opening of a narrow and short valley in order to skirt another hill, much wilder, rockier and steeper, with fewer trees, which was reminiscent of the terrain of the Corsican scrubland, save for its color, which was uniformly yellow with regard to the vegetation and gray with regard to the soil and the rocks.

Suddenly, the base of that hill was subject to a fracture, a retreat analogous to the acute angle made in a cake or round cheese when a triangular slice is cut and removed. The Nocturnals went into that angle, whose steep edges extended to an abrupt cliff-top.

At the back, which was about a kilometer from the periphery, an enormous arch offered an entrance to an exceedingly spacious cavern to all-comers.

"Good! Here we are at last!" said Fageat. "No trace of masonry, nor any construction or consolidation whatsoever. At the first sight of their habitat, the Nocturnals seem to me to be completely ignorant of architecture and masonry."

They went through the cavern from end to end in a straight line. A second arch appeared, much lower and narrower than the first. All the same, it gave easy access to the three entrants, still walking abreast. After twenty paces, however, the corridor, relatively high and wide for a natural subterranean tunnel, made an abrupt turn, and Fageat found himself in total darkness.

"Uh oh!" he said. "Time to light up. I'm neither the Nyctalope who can see clearly by day that Saint-Clair is, nor the kind of night-dwelling animal that the Rhean Nocturnals are." And he pronounced, imperiously: "Ma! Ma!"

His companions' halt was immediate, as was his own.

"Good!"

During the many hours he had spent in the *Olb.-I* in the sole company of Ggo and Rrou, the engineer had anticipated many things, including the fact that in the subterranean world of the Nocturnals he would need a means of lighting that was adequate for him but tolerable by the Nocturnals' eyes, which

137

all light wounded seriously save for the phosphorescence used by the Diurnals and pale moonlight or starlight. He had therefore carried out trials, putting increasingly thick layers of blue paint on the convex glass of one of the powerful portable electric lamps equipped with hooks that permitted them to be attached to any part of a man's garment or to his belt. He had soon arrived at the point at which the electric light, tinted and muted by the paint, did not offend the sensitive eyes of the Nocturnals, while providing an illumination sufficient for him to have an adequate visual range.

In addition, he was furnished with a powerful electric torch, uncamouflaged, which he could use if he were in danger and if it were in his interest to blind the Nocturnals painfully.

Thus, with his lamp suspended in the middle of his torso, Ariste Fageat switched it on, and a beam of pale blue light sprang forth in front of him, spreading out. He resumed marching immediately; the two Nocturnals immediately did likewise. The tunnel was still wide enough for the here marchers to remain side-by-side in single line.

The corridor was very sinuous, its height and width varying in dimension; it showed no sign of human—or, rather, Rhean—intervention or labor. Nothing, as yet indicated that the Nocturnal race made any kind of effort to ameliorate the conditions of its natural existence, but the evenness of the ground and the smoothness of the slightly-porous rock of which it was comprised provoked a thought in Fageat's mind.

For hundred of thousands of years, no doubt, multitudes of Nocturnals have passed this way, and the tread of their bare feet, almost as solid and rough as the hoof of a wild horse, has transformed the ground to the extent of making it a velvet carpet! No dust; the rock never crumbles.

As he made these reflections, Fageat began to hear sounds other than that of his own footfalls and the more muffled tread of his companions—and that changed the course of his thoughts.

We're getting close to the inhabited grottoes, he said to himself.

138

While continuing to walk, he listened harder, trying to identify the sounds that were reaching his ears—but it was only a dull murmur, like that produced by a high, broad waterfall.

A subterranean river? he wondered.

It occurred to him to study his companions. Alternatively, he looked at Rrou and Ggo, immediately observing that the Nocturnals were animated by a similar curiosity in his regard, and clearly distinguished in their eyes a kind of excitement, suggestive of a greater animation in their attitude and gait.

The creatures are jubilant at the prospect of the success they'll enjoy with their tribe, he thought, *by virtue of returning in my company, one of them carrying a unknown biped.*

Suddenly, however, as thy rounded a sharp bend in the subterranean tunnel, the sound of falling water became deafening; for paces further ahead Fageat stopped dead, crying out in an imperious voice: "Ma!"

Docile I spite of their increasing overexcitement, Ggo and Rrou stopped.

Then, searching the darkness with the pale beam of his electric lamp, which went from one side to the other as he moved his torso, the Terran tried to take account of the place.

He found that he was on the threshold of a grotto that he judged to be immense, for its walls and vault extended into darkness. To his right, at the limit of the range of the muted electric light, was the waterfall, a enormous mass emerging from a high orifice, too narrow for the light too reach it, and falling into a huge basin, doubtless very deep, from which the excess flowed away in a natural channel, the water running at floor level twenty paces in front of Fageat. To the right the rock-face rose vertically until it formed a parapet at the top of the cascade. To the left, however, there was a sort of quay about 15 meters wide.

Having seen all that, the Terran made a gesture.

"A!" replied Ggo and Rrou, in unison—which meant "yes."

Fageat's gesture had simply pointed at the quay.

"Well then, let's go!" he said—and all three of them set out along the broad ledge, equidistant from the rocky wall and the channel.

Immediately, however, the Terran perceived that the Nocturnals were accelerating their pace, lengthening their stride and tending to draw away from him. The prudent and adventurous Fageat did not want to tire himself out—he wanted to arrive in perfect physical shape and total mental lucidity before the Nocturnal people. He therefore took hold of Ggo's arm and Rrou's shoulder, to either side, and held them back, breaking their progress.

They understood, and meekly remained thereafter in a straight line with the Woo, who continued to advance at what had become for him, an ordinary pace, given the lightness and increased strength that the plant Rhea conferred upon him.

It was not for long, though. Five minutes had not yet gone by when Ariste Fageat said to himself: *Here we are, at last!*

And he made sure that his two principal weapons, the powerful electric torch to his left and the automatic pistol to his right, could move freely in the open holsters attached to his belt, and could be ready and aimed in his hands within three seconds.

Chapter IX
The Ambush

However well a criminal calculates, his solutions are rarely exact, because he is almost never in possession of all the facts of the problems he wants to solve.

Fageat estimated that the effect of the soporific administered to Saint-Clair, Véronique and their companions would last at least 15 hours—but he did not know that the Nyctalope, in the course of his travels through the countries of the Earth, had accustomed himself to a certain number of poisons, as Mithridates the Great had once done, and he also did not know that His Excellency Gno Mitang, exposed to many assassination attempts in the Asiatic style, had applied the same immunization process to himself while young. Even so, the narcotic employed by Fageat, a product of modern chemistry, was not without effect on the Nyctalope and the Japanese—but that effect, brutal at first, did not last as long as the criminal had expected.

Indeed, why was Fageat not a criminal through and through—which is to say, a poisoner? It would have been as easy for him to kill his victims as to put them to sleep. It was doubtless because his conscience was not yet completely corrupted, and perhaps also because his temperament, as an adventurer, wanted to have what is known as "the pleasure of risk." Then again, he was courageous and proud; he enjoyed a contest. To allow Saint-Clair and his companions to live, while betraying them and abducting their Mademoiselle d'Olbans, was to run a risk, to leave an enemy a chance. At that price, Ariste Fageat avoided despising himself, and gave himself a reason to admire himself.

At any rate, Gno Mitang was the first to wake up, long before the minimum of 15 hours had elapsed.

At first, he was astonished; his aching head felt heavy and his tongue rough. He thought: *But we only ate and drank perfectly healthy foodstuffs and beverages.*

He sat up and let himself slide out of his bunk. When he was standing, he had to put his hand on the wall of his cabin to support himself, for his legs were tremulous.

Uh oh! That's not normal...why?

He clicked his tongue against his palate, salivated, and tasted the saliva.

Bizarre! It reminds me of what I felt in my mouth when I came round after the operation on my wound. I didn't eat or drink anything different from Saint-Clair, Mademoiselle d'Olbans and everyone else. Let's see...?

Using both hands to prop himself up, Gno went first to the Nyctalope's cabin. Drawing aside the heavy curtain, he heard:

"Ah, Gno! Why are you here? What's happening? I don't feel well. Ah! You too...?"

"Me too," replied the Japanese, letting himself fall on to the bunk at the head of which Saint-Clair was sitting up, vigorously rubbing his forehead, temples and neck with a washing-glove steeped in ether.

"Here," said the Nyctalope. "Do as I'm doing. Nothing like it to dissipate the fuliginous vapors of bad sleep." And he put the washing-glove in his friend's hand, with the flask of ether. Then, almost immediately, he added: "But why that bad sleep, Gno? And me and you, my old friend, both so robust? Why? And why the two of us?"

"Perhaps the others too," risked the subtle Japanese, wiping his face, his forehead, his temples and his neck with the odorant, volatile and benevolent ether.

"Yes, I thought of that when I saw you," Sat-Clair replied, swiftly. "Let's go see Véronique!"

Sufficiently reanimated and invigorated no longer to be at risk of losing equilibrium, the two friends stood up and went at the same pace to Mademoiselle d'Olbans' cabin.

In a loud voice, Saint-Clair pronounced, in an almost-imperious tone:

"Véronique! Véronique!"

Absolute silence.

After 30 seconds, Saint-Clair drew the curtain with an abrupt gesture. The bunk was empty.

"Uh oh!" groaned the Nyctalope.

From then on, everything moved rapidly and abruptly.

Ariste Fageat's cabin was also empty. In the crew quarters, the hammocks to which the two gorilloid Nocturnals had been tied were similarly empty. As for Vitto, Soca and Jean Margot, they were sleeping like healthy brutes stunned by alcohol… or by a powerful soporific.

Oh, they were wide awake now and very lucid, Gno Mitang and LeoSaint-Clair! And they understood what they needed to understand—which was quite straightforward, made manifest by a hundred obvious clues.

"Abducted! He's abducted her, with the complicity of the two Nocturnals!" said Gno, in a dull voice, tremulous with anger.

As for Saint-Clair, he was in such a state of furious agony and tortuous rage that he could not pronounce a word to begin with, as rigid as a bar of iron from head to toe, his eyes fixed like enamel, his teeth clenched, his jaws so taut that his entire face was unrecognizable.

They were standing there, face to face, in the middle of the crew quarters, violently lit by all the electric lamps in the ceiling, between the three hammocks in which Soca, Vitto and Margot were asleep and the two empty hammocks from which the ropes that had secured the Nocturnals were hanging down.

For two, three or perhaps five minutes they remained there, immobile and mute.

Less sensitive than Saint-Clair, and less afflicted in the heart, Gno Mitang was the first to make a gesture and resume speaking.

"Leo," he said, tapping his friend's left wrist with a firm but gentle hand, "I don't want you to go after them alone. I'll go with you. You can leave a brief explanatory note for Vitto, Soca and Margot, with your instructions—your orders. They'll wake up, read it, and obey. And the two of us can leave, can go."

Saint-Clair shivered. His body relaxed; his eyes became human again; his face became his own face again.

"Yes, we'll leave right away!" he said, in a contained, menacing and terrible voice. Oh, the last vapors of the soporific drug had been thoroughly dissipated!

It took them a full hour however, to dress lightly, and to equip and arm themselves completely. Given what they had learned from the Diurnals in their city with regard to the Nocturnals, they believed that they needed to find Fageat and save Véronique without waiting for Vitto, Soca and Margot, who would receive orders to follow them and help them to reduce the savage tribes of Nocturnals to impotence, at least in that region of Rhea.

After writing his instructions for the three sleepers on a large sheet of paper that as pinned up beneath the only electric light they left on in the crew quarters, Saint-Clair and Mitang made a careful check of everything that they were carrying, either in their pockets, buckled or fastened to their clothing, or in cartridge-belts and knapsacks.

"Nothing missing," said the Nyctalope.

"No, nothing," confirmed the Japanese.

"Let's go!"

They went out of the *Olb.-I*, having made sure that all the portholes were tightly closed inside and out, as well as the doors. In their absence, the interplanetary vehicle would be inviolable, save by Fageat and with his key—but the traitor's return was the most improbable thing in the world, at leas for a few days.

The Diurnals of the city had never entered the subterranean domains of the Nocturnals willingly. Those who had been taken there as captives had never emerged again; none of them had ever reappeared. The Rheans of the day were therefore entirely ignorant with regard to the existence of the Rheans of the night, their enemies and their abductors since time immemorial.

Often, however, after an attack on their city, the Diurnals had followed the retreating savage hordes at a distance, so the location of the entrance—unique, they thought—to the subterranean habitations was well-known.

During their sojourn in the city, Saint-Clair and Mitang had drawn a map of the region according to the precise information given by the Diurnals. Not only did they consult that map before leaving the *Olb.-I*, but the Japanese brought it with them, carefully folded and enclosed in one of the four cartridge-cases fixed to his belt.

It was, therefore, without difficulty and after several hours of rapid march, but at a pace calculated to avoid fatigue, that the two friends arrived at the large arch hollowed out by nature in the base of a hill in the wildest part of that mountainous region.

It was not yet daylight, but bright gleams in the east were advertising the imminent dawn. Turning his back on that auroral enchantment, Saint-Clair and Mitang went into the first cave without hesitation.

"Wait!" said Saint-Clair, suddenly.

"What can you see?" asked Gno.

"Look."

Saint-Clair pointed at the ground with his index finger.

There, the ground was covered with a kind of fine sand, doubtless falling from the vault, which was crumbling imperceptibly. On that sand thousands of traces were visible—the imprints of huge bare feet. Precisely because of their number, however, they formed a kind of continuity, over which imprints other than those of Nocturnal feet had been strongly marked.

"Fageat's boots!" murmured Gno Mitang.

"Yes."

"I was sure that we were on the right track."

"And that, my dear Gno, legitimates our certainty. If the subterranean tunnel beginning over there is unique, we only have to follow it, without consulting the ground—but if there's a bifurcation, and even if the ground doesn't remain uniformly dusty, we'll find Fageat's footprints. Good. Let's go!"

Being a nyctalope, Saint-Clair did not have to use any light at all when he went into the dark region of the subterranean tunnel. Gno, on he other hand, was blind from then on. Nevertheless, as the light of a torch-beam might have revealed their presence prematurely, the Japanese did not switch one on. He was content to grip Saint-Clair's right hand with his left hand, and the two friends continued to walk at the same rapid pace, accustomed as they were to move in that fashion, one guiding the other. They had done it so often before in the course of their numerous adventures!

They did not stop once, having not encountered any difficulty, before reaching the vast grotto with the waterfall, the pool, the natural channel and the quay continuing to the left.

The darkness was absolute; Gno Mitang could hear the rumble of the cascade, but he could not see anything. The Nyctalope described the place to him in a few words, concluding:

"There's no other route than the quay extending to our left, alongside the water, between the channel and the all of the immense cave. There's no dust here; the rock in the vault isn't the sort that crumbles—but I have no need, here, to see footprints. I repeat: there's no other route."

"Good," said Gno. "Onwards?"

"Yes."

The Nyctalope glanced at his wristwatch from time to time, to measure distances; his stride and that of his friend, equal and constant in rhythm, served as secondary data for the calculation of the decameters, hectometers and kilometers they covered. That knowledge of matters of space and time might be useful for the return journey.

The march along the channel went on for a quarter of an hour without the aspect of he place changing at all—but suddenly, he channel and the quay separated; which is to say that within the range of Saint-Clair's vision, a hundred paces ahead of him and Gno, the subterranean river disappeared into a tunnel to the right, without a quay of any sort, while the subterranean pathway curved to the left into a new tunnel, relatively straight and low.

"Halt!" whispered Saint-Clair, pausing.

For, at the same time that he had seen the bifurcation, he had hard noises that were not those of the attenuated murmur of the now-distant waterfall, nor the footsteps of Gno and himself on the rocky ground.

"Listen! Can you hear that?"

"Yes, I can hear it," replied the Japanese.

There was a brief silence.

"One might think that it were a hymn," said Saint-Clair.

"Yes… without musical accompaniment… like the one we heard in the Diurnals' city."

"Oh! Gno, my friend—might it be to enjoy the Diurnal's admirable singing that the Nocturnals make war on them? A war in which the Nocturnals never kill a Diurnal, even though many of them are killed? A war that has no objective but to lure the Diurnals from their city, seize them, carry them off and imprison them underground, in darkness, forever… in order to hear them sing?"

"It's quite possible," said Gno Mitang. "That would prove that the Nocturnals aren't completely savage brutes."

There was another pause, during which the two friends listened, meditatively.

Suddenly, Saint-Clair said, in a harsh voice: "That's curious. It seems to me that that ought to reassure me somewhat on the subject of Véronique—but on the contrary, it makes me afraid. Véronique has a moving contralto voice, which has been sufficiently trained to serve her well. Fageat knows that. He might utilize Véronique's voice and talent to increase his

147

own prestige in the eyes of the Nocturnals. If the Diurnal captives sing, Véronique risks being forced to sing too..."

Gno squeezed his friend's hand. "Oh, my friend, how you love her! And how much you must be suffering from knowing where she is, and, above all who she's with! I understand—but your hypothesis is as hazardous as it's specious. Shall we go on?"

"You're right, Gno—but pay attention to the pressure of my hand. We're no longer far from the habitation of the Nocturnals. If I squeeze your fingers, stop and keep still. If I pull downwards, lie down flat on your stomach."

"Agreed!"

"Good."

And the two men resumed their march, after the Nyctalope had described the new dispositions of the location to the Japanese.

Relatively low and narrow by comparison with the tunnels they had followed thus far, this one as extremely sinuous. By virtue of a strange acoustic phenomenon, the chant could sometimes be heard more amply and clearly, and sometimes faded away, becoming vague and almost imperceptible, although there was no doubt that they were drawing closer to its source.

Suddenly, however, the song burst forth with such sonority, in several choirs of distinct voices, that the Nyctalope, although he could see nothing ahead of him but yet another bend in the tunnel, squeezed his companion's hand.

For several minutes they listened, still and silent, gripped by admiration. Then Saint-Clair leaned toward Mitang's ear and whispered:

"Twenty paces ahead of us, Gno, there's another sharp bend in the tunnel. I think that immediately thereafter we'll emerge into a subterranean hall, where the male and female Diurnal singers are gathered. For you're still thinking what I'm thinking—that theses magnificent and sweet songs have exactly the same quality as those the Diurnals sang for us in their city."

"I'm certain of it," Gno replied.

"Then let's go forward prudently. Once we're past the bend, perhaps I'll be able to see Véronique. Perhaps these songs are in her honor. The Diurnals know so little—and were only able to tell us very little—about the Nocturnals!"

"Let's go," said Gno Mitang. "Everything is possible, in spite of Ariste Fageat!"

That abhorrent name struck Saint-Clair like a whiplash.

"Let's go!"

And once again, the two friends resumed their march.

The Japanese counted the paces: 23. And there, under the impulsion of the Nyctalope, there was a 90-degree turn to the right. Another eighteen paces, following a semi-circle.

Suddenly, Gno felt the pressure and the downward thrust of Saint-Clair's hand. Instantly, the two friends were lying prone, side by side—and the more astonished of the two was Gno Mitang, for he could now see!

Ahead of him there was no longer the absolute darkness, as in the long journey through the subterranean tunnels. Nor was it daylight, though, or even light analogous to terrestrial artificial light.

In the depths of a troglodytic hall, whose immensity was lost in darkness on all sides, there was a nucleus of phosphorescence, as if placed on the ground, as well as an enormous pedestal—or, rather, a long, broad and tall semicircular stage. And on hat stage, with several tiers, were grouped, in unequal ranks, several hundred Diurnals, not phosphorescent themselves but softly and magically illuminated by the phosphorescent radiation of the stage.

And they were singing, in a prodigious assembly of various choirs.

Gno Mitang could not see, although the Nyctalope could, that in the darkness of the vast grotto, around the stage and extending all the way to the most distant walls, a multitude of Nocturnals was assembled, sitting, lying or kneeling, in all the attitudes of wakeful rest, in a comfortable and attentive immobility. Al those Nocturnals were listening, as if in ecstasy...

The Nyctalope looked everywhere, searching for Véronique—but he could not see her, nor Ariste Fageat.

He was putting his head close to Gno's, in order to whisper in his ear, when the greatest, the most unexpected and most ominous surprise struck him like a thunderbolt.

Ariste Fageat was an imperfect criminal, like the majority of criminals, but unlike the great majority of them, he was intelligent in the logical anticipation of events. The first hours that he spent in the world of the Nocturnals were judiciously employed.

Firstly, he allowed Rrou sand Ggo to explain themselves and him, as fully as possible, to the numerous and soon innumerable Nocturnals they encountered, who assembled and came running, clustering around them, and finally immobilizing them. To half a dozen "chiefs" one of whom was indubitably the "supreme chief," the Woo of that population, Rrou and Ggo spoke for a long time, not because they were making long speeches—the Nocturnal vocabulary being very restricted—but because they each repeated their extraordinary story and their difficult explanations several times over.

Then Ariste Fageat thought it useful to make, by the light of his camouflaged lamp, held twenty paces away from Rrou, a few demonstrations of the mortal power of his rifle and pistol. For that purpose, Ggo had brought two quadrumanes from a reserve stock of those living animals, which the Nocturnal carefully maintained in their grottoes.

After that, Fageat thought it equally useful to acquaint the Nocturnals with the binding, unbearable light of his uncamouflaged electric torch—and he saw immediately that all the Nocturnals present, headed by the chiefs, recognized him as a great all-powerful Woo, come from the extrarhean world represented in the minds of Noturnal Rheans by what Terrans called the moon, the Earth and the stars.

"Good!" he said, with satisfaction. "Here I am, tranquil in my power. And now, let's insure against the probable—the certain—arrival of the Nyctalope and his companions. Time's pressing. Better to make my troops wait for hours than be a single minute late!"

And to the chief of the Nocturnals, whose name was Tugg, he explained via Rrou and Ggo that although he, the "great Woo Fagg"—that was the Nocturnally-pronounceable name he had given himself—was animated by the best sentiments toward the world of the Nocturnals, his companions, five in number, wanted, by contrast, to fight the Nocturnals on behalf of the Diurnals. So he, Fagg, had to make arrangements so that the five enemies, when they arrived, would be put beyond the possibility of doing any harm in the blink of an eye.

The chief, Tugg, approved vehemently—and Fageat gave his orders to Ggo and Rrou.

Meanwhile, Véronique was still asleep, lying down now but on a very strange bed! When Fageat had deemed that walking was no longer possible in the midst of the Nocturnals surging from all directions in the immense grotto, primarily remarkable for the astonishing phosphorescent stage, and that a long pause and negotiations had become necessary, he had headed straight for the enormous stage, with twenty steps arranged as an amphitheater.

At the foot of the stage he had stopped Rrou and Ggo, and at the same time, the entire increasing multitude, bewildered, uncomprehending and admiring, had been immobilized, amid a great rumor of exclamation and brief phrases spring from every mouth.

Then Fageat had touched the surface of the fist phosphorescent step with his right hand. It was about a meter above the rocky soil of the grotto, which was uniformly flat and smooth.

Saint-Clair was mistaken, he thought, *in believing that the phosphorescence of the city walls was a Diurnal defense against the Nocturnals, since the Nocturnals have set up a kind of amphitheater here. It's rather that the Diurnals, blind by night, have coated their buildings with the phosphorescent substance in order to illuminate their own offensive and defen-*

sive actions against the Nocturnals. But what's the reason for this phosphorescent installation here?

He turned to Rrou and Ggo and made them understand, by means of gestures, that he wanted Véronique to be laid down there, but that the bed was too hard. Rrou, who was carrying the young woman, did not move, but Ggo spoke to a group of Nocturnals pressing behind him. The few brief words were repeated and transmitted far to the rear, and soon, above the heads, hundreds of hands passed from one to another a quantity of furry pelts, which Fageat immediately recognized as the skins of the little quadrumane monkeys. A thick layer of furs was arranged on the first step, and Rrou gently laid his sleeping burden down upon it.

It was only after that had been done that Fageat gave his orders to Rrou and Ggo—precise and simple instructions, which he repeated several times in order to be better understood. Wanting to keep his two habituated and comprehending companions with him, however, he had his instructions transmitted to the chief Tugg. The latter had to be eminent within the tribe as much for his intelligence as his stature—which, as well as being admirably proportionate to his body's girth, surpassed by a head that of the dozens of Nocturnals that Fageat could see around him.

Tugg understood immediately. He replied by a mime and words that signified, in sum: "I'll organize that myself."

And he went to do so. He disappeared into the crowd, which opened up before him and closed again behind him.

Secondary woos—doubtless clan chiefs of the Nocturnal people of the region—then formed a semicircle around an empty space, in the middle of which only Fageat, Rrou and Ggo remained: an attentive, respectful, curious and admiring semicircle, behind which the innumerable host of Nocturnals was now silent. Undoubtedly, the most distant had learned from their neighbors about the unprecedented phenomenon come from another world, which, in its omnipotence, was the master of light and death. By word of mouth the fantastic news was transmitted.

"Perfect!" Fageat pronounced, in a low voice. "Now it's just a matter of waiting for Véronique to wake up. In the meantime, though, the time won't be wasted if, via Rrou and Ggo, I obtain as much information as possible about the state of things."

It was easy for him to jump up and sit down on the step among the animal skins beside Véronique. Then, in a dominating fashion, he turned to Ggo and Rrou, who remained standing, to the semicircle of woos and, finally, to the several rows of Nocturnals vaguely lit by the amphitheater's phosphorescence. He was clearly in view, not only to them but to the whole multitude hidden in the darkness of the immense grotto, whose vault and walls he could not see, so distant were they.

Deliberately, using gestures and his voice, he set about interrogating Rrou and Ggo.

That bizarre conversation had been going on for exactly sixty-seven minutes—Fageat had consulted his wristwatch—when the chief Tugg reappeared. Immediately, he spoke to Ggo and Rrou, and they informed Woo Fagg that everything was arranged as he had prescribed at the entrance to the grotto.

"Very good!" said Fageat, loudly and with satisfaction. "Now, put on a concert for me, since the Nocturnals capture Diurnals to make them sing and not to eat them, as we Terrans first assumed, as Diurnal society has always believed, and as Saint-Clair and the others probably still believe too."

Through the intermediary of Ggo and Rrou, he made Tugg understand what he wanted.

The first consequence of Fageat's desire was that, less than an hour later, Saint-Clair and Gno Mitang, arriving at the threshold of the immense grotto, heard a sweet and magnificent song, and saw hundreds of Diurnals, by reflected phosphorescence, arranged in standing positions on all the steps of the phosphorescent amphitheater far away from them in the depths of the grotto.

Another immediate consequence of the instructions and orders given by Fageat and carried out by Tugg, however, was this:

Lying at the entrance to the subterranean tunnel, whose floor overlooked a gentle slope leading down to the floor of the grotto, the Nyctalope and the Japanese were all eyes and ears when a heavy weight fell upon their backs. The weight did not crush them, but it kept them lying face down. At the same time, their arms were seized and drawn backwards brutally. Their wrists were brought together and tied, and the cord used for that was passed underneath them, around the waist, and knotted once again to the wrists.

A moment later there was no more weight or constraint.

The Nyctalope had contrived to turn his head, to see how Gno Mitang was being treated, in order to understand how he was being treated himself.

He breathed in, shifted, and got into a kneeling position. He leaned toward his friend, who was still lying motionless on the ground, and who was blind in the surrounding darkness—for the phosphorescent light of the amphitheater did not reach that far. In the calm, firm and warm voice he employed in grave circumstances, he said:

"Gno, my friend, from a hiding place that, unfortunately, I didn't see, gripped as I was by the spectacle, two Nocturnals leapt upon us. Four others helped them, adroitly. Three are standing to your left, three to my right. They've secured our wrists and arms tightly, but our legs are free and I can see for both of us. Stand up. I'm standing up."

Gno Mitang obeyed without saying a word, while Saint-Clair got to his feet and went on:

"I'm beside you, shoulder to shoulder. You're not hurt? They haven't broken anything or pulled any muscles?"

"No, I'm not hurt. The cord doesn't seem as tight around my waist as when I was lying down. All right—what do we do, Leo?"

In making this reply the Japanese spoke normally, in a voice that was soft and yet firm, almost incisive.

"Good," said Saint-Clair. "I'm content. After all, these Nocturnals could have killed us, strangers as we are, on Fageat's orders. The traitor's letting us live, at least temporarily. He'll doubtless want to enjoy his victory and show me Véronique held captive. Criminals have these imprudences. Let's maintain hope, Gno!"

"While you can see, Leo, I never doubt a triumphant outcome."

That was said with the most perfect simplicity. Saint-Clair adopted the same attitude; he too did not doubt that he would win the formidable contest, if Fageat let him live long enough to turn the situation around.

There was a brief silence. The two Terrans and the six Nocturnals did not move. Then Saint-Clair said:

"Gno, you just said that the cord isn't as tight around your waist. Now, it's the same one that binds your wrists. We're going to walk straight ahead. My shoulder will maintain contact with yours. By imperceptible movements of the arms and wrists, try to ascertain whether the cord can be loosened. I'll do the same. I say 'imperceptible' because we mustn't forget that the Nocturnals are nyctalopes, and are even better ones than me, for certain. They're probably watching us closely. For the moment, they only have eyes for our faces and our equipment; they're not looking at our arms or wrists. I'll warn you if that changes. Are you ready? Can we walk?"

"Yes."

Already, by the attitude of the tightly-packed crowd of Nocturnals that opened in front of him and Gno, the Nyctalope had realized that these beings with the appearance of large terrestrial gorillas had a very keen intelligence. While they walked, he said to Gno:

"It's probably only a short time ago that the Nocturnals pullulating here were informed of our existence, extremely exorbitant from their viewpoint. Fageat must have made it clear that one of his companions can see in the dark, for our assailants, who are presently framing us as guards, don't seem astonished that we're advancing without hesitation, although the short-range radiation of the distant phosphorescence, though visible to our eyes, isn't reaching us yet. As for the crowd of Nocturnals, each of them is looking at us with an avid curiosity, but without overmuch amazement or any hostility. It's true that we don't represent any threat or peril to them, since we can't make use of our hands..."

The Nyctalope fell silent.

Gno Mitang continued the expression of his thought, as often happened between them:

"Their intelligence is keen and prompt, for Fageat can only have talked to a few of them, and not for long, but what he has made them understand has expanded rapidly through the entire host."

"Yes, that's right," said Saint-Clair.

"There are hundreds of them in this grotto?" the Japanese queried.

"Oh, thousands," the Nyctalope replied.

Meanwhile, they walked on; the crowd opened before and closed again behind them and their six guards. In the distance, on the stage in the amphitheater, the phosphorescent Diurnals continued singing, as if nothing new had happened or was happening.

It was a prodigious song, as musically sonorous, multiple, varied, melodious and harmonious as a great orchestra in Paris or Bayreuth—richer, in any case, than the most celebrated church choirs and choral societies of the civilized terrestrial world.

Suddenly, Saint-Clair saw in the distance a tall dark form standing up, doubtless on the first tier of the amphitheater. It was a Nocturnal more colossal than the rest, outlined against the phosphorescence of the steps and the Diurnals. It raised its arm and uttered a guttural cry. Instantly, the song ceased, like that of a phonographic disk suddenly stopped dead.

Intuitively, Gno Mitang said:

"That must be because of us."

"Probably," said Saint-Clair—but immediately added, in a different tone: "Gno, my wrists have a little play within the knots of the cords. What about yours?"

"Mine too."

"Let's walk more slowly, giving ourselves time. Let's not arrive too soon at where I hope Véronique and Fageat at. I'm slowing down."

"Good."

The Frenchman Saint-Clair, the Nyctalope, and Gno Mitang, the Japanese warrior, diplomat and politician, both great travelers and adventurous explorers, had certainly experienced emotions of every sort in the course of their often-perilous adventures, charged with mortal menace: vast, profound and violent emotions... but never—no, never—as much as they did at that moment, the most prodigious of their existence.

For both of them, there was the planet Rhea and its entire world, so unfamiliar and so mysterious. For Saint-Clair, there was also Véronique—Véronique, whom it was necessary to save. But did she not count also for Gno Mitang, Saint-Clair's friend? Yes, certainly. And for both of them, again, there was Fageat, who had to be punished.

But the possibility that the Terrans could stay alive in the Rhean world, the salvation of Véronique and the punishment of Ariste Fageat all depended on the answer to one question: could Saint-Clair and Gno Mitang free their hands soon enough? Soon enough—which is to say, a few seconds before finding themselves confronted by Fageat, on his guard, free and armed, with prompt reflexes and a conscience without scruples. For if the criminal glimpsed, on the part of both or only one of the captives, the slightest suspect movement, and had time to aim his pistol, he would undoubtedly fire to kill both Saint-Clair and Gno Mitang, in order to save himself and have Véronique to himself.

All of that went through the minds of the two friends at that moment, and they had no need to say it aloud; each knew that the other was thinking it, and that he would lose none of the calm, self-composure, lucidity or energy that were more necessary than ever.

Suddenly, Mitang said:

"Leo, the darkness is no longer complete for me. The phosphorescence is perceptible. I'm beginning to see what's around me, you..."

"Good," said the Nyctalope. "What about your hands?"

"No tangible progress for a few moments. You?"

"Me neither. Let's slow down further."

"Yes. Pretend to be gripped by curiosity regarding one of the Nocturnals."

"We might even stop."

"Why not?"

They both stopped, as if startled by the sight of a Nocturnal that, by virtue of an extraordinary anomaly, was much smaller than all the rest. Its stature only just matched that of Gno, who was not tall.

Gno Mitang had not been mistaken, two minutes earlier, when he had said, at the abrupt cessation of the Diurnals' song: "That must be because of us."

Thanks to his height, and because he had never ceased to watch the entrance to the first grotto of the subterranean domain of which he was the king, the Nocturnal Tugg had seen the movement and then the drawing apart of the crowd and had understood that the supreme Woo's "evil companions" had been overcome and captured, and were being brought to him. Immediately, by means of a mime, gestures and words that Fageat understood very well, he had given the expected notification.

"Already!" the engineer had exclaimed.

Then, thinking what he ought to have thought before, he muttered:

"I'll wager that the Nyctalope and the Japanese woke up first, earlier than I had calculated." Cheerfully, he added: "So much the better, then! The sooner we get it over with, the better. Then again, it's as well that everything is settled before

Véronique wakes up. Afterwards, I'll only have to deal with Vitto, Soca and Margot, which is nothing. The only one dangerous to me is the Nyctalope—and, secondarily, the Japanese. Come on! Enough singing—let's get to the action!"

He made Tugg understand that he wanted the Diurnals, while remaining in place, to stop singing. Immediately, the Nocturnal chief stood up on the first step and uttered a cry.

Silence fell instantly, on the steps of the amphitheater and in the depths of the grotto, but not in the rest of the vast excavation. Around the extraordinary newcomers, Nocturnals were exchanging their impressions, thus making a dull rumor that was propagated to the limits of the grotto like wavelets on a deep pool of water into which a heavy stone has fallen, followed by other stones falling successively closer to the bank—the bank here being represented by the semicircular base of the amphitheater

There was a pause, which Fageat observed. *What's happening?* he wondered. *Why aren't they coming forward any longer?*

The pause was brief, however, and the progress of the Terrans, invisible in the crowd because of their relatively restricted height, resumed at a slow pace.

Impatient and nervous, Fageat had the idea of standing on the same step as Tugg, but he thought that it might compromise his dignity, and therefore remained seated.

I'll see them soon as the crowd parts, he told himself—and that happened two or three minutes later.

The progressive separation of the crowd suddenly formed a double hedge between the group of newcomers and the space left vacant in front of the amphitheater. Ariste Fageat saw Saint-Clair and Gno Mitang at the same moment when the Nyctalope and the Japanese saw the traitor.

With an instinctive gesture, Fageat drew his pistol from its holster and held it in his right hand, resting on his thigh.

The Nocturnals might not have tied their wrists properly, he thought. *At the first suspect movement, I'll fire.*

Saint-Clair and Gno Mitang saw that, and divined the thought. Without interrupting their march, they looked at one another and shrugged their shoulders. Alas, during the brief halt before the singular dwarf Nocturnal, neither of them had been able to loosen the cords that rendered them incapable of action. Their wrists had some freedom of movement within the double or triple bracelet, but not sufficient to free a hand, even the left. The indignant fury of the Nyctalope and the cold rage of the Japanese were at their peak when they finally came to a halt three paces from the step on which Véronique d'Olbans lay asleep in the midst of a heap of furs, between a colossal standing Nocturnal and Ariste Fageat, sitting on the edge of the step, his legs crossed and dangling, with his left thumb tucked into his belt and his right hand resting on his thigh, holding the pistol pointed in their direction.

Saint-Clair and Gno Mitang had such self-control, however, that nothing betrayed the cold rage of the one or the burning fury of the other. The two faces retained the same severe and scornful calm. There was a rapid change in Saint-Clair's features for a second or two—a change of complexion and a painful softening of his gaze.

"Véronique," he sighed.

But that was brief, and his terrible eyes fixed themselves on Fageat.

Immediately, the duel was engaged: the duel that was inevitable. In conformity with his character and habits, the Nyctalope attacked first. In a tone of contained violence, with an inimitable hauteur, he said:

"Fageat, you're a traitor. At the very moment when you were meditating, in Maxime d'Olbans house, begging me to accept you aboard the *Olb.-I*, your treason began. I wanted to be generous. I didn't heed my instinctive antipathy. I only took account of your technical abilities. You've betrayed Monsieur d'Olbans, your good master; you've betrayed me, the leader who trusted you and has treated you benevolently. You've betrayed your companions, who thought you worthy of them. You've betrayed the illustrious man who did us the honor of becoming one of us, His Excellency Gno Mitang. As for Mademoiselle Véronique, you have dared... you have dared...!"

He fell silent, his voice strangled. He could no longer contain his fury at being powerless to do anything but pronounce vain words—and he stiffened, his teeth clenched and his jaws contracted.

Then Fageat, with simultaneous insolence, fatuity, bravado, anger and ferocious joy, said:

"Oh, what I have dared thus far is really very little—nothing, even—by comparison with what I shall dare when Mademoiselle Véronique has woken up, and is fully conscious, endowed with speech, capable of defensive reflexes..."

He laughed, with inexpressible vileness.

"Miserable coward," pronounced Gno Mitang. "And a ridiculous fool, who believes Mademoiselle d'Olbans capable of surviving certain insults—such as, for instance, the lust of a man like you. And, finally, stupid and brainless enough to imagine that a dozen clips for his pistol and rifle and twenty batteries for his lamp and electric torch will suffice for him to ensure a lifetime of domination in the double society of the momentarily-subjugated Nocturnals and the Diurnals, with whom you will also have to reckon with us gone. Your treason will not pay; treason never pays. It provides a temporary illusion of being richer in future than one is at present. Ariste Fageat, my friend Saint-Clair was right when he called you a traitor; for myself, I've told you, no less pertinently, that you're a coward, a fool and an imbecile. It's not in the character of Saint-Clair and myself to say such as much, especially when words are futile, but the circumstances excuse the exception we have made. And all is said, isn't it, my dear Leo?"

"Indeed, my dear Gno, all is said!" pronounced the Nyctalope, in his most placid voice.

"So, let's be quiet then, and await the realization of what Ariste Fageat has undoubtedly planed in our regard."

Even when one is the only person who can understand what certain people say to them, one suffers in hearing the truth laid bare.

Fageat was not an insensitive brute; he suffered. And he understood that if Mademoiselle d'Olbans had heard what Saint-Clair and Gno Mitang had just said to him, he would not have had the starring role. That comprehensive suffering modified his homicidal plan. An idea occurred to him: it would be better to employ cunning, to make up an improbable story, to dupe Véronique, to make her admire him and then to remain her "last resort" on Rhea.

So, the traitor made no reply either to the Japanese or to Saint-Clair. With a gesture he summoned Rrou and Ggo, who were standing a few paces away, at his disposal, looking at the two captives in a hostile manner. He spoke to them, as he already knew how to talk to the Nocturnals. They understood, and spoke in their turn to the chief Tugg, who approved.

Immediately, Saint-Clair and Gno Mitang were grabbed by the shoulders by four of their guards. They were irresistibly shoved and dragged along the semi-circular base of the amphitheater, and then into the midst of the crowd, which opened before them and closed behind them as they passed.

It was so brutal and so rapid that the two friends scarcely had time to bid farewell to Véronique d'Olbans, who was still unconscious, with a glance.

Chapter X
Actions and Reactions

Although he was able to make himself understood to some extent by the Nocturnals, given the relatively summary knowledge of their language that he had, Ariste Fageat was unable to make all his ideas clear to them. He could, in sum, only make them obey him in a simplistic manner, however willing they were.

That was why Tugg thought that he was acting correctly and sufficiently when he ordered the two Terrans captives to be taken to the grotto specially reserved for the existence, henceforth subterranean, of the Diurnals.

The numerous choristers that Saint-Clair and Gno Mitang had heard and seen in the phosphorescent amphitheater only comprised about a quarter of the Diurnals presently living in the Nocturnals' domain of that Rhean country. The winged Rheans were habitually lodged in another large cave, and only emerged in order to sing in the amphitheater, or, when they died, to be buried by night in some isolated place in the rugged hills.

All that, Saint-Clair and Gno Mitang were soon to learn in detail, but they had a sudden and rapid intuition of it as soon as they arrived in the "Diurnals' grotto"—for that was evidently where Tugg and the six guards had brought the two prisoners.

It offered a characteristic aspect by which Gno, although he was no nyctalope, was struck, because the grotto was illuminated in its entirety by columns made of the hardened phosphorescent clay with which the Diurnals' cities and the amphitheater in the great grotto were constructed. Those columns, twenty in number, were set at equal intervals, and rose fro the floor to the vault. Everywhere between the columns, innumerable "monkey" hides were heaped in various thicknesses, and to those makeshift beds and seats, Diurnals were lying or sitting. Others were walking in wide aisles contrived between the orderly rows of heaped pelts.

"Look!" said Saint-Clair. "The subterranean river reappears here."

"And the Diurnals drink from it," said Gno.

The river ran to their left, in a narrow rectilinear channel, beyond which rose the wall of the grotto itself. Many of the Diurnals were kneeling on the edge, picking up water in their cupped hands and drinking it. That did not last long. They soon got up again and, walking or flying, returned to strolling, sitting or lying down, isolated, in couples or in groups. The majority were talking among themselves. A few were humming or singing in low voices. A large number were crowding around shallow vats made of phosphorescent clay.

Guided by Tugg, who was preceding them, and followed by the six Nocturnals who had attacked them and never ceased o serve as their guards, Saint-Clair and Gno Mitang passed close by one of these vats, and were able to see that it was half-full of the shell-less nuts that constituted the sole nourishment of the Diurnal Rheans.

Naturally, the arrival and progress through the cave of the two extraordinary beings, bound and evidently captives of the Nocturnals, provoke tumultuous movements among the Diurnals, which soon spread throughout the grotto. They creased eating, drinking, singing, strolling, sitting or lying down, and gathered round, forming a crowd. Soon, the two Terrans were advancing along a narrow path bordered on one side by the channel and on the other by the rapidly-compacting crowd of Diurnals, all silent with astonishment. Those in the more distant rows leapt on to the shoulders of others, all of them watching the unprecedented, extravagant and incomprehensible spectacle of two unknown beings being led by the Woo Tugg and six Nocturnals of the "orderly service."

At the far side of the cave, to the left, near the channel, Tugg pointed out to the two new captives a narrow excavation, not very tall, into which, comprehending the gesture, Saint-

Clair and Gno entered meekly. Showing that they understood what as expected of them, they sat down on the ground, lowering their heads, seemingly resigned.

"If they leave us here alone, we're saved," said the Japanese.

"And we'll save Véronique," added the Nyctalope.

And, in fact, they were left there, alone and unguarded!

In the simplicity of his mind, Tugg doubtless thought that he had carried out the great Woo Fagg's orders adequately. He knew, in any case, that no one escaped from his subterranean domain. The exit was a long way away. To get to it one had to traverse the entirety of the great hall of the amphitheater and force a way through the barrage of Nocturnals of the orderly service who guarded the exits continuously. He was doubtless also in haste to return to Fagg and the sleeping being—a haste shared by the six guards. Finally, Saint-Clair and Gno did not take long to discover that the custom was to lave the Diurnals alone in the cave, from which they only emerged in order to sing in the amphitheater or to be carried away, dead, in the arms of a galloping Nocturnal. Furthermore, Tugg did not know that the two enemy companions of Woo Fagg had spent more than a day in the Diurnal city and had acquired a sufficient knowledge of their language to enter immediately into an amicable relationship with the most intelligent of the numerous winged captives.

Two or three minutes after Tugg and the six guardians had turned their backs and left, the Nyctalope got to his feet. Over the crowd of Diurnals packed in front of him, he saw the Nocturnals disappear into the darkness of the tunnel leading to the great hall.

"Get, up, Gno!" he said. "Talk to the Diurnals on your side; I'll talk to the others. Our first objective is to get rid of these cords."

"Yes," said the Japanese.

It was relatively easy to make the Diurnals understand that they were two of the new beings who, during a recent assault by the Nocturnals on the city, had sided with the defenders against the attackers. Then the two friends succeeded in making it known that they had spent some time in the city itself. Finally, they convinced their wonderstruck listeners that they had come into the underworld in order to free the Diurnals from Nocturnal tyranny forever...

Turning round to display their bound wrists and arms, Saint-Clair and Gno asked to be released.

All that took time of course, the repetition of words, a varied mime and numerous movements of the head, torso and even legs, fortunately visible to the Diurnals by virtue of the radiation of a nearby phosphorescent column.

The essential thing was, however, that, in the end, what the Terrans wanted to express was understood by the Diurnals. The hands of the winged Rheans were much more vigorous than the general appearance of their slender bodies suggested, and their fingers were extremely dexterous. As soon as Saint-Clair and Gno had been understood, their desire was satisfied in less than a minute; the two cords were untied, unrolled and thrown on the ground.

"Ah!" said Saint-Clair. "We're free to act."

"Yes," said Gno, "and let's not neglect anything. Pick up your cord, and I'll take mine. We'll coil them around our waists; they might be useful to us."

"Of course!" They rapidly did as the Japanese had suggested.

"And now, without another moment's delay, we march against Fageat, don't we, Gno?"

"Naturally."

A word and a gesture from Saint-Clair sufficed for the crowd of Diurnals, silent again, to open up before them. There was no doubt as to the route to follow: along the channel to the bifurcation with the tunnel that had brought them here. The phosphorescent columns provided enough light for Gno Mitang to walk without hesitation beside Saint-Clair—but in the sinuous tunnel, the darkness became opaque, and the Nyctalope grasped his friend's right hand in his left.

"We're alone now," whispered Saint-Clair. "None of the Diurnals is following us."

"Fortunately, you're as nyctalopic as the Nocturnals!" said Gno Mitang, after a burst of relieved laughter. "On Rhea as on Earth, my dear Leo, you're the King of the Night."

"A fine title, Gno—I accept it."

And he too laughed in relief. Henceforth, they were finished with the desperate emotion that had chilled them momentarily when they had first arrived before Fageat without having been able to free their hands.

Confidently, "on their toes," as Margot would have put it, they increased their pace, the Japanese having long since become accustomed to adapting himself to the Nyctalope's stride in spite of darkness and whatever the terrain.

Here, the ground was flat and smooth, permitting him to walk without apprehension.

Meanwhile, the situation in the grotto of the amphitheater had been considerably modified.

After Tugg and the six guards had taken Saint-Clair and Gno Mitang away, Ariste Fageat remained perplexed, sitting on the step beside the recumbent Véronique, still contemplated with an admiring curiosity by the Nocturnals. The first rows of the crowd were being maintained at a respectful distance by Rrou and Ggo, very proud of their role in such extraordinary circumstances.

Fageat set about reflecting. In accordance with his mania, he embarked on a quiet monologue.

"I've no further need to worry about the Nyctalope and the Japanese. I don't have to decide right away what to do with them—that will depend on a great many things! First of all, Véronique's attitude toward me...

"Yes, but what about me? How shall I conduct myself with regard to Véronique? What shall I tell her when she wakes up? The truth? Get away—that would be idiotic. With all her body and soul she'd have nothing for me but hatred, scorn and repulsion. Certainly, I could use force, if it pleased me and when it pleases me, and impose my will upon her—but then, as the Japanese demon said, she'd kill herself brutally or let herself die, depending on the degree of physical liberty I allowed her. A passive woman, as if dead already...no, that's not what I dreamed of on Earth, when I thought about Véronique d'Olbans night and day."

He interrupted himself, crossed his legs, gazed at the unconscious beauty, and then resumed:

"I ought to tell her a story, something that will give me, in her eyes, the merits of a savior and a hero, but also, for the sake of plausibility, those of a skillful diplomat, a subtle negotiator, who has been able to tame the Nocturnals, at least to a certain point. Yes, that's what I need to do. But how? What story can I make up that will be plausible to her and fit in well with out apparent situation in the society of the Nocturnals? I have to find one. I have time to search, to plan, to bring Rrou and Ggo into my plan; they understand me well enough to play the role I give them adequately...

"Here, though, I'm not at ease. That crowd of Nocturnals... those Diurnals on the steps... I need to be alone, so that Véronique finds herself alone with me when she wakes up. Let's see—there must be caves in this underground city that are less vast, more intimate. That's what I need: a retreat that I can hasten to render comfortable, if I dare employ that word, and which I can make, at least temporarily, the private habitation of Mademoiselle Véronique d'Olbans and Monsieur Ariste Fageat. Yes, to bring about that small amelioration of the present situation—and then, I hope my imagination will provide the eventual necessities... let's go!"

In a loud voice, he called:

"Rrou! Ggo!"

They came to face him, very attentively.

This time, however, it took him some time to make them understand what he wanted. He strove to find the most expressive gestures, to make them pronounce the words that might translate his thoughts. He went so far as to draw a diagram on the ground with the blade of his hatchet: an approximate plan of the immense cave where they were and corridors to other, hypothetical caves, one of which was much smaller than the rest...

Finally, the two Nocturnals understood, and they replies did not take long to inform Fageat that his desire was easily realizable.

"Right away!" he said, to himself—and he put the unconscious Véronique into Ggo's left hand and right arm while Rrou opened a path through the crowd and set off in the lead.

It was at that moment that Tugg appeared, followed by six colossi almost as tall as him. Fageat saw them, and was not content.

"Damn it!" he swore. "Saint-Clair and Mitang have been left without surveillance, without guards! It's true that the brave Tugg doesn't know the Nyctalope, though, and that, on the other hand, I'm incapable of making the Nocturnals understand all my ideas. Let's try."

First, he shouted:

"Rrou! Ggo! Ma!"

His two valets halted, Ggo laden with Véronique and Rrou frozen in the gesture of parting the crowd. Fageat caught up with Rrou, who was his interpreter in trying to make Tugg understand, firstly, that he must send the six guards to maintain strict and constant surveillance over the two captive adversaries, and secondly, that he, the great Woo Fagg, wanted to be provided with a place of his own, some way away from the large caves where the Nocturnals lived communally.

Tugg understood right away. He sent the six guards back to the Diurnals' grotto, with severe and precise instructions, and started walking himself in the direction in which Rrou had opened a path through the crowd. Ggo followed, carrying Véronique, then Fageat, who switched on the veiled electric lamp fixed to his torso. Rrou brought up the rear.

Almost a quarter of an hour later, having gone through two other large caves and a short tunnel, the little procession arrived in an excavation much smaller than those already familiar to Fageat. The Terrand was surprised to find that this "habitation" was illuminated by a phosphorescent column, and that it included three natural steps, on the third of which four Diurnals were lying on monkey-hide beds.

In response to Tugg's gestures and cries the Diurnals stood up, and by the movements they made Fageant understood that they would obey the Nocturnal chief, who was expelling them, sending them elsewhere.

He had an idea.

"No" he said, swiftly. "No!"

He succeeded fairly easily in making it understood that he wanted the Diurnals to stay, that they would be agreeable and useful company for his "wife" when she woke up. That done, he undertook a different mime to communicate that Tugg ought to leave, and that, in case of necessity, Ggo and Rrou would serve as envoys, couriers and agents of liaison.

Without manifesting the slightest ill-humor, Tugg obeyed, turning his back and disappearing into the darkness of the tunnel.

"There!" said Fageat. "I'm settled for the moment."

He uttered a deep sigh and passed his hand over his forehead, which was streaming with sweat. Suddenly, he felt very tired. His watch aboard the *Olb.-I*, his feverish activity before is departure with Véronique and the two Nocturnals, the hours of walking to the subterranean passages, and then to the caves, the mental effort of making himself understood, deciding at every moment upon the opportune course of action, and envisaging the eventually realizable outcomes, would have exhausted the most vigorous and durable of men. And even though he was very lightly dressed he was too warm, and was breathing with difficulty in the relatively impure and heavy atmosphere of the underworld.

"Come on, come on!" he muttered, chiding himself. "This isn't the moment to weaken. I have to rest lucidly until Véronique wakes up. Yes, I need to rest, while staying keenly alert. I know so little about the world I'm in, about the Nocturnals, about their possible reactions. Come on, damn it—buck up!"

170

And having got a grip on himself, he pronounced a few words that he knew of the Diurnal language, vaguely adequate to the situation.

Standing on the second step of the cave, the four winged Rheans were frozen with astonishment and incomprehension at the sight of the extraordinary unknown beings who had arrived in their "apartment" with the chief Tugg and two other Nocturnals. Slender in their clinging garments, illuminated by the radiation of the phosphorescent pillar, still motionless, their inexpressive eyes went from Fageat, who was trying to speak to them, to Véronique, still carried by Ggo. Perhaps they understood what was being said to them, but they did not give any sign of it. They seemed utterly bewildered.

That, at least, was what Fageat thought. "All right!" he said, shrugging his shoulders. "The essential thing is that they stay here, at Véronique's disposal. She spent more than thirty-six hours with the ones in the city; she'll know better than me how to make herself understood."

He climbed up to the third step, took a few hides from one of the four beds, threw them on to the first step, and then went down to arrange the pelts so as to form, in a corner of the grotto, as far away as possible from the tunnel entrance, a kind of thick and deep divan with a back. He had Véronique deposited on the divan, no longer lying down but in a sitting position, her head supported by a cushion made from several rolled-up hides. He examined the young woman's face at close range, and, on a whim, touched hr lips with a kiss. She did not quiver; serene and vaguely smiling, she was profoundly asleep, but calmly, with no sign of distress.

"Be patient! Be patient!" Fageat said to himself, not without a certain nervousness.

He looked around slowly, in order to acquaint himself more thoroughly with the cave that would be his habitation, and that of Véronique, at least temporarily. Pulling himself together, he sniggered:

"Our nuptial chamber!"

The excavation was approximately square. It was primarily due to the unfathomable caprices of nature, and owed relatively little to the industry that the Nocturnals had undertaken in providing the necessities of life for the Diurnals imprisoned there. That "relatively little" consisted, firstly, of the phosphorescent column, made of superimposed fitted blocks of the rapidly-hardening clay, which Fageat knew, thanks to the Diurnals brought to the *Olb.-I*, to be extracted from inexhaustible quarries and fashioned by hand; secondly, of a sort of trough, also made of phosphorescent clay, containing a fairly large quantity of the shell-less nuts that were the Diurnals' sole nourishment; and thirdly, the numerous hides of the quadrumane monkeys, piled into four beds on the third step.

The steps themselves were entirely natural in formation, the first rising scarcely two meters from the inner surface at one extremity of which the access tunnel opened. Each of them had almost the same height, of about a meter, and the same width, of between three and four meters; their length was about twelve meters, which made the interior of the grotto into a visibly angular cube.

These relative restricted dimensions permitted Fageat to see everything within it, the light of his electric lamp, although attenuated and blue-tinted by the camouflage, carrying at least twelve meters.

One other, but important, detail was that a hole beside the opening of the tunnel gave passage to a steady flow of water which fell about fifty centimeters into a natural bowl, in a fresh and crystalline stream. The overflow ran down a brief slope terminating in a thin crevice, into which the water disappeared. There too, nothing was due to the labor of Nocturnals or Diurnals; that was obvious. Nature alone had amused herself in creating that spring, a trickle of water doubtless derived from the great subterranean river running in capricious channels from grotto to grotto.

Finally, two paces to the left of the fountain, a kind of high black niche was hollowed out. Fageat went to explore it. The reflections of the column's phosphorescence just about reached it. At the back was a hollow in the rocky floor—a basin in which Fageat's lamp caused running water to gleam. The Terran burst out laughing.

"A lavatory!" he exclaimed. "Well, when Nature takes the trouble to think about vermin like humans, Rheans, and doubtless inconceivable myriads of millions of other planets, she does things well."

He went back to the cave, and drank from the fountain. As he passed by he took a handful of nuts from the trough and started chewing them for a few minutes, standing motionless in front of Véronique.

Then, in his clarified mind, the idea that had occurred to him when, on entering the cave, he had prevented Tugg from sending away the four Diurnals—the idea that the mere sight of the four Diurnals had inspired in him, at least hypothetically, in principle—began to develop.

"Very good," he said. "That's it! It's impossible that it won't pass muster. Everything in the story hangs together. In Véronique's eyes. I'll be the hero, the savior, the only hope."

Thus spoke Mademoiselle d'Olbans' abductor, while freeing himself of a considerable part of his equipment, which he went to hide in a corner under some monkey-skins. All he kept about his person were his belt, his holstered revolver, the sheath of his electric torch and the lamp fixed to his torso. Then he consulted his wristwatch. He made a rapid mental calculations and pronounced:

"Employing our terrestrial vocabulary, adapted to Rhean astronomical conditions, it's 8:15 p.m. on September 9."

It was at that moment that Véronique woke up.

Two kilometers away, but exactly at the same moment, Saint-Clair, walking with Gno through the darkness of the tunnel leading from the Diurnals' grotto to the grotto of the amphitheater, saw several Nocturnals rounding a bed 50 paces in front of him.

"Alert!" he whispered to Gno. He pushed him against the wall of the tunnel and flattened himself against it too.

173

"It's our six guards coming back," he said, in a low voice. They haven't modified their stride, so they haven't seen us. Take out your electric torch, my friend, and when I switch mine on, light it. At a stroke you'll be able to see clearly and we'll blind the Nocturnals."

"Yes," said Gno. "Let's hope that this sort of weapon is sufficient. I wouldn't like to have to make use of my pistol to shoot down any of the troglodytes, who seem to me, fundamentally, to be good enough fellows, but simply passionate music-lovers—lovers, that is, of the Diurnals' songs..."

"I agree entirely," Saint-Clair concluded. Immediately afterwards, he added: "I think that they can see well enough in the dark that they won't get close to us without seeing us, for we're only concealed by a slight projection in the rock. Nevertheless, I'll let them come... if they look straight ahead, they might go past without having seen us, because of the width of the tunnel. They're well-grouped in the middle..."

The Nyctalope, leaning forward slightly, could see the six Nocturnals quite clearly. The Japanese could hear the muffled sound of their footsteps.

They were no more than five or six meters away when ne of them raised his arm, stopped dead and shouted: "Ogr!"

The two fiends immediately heard a precipitate exchange of hash monosyllable.

"Gno!" said Saint-Clair, loudly. "They're coming!"

He pressed the switch of the powerful electric torch that he was holding in his left hand. Gno did likewise. Two lances of violent light sprang forth, zigzagging for a few seconds, and, well-aimed, struck the faces and eyes of the six huge Nocturnals one after another, and then swept back again.

What howls of agony! What terrified leaps! With their enormous hands covering their eyes and their whole faces, the six Nocturnals fell down, flattened against the ground, panting and moaning.

"Poor devils!" said Saint-Clair, pityingly. "Let's hope that the painful blindness will only be a kind of whiplash, with no other consequence, not an incurable injury."

"Yes, and let's get on," said Gno, swiftly.

They stepped over two or three of the recumbent bodies, and, in darkness once again, holding hands, they resumed their march, having decided with a tacit accord only to use the electric torches in case of necessity, in order to make the batteries last as long as possible.

Without any further incident they arrived at the threshold of the grotto of the amphitheater. The crowd of Nocturnals had their backs to them. The pale radiation of the phosphorescent steps laden with Diurnals did not reach that far. Saint-Clair informed Gno, and, spotting a rocky block once detached from the natural wall, which formed a pedestal, he climbed up on it, and easily hoisted Gno up with both hands.

From there they could look down on the host of Nocturnals. The rumor of curt conversations rose up from the entire unmoving crowd. Suddenly, however, Saint-Clair said, in a tremulous voice:

"Gno! Véronique and Fageat are no longer there!"

"So I see." The amphitheater was, in fact, near enough for the Japanese to distinguish the details of its luminous steps.

Immediately, the Nyctalope continued:

"There's a stir at the back of the crowd, beyond the amphitheater...someone's fraying a passage through it. It's the big Nocturnal, undoubtedly the chief of the population, whom Fageat called Tugg. Can you see him?"

"Yes."

"He's alone," said the Nyctalope. "Perhaps he's coming back from accompanying Fageat to some retreat, to which he's taken Véronique?"

"It's probable. Did you notice what direction he came from?"

"Yes."

"Then that's where we need to go—but we have to get through that entire crowd."

"Easy! We'll open a path with out electric torches."

Then they saw Tugg jump on to the first step, exactly where Fageat, seated beside the recumbent Véronique, had received them. The huge Nocturnal raised and arm and shouted. Instantaneously the rumor of the crowd fell silent, and the lyrical song of the Diurnals immediately rose up, without any the need for any "conductor."

The song was such a marvel that, in spite of their anguished preoccupation with the subject of Véronique, the two friends were gripped by the same admiring emotion that had immobilized them on their arrival, before they had been flattened by the Nocturnals leaping on their backs.

For a few minutes they were ecstatic, like Ulysses' sailors on hearing the song of the sirens.

Saint-Clair was the first to break that hold, and said with contained vehemence:

"Enough, Gno! Don't listen. And let's not hold back. We need to get to Véronique right away."

"Let's go!" said Gno, in the same tone. "Electricity?"

"Yes!"

"We'll march side by side—but keep an eye on our rear. Nocturnals untouched by the light mustn't be allowed to attack us from behind and knock us down!"

"Certainly not! This time, we'd be doomed!"

"And so would Véronique!"

"Let's go."

It was a nightmare journey. Only the human imagination, exercised in inexplicable mystery, in the incomprehensible enigma of the craziest dreams, can realize such a phantasmagoria, in which the impossible and the real are amalgamated, in which the horrible and the grotesque are entangled, and which is a formidable torture because the victim of the dream believes, subconsciously, that he will never get out of that Gehenna.

Having switched on the two powerful torches simultaneously, Gno Mitang and Saint-Clair leapt down from their pedestal together. Instinctively, they howled: "Oooh! Aaah!"

The nearest Nocturnals turned round, and were immediately struck full in the face, in the eyes, by the electric beams, as unsustainable for them as the Sun's rays in broad daylight.

Did they understand? Had they been informed that the great Woo Fagg, on his marvelous arrival, had given a demonstration of his power of light and death?

The Nyctalope and the Japanese, of course, did not ask that question. They advanced side by side at a rapid pace, often glancing behind them, without stopping, whipping the crowd at head height with the rigid lash of their electric beams, in front of them first, then to the sides, and then behind them, and henceforth all around the moving block that they formed, there as a demonic racket of atrocious screams, an infernal moving chaos of living bodies that were bounding, recoiling, falling down and writhing in heaps on the ground.

Always, after the first painful stroke, the huge hands were plastered against the faces before the disorderly collapse of the body: an instinctive, but belated, gesture of protection—for the luminous jets, incomprehensible, or at least unexpected and always unsustainable, struck with a rapidity, a continuity and a mobility against which none of the crazed Nocturnals thought of defending themselves by simply turning their backs.

The initial reflex of the unfortunates afflicted, and then the others who saw the invincible evil coming, was to leap backwards—with the result that soon, throughout the immense grotto, there was a terrible tempest of violent bodies pressing and colliding with one another, throwing one another into the air, crushing one another, shoving one another and being shoved, like the confused waves of a furious sea in which the winds and currents are in conflict...

Saint-Clair and Gno Mitang were impassive at first as they advanced into the tumultuous gap that the electric beams opened up in front of them. Immediately, however, the song of the Diurnals broke off. The Nyctalope had but one thought: not to deviate in his course; to go straight ahead in the direction from which he had seen the giant Tugg arrive. He had one reference-point: the amphitheater, which he needed to keep to his left, always at the same distance, which he had estimated at approximately thirty meters.

In spite of the Nyctalope's fixed determination, however, and in spite of the determination that the Japanese had to ensure, by means of frequent half-turns, of the security of their rear, the two friends gradually lost their grim impassivity. The task they were accomplishing, which they had to accomplish, was truly too horrible. Its nightmare effects were repeated, superimposed and propagated in such cataclysmic proportions!

Deafened by the unspeakable howling, jostled by the writhing of the Nocturnals fallen at their feet, suffocating in that atmosphere already heavy, into which thousands of hairy bodies sweating in anguish were discharging their odors, Saint-Clair and Gno Mitang soon felt as if their heads were on fire, their nerves exasperated, their chests oppressed, their throats wheezing...

Pitilessly, however, they went forward, on and on, fighting with all their conscious and lucid minds against the deadly impression of nightmare that overwhelmed them, repressing their physical malaise with all of their will-power—and finally, they reached, at the far side of the immense cavern, a place where there as no longer a single Nocturnal in front of them, and where the crazed masses behind them were retreating, trampling fallen bodies.

"There! That must be it!" exclaimed the breathless Nyctalope.

The two electric beams extended freely into the black hole of a relatively narrow gallery.

"Gno! Turn your back to me and walk backwards. Or, rather, no! Here, take my torch, and light your forward march as normal, three paces before me, and prevent anyone from following us by directing the other beam behind you. Understand?"

The Japanese was much less excited than the Nyctalope.

"How could I not understand, my dear Leo? Calm down and go forward. I'll follow you, sand my rear-guard will never cease to be luminously effective. But calm down, I implore you! You'll be facing Fageat before long—and he's armed!"

"Thanks, Gno!" said Saint-Clair, with grave firmness.

He handed his illuminated electric torch to his friend. Then, moving normally, he took his pistol from its holster, disengaged the safety-catch, checked the mobile chamber and made sure that there was already a bullet in the breech, ready to be fired—and, retaining the weapon in his right hand, he went into the tunnel.

Twenty minutes earlier, in the little cave with the three steps and the phosphorescent pillar, before the unexpressive eyes of the attentive Diurnals, reflecting on phenomena that they did not understand, and before Ariste Fageat, quivering with desire, Véronique had woken up.

At first her gaze was that of a sleepwalker; she did not move her head or her hands, and did not make the slightest effort to stand up, slumped as she was, propped up by the monkey-skins.

Soon, however, her eyes assumed a gaze—and they saw Fageat standing almost immediately in front of her, and then the four Diurnals sitting huddled together, and finally the phosphorescent column.

There was a moment of uncomprehending perplexity, with a sensation of heaviness in her head, softness in her limbs and a bitter taste in her mouth.

Suddenly, however, a desire to know, to understand, animated her eyes, and caused her body to sit up straight, while her hands, with an instinctive gesture of modesty, closed upon and buttoned up her pajama jacket to the neck—for Mademoiselle d'Olbans, barefoot and bare-headed, her hair hanging loose, was only clad in night-pajamas.

An instant later, her gaze was gravely fixed upon the engineer, and she said, curtly:

"What am I doing here? Where are we? What's happened?"

Fageat bowed respectfully, sketched a gesture intended to appease, and, in a voice that was emotional for reasons other that those which Mademoiselle d'Olbans could yet imagine, said:

"It's a long story, Mademoiselle—and very extraordinary. We've all been captured, inside the *Olb.-I* for those who were asleep and in the immediate vicinity for those who were awake and went out to see what as happening…"

He stopped, a trifle breathless.

"Captured?" cried Véronique. "How? By whom?"

"By the Nocturnals!" Fageat replied, with a kind of hateful violence.

"But how?" Véronique insisted. "How? That's incredible… crazy!"

Then Fageat could not help a snigger that was supposed to be bitter but was merely insolent:

"Crazy? Incredible? You can't see, then, that you're in one of the Nocturnals' caves? Imprisoned, like these four Diurnals, like me..."

Véronique attached her own thoughts, logically, to Fageat's:

"What about Saint-Clair? Gno Mitang? Vitto, Soca, Magot? Why aren't they here with me, and you? Where are they?"

"Oh, Mademoiselle!" exclaimed the engineer, with a grand gesture of his arms, "let me tell you how it happened…my story will answer all your questions..."

"Well go on, then! Tell me!" the young woman spat out, with a hysteria of which she immediately became conscious and for which she reproached herself, so effectively that, to calm herself down, she had the idea of looking at the four Diurnals, whose delightful faces, turned toward her, were taut with attention and curiosity, but whose unexpressive eyes were incapable, alas, of giving her any comfort.

Nevertheless, the sight of those four beings, so peaceful, delicately pink in the light spread by the phosphorescent column, immediately did her good. She turned back to Fageat and said, in a calmer voice:

"I'm listening."

"Well, this is what happened," began the engineer, in a tone that was more casual than was appropriate to the terrible significance of the story that he was about to tell, which he had been preparing meticulously since Tugg had left him there. "You remember, Mademoiselle, that after dinner, you all went to bed and I took the first watch?"

"Yes, yes..."

"An hour went by. You were all asleep. Suddenly, I heard strange noises around the *Olb.-I*. I listened, but, being unable to identify them, I had the idea of opening a porthole, in order to hear better—and also to see better, for I couldn't see anything through the crystal, misted as it was by some kind of humidity. So I opened a porthole and, in truth, without realizing that I was committing an idiotic imprudence, I put my head outside. Immediately, I was grabbed by the neck and shoulders. I was able to cry out. I was released, and cried out again. Immediately, I was grabbed again—but Monsieur Saint-Clair had heard. The light of his electric lamp put my assailants—who were Nocturnals—to flight.

"Monsieur Mitang arrived. Monsieur Saint-Clair ordered me to arm myself and equip myself. He went out, and Monsieur Mitang went with him—but they must have been attacked from behind, for moments later the *Olb.-I* was invaded by the Nocturnals, who overwhelmed me before I was able to light a single electric lamp. I was only illuminated by the green light of the central compartment. I think Vitto, Soca and Margot were surprised in their hammocks; I didn't see them.

"Before my eyes, a Nocturnal picked you up, deeply asleep, in his arms. I was able to glimpse Monsieur Saint-Clair and Monsieur Mitang being carried away, like you and me. What a gallop through the woods, all the way to the hills! I was pressed by two enormous hands against the breast of a Nocturnal. Suddenly, there was a vast hole at the base of a hill, a cavern, total darkness, and the gallop continued through interminable tunnels. Finally, I was deposited here, and left here, with you, who were laid down on those furs, and these four Diurnals with insignificant eyes.

"I hadn't been disarmed, and the equipment that I had only just had time to buckle on—very little, as you can see—

hadn't been touched. As my limbs had been left free, however, and I have a powerful electric torch and my pistol, I'm not entirely demoralized, Mademoiselle. And although I'm the only one able to fight, to defend you and save you, I'll succeed, for the electric torch and the pistol, judiciously employed, are the weapons by means of which—you with the torch and me with the gun—we'll overcome the Nocturnals, opening up a path through their midst, terrorizing them, even forcing one of them to guide us to the exit from the tunnels..."

There, Fageat fell silent. Yes, he had reached the end of his story, but most of all it was because he could not go on. He could not go on because he could see in Mademoiselle d'Olbans' eyes that she did not believe him.

Simply, and in a firm voice, she said, scornfully:

"You're lying. I sense that nothing you're saying is true."

But the young woman had to make a great effort to say that. Precisely because she was convinced that the man was lying, she was afraid—afraid of Fageat, whose gaze had too frequently sent shivers of repulsion through her back at Les Pins.

She remembered! And now, in the anguishing enigma of the situation, she understood that she was at the mercy of that enemy, free in all his limbs and armed, with whom she found herself alone, as a consequence of unknown events whose mystery threw her into confusion. But Mademoiselle d'Olbans had character, energy and self-control. Rejecting the fear that she felt spreading within her, mentally and physically, she put on a brave face, stood up and thought hard...

Standing thus on the first step, she was level with the four Diurnals sitting on the second step. She sensed the delicate natural perfume that emanated from their healthy bodies, unacquainted with any malady. And that caused her to think:

Alone? No, I'm not alone. I can talk to these Diurnals in such a way that they'll understand me well enough. I've spent hours in their city. They'll defend me. Although slender in appearance, they're strong—and I'm vigorous. Unless he makes use of his pistol to kill us all, Fageat won't have the upper hand against five of us.

That lightning-fast thought rendered her all her courage and usual presence of mind. *It doesn't really matter what happened*, she said to herself then. *The future will make the facts clear. I only need to think about the present, and the present is the struggle against Fageat, after reaching a rapid understanding with the Diurnals.*

Immediately, she spoke again:

"Yes, you're lying," she repeated. "Your laborious lie must be hiding an abominable perfidy."

Fageat laughed, brutally. He had just thought:

I was very naïve to think that my story would hold up! And very stupid to want to play the noble knight when, without much embarrassment, I'm the master! I made a mistake—so what! Won't I obtain much more pleasure from imposing my will than by playing the dandy in the hope of a reward? Let's throw away the mask!

And he began to laugh.

Then he gave voice, by means of a violent flood of words, to the obsession that had been torturing him for weeks and months. He was abominable in his cynicism, frightful in his sadistic joy...

But Véronique was not listening. She did not even hear him. All her mental labor consisted of recalling the words of the Diurnal language that she had learned aboard the *Olb.-I* with the winged Rheans. She recalled the words, chose those which, at the present moment, had the most useful signification, the most adequate to the extraordinary circumstances.

Abruptly, with a supple effort of her entire body, she sprang up on to the second step, and was immediately behind the seated Diurnals, who rose to their feet in response to the cry she uttered as she leapt. Rapidly, she spoke to them in their own language, words that signified:

"I'm a being of the same nature as you. I know your city. My companions and I come from a star in your sky. We saved Diurnals whom the Nocturnals were abducting. This man, this being of our species, has betrayed us and allied himself with the Nocturnals against us and against the Diurnals. Help me, until our leader, the most powerful being in the world, arrives. He will save us. He will vanquish the Nocturnals, who will no longer attack your city..."

And those rapid, but not precipitate, words, articulated with care, Véronique repeated, in order that she might be better understood, while Fageat, carried away by his passion, vociferated, ironically and menacingly, expressing his intentions violently and indecently, rejoicing in the certainty of his triumph...

The Diurnals were listening to Véronique, their comprehension gradually increasing—and the bewildered Ggo and Rrou, hidden in a shadowy corner, were beginning to comprehend Véronique and not understanding a word of what Fageat was saying.

But then other sounds were heard than those of human voices. From the gallery came a kind of gust compounded of a dull rumor. That rumor quickly grew, seemingly extending, rising and spreading, and was soon and extraordinary din such as neither the Nocturnals nor the Diurnals had ever heard.

Véronique fell silent. Fageat stopped talking. None of them was listening any longer to anything but the din.

The engineer guessed immediately what was happening.

"Great gods!" he swore, giving no further thought to Véronique. "The Nyctalope and the Japanese have escaped. They're taking action!"

"Ah!" said Véronique, astounded.

Fageat had but one thought now: to intervene right away; to kill Saint-Clair and Mitang, whom he envisaged simultaneously victorious over the terrorized crowd of Nocturnals but fully occupied, hampered by that very fact.

He put his left index-finger to the switch of the lamp on his breast, clutched the heavy pistol in his right hand, and launched himself into the tunnel.

Perplexed, Rrou and Ggo did not budge.

The encounter took place half way along the corridor.

Fageat saw the beam of the torch that Gno Mitang was directing forwards. He saw nothing else, because Gno and Saint-Clair were invisible, still too far away for his own lamp, attenuated and blue-tinted by the camouflage, to render them visible to him.

At the same moment, however, the Nyctalope saw Fageat. His reflexes were prompt. He leapt backwards, snatched the torch out of Gno's right hand and extinguished it.

Already, two shots had rung out in quick succession.

But Fageat had only fired by guesswork.

"Get down, Gno!" said Saint-Clair. Flattening himself against the left-hand wall of the tunnel, able to see clearly in the darkness thanks to his nyctalopia, he raised his right hand, holding the pistol.

I can't kill him, he thought. *Life will punish him more than death. But I have to disarm him.*

In the distance, no longer able to see anything, Ariste Fageat did not continue firing. He stood still, slightly to one side relative to Saint-Clair, with his right arm raised, ready to fire...

The Nyctalope took careful aim...and fired.

Fageat uttered a cry; his left hand went to his right arm and grasped it, while the armed hand opened and dropped the pistol.

Coldly, Saint-Clair fired again.

This time, the bullet went through Fageat's left hand as well as his right arm, which was already grievously wounded by the first bullet.

Then Saint-Clair said placidly:

"Gno, my friend, get up, switch on the light and come on. The swine is out of the fight."

It was Gno Mitang who picked up Fageat's pistol. Meanwhile, Saint-Clair said, in his terrible dry voice:

"Come on, you—forward march! Your wounded arm and hand won't prevent you from making use of your legs."

Mad with rage, humiliation and the despair of having lost Véronique, however, Fageat coughed and groaned:

"Kill me! Kill me, then!"

"No," said Saint-Clair, curtly—and he expressed the thought that he had had before firing. "More and better than death, life will provide your expiation." Then, in a different tone, he continued: "March! March all the way to Mademoiselle d'Olbans! Don't you have the courage to accept your defeat with dignity?"

"Ah! Cursed that I am!" exclaimed the vanquished man—and, turning his back on Saint-Clair, he marched. The Nyctalope and Gno Mitang followed him, pistols holstered and torches in hand, one lit, the other switched off.

Suddenly, Saint-Clair saw a phosphorescent pillar in the distance.

"Would you care to extinguish the torch, Gno?" he said. "It's possible that Nocturnals are already in company with Mademoisele d'Olbans—best not to drive them crazy unnecessarily. Only light up again if they show signs of attacking us."

A moment later, however, he stopped dead, and said in an ardently emotional voice:

"Ah! I can see Véronique… with Diurnals. Véronique!"

He launched himself forwards. Without intending to, he bundled Fageat out of the way. He ran. He leapt.

"Halt, Fageat!" commanded Gno Mitang. He shoved the engineer into a crack in the wall, and followed him into it. With satisfaction, he observed that unless he leaned a long way forward and stuck out his head, neither he nor Fageat could see into the grotto, of which he had so far only perceived the phosphorescent column.

What an embrace! What a kiss!

Oh, it was no longer Mademoiselle Véronique d'Olbans and Monsieur LeoSaint-Clair who came together then, but two lovers, who had loved one another for a long time, but who had never said so, who had thought that they might have lost one another, and who had found one another again, and were only thinking about one another, only living those moments for themselves...

"Véronique!"

"Leo!"

She was weeping while laughing. He was laughing with his eyes full of tears. They held one another in their arms, hugging one another. They kissed one another on the lips, the cheeks, the neck, and on the lips again.

"My God, Leo, how happy I am!"

"I'm crazy with happiness, Véronique!"

They did not say any more. Looking at one another at close range, eye to eye, they calmed down, smiling. Gently, they relaxed their embrace.

Still holding her in his arms, he said:

"I'll explain it to you, Véronique. It's quite simple. But although you're saved from Fageat, we're not entirely saved from the Nocturnals. We have no time to lose."

"You're alone?" she queried.

"No. Gno's with me." He turned his head and laughed lightly. "A discreet friend!" he said. "When I hurled myself forward, he must have stopped Fageat and held him back. He knows me thoroughly; he understood that having found you, after having feared losing you, I'd need a moment alone with you..."

Tenderly mocking, Véronique replied:

"You're forgetting these four admiring Diurnals and those two petrified Nocturnals over there..."

"Indeed!" said Sant-Clair, laughing.

He saluted the Dournals with the word "Vahiné"—which meant "Have a nice day," and was equivalent to the terrestrial "Bonjour" with an extra nuance of smiling cheerfulness. To the Nocturnals, he intimated with a broad an authoritative gesture, an instruction not to move. Did they understand? At any rate, they remained rooted to the spot, rigid on their colossal legs.

Then Saint-Clair called:

"Gno, my friend! Gno!"

Thirty seconds later Gno Mitang kissed the hand that Mademoiselle d'Olbans held out to him, and pronounced a few polite formulae, smiling. Then he said:

"It occurred to me to make ligatures for Fageat's left fore-arm and right arm, to restrict the blood-loss. I ordered him to sit down on the ground in a fissure in the tunnel—and to prevent him from playing the idiot, I tied his legs together with the cord that the Nocturnals had gifted to me. We can pick him up on the way back."

"Very good, Gno—thank you," said Saint-Clair.

In a different tone, speaking to Véronique as well as the Japanese, he added:

"We have to act without wasting time, but not at hazard. We already know enough of the Diurnals' language, I believe, to have a useful conversation with these."

"I think so too," said Véronique.

"Indubitably," said Gno.

"Well then! Ask them to sit down, Véronique. Let's sit down and talk."

No noise was coming from the great grotto of the amphitheater now; surrounded once again by natural obscurity, the Nocturnals had calmed down; to least, they were no longer crying out. Nothing could be heard in the little grotto but the trickle of the water falling into its bowl and overflowing smoothly into the crevice.

The Diurnals sat down. In their dark corner, the Nocturnals remained still. Then Saint-Clair attempted to converse with the four winged Rheans, who were sitting in a row in front of Véronique, Gno Mitang and himself.

Conclusion

Aboard the *Olb.-I*, a few hours after the departure of Saint-Clair and Gno Mitang, Vitto and Soca woke up almost at the same time, shaken by Jean Margot, who immediately said to them:

"Stir yourselves! Your heads are heavy, eh? Mine too, damn it—but it soon passes. It'll pass even more rapidly when you read this."

With a gesture, he showed them the piece of paper pinned to the wall underneath an electric lamp.

Thick-headed but hurriedly, the two Corsicans slid from their hammocks to the floor, took three steps, stopped with their heads raised, and read what was written on the piece of paper.

Doubtless after being assured of a certain comprehension and obedience on the part of the two Nocturnals, Fageat has left with them, abducting Mademoiselle d'Olbans. It's probable that we've been drugged by Fageat, to various degrees, during the evening meal. Gno Mitang and I are going after the traitor. Guard the Olb.-I *and, if necessary, defend it. If we have not returned in two Rhean days, act as you think best, all three of you. Our objective is the great cavern in the western hills, where the Diurnals indicated to us that the entrance to the Nocturnals' underground dwellings is located.*

S.-C.

"Oh, that swine Fageat!" exclaimed Soca, furiously.

In important brutal circumstances, Vitto never said anything.

As for Margot, still pale with indignation and anger, he said, violently:

"I'm not surprised. I've always thought he was a dirty swine, in spite of his technical abilities."

The three men immediately organized themselves so that they could keep watch and rest alternately during the seventy-two hours comprised by two Rhean days.

Absolutely nothing troubled the peaceful clearing in which the *Olb.-I* had landed. Through the open portholes, or when they walked around the *Olb.-I* to stretch their legs, Vitto, Soca and Margot did not see any living beings except for the impassive large white birds and, fleetingly, frightened quadrumanes rapidly climbing into the trees.

At first, Margot and Soca chatted, a trifle feverishly, formulating a hundred hypotheses, while Vitto kept quiet. Then the talkers wearied of futile chat, and there was almost absolute silence, until the seventy-second hour of waiting, at the fourth minute of which, Vitto, who was then on watch, abruptly cried:

"Alert!"

Almost immediately afterwards, however, he added:

"Praise God! It's the Boss!"

The Sun had risen two hours earlier. Vitto, Soca and Margot bounded from the vehicle into the clearing, which the broad beams of the sun's rays were traversing horizontally.

The three men ran forward.

"Mademoiselle! Monsieur Mitang!" they cried.

"Oh, Fageat!" muttered Margot. "Wounded! Good!"

"And Diurnals!" added Soca, merrily.

With what glad ardor their hands met and shook one another. What speeches!

Finally, Saint-Clair said:

"Come on, calm down. Into the *Olb.-I*, quickly. Vitto, Soca, Margot, we're dying of hunger. A good cold meal, at the gallop!"

"And what shall we do with him?" said Margot, coldly, pointing at Ariste Fageat, who, with his right arm in a sling and his left arm above the right on his breast, was standing to one side, head bowed, with his back against a tree.

He was bizarrely semi-clad; to make the bandages they had used his own shirt, partly ripped up, and his neckerchief;

the straps were made of the same pink fiber with which the Diurnals made their body-stockings and bonnets.

All eyes turned toward the traitor.

Saint-Clair replied:

"That's fair—all three of you have the right to know, without delay. I could have killed Fageat, who had just shot at Gno Mitang and myself. I only wounded him, in order that life itself can be the sanction of his crime. To imprison him in the *Olb.-I* is impossible, and it's more impossible still to let him live with us. I've agreed with the Diurnals that they'll isolate him in one of the small buildings in their city. A human being might well be able to live eating nothing but Rhean nuts; those admirable fruits contain all the elements indispensable to perfect nutrition: fats, calories, vitamins. He'll be permitted two hours exercise every day in the gardens inside the city. These Diurnals will take him away, taking everything from the *Olb.-I* that belongs to him—except, of course, for weapons. The Diurnals, who are immune to diseases, microbial and otherwise, are familiar with injuries and know how to tend and cure them. That's it for Fageat. The Diurnals will take him away immediately. While you and Mademoiselle d'Olbans prepare our meal, I'll do his packing personally."

Having said that, in a tone of sad severity, Saint-Clair headed for the *Olb.-I* at a rapid pace. Gno and Véronique were at his sides. The four Diurnals surrounded Fageat, who sat down on the ground, signifying by that movement that he would not go into the vehicle.

Saint-Clair, glancing back, saw that, and stopped momentarily.

"As you please, Fageat," he said. "Margot will bring you the package of your belongings. We'll only see one another again in a year's time, when we'll be leaving for Earth!

Rapidly prepared by Véronique, aided by Vitto and Soca, the meal was tasty and copious, thanks to the provisions of refrigerated conserves stored on the *Olb.-I* in cans and bottles. It was a champagne lunch. What relaxation and joy, after so many hours of threat and drama!

Then, over the odorous coffee, outside on the grass of the sunlit clearing, while the smoke of cigars and cigarettes dispersed in the pleasantly warm, calm and light air of the planet Rhea, Saint-Clair gave a brief but complete and very animated account, for he benefit of Vitto, Soca and Margot, of the adventures that he and Gno Mitang had undergone before arriving at the small cave and finding Mademoiselle d'Olbans.

He concluded:

"Afterwards, Mademoiselle d'Olbans, Gno Mitang and I chatted with the four Diurnals incarcerated in the cave. They were being held apart from hundreds of other winged Rheans detained in the underworld because they belong to an elite class of the Diurnal people, which only has two constituent classes: composers and singers. Equal with respect to all the forms, obligations and customs of social life, the members of the two classes only differ in that the composers imagine and make up sings, orchestrate them while teaching them and having them repeated, but then withdraw and leave the care of directing their execution to the choirmasters..."

"Curious," said Soca. "We didn't learn that in the city."

"Oh, there are many other things yet to learn!" Saint-Clair replied, and continued: "These four Diurnals, greatly revered by the Nocturnals, soon put us in communication with one named Tugg, a kind of king of the Noctrunal people of this region. This communication was established between the small and large grottoes through the intermediary of two Nocturnals we had captured, and whom the traitor Fageat had made his accomplices, named Rrou and Ggo. Fortunately, Tugg had not been afflicted by the rays of our electric torches during our tumultuous traversal of the great grotto..."

"Ah! Forgive me for interrupting you, Monsieur," said Soca again, "but what is the ultimate effect of a powerful light, natural or artificial, on the Nocturnals' eyes?"

"A pertinent question," said Saint-Clair, smiling. "This is the answer: any light surpassing the intensity of the Rhean phosphorescence with which we're familiar is intolerable to the Nocturnals' eyes. The beams of our lamps or portable torches have the same effect on them as the light of the sun as soon as it appears in a clear sky above the horizon. Instantaneously, the Nocturnal is dazzled and feels an unbearable pain in the eyes—hence the instinctive gesture of putting the hands over the eyes and lying face down. The pain and dazzlement remain intense for two or three minutes, and then begin to abate; after a quarter of an hour or so, the Nocturnal is no longer in pain, and becomes clear-sighted again—in the dark, at least.

"If light strikes again, the second affliction is crueler and more durable than the first. A third and a fourth can render the Nocturnal blind, for the eyes are materially burned, and mad, for the intolerable pain only ceases with death. In living Rhean memory, however, few Nocturnals have suffered that terrible fate; it requires a rare combination of successive circumstances to expose an unfortunate to sunlight several times over in a relatively short lapse of time—and you can well imagine that the Nocturnals, by instinct and education, know how to avoid committing imprudences and exposing themselves to that torture—which is sometimes, but very rarely, inflicted by the Dournals when they are able, exceptionally, to capture one or two of the Nocturnals that attack their cities by night."

There was a pause, and then Saint-Clair resumed:

"So, we were able to summon King Tugg to the small cave. Diurnals imprisoned even for a few months, as the four composers were, are easily able to learn the simple language of the Nocturnals. One of the four, the most intelligent, served as our interpreter; we knew enough words in the Diurnal language to express our thoughts clearly. In brief, these are the essential elements of the three-way pact that has been concluded between Terrans, Diurnal Rheans and Nocturnal Rheans..."

Saint-Clair liked to smoke a good cigar. The one that he was smoking at present was excellent. And he knew that, even while talking, he must not let it go out. He took advantage of interruptions occasioned by an interlocutor, or interrupted himself, in order to breathe in, savor the delectable smoke momentarily, and exhale it slowly. That was what he did, in spite of the impatient avidity of his listeners—not merely Vitto, Soca and Margot, who knew nothing of what he was about to say, but also Véronique and Gno Mitang, who were both taking pleasure in hearing the Nyctalope provide a focused, clear and definitive depiction of a series of successive images that only tended to reappear to them, at a distance, as incomplete and sometimes incoherent sketches.

Having taken a drag, Saint-Clair resumed speaking:

"As I said, it's a three-way pact, with a few brief articles. Firstly, the Diurnals and the Nocturnals, the former from sunrise to sunset and the latter during the night, will be at our disposal to help us organize, in this region, our life as explorers of the planet Rhea. The first action of that collaboration will be the transportation, tomorrow night, of the *Olb.-I* to a hill, beside a powerful waterfall, which will serve to power our various electrical apparatus, including our interplanetary projector."

"Bravo!" cried Margot, the specialist electrician.

"Secondly," Saint-Clair continued, "peace is initiated between the Nocturnals and Diurnals of this region. For many centuries, the former have only been attacking the latter in order to capture the largest possible number so that they might hear them sing. These aggressions were frequent because, in the imprisonment of subterranean darkness, in spite of the care lavished on them by the Nocturnals, the Diurnals declined rapidly and soon died of consumption and languor. The imprisoned choirs thus had to be frequently reconstituted by the arrival of further captives. Well, no more! Often, if not every night, either outside on the plain or in the grotto of the amphitheater, Diurnal choirs, which are various in kind, will go in turn to give vocal concerts to the Nocturnal people. In payment, the Nocturnals will deliver to the Diurnals large quantities of furs, a movable commodity highly valued by the winged Rheans, who have a horror of hunting quadrumanes.

"In consequence, in this region, there will never again be war, if, as I believe, the Rheans are wiser than Terrans—and I

194

hope that during the year of our first sojourn on Rhea we shall be able to expand that peace over the whole extent of the planet."

"That's marvelous," said Soca, delightedly.

"For sure," approved the laconic Vitto.

Saint-Clair took another puff on his cigar. Then, with gently irony, to which he often resorted when joy reigned within him, he said:

"And that's all! The three-way Terrestrial-Rhean pact has but two articles, which can be summed up in three words: comprehension; cooperation; peace."

This account of the interplanetary adventure of Saint-Clair and his companions, summary although sometimes melodramatic—by reason of the passionate and dramatic turmoil provoked Ariste Fageat—could end here. What followed the events of those first few days of the life of the Terrans on Rhea no longer belonged to the domain of adventure but to that of science.

Does not the progress of science though the centuries, however, comprise the increasingly prodigious chapters of the veritable adventure?

The sojourn of the Terrans on Rhea lasted a year. It is the subject of a very voluminous communication made by Gno Mitang and Leo Saint-Clair to the Académie des Sciences—a communication that is still confidential and will remain so while scientists and linguists work to translate it into all the languages of the civilized terrestrial world.

It is impossible for us to offer here even an exceedingly humble and succinct summary of that important scientific work, but we can extract a few essential items of information from it, in order to satisfy, at least in part, the legitimate curiosity of our readers. As for the part—undoubtedly the largest, alas—that we leave in darkness, the exercise of their imagination might assist them to await the publication of the official work of Messieurs Saint-Clair and Gno Mitang.

What follows are a few important details regarding the life on the planet Rhea, and, thereafter, a brief account of the return of the Terrans in the *Olb.-I* to their native planet.

To begin with, the essential character of life on Rhea, on which the communication of Saint-Clair and Gno Mitang insists at length, is that on that planet, fire does not and cannot exist. Lightning is unknown there; the intrarheal fire does not manifest itself in any fashion—whereas the Earth is punctured by volcanoes—and, finally, none of its vegetation, however dry, is combustible.

Thus, the civilization of the Diurnal Rheans, very advanced in other respects, and the less developed civilization of the Nocturnal Rheans, do not involve any of the aspects that depend, on Earth, on the existence and usage of fire. There are no weapons, save for the flint ax-heads attached to wooden shafts that the Diurnals used in defending themselves against the Nocturnals, who use nothing themselves as a means of attack, fighting, capture and destruction but their strength, their agility and the suppleness and vigor of their limbs. There is no industry, save for architecture, with no other tools than hands and no other materials than the inexhaustible clay found in all the regions of the planet, in valleys and the deepest depressions in the plains, and the fabrication of vestments, the body-stockings of the Diurnals and the loincloths of the Nocturnals being woven from vegetable fibers. There is no industry, nor any agriculture or commerce, with respect to nourishment, the Diurnals living on "nuts" produced every year by billions of trees and the Nocturnals nourishing themselves on the raw flesh of the quadrumanes that pullulate on Rhea even more than the millions of insect species on the Earth.

On Rhea, there are no beasts of burden that draw vehicles, carry packs or are saddled for riding. Travel is, in any case, infrequent, because each region, delimited by rivers or chains of hills, is effectively isolated, and journeys are made on foot.

The temperature is maintained at summery levels throughout the day, and spring-like levels at night by the heat of the Rhean mass itself—a heat whose source and nucleus the Terrans were unable to discover. They observed that in the clay-filed depressions, geysers suddenly bust forth in places, randomly in space but at regular intervals in time, which do not project water but only vapor. It is these vapors that form the thick clouds that rise up to heights varying, according to the region, between eight hundred and a thousand meters, where they are gripped, cooled and carried away by the inexplicable perpetual wind that envelops the entire plant, rotating at great speed from west to east, creating a kind of formidable maelstrom at the poles, beneath which life is impossible. That wind remains inexplicable, so far as Saint-Clair and Gno Mitang are concerned.

There is no art or literature among the Nocturnals, who spent half the night hunting and have no other intellectual enjoyment than listening to Diurnals sing. By contrast, the Diurnals are ingenious and knowledgeable architects, sketchers and writers; the dried leaves of a kind of water-lily serve them as paper; their sole implement for drawing and writing is a stylus made from the hardened tip of a plant analogous to the terrestrial bulrush. They have museums, libraries and archives, but their great art is music; Rhean voices, abundant in richness and extensive in register, replace the instruments devised on Earth by human genius and fabricated by human industry.

There is no "social question" or "class struggle." Among the Diurnals the not-very-numerous elite arises from an entirely natural selection, some Rheans revealing themselves a composers between the ages of fifteen and twenty years. After a few months of spontaneous evolution, their talent achieves perfection, but without monotony, for the inspiration of each one is infinitely varied. Among the Nocturnals, absolute equality, under a sort of regency, which is very casual and elementary in its administration; there is one chief, who, until his death, has no competitor because he has no advantage of

197

any kind by virtue of being the chief. On his death, he is simply replaced by the tallest Nocturnal in the tribe.

Neither among the Diurnals or the Nocturnals is there any marked difference in mental intelligence; rivalries and ambitions are unknown. In the most natural fashion, everyone acts for the community and the community acts for every individual. It is an integral communitarian regime, no one having needs and desires different from anyone else. Physiologically, the Diurnals and Nocturnals are much like humans, but have no diseases. A rapid infancy, a long youth, a similarly extended prime, and a brief old age; death arrives without suffering after a few days of cheerful languor, among the Nocturnals as well as the Diurnals.

In sum, happiness: a happiness that, prior to the arrival of the Terrans, was only troubled among the Diurnals by the fear inspired by the Nocturnals, and among the latter, by the tyrannical need to hear the former sing, often and at length. Hence, warfare! Warfare to which the mediation of Saint-Clair the Nyctalope put an end, within an hour, after centuries of hostilities.

Yes, happiness!

For it is not true that intelligent beings need disease in order to enjoy health, evil to appreciate good, poverty to savor abundance, or war to love peace. The Rheans are evidently superior to Terrans, in the sense that they benefit from conditions of existence that have allowed them to avoid creating, on their planet, morally and materially, everything that creates the agony of the human condition, interminable and incessantly renewed on Earth.

But we, who have just written all that in accordance with what we have been able to discover about the scientific communication of Saint-Clair and Gno Mitang, must stop there, for it is not permitted for us to deflower that communication further. We are, however, authorized to recount, by way of conclusion, how the *Olb.-I* and its occupants left Rhea to return to Earth.

During the Rhean night dated, in the terrestrial calendar the ninth and tenth of September, the *Olb.-I* was transported from the clearing where it had landed to a place situated between two hills where there was a significant waterfall.

In order to supervise that difficult operation, Saint-Clair stationed himself to the right of the vehicle and Gno Mitang to the left. The former had under his command the chief Tugg, seconded b the intelligent Rrou. Two Diurnal composers acted as interpreters. A hundred Nocturnals divided between the right and the left, carried out the operation. First they lifted up the front to the *Olb.-I*, and trees trunks stripped of their branches by hatchets were passed underneath the vehicle. Then the same was done at the rear. Thus, the interplanetary vehicle rested upon a kind of enormous stretcher, constituted by the tree-trunks, which were roped together. The hundred Nocturnals took hold of the handles of the stretcher and, thanks to their Herculean strength, lifted the enormous burden without difficulty. Meanwhile, Vitto, Soca, Margot and six Nocturnals opened a pathway through the wood by felling trees with their axes. The journey was approximately six kilometers. The *Olb.-I* was in place, near the waterfall, before the first light of dawn. Then all the Nocturnals returned to their subterranean dwellings.

The Terrans and the two Diurnals took a few hours' rest in the vehicle. Then, after a frugal but substantial meal, everyone except for Véronique and the Diurnals began the work of setting up the apparatus that would, thanks to the waterfall, furnish enough electricity to aliment the formidable interplanetary projector occupying the entire rear end of the *Olb.-I*, by means of which Saint-Clair would be able to communicate with Maxime d'Olbans.

Those communications by optical telegraphy between Rhea and Earth were established at the first attempt, but they could only be carried out and repeated on rare occasions because of the conditions of astronomical position and atmospheric clarity that were necessary to them.

The principal goal had, however, been attained: that of keeping Monsieur d'Olbans and the terrestrial world up to date with the life of the Terrans on Rhea. That existence was to last exactly 366 days—which is to day, until the period, merely seven times twenty-four hours long, during which the return of the *Olb.-I* to Earth would be possible.

But how would that return be possible?

This is an appropriate moment to report a conversation held between Monsieur d'Olbans, Saint-Clair and Gno Mitang, in the presence of Véronique, Vitto, Soca, Margot and Fageat at Les Pins on the eve of their departure on the interplanetary voyage.

The question had been initially raised by Véronique in a preceding conversation. Launched on to another subject, Monsieur d'Olbans had not replied. It was presented a second time by Gno Mitang in these terms:

"Now that the interplanetary voyagers have been selected, is it not appropriate to consider their return? We know that everything is ready for the journey from the Earth to Rhea, but what have you anticipated with respect to the return from Rhea to the Earth?"

Maxime d'Olbans laughed softly. He made an apologetic gesture and said, amiably:

"Scientists, particularly astronomers, have these distractions. I confess that yesterday, that question found me at a loss when Véronique formulated it. Since then, however, the problem has made progress in my mind. I'm surprised that I didn't think of such a simple solution immediately—a solution given to us by the knowledge and calculation of the natural actions and reactions of the planet Rhea and the planet Earth on the metal Z-4. My temporary negligence evidently emerges from the fact that in the course of our studies and endeavors, neither Saint-Clair nor I had thought about the return journey, so preoccupied were we with the matter of getting to Rhea. But really..."

He broke off and, fixing his affectionate gaze on the Nyctalope, said:

"Let's see, my friend—have you, like me, neglected..."

"Absolutely!" Saint-Clair affirmed. "I didn't give it any more thought than you—but I believe that, like you, I can now reply to Véronique's question, repeated by Gno Mitang."

"Aha!" said Monsieur d'Olbans, laughing again. "Well then, reply! We're listening."

"My God!" the Nyctalope exclaimed, smiling. "The solution is, indeed, extremely simple. The astonishing thing is that it didn't impose itself upon us in the course of our work. And since you've done me the honor of wanting me to formulate it, here it is." He paused, and then continued: The power of attraction of Rhea on the Z-4, and hence on the *Olb.-I*, will begin to enter its period of maximum intensity on August 30, at 6 p.m. That period will last for 24 hours, increasing slightly with each passing minute. Afterwards it will decrease, to become negligible after about six month—after which the power of attraction of the Earth on Z-4 will get the upper hand, and will intensify progressively for six months until it attains its maximum. Then again, the predomination of the Rhean attraction by virtue of the position of the new planet relative to the Earth will begin to increase. Well, as you can see, it's as obvious as it is simple. While the terrestrial attraction is at its strongest, all we have to do, a few days before the maximum, is to open the panels closed over the Z-4 partially coating the *Olb.-I*, having first placed it in the appropriate position relative to the Earth...and we'll come back in exactly the same manner than we left..."

It was done as Saint-Clair had said.

In the course of their sojourn on Rhea of approximately a year the Terrans had explored the entire planet—all of the regions between the polar caps swept by the deadly wind, which resembled one another to the point that, by comparison with the Earth, Rhea appeared monotonous, being relatively sparsely populated, and extremely poor in flora and fauna, in diversity if not in quantity. There were no flowering plants except the "water-lilies" and the "nut-trees," no animals except the inedible white birds and the edible quadrumanes, and no fruits except the "nuts." The nuts, however, the nutriment of the Diurnals, and the quadrumanes, the nutriment of the Nocturnals, were superabundant, and reproduced so prolifically that, even with twice as many consumers, there would never have been any threat of famine.

The Terrans did not even think of introducing on Rhea the slightest element of what, on Earth, would be called "civilization." It was unnecessary, since the Rheans, Diurnal and Nocturnal alike, lacked nothing for their material life, and also impossible, since all terrestrial civilization depends on fire, which is unknown and uncreatable on Rhea.

The good that Saint-Clair and his companions did, and did well, which they accomplished perfectly, and seemingly conclusively, was to achieve rapid and total pacification between the Nocturnals and the Diurnals. And that pacification had, from the first weeks onward, one enormous consequence: the abandonment of the cities, henceforth unnecessary since they were merely a refuge and a defense, and the adoption by the Diurnals of a rural way of life, continuous existence in the open air being possible and agreeable, thanks to the equality of a warm temperature, the fact that it only rained in the valleys between the hills and never on the plain, and that sufficient comfort was provided for the Diurnals by constructing soft beds under the trees with the quadrumane skins that the Nocturnals gave them in exchange for their quotidian concerts, in the open by night and in the grottoes by day.

Thus, the Terrans did useful work on Rhea, which, we hope, will also be useful on Earth by virtue of the example provided for humans by the Rheans.

On the date fixed for the departure to Earth, which took place during the Rhean night, an innumerable multitude of Diurnals and Nocturnals, from all regions of the planet came to salute their marvelous guests alternately, with their songs and their cries.

And in the same time that it had taken to travel from Earth to Rhea, the *Olb.-I* returned from Rhea to Earth.

Saint-Clair and Gno Mitang on the one hand, and Maxime d'Olbans on the other, had made their calculations so scrupulously that the interplanetary vehicle landed within two hundred meters of the spot where it had taken off, on a landing-ground two kilometers in diameter, which Maxime d'Olbans had prepared scientifically with that landing in view. The vehicle's powerful brakes functioned perfectly, the "fall" being, in any case, slowed down considerably by special electromagnetic discharges that interposed a solid and elastic mattress of invisible waves between the bolide and the terrestrial surface. Nothing was broken during the landing, and the *Olb.-I* settled gently upon its landing-frame.

In order to avoid an invasive crowd, Monsieur d'Olbans had only made the date and hour of the *Olb.-I*'s return known to his intimate friends, Monsieur Lamurat, the Prefect of the Sarthe, Dr. Serres, the local physician, Maître Blanquer, the notary resident in Longpré, the commune in whose territory the estates of Les Pins is situated, and finally, Professor Charpin, the directory of the Paris Observatory.

The interplanetary voyagers were therefore welcomed to Earth in the strictest intimacy, and were quite content with that. The scientists, journalists and innumerable curiosity-seekers could wait until later!

Is there any need to paint a picture of that welcome? To describe the hours that followed? No, our readers can easily imagine all that.

Let it suffice for us to say that Ariste Fageat, forgiven and repentant—a year of living among the Diurnals had improved him considerably!—resumed his functions as steward of the Les Pins estate, and that, genuinely without bitterness, he attended the marriage of Leo Saint-Clair and Véronique d'Olbans, three months after the *Olb.-I*'s return.

Thus, the most extraordinary adventure of modern times was accomplished, not only without the death of a single human being by virtue of the adventure itself, but with general and individual consequences that were highly beneficial, under the triple heading of peace, redemption and love.

Jean-Marc & Randy Lofficier:
Return of the Nyctalope

The life—the life that I saw before me,
so vast, so rich in promises,
tasks, exploits... and so beautiful!
To die... the future life... eternal life... yes.
Leo Saint-Clair
Enter the Nyctalope

Chapter I
Claude Marécourt's Experiment

By the summer of 2014 CE, as man counts time on Earth, Rhea was approaching the Kuiper belt. Already in the sky, one could see the Oort Cloud spreading its white mantle across the horizon.

In the Great Northern Desert, life was sparse and difficult. There was no rain and, therefore, not enough food to support much fauna. Other than the few insects with strange, reddish carapaces, which chirruped randomly, no one could have called this place "home." Yet, in the midst of this arid desolation stood a large, low-roofed, camouflaged building—nothing more than concrete walls slapped together to protect its inhabitants from the ravaging winds which continually battered the desert. Its purpose was merely functional: it was a base of some kind, not designed for permanent habitation.

A sophisticated, spherical airship hovered just above it. Below, on the roof of one of the buildings, three men dressed in drab, grey overalls, their eyes protected by dark goggles, were supervising the loading of several boxes into the hull of the ship via a tractor beam.

After the boxes were loaded, one of the men spoke into a communication device attached to his wrist:

"Survey Team 1 to *Oxus*, do you copy?" he asked.

"I hear you, ST-1," answered a man's voice. "What's up?"

"These are all the samples from our survey of this region, Monsieur De Soto," said the first man. "Everything checks out fine."

"Good. Koynos will be pleased. So far, everything's gone very smoothly. Keep up the good work, ST-1. *Oxus* over and out."

The airship gained altitude, then made a sharp turn and zoomed away towards the north.

Inside the east wing of the desert base was a vast laboratory, cluttered with scientific devices and bathed in orange light. There, Claude Marécourt was working on the prototype of a new matter-to-anti-matter converter powered by *heliose*, that strange mineral found only on Rhea.

Claude had been the youngest experimental physicist to ever have been hired by CERN in Geneva. Then, soon afterward—only three years prior—he had been invited to meet a man named Koynos in an expensive restaurant in Nyon. Curious, Claude had accepted the invitation.

Koynos was a tall, pale, muscular man with blonde hair and blue eyes. He seemed strangely ageless, and could have been anywhere between the ages of 30 and 50. He had been direct, not waiting for coffee and liqueur before discussing the reason for his invitation.

"I represent an organization of scientists and explorers known as the *New Fifteen*," he had told Claude. "I'm looking for a physicist like you."

"I already have a job," Claude had replied.

"On Earth, yes," had said Koynos, smiling. "The job I'm offering to you is located much further away…"

Thus young Claude Marécourt had learned of the existence of the wandering planetoid known as Rhea, which had been first visited in 1935 by that prodigious French adventurer Leo Saint-Clair, sometimes known as the Nyctalope.

"Although I never met Monsieur Saint-Clair myself," commented Claude, "I know he once rescued my grandfather during World War II...[6] How can he still be alive? He must be incredibly old..."

Koynos had only smiled mysteriously, and gone on to explain that the Nyctalope had once had his heart replaced by a synthetic organ that had possibly granted him an extended lifespan beyond that of ordinary mortals. But no one seemed exactly sure of the reasons for his seeming agelessness. There were conflicting stories. In any event, Leo Saint-Clair had secretly returned to Rhea during the darkest days of World War II, when he had feared the world might fall beneath the Nazi heel, in order to establish a small but permanent and peaceful human settlement.

It was to Rhea that Koynos proposed to take Claude.

"But Rhea must be almost out of the Solar System by now," had objected Claude. "How can we possibly go there? We don't have that kind of technology..."

"On the contrary, we do—I mean, the New Fifteen have a craft capable of reaching Rhea in just under a year."

"But no human science can..."

"Did I say it was based on *human* science?" Koynos had replied.

That, of course, had clinched the deal. A young genius like Claude Marécourt could hardly pass up the opportunity to travel to the outer regions of the Solar System and explore a strange, new world.

After Claude had joined the New Fifteen, who were headquartered nearby in the Swiss Alps, Koynos had told the young scientist that they theorized that Rhea was an artificial world, a giant spacecraft built by a mysterious race whose

---

[6] See *The Nyctalope Steps In*.

descendents had devolved into the gorilla-like Nocturnals and the bat-like Diurnals that Leo Saint-Clair had met during his first journey.

The goal of the New Fifteen was to uncovber its secrets, and, for that, they needed the help of an anti-matter specialist like Claude Marécourt.

Eighteen months later, the New Fifteen's ship, a complex, spherical contraption christened the *Oxus* by Koynos, reached Rhea.

The crew was comprised of the fifteen leaders of the organization—Claude had been given the number Nine; Koynos was, of course, Number One. They had been extremely careful, so they were not detected by Olbansville, the Nyctalope's human settlement located in the Southern hemisphere near the Equator, named after the French scientist who had designed the first ship to travel to Rhea in 1935.

Their mission, as defined by Koynos, was to survey the planet and discover its scientific mysteries, especially the secret of its propulsion, atmospheric field and the radiant energies which kept the planetoid alternatively bathed in day and night in an 18-hour day circadian pattern.

Half of the crew, led by Frederic de Soto (Number Two), had gone out to explore Rhea in powerful, tank-like vehicles, while the other, supervised by Dr. Eva Steilman (Number Five), worked on scientific missions. Koynos, too, had gone out, for his own purposes—no one knew exactly where.

During the journey, Claude had often wondered who Koynos really was, and what his ultimate goals were. That he was human, there was no doubt in his mind—but he also seemed more than human, different from the rest of the crew, who were, in every respect, ordinary geniuses, if one could say such a thing. Piercing together various bits of water-cooler gossip, the young physicist had gathered that everyone on board, like himself, was somehow connected to the mysterious Nyctalope who had saved his grandfather's life. But why?—he still had no idea.

Koynos and his secrets remained as obscure eighteen months later, as they had been the first time Claude had met the man in Nyon.

Inside his laboratory in the desert base, Claude was putting the finishing touches to his converter.

"I've got to remember that this is an entirely new design," the young physicist muttered. "I hope the crystal lattice will hold up under the stress. If something was to go wrong... No, better to not even think about that..."

Entirely focused on his work, Claude failed to notice a tiny red insect which had been fluttering around the room, and which had just landed on the physicist's sleeve. From there, the insect jumped onto the converter.

Had Claude been able to examine it with one of his instruments, he would have discovered that the creature was not entirely natural, but was made up of several bionic parts.

As Claude pulled a particle projector down from the ceiling, the fake insect crawled inside the converter through a small opening. Once inside, the strange beast unfolded and began to transform into a sinister-looking device, which clamped itself onto the lattice's central connector.

"I'll plug in the particle projector and give it a dry run," said Claude, starting the device.

A beam radiated from it and hit the lens of the converter, which immediately began emitting a strange sound, then exploded with a silent flash of white light.

As the converter began to melt and turn into a spiky, gooey black mass, a small energy bubble created by the explosion raced from the machine to the floor through a series of cables. All of this was unseen by Claude, who was not hurt, but still blinded by the explosion.

Had the young physicist been able to follow the tiny energy bubble, he would have seen it race from circuit to circuit, run through memory chips and power lines, deeper and deeper inside the complex network of technical wonders that was the secret core of the wondrous artificial world, Rhea.

The bubble finally reached a small, golden sphere at the center of a huge shaft, connected on four sides by complex, mechanical arms.

It triggered a series of short circuits as it traveled along one of the arms, which, upon its contact, also transformed into the same black, thorny substance as Claude's converter.

Finally, when the bubble hit the gold sphere, it cracked—but did not shatter.

Then, there was silence at the heart of Rhea.

Meanwhile, much farther away in the desert, a tank-like vehicle was rushing towards a destination known only to its driver. Inside, at the commands, sitting in a large, pod-chair, was Koynos himself, clad in soft leather, wearing an aviator's helmet. His blue eyes were attentively watching a series of instruments mounted in front of him, while his pale, elongated hands, were gripping the steering-wheel.

Suddenly, a voice came cracking out of a loudspeaker:

"De Soto to Koynos. Come in, Number One! It's an emergency!"

Koynos flicked a switch.

"Koynos here. I hear you, Frederic."

Aboard the *Oxus*, Frederic de Soto emitted a sigh of relief. He, too, knew nothing of Koynos' true purposes, but he was all too aware that the fate of their expedition depended on their mysterious leader.

De Soto, a brilliant engineer who had made his fortune in South America, had initially joined the New Fifteen, motivated by the vague desire to meet and possibly harm Leo Saint-Clair, whose family had been feuding with his for centuries. Unlike Claude Marécourt, he knew what few people in the world were aware of: that the Nyctalope was still alive and well, having barely aged since he had destroyed his great-grandfather Dominique de Soto a.k.a. Gorillard, in 1930. But that was ancient business. Frederic had soon forgotten his plans for revenge, and thrown himself whole-heartedly into the Rhea mission.

"Koynos, at last!" he said, barely hiding his concern. "I was afraid you wouldn't answer."

"Secrecy is vital to our mission, Number Two," replied Koynos. "Why are you breaking radio silence and risking detection by Olbansville?"

"It's that business with the new converter. I'm afraid it's turned out badly."

"What happened?"

"There was a particle explosion at the base."

Koynos experienced a shock. This was entirely unforeseen and could change everything.

"What caused it?" he asked.

"It seems that Number Nine, I mean, Claude Marécourt, was involved. If you remember, I advised against recruiting someone so young and inexperienced..."

"And I disagreed," said Koynos sharply. De Soto's tendency to always throw blame on others was a constant irritant to him. "What measures have you taken?"

"We've tried to cloak the explosion, but it's bound to have been detected by the scientists at Olbansville."

Koynos' fist hit the armrest.

"Damn! The Nyctalope is going to learn we've infiltrated his private little world before we've had time to complete our survey. Find out exactly what happened and report to me asap, Number Two. Koynos over and out."

In his anger, Koynos had blurted a crucial fact that had not escaped Frederic de Soto's notice.

"The Nyctalope is returning to Rhea?!"

Chapter II
The Nyctalope Is Back

In the Southern Hemisphere of Rhea, close to the equator, virtually at the same spot where the *Olb-I* had landed in 1935, stood Olbansville.

The somewhat pretentious name really applied only to a settlement of about fifty white buildings, made of glass and concrete, which had been built by Pierre Saint-Clair, the Nyctalope's own son, according to designs inspired by the great French architect Le Corbusier. Today, they looked somewhat dated, like the "City of the Year 2000" as imagined in the 1950s, which is when Olbansville had been built.

Its inhabitants were aware that they were special: they were the first pioneers of the Human Race to leave the boundaries of the Solar System and travel to the stars.

After his first trip to Rhea, Leo Saint-Clair had left the *Olb-I* in a secret base, hidden under the Moroccan desert, which had been built in the heady days of the CID. When his beloved France had lost World War II, and the Nazi menace looked like it might well prove unstoppable and conquer the world, the Nyctalope had made the fateful decision to preserve the values of Eternal France and, at the same time, embark on an ambitious plan of truly cosmic proportions.

The French Martian Colony had been a tragic failure, but Rhea would prove a far more hospitable home—and vehicle! For with it, or rather *on it*, it was possible to travel to other stars and spread the Human Race throughout the galaxy!

Thanks to the resources of Free France in North Africa, three more spaceships had been built according to Leo's exacting specifications: the *Olb-II, III* and *IV*. Then, the Nyctalope had personally selected the future colonizers of Outer Space. They included his faithful Vito and Socca, of course, Véronique d'Olbans and their son, Marc—her father had passed away only a few months before the fateful journey—several members of the De Ciserat family, Pierre, Saint-Clair, his oldest son, still fresh from serving under General De Gaulle, Toru Mitang, the son of his friend Gnô, as well as their wives and children, and other scientists and explorers, all chosen for their bravery and ideals.

In 1941, the colonists had reached Rhea, which was then located near the Asteroid belt. By unanimous decision, their first settlement had been named Olbansville, after Leo had modestly rejected the name of Saintclairville proposed by his friends.

Relations were quickly established with both races of Nocturnals and Diurnals, favorably predisposed towards the French, and research had begun into the mysteries of Rhea's propulsion, towards the goal of cutting down the time it would take to cross the great distances between the stars. Everyone knew that this would be a project that would take several generations.

The Nyctalope had returned to Earth—alone—in the *Olb-1*, while Rhea pursued its journey towards the outer planets of the Solar System.

Seventy years passed; then in 2011, Leo Saint-Clair received a telepathic SOS from Rhea. The mental call was brief, but indisputable. It emanated from Akira Mitang who, no doubt, was a descendant of his old friend, and had cultivated the same psychic powers that Leo and Gnô had acquired in Tibet so long before.

The Nyctalope had not expected to hear from Rhea ever again. He alone knew that he had had to return to Earth to protect his homeworld from the one threat that could not be defeated by any other earthly inhabitant:

The Martians.

Only Leo Saint-Clair knew, from personal experience, that Mars was an inconceivable threat, a permanent danger waiting to devour Humanity. As the one who had awakened the Martian menace, it was his duty to protect Earth from it.

213

At the time he received the psychic SOS from Rhea, he had, in fact, just vanquished another Martian threat, at great emotional cost to himself.[7]

As he recovered, he had begun a romance with a young woman named Gisèle d'Holbach. In her late twenties, she had striking blue eyes and black hair cut in a short "bob." She was his liaison with the department of French Intelligence, which occasionally employed his services.

Leo had no need of money or a secret identity; however, for convenience and courtesy, the French Government period-ically issued him a new set of papers, every time moving his birth date forward in order to hide his agelessness. He was now a comfortable, perennial 44.

Leo continued to serve his beloved France every time they asked him to perform a mission. His secret was known to only a handful of officials—not even the President knew of the "forever man" in the service of his nation—and that was fine with Leo. For his part, he had told no one about the Rhea colony. Those who knew were long since dead and Leo had not deemed it wise to bring new parties into his confidence.

After Leo received the SOS from Akira Mitang, he knew he had no choice but to travel to Rhea. His own private re-search enabled him to boost the speed of the original *Olb-1*, which remained safely hidden under Morocco's desert sands; but he knew it would still take him more than two years to reach the planetoid for, according to his calculations, Rhea was approaching the outermost fringes of the Solar System.

As for what awaited him there, and the likelihood of his return, it was impossible to speculate.

It was also impossible to disappear without a trace and leave France—Earth—unguarded. Reluctantly, Leo had been forced to share his secret with Auguste Pichenet, the Head of the French Intelligence Service which employed him. Pichenet had listened, managing to not look incredulous—he was gifted with a vivid imagination, which was rare in the military—and

---

[7] See "The Ides of Mars" in *Night of the Nyctalope.*

had given Leo his blessings, but had insisted he take Gisèle with him.

At first, Leo had argued, but he had quickly seen the wisdom of the request: who would want to spend two years alone in a spaceship? He had occasionally thought of proposing to Gisèle, thus making her his sixth wife, and the trip might be just the opportunity he needed to decide whether he wanted to take his relationship with the young woman to the next level.

After almost 30 months of travel, the *Olb-I* at last was orbiting around Rhea.

In Olbansville, in the building that served as transmission center and control tower, a radar operator sat behind a console. Behind him stood a short, rotund Japanese man with remarkably piercing dark eyes. He was dressed in black slacks, white shirt, and wore a tricolor sash around his belt, proclaiming him to be the Mayor of Olbansville.

"I've just spotted the *Olb-I* entering orbit, Monsieur le Maire," said the operator, pointing to a blip on his screen

"Thank you, Monsieur Pilou," replied Akira Mitang. Then, grabbing a microphone and clearing his throat, he announced over the P.A. system: "All stations, please stand by for a priority one communication. This is your Mayor, Akira Mitang, speaking. The Nyctalope is back. The heads of all families should report to the Landing Pad immediately. Repeat: the Nyctalope is back!"

Outside, on a platform that served as landing pad, a dozen technicians rushed to prepare for the spaceship's arrival. Meanwhile, a colorful throng of men and women, dressed in various attires, from military to casual, had emerged from the buildings to watch the much-awaited event.

All those who had known Leo Saint-Clair personally had passed away long ago; the man had become a legend for the denizens of Rhea. His return was by far the most important event ever in the history of the colony.

215

"Landing Pad, are you ready?" asked Mitang in the control room.

"We're standing by," replied one of the technicians, speaking into the microphone connected to his helmet.

In the control room, the monitor screen showed the *Olb-I* starting its descent.

"Engage guidance beam, Monsieur Pilou," said Mitang. "And tell them to correct their trajectory by three degrees."

"Guidance beam engaged. Trajectory corrected."

Slowly, majestically, like a tennis ball on top of an invisible water sprout, the *Olb-I* appeared, first as a small dot in the sky, then growing larger and larger as it approached the ground. Its shape was roughly that of an old-fashioned rocket, 40 meters tall and 10 meters wide. Inside, it contained two large cabins, the bridge, a recreation room, and four storage rooms. A crew of six could live comfortably in it for a year. Leo and Giselle had been its sole passengers for over two years.

"The ship's in position, Monsieur le Maire," confirmed Pilou.

"Prepare to land."

The *Olb-I* delicately settled onto the landing pad, its three fins fitting snugly inside the gantries. The waiting crowd became even more excited, with people jostling each other to get a better view.

Akira Mitang came out of the control tower, followed by two officers in full French Army colonial uniforms, each carrying a garland of flowers.

"Please let us through," said the Mayor, politely pushing his way through the crowd.

As they reached the edge of the Landing Pad, Mitang turned to his first officer, a tall man with dark hair, blue eyes, and a noble bearing.

"Monsieur de Ciserat," asked the Mayor of Olbansville, "is the Orchestra ready?"

"Of course, Monsieur." Ciserat turned to a makeshift orchestra which had stood patiently to the side, and waved his hand. "You may begin, gentlemen."

The Orchestra began playing the *Marseillaise* just as Leo Saint-Clair and Gisèle d'Holbach emerged from the ship, being carried to the ground on a small elevator platform, which rose up again after having deposited its two passengers.

For such an important occasion, Leo had chosen to wear formal attire, consisting of a black silk jacket, pants, white shirt and tails. He thought he looked like his father, when the latter had been received at the Court of Tsar Alexander III in Moscow in 1892.

Gisèle, by contrast, wore a modern black overall with belts and many pockets, of the type favored by the agents of her service.

Once on the ground, the Nyctalope raised his arm to salute the crowd, which went wild at the sight.

"Thank you, my friends! Thank you very much!" he said. Then proudly turning towards Gisèle, he added: "Welcome to Rhea, my dear. The most wonderful planet in the universe!"

At that moment, Akira arrived and gestured to the officers to place the garlands over their honored guests' head.

"I'm Akira Mitang, Mayor of this settlement, Monsieur Saint-Clair. I'm honored beyond words to welcome you back to Olbansville."

Leo extended a warm hand shake to the man he immediately recognized as the descendent of his long-time friend, Gnô Mitang.

"The honor is all mine, Akira. And please call me Leo. This lady is Gisèle d'Holbach, my trusted companion."

"Mademoiselle," said Akira, bowing deeply.

"This is... all so... amazing," said the young woman.

Gisèle hadn't stopped mentally pinching herself since they had landed. She had just set foot on an alien world—it was a mind-blowing concept. She was actually standing on a planet about to leave the Solar System. This was such an awesome experience that she could hardly contain her excitement.

When she watched Leo, and how he took everything in stride, as if it was no big deal for him—and indeed, perhaps it was—she realized with a pang how much of a gulf separated them—and not only years.

It was one thing to accept that the man who had become her lover was born in 1877; it was another to realize that he had walked on alien worlds a long time before she was a mote in her grandparents' eyes!

Sensing his companion's sense of displacement, Leo took her hand and squeezed it to comfort her.

Meanwhile, Akira introduced his aide-de-camp:

"This is Monsieur Marc de Ciserat, my First Officer; he is ready to give you a tour of the colony."

The Nyctalope understood right away that this was the ideal pretext for Mitang to have a private conversation with him, and also to relieve Gisèle of her stress, so he enthusiastically supported the suggestion.

"That's an excellent idea, Akira. *Ma chérie*, go with Monsieur de Ciserat. This is your first time on Rhea; you should enjoy yourself. You don't mind, do you, Ciserat?"

"Not at all! It will be my pleasure, Monsieur!" said the officer, saluting.

Then, after Gisèle had gone with the young officer, Leo turned to the Mayor and asked:

"So what is it, Akira. Why have you called me back after so many years?"

"I'm very sorry, great Nyctalope, but we've detected intruders in the northern hemisphere."

"Intruders? You don't mean…?"

"Yes. Intruders from Earth. And just before you arrived, there was a disturbing incident. We detected a small antimatter explosion somewhere in the great northern desert, near the pole."

"What!" exclaimed Leo.

"We don't yet know the cause, but our scientists think it might affect the engines that propel Rhea…"

"Damn!" The Nyctalope raised his arm and addressed the crowd. "May I have your attention? I'm deeply touched by your warm welcome, but you must all return to your stations—at once!" Then, he added for the Mayor's ears: "You did well to summon me back, Akira. We'd best not rush to any hasty conclusions, but this looks serious indeed!"

Chapter III.
A Gathering of Schemers

Since the Earthmen had first visited Rhea in 1935, the Nocturnals had made great progress. The intervention of the Nyctalope had enabled a lasting peace to be built between them and their brethren, the Diurnals, who existed in a loose confederation of far-flung cities on the surface of the planetoid.

The Nocturnals, on the other hand, were gregarious creatures. With the help of the Earthmen, they had unified and gathered in ever-growing cities located in the night-dark caverns of the planet. Being more technologically-minded than their surface cousins, they had taken to scientific progress like a fish to water. One of the theories popular amongst the French colonists was that the Nocturnals were descended not from the servants of the mysterious race who had built Rhea, as had been originally believed, but might well be the degenerated descendents of the Builders themselves. If so, the reason why they had devolved remained a mystery.

As the decades passed, the Nocturnals had further congregated to create their first capital, the great city of Qotwaa, located in the northern hemisphere, inside a gigantic network of interlinked caverns. The city itself managed to look both futuristic, yet strangely medieval at the same time. In the largest cave was the palace of its undisputed ruler, King Kkal. He was tall and hulkish; even amongst ape-men, his stature inspired respect—and fear.

Deep below the palace was Kkal's inner sanctum and secret laboratory, where he was presently pacing, surrounded by his two faithful retainers, the equally tall but lanky Chamberlain Ddôl and the short and rotund Chief Scientist Ppy, whose head was shaped like the top of a mushroom and who wore a

220

small magnifying glass slide attached to the top of his skull in front of his eyes (instead of Earth glasses).

There was a strange pattern on the floor; a glowing ball of light hovered directly above it.

Kkal interrupted his pacing around the pattern and, followed by Ddôl, headed towards a dais, which supported a column of light and where a makeshift console on the side was attended by the frantic Ppy.

"What's going on, Ppy?" asked Kkal.

"I think I finally succeeded in damaging the control sphere, O Great King," replied Ppy.

"Really? Show me."

Ppy turned a wheel and depressed a lever on his console. Images of the strange insect that had penetrated Claude Marécourt's converter began to appear and the scene unfolded to show the fateful explosion.

"Our little saboteur did a good job," said Kkal, grinning. "Manipulating that young human into causing the explosion was a stroke of genius, even if I do say so myself. The accursed force field that protects Rhea's Core and its great engines still stands, but now it should be vulnerable to our ally's magic…"

Kkal turned around and shouted: "Vôo! Where are you, Vôo?"

Ppy looked frightened, and even Ddôl's usually inexpressive face showed some apprehension. "Vôo" was the name of the Master of the Nine Hells in the legends told to children when they were small. The fact that their new ally had introduced himself under that name still caused them not a little discomfort.

Suddenly, a tall, humanoid figure, dressed all in red, and wearing a silver mask shaped like a demon skull to cover his face, emerged from the glowing ball of light.

"I'm here, Kkal," said Vôo, materializing.

"Are you ready? I can't wait to access the Core. The power of the great engines will make me master of Rhea!"

"We can but try."

A beam of violet light issued from Vôo's mask and hit the pattern on the floor. Kkal, Ddôl and Ppy looked on with interest—the latter, however, with much concern contorting his face.

Slowly, a warp opened in the pattern and pure, white light, almost insupportable for human eyes, appeared. Ppy's "glasses" became dark and he handed two identical protective eye-coverings to his partners, who put them on.

"Rhea's Core," said Kkal, awe-struck.

Suddenly, there was a spark, followed by an explosion. The white light was replaced by a huge burst of flame which almost hit Ppy, who jumped back, screaming.

The lights in the cave died.

"I have failed," said Vôo, matter-of-factedly.

"By the horn of Ggorn!" muttered Kkal. Then, turning towards the frightened scientist. He barked: "The lights! Turn on the emergency lights!"

Ppy rushed to obey, scrambling maniacally over his console. As the lights returned, Kkal, followed by Ddôl, climbed from the dais and walked towards Vôo.

"What good is it to ally myself with you, stranger, if you can't deliver what you promised?" he spat. "You told me you could break through the force field that protects the Core!"

"True, I can. But the field is strong. I require more time."

"I don't have more time! Olbansville's imperial rule has already gone on for too long. And now, the Nyctalope has returned. But soon, that sanctimonious, self-appointed 'King of the Night' will learn that I, Kkal, King of the Nocturnals, have decreed that his reign is over!"

"I hate the Nyctalope too—more than you can ever imagine—but I must advise caution. Great king. I know Leo Saint-Clair. To defeat him will require subtlety. But I know I will eventually triumph."

"You'd better," spat Kkal, walking towards an elevator. "I've sworn to free this world from French colonial domination, and I'll let no one stand in my way."

Ppy rushed to catch up with his master. Together, the three ape-men entered the elevator, which went up.

Vôo was alone in the cavern. From behind his mask issued an evil, contemptuous chuckle.

"Ha! Kkal is a fool. The secret of Rhea's engines shall belong to me, and me alone. I will kill the Nyctalope and destroy that pathetic, puny world of his. *I, Lucifer, will be victorious at last!*"

Then, he vanished as he had appeared, with only the small glowing ball of light remaining behind as a silent witness to his presence.

Chapter IV
Gisèle's Curiosity

In the Control Center in Olbansville, the Nyctalope had taken command, sitting in the controller's chair, the loyal Akira Mitang standing by his side.

Before them were half a dozen large screens and consoles manned by operators.

"Summon our agent in Choon Ya, Monsieur Pilou," said Akira. Then, he explained to the Nyctalope: "That is the Diurnal village closest to where we detected the anti-matter explosion. Perhaps they'll know something. I'd like to hear his report."

The Console Operators below busied themselves at their machines. Suddenly, the giant screens filled with static, then the image of a wizened Diurnal appeared. His face was covered with ritual tattoos that indicated his mastery of the most arcane rituals of his race, and his appurtenance to five of the planet's seven major clans. Like all his brethren, he had big almond-shaped blue eyes with gold pupils, but no eyelids or eyebrows.

"His name is Jaffa M'Deni," whispered Akira in Leo's ear.

"Ah, my good Jaffa! Tell me: how are things in Choon Ya and the Great Northern Desert?"

"*Diffidently*, your Overlordship," replied the old Diurnal. "The blondels are a bit *prostive* at this time of the year."

"Forget the blondels," said Leo. "Have you noticed anything unusual in your region?"

"No, your Overlordship, I *forebode* nothing."

"Yet, Olbansville has just detected an anti-matter explosion near your village. Surely..."

"A what, your Overlordship?" interrupted Jaffa.

"A... A big white light..." said Leo, frustrated.

"Ah! The breath of the gods!" said the bat-man.

"Yes. The breath of the gods. Surely, you must have noticed something of the sort?"

"No, not a *wobble*, your Overlordship."

Leo sighed.

"Very well. Remain alert and notify Olbansville immediately should anything unusual occur."

Jaffa M'Deni bowed his head, and disappeared from the screen.

"Now," said Leo, "let's contact your agent with the Nocturnals. I never fully trusted those hairy deviants…"

Meanwhile, elsewhere in the colony, Marc de Ciserat was still with Gisèle, continuing their tour. They reached a semi-spherical, steel-grey building, and stood in front of a large set of double metal doors.

"This is our Map Room," said Marc, opening the door.

The young officer turned on the light. The room was empty except for a giant, three-dimensional model of Rhea, and several miniature projectors, which constantly updated the features of the globe. All were connected by cables to intricate machinery on the ceiling.

Watching the globe, the color of gold and burnished brass, slowly rotate before her eyes, Gisèle could not help but express both admiration and curiosity.

"This… is Rhea?" she asked.

"Indeed, it is, Mademoiselle," said Marc. "Or rather, a constantly updated projection of the real thing."

The young officer typed a command on a small control panel keyboard.

"Let me demonstrate."

The hologram appeared to fragment, then expand, enabling the viewer to have a closer look at the planet.

"Rhea is one-sixth the size of Earth," commented Marc. "As you can see, it's mostly a desert, buffered by strong winds circling the planet. There are a number of interconnected lakes and rivers centered, as you can see, mostly around the Equator. Most of the water here lies underground. There are no tall mountains to speak of, only rugged hills, and tundra-like plains and deserts. There is a forestry belt near the Equator, where the first expedition landed. This is where we are: Olbansville…" Marc pointed towards a dot on the map, then at the neighboring region. "These forests are mostly composed of very tall trees which look like yellow poplars. They're inhabited by a native species of bird called blondels… There are few animals on Rhea… Certainly no farm or industrial animals… This, here, is Suwa Jem, the first village of Diurnals we encountered, and a little to the south, near the edge of the forest, under that mountain range, is Chunda, where we first made contact with the Nocturnals…"

"What about the natives?" inquired Gisèle.

"There are two races of Rheans: the bat-like humanoids we call Diurnals, who live on the surface in villages spread around the equator. They're artistic and peaceful, and like to trade between their city-states. Before the Nyctalope arrived, they were often attacked by the Nocturnals, a gorilla-like species who live underground in vast networks of caves located under the hills in both the northern and southern hemispheres. But the Nyctalope made peace between the two species and made them sign a Treaty. Today, the Nocturnals have unified in a sort of loose confederation ruled from here…" continued Marc, pointing at a dot in the northern hemisphere, "…Qotwaa."

"Why were they at war?"

"The Nocturnals are more like engineers or scientists, if you will. Their underground cities are quite impressive to visit, especially since there is no fire on Rhea and virtually no metal, so everything has to be manufactured from clay and chemicals. But they have no art, no music, no culture, so they would kidnap the artistically-minded Diurnals for their own entertainment."

"How revolting!"

"Well, that's all in the past now. Besides, the Diurnals are daysiders and the Nocturnals nightsiders, so they cohabit and trade, but they don't visit each other very much."

"What do you mean by daysiders and nightsiders?"

"You hay have noticed during your approach that Rhea is protected by a force field that keep its atmosphere in, and deadly space radiation out. That field also provides a circadian rhythm as half of it radiates light during the "day" and rotates around the planet every 18 hours. Thus we have short days of nine hours. On the other side of Rhea, the field is transparent and enables us to watch the stars and experience night."

"That's amazing. What powers such a fantastic device?"

"Frankly, we don't know. Clearly, Rhea is powered by some mighty engines, buried deep inside the planet. There are two openings at the poles, but they're protected by fierce maelstroms that are virtually unbreachable. We've asked the natives, but they have no written history. As far as they know, it's always been like this. Several years ago, the Nyctalope's grand-daughter, Xavière Saint-Clair, and Professor Henri d'Olbans tried to gain access to Rhea's Core through the North Pole opening, but Xavière perished in the process. Henri has kept trying, but without success so far. In the end, our resources being limited, it was decided to wait until our colony had grown stronger."

Meanwhile, in the Control Center, the Nyctalope was continuing his investigation into the current state of affairs on Rhea.

"So, the Nocturnals are now ruled from Qotwaa?" he asked Akira.

"Yes," responded the Mayor. "The city has grown mightily since you were last here. Its king is a smart but devious fellow called Kkal. I don't trust him a bit, so I've posted an agent, an ambassador if you will, to keep us abreast of what he's up to. His name is Ludo Corsat. He's the grandson of your faithful retainer.""

"I never had a better a man in my service," said Leo. "Let's call him."

Soon, the face of a handsome young man with dark hair and brown eyes appeared on one of the screens.

"Mayor Mitang is correct, Great Nyctalope," he said. "King Kkal is definitely up to no good. There are rumors that he's trying to gain access to Rhea's Core."

Leo raised a skeptical eyebrow.

"Bah! He's a fool. He doesn't have the technology for it."

"Not by himself, no. But the same rumors claim that he's recently acquired an ally."

"Hmm. A new wrinkle. Do you know who this ally is?"

"Not yet, Monsieur. But I'm working on it."

"I don't like the sound of this, Monsieur Corsat. Learn everything you can, then report back to Olbansville."

"Yes, Great Nyctalope!"

"And, Corsat, it wouldn't do for you to end up in one of Kkal's nasty, little dungeons."

"I understand, Monsieur."

The screen went dark. Saint-Clair turned to Akira.

"This is serious. No one should be allowed to break into Rhea's Core before we do. Especially not this Kkal. I've got to get to Qotwaa at once."

"I'll have one of our new mygale battletrucks prepared. No need to take any chances. Will you travel alone?"

"Yes, of course."

Suddenly, the doors opened, and Gisèle d'Holbach entered, followed by a slightly embarrassed Marc de Ciserat.

"Gisèle! What are you doing back here so soon?" asked Leo, surprised.

"I wanted to see the Control Center. Is that so surprising?"

"I'm sorry, Monsieur," said Marc to the Nyctalope, apologetically. "I've tried to explain to the Mademoiselle that you were..."

"It's all right, Monsieur de Ciserat," replied Leo, dismissively. "Mademoiselle d'Holbach is welcome everywhere in this colony." Then, he turned towards the young woman, and added: "By the way, there's been a minor change in plans, *ma chérie*. I've got to go to the ape-men's capital city for a few days to take care of some details personally."

"Oh, good!" said Gisèle, excitedly. "That's Qotwaa, right? I can't wait to see it."

"Er, I'm afraid not, *chère amie*. This is something I've got to do alone."

Gisèle frowned and her blue eyes darkened.

"Don't be absurd, Leo! Of course, I'm going with you. That's one of the reasons I came here in the first place, remember?"

"I'm sorry, but I can't allow it. Not yet, anyway." Leo marked a pause. "Besides, it'll be terribly dull. You'll find things here much more entertaining. Marc can show you the hills of Chunda and..."

"Don't patronize me, Leo Saint-Clair," said Gisèle in a low, but unmistakably dangerous tone. "You forget who I am. I'm quite capable of looking after myself."

But the Nyctalope stood his ground.

"Please, Gisèle, don't be difficult. I promise, as soon as I take care of these loose ends, I'll send for you."

He then got up and walked towards the door, gesturing to Akira.

"Show me to that battletruck, Monsieur Mitang."

What he didn't notice was Gisèle muttering under her breath: "We'll see about that..."

Chapter V
Flight Into Nowhere

Claude Marécourt was afraid.

Since the scientist had joined the organization of the New Fifteen, he had come to realize that it was not a harmless club of benevolent do-gooders, but an implacable machine designed to serve only the aims of one man, its leader, the mysterious Koynos.

And what Koynos' purpose was, no one knew

After he had joined the New Fifteen, Claude had been witness to a particularly merciless execution. One of the scientists, the former No.8, a small, meek Englishman, had either decided that he could make more money selling the organization's scientific secrets to an American corporation, or he was afraid to go into space, perhaps both. Somehow, Koynos had gotten wind of the man's treachery, and before No.8 could leave Switzerland, his throat had been slit by the fearsome No.4, Koynos' executioner, a giant of a man named Malterre. Then the body had been vaporized in one of the base's generators.

Koynos is going to kill me, thought Marécourt. *There's no telling what kind of damage that explosion might have caused...*

The young scientist walked briskly down the metal corridors, trying not to attract any unwelcome attention. At the end of the base was a vast hangar where he knew he could "borrow" a travel-sphere, a transparent spherical vehicle with a built-in gyroscope, which could roll over any surface and travel at great speed. The crew had nicknamed them "hamster balls" because, once inside, one felt a little like one of those friendly rodents.

I've got to get out of here, thought Marécourt, as he entered the hangar. Fortunately, it was deserted. *Maybe I can get*

*to Olbansville? Somehow, they'll get me off this horrible plan-
et...*

Marécourt got into one of the hamster balls and started
its magnetic engine. A faint vibration ran through the vehicle
while the gyromotors came to life. He then remotely activated
the opening of the great metal door, revealing the vastness of
the great northern desert outside.

Suddenly, a man entered the hangar. Marécourt shuddered because he had recognized the imposing silhouette of
Malterre.

"Going out for a spin, No.9?" asked the giant. "Could I
see your pass?"

Instead of obeying, Marécourt pushed the starter button
on the gyrosphere which zoomed towards the hangar door,
almost running over Malterre.

"Marécourt's lost his mind!" shouted the giant into a
communicator on his shoulder. "Alert!"

Claude drove off into the desert. Malterre pulled out a
gun and fired a shot. The bullet hit the gyrosphere, apparently
causing no damage.

The vehicle quickly disappeared over the horizon towards the south.

"ST-1 to *Oxus*! Emergency!" shouted Malterre into his
communicator.

The *Oxus* was gliding through a canyon. Frederic de Soto, No.2, heard Malterre's report and immediately called his
master.

"No.2 to No.1, do you hear me? I'm afraid I've got more
bad news, Koynos."

Inside his tank-like vehicle, the leader of the New Fifteen
picked up the communication.

"What is it this time, Frederic?"

"Young Marécourt's panicked. He must've been afraid
you would blame him for the explosion, so he's run away."

Koynos swore silently under his breath, then replied:

"Go after him. If he falls into the Nyctalope's hands before I'm ready, our entire mission here will be jeopardized."

231

"Why don't we just let him go?" asked de Soto. "After all, Marécourt knows nothing of your plan."

"Maybe so, but Saint-Clair is no fool. If he gets holds of Marécourt, it won't take him long to get the full picture."

"Even so, what could he do? The ones you serve are beyond even his powers…"

"I learned the hard way to never underestimate the Nyctalope, No.2. No, my friend, find Marécourt and get him off Rhea before he causes us any more headaches."

"Understood, No.1. I'll start the search immediately!"

The *Oxus* left its position and zoomed off.

"And, Frederic, when you find Marécourt, don't be too harsh on him," added Koynos, before shutting the comlink.

Chapter VI
The Dastardly Digger

Once his mind had been made to go to Qotwaa, the capitol of the Nocturnals in person, the Nyctalope moved quickly.

Olbansville was located in the southern hemisphere, east of Lake Flammarion; Qotwaa was in the northern hemisphere, westward, beyond the Mariposa Mountains. For a trip of that magnitude, Saint-Clair had commandeered Olbansville's mightiest vehicle, the *mygale*, an all-terrain battletruck which could move on wheels, tracks and even eight artificial legs like its spidery namesake. It was the size of a Greyhound bus, powerfully armed with cannons and electroguns, and even came equipped with a small medibloc.

Leo had been traveling for a day and a half, staying in regular contact with Olbansville hourly, when he heard a small, creaking noise coming from the back of the vehicle.

Grabbing his gun, the Nyctalope left the control module and walked down a narrow central corridor leading towards the pantry.

"All right, whoever you are, come out!" he said menacingly.

The lid of a large, trunk-like wicker basket, which was supposed to contain gifts for the Rheans Leo was planning to meet, opened and Gisèle d'Holbach's somewhat embarrassed face emerged.

"Gisèle! I ordered you to remain in Olbansville!" said Leo, indignantly.

"You don't control me, Monsieur Saint-Clair! No one gives me orders. Not even you!"

"How did you manage to find your way in here?" asked Leo.

"Easy," replied Gisèle, smiling. "I asked that handsome young officer of yours."

"You mean, de Ciserat? I'll wring his neck when I get back!"

"Don't be silly. He's a smart young man. He only wanted to be helpful."

"Ha!"

Then, Leo reconsidered the situation. While he was annoyed that Gisèle had disobeyed his orders, he was nevertheless happy to have a companion for the long and most likely boring journey to Qotwaa. Besides, he was secretly proud of his status as "King of the Night" and would enjoy showing the wonders of what he thought of as "his planet" to the young woman. So he said:

"As always, I'm impressed by your resourcefulness. Now the question is, what am I going to do with you?"

Gisèle climbed up and out of the basket and started walking towards the control module.

"Since you can't send me back, you might as well enjoy my company. Besides, I'm pretty talented, as you well know," she added in a flirtatious tone.

The Nyctalope smiled in spite of himself.

"I guess it's pointless to argue."

Half-a-day later, the mygale had crossed the equator and was moving along a row of giant mounds, not unlike African termite hills.

"This mygale of yours is very impressive," said Gisèle, sitting in the co-pilot's chair, looking at the controls.

"It was especially designed to travel across the surface of Rhea. I'm planning to reach Choon Ya tomorrow; that's where I'll make contact with Jaffa M'Deni, one of my best agents among the Diurnals."

"The bat people, right?"

"Yes. You'll see, they're quite a sight."

Leo then grabbed Gisèle's hand and took it in his.

"I must admit, I'm not unhappy to have you here. This might turn into a fun trip, after all."

"Uh-uh," smiled Gisèle, familiar with Leo's romantic moods. "I can see your concern from here... But seriously, what's so important about this trip to Qotwaa?"

"I can't tell you yet," said Leo, all business again. "If Rhea has been invaded by strangers... It needs investigating...There are secrets that must be protected..."

"Secrets? What kind of secrets?"

"Secret secrets," replied Leo, evasively.

Gisèle frowned, but didn't have time to speak up. A sharp blow from outside had just shaken the mygale which stopped dead in its tracks.

"What's happening?" asked the young woman.

"I don't know," said Leo. "We seem to be under attack. Let's take a look."

The Nyctalope looked at a screen, then exclaimed:

"Damn! We've stumbled across a Dastardly Digger!"

The Dastardly Digger, a hulking figure of a giant, had just thrown a rock at the vehicle. It was obviously intended as a warning shot, because he returned to digging inside the nearest mound, chewing on something abominable.

The Nyctalope started the vehicle again, hoping to avoid conflict. But the Digger pulled his head out the mound and turned to look back at the mygale.

He looked like a cross between the two Rhean races: he had the bulk and savage red eyes of the Nocturnals, and the claws and wings of the Diurnals. He also sported a deadly row of razor-sharp fangs, which gleamed into the pale rhean "sunset."

"He must think we're after his larder," said Leo.

"His *what*?"

"Dastardly Diggers—a loose translation of the term used by the natives—are mutants who feed on the mummified bodies piled in those mounds. According to Rhean history, they were exterminated during the last Great Crusade that saw the two races join forces to get rid of the brutes. It's one of the most exciting moments in Rhean history, and the subject of many operatic songs amongst the Diurnals."

"Yuck!" said Gisèle, making a face. "That's disgusting."

"True. But in a world like Rhea, certain ecological balances need to be maintained—even if it means offending our more refined sensibilities."

Leo straightened up in his chair.

"I'm afraid he won't let us through without a fight."

"I don't mind. He's a repulsive brute!"

The Dastardly Digger roared and rushed to attack the mygale. The vehicle shot a powerful explosive shell which hit the creature's chest bull's eye and caused it to fall to its knees.

"Maybe now he'll leave us alone," said Leo, his hope tempered by skepticism.

The mygale turned and began to slowly drive away. But the Dastardly Digger got back to its feet, roared again, and struck a powerful blow to the vehicle's back, causing it to shudder and stop.

"*Aie*! Can't... you do... something?" said Gisèle.

"I'm trying," replied Leo, pushing buttons wildly.

The Dastardly Digger now struggled with the mygale's back, trying to pull it open like an oyster.

"We're in luck," said Leo. "None of the hydraulics have been damaged!"

Suddenly, the mygale's eight artificial legs sprang from the underbelly of the armored vehicle and lifted it up in the air.

"Our hairy friend is in for a bit of a surprise," said Leo.

A powerful bolt of electricity fired by one of the electroguns at the back of the mygale forced the Digger to release its hold on the vehicle. Screaming, the creature fell onto the desert sand. Then the mygale reared up and, like a mule, delivered a powerful kick to the Digger's head.

"That should take some of the wind out of him," said Leo.

"I don't know," said Gisèle, studying the monster on one of the screens. "He doesn't look that winded to me."

Indeed, the Dastardly Digger now picked up a big rock that had been lying on the desert floor, and prepared to throw it at the mygale.

"Uh-oh. It looks like I was right."

The Digger threw the rock, but the mygale fired another explosive shell which shattered it in mid-air.

Now, the two combatants circled, carefully observing each other.

"What now?"asked Gisèle.

"I've got to end this," said Leo. "We don't have time for..."

Interrupting the Nyctalope, the Dastardly Digger roared and again threw itself at the mygale, encircling the vehicle in a crushing armlock designed to crush it. But Leo fired two more shells from the right and the left cannons that hit the monster's arms, forcing it to release them.

By now, the Digger's face showed severe strain, and its body was bleeding profusely from multiple places. Leo thought that at least one of the creature's arms had been broken by his last attack. The Digger studied the mygale warily for what seemed to be a long time.

"We can't take much more of this," said Leo, checking on the damage.

Suddenly, the Dastardly Digger straightened up, let out one final mighty roar, and thumped his chest with his fists like a gorilla. Then, he turned around and, after a last hate-filled glance at the mygale, walked away from the fight.

"Oof! I guess he had his fill after all," said Leo, wiping sweat off his forehead.

"I wish I'd had your mygale back when I was running guns in Mali," said Gisèle, admiringly. "It would have come in handy."

She then snuggled closer to the Nyctalope.

"Yes, I'm quite proud of it," said Leo. "A real engineering feat."

"Let's not talk about engineering," said the young woman, beginning to undo Leo's top collar buttons. "That fight was something, wasn't it? I'm sure your Jaffa what's-his-name won't mind if we're a little late..."

She kissed the Nyctalope passionately.

Chapter VII
The Perils of Choon Ya

High in the sky flew a bird with a long, cigar-shaped body, a small beak, and short square wings, entirely snow-white. The creature mostly glided through the air, creating an impression of extraordinary lightness.

The bird seemed focused on the mygale, still at a dead stop on the desert below. If an observer had been able to approach the bird in flight, he might have detected something that looked like a camera lens in one of its eyes.

And indeed, it was.

The scene being observed by the strange "spybird" was being relayed to, and broadcast inside, the column of light in Kkal's sanctum. There, it was being watched with great interest by the King, his Chamberlain Ddôl, and the mysterious "Vôo."

"It seems the Nyctalope has left Olbansville and is coming here in that overgrown rust bucket," said Kkal. Then, turning towards the Vôo, he asked: "What should we do now?"

"We must act at once," replied the scarlet-clad figure. "We must stop the Nyctalope."

"The thing is, I'm not ready for an open conflict with the French—yet."

"If we don't stop the Nyctalope and he uncovers our plans, we'll suffer a calamitous setback."

King Kkal thought for a minute, contemplating his options. Then, having made up his mind, he barked:

"Right. You want action? I'll show you action!" He turned to the Chamberlain. "Ddôl, alert our agent in Choon Ya. Tell him to destroy the Nyctalope!"

"Welcome to Choon Ya, *ma chérie*" said the Nyctalope.

238

As the mygale drove over the last hill, the village of Choon Ya came into view. Everything, including the city's enclosing wall, was a uniform silver-gray. Nowhere could doors or windows be seen, but every building had an indented pyramidal roof, and, at the top, instead of the tip of the pyramid, there was an entrance and exit "door" with convex panels and lock that Leo and Gisèle could make out quite clearly.

The buildings were large and small, round and oblong, triangular and square; the streets below were sinuous and maze-like. Normally, there would have been numerous Diurnals entering or emerging from the edifices, circulating on foot in the streets, or launching themselves into the air from the top of the ramparts, crossing the river in a descending glide and landing on the plain outside the walls.

But not today. Today, Choon Ya appeared to be deserted.

"That's odd," said Leo. "Where are all the villagers?"

The mygale drove under a gate-like arch and entered the city

"Maybe we came in at the time of their daily *siesta* or something like that?" said Gisèle.

"Don't be silly. Why is the city empty?"

Suddenly, they saw and heard some sound-and-light activity at the end of a long avenue.

"It's not empty," said Gisèle. "What's going on over there?"

"Let's find out."

The Nyctalope drove the mygale towards the source of the mysterious phenomenon.

They arrived at what looked like a town square, round in shape, surrounded by a colonnade, from which radiated seven avenues. In its center, on a dais, stood a bizarre figure dressed in eccentric, multicolored clothes performing a strange juggling ritual with two crimson rings and wands in front of the gathered villagers, while chanting an incomprehensible melody. The hypnotized villagers swung their heads from side to side in accord with the music, a glazed look in their eyes.

"What the Hell is going on?" exclaimed Gisèle, taken aback by the strange ceremony.

The Nyctalope frowned, for he had just recognized the colorful juggler. He shared his discovery with his companion.

"It's our agent, Jaffa M'Deni."

"What is he doing?"

"Performing some kind of ritual, I suppose... Seeding Day or something like that."

"I don't like him. He looks... strange."

"That he is. But he's also been our operative in this city for many years. Let's go and talk to him."

The Nyctalope pressed a button and a holographic image of him sitting in his command chair appeared just in front of the mygale. He raised his hand in a salute and said:

"Greetings, Jaffa M'Deni!"

Jaffa turned around and, on discovering the mygale and the image of its driver, grinned an evil grin.

"Nyctalope! I had been *exponding* you with great *malevance...*"

"I don't like this," whispered Gisèle into Leo's ear.

"Neither do I," he whispered back. "I've never seen him like this."

Jaffa recaptured one of his crimson rings with a wand, twirled it a few times, then, suddenly, hurled it towards the mygale.

"Die, Nyctalope, die!" he screamed.

"Leo! Do something!" shouted Gisèle.

"I don't believe it," said the Nyctalope. "I've never seen anything like it!"

As the crimson ring zoomed ever faster towards the mygale, the Nyctalope pushed a button. An energy beam shot out of one of the cannons and hit the ring, which exploded in mid-air.

"It would seem that Jaffa M'Deni has turned traitor," said Leo, with a note of sadness in his voice.

"Isn't that obvious?" said Gisèle, angry. "I think you should smash that little worm to a pulp."

"Uh-uh. He is using Builders' technology. God knows where he's got it from, but I can't match it. The mygale doesn't pack that kind of firepower. But everything has some value. At least, it confirms my suspicions... We'll be lucky if we get out of here in one piece though..."

At the Nyctalope's command, the battletruck turned around and prepared to flee. But Jaffa had other ideas. He plucked the other crimson ring out of the air, while cursing:

"You can't *crapete* away like this, Nyctalope!"

And just as the mygale drove into a side street, Jaffa used his waqnd to throw his second ring towards it.

The ring chased the vehicle like a heat-seeking missile and finally hit the back where the engine was. Almost immediately, there was big explosion.

Unseen by the crowd, however, the control module detached seconds before the explosion, flew through the air, and landed with a thud on the ground below after bouncing a few times. It finally reached a halt by bumping against a wall.

The Nyctalope, battered, bruised and disheveled, extricated himself from the wreck, helping Gisèle by giving her his arm.

"Are you hurt, *chérie*?"

"Not really... Just a little startled."

Gisèle looked at the wreck and shook her head in wonder.

"You really built that mygale well... Amazing..."

Meanwhile, the Nyctalope stepped back inside the wreck and returned carrying a small briefcase.

"We can't stay here," he said. "It's only a matter of minutes before Jaffa finds us."

Indeed, Jaffa had been running towards the site of the explosion and, when they raised their heads, they saw him coming towards them.

"Nyctalope! Nyctalope! Where are you, you little *lanske*?"

Realizing that he had not spotted them yet, Leo pulled Gisele towards a tiny alley and they began running through the maze-like streets of Choon Ya.

"Let's get out of here. We've got to get to Qotwaa quickly. Fortunately, we're near the riverfront... Faster, *chérie*, or we'll miss the boat!"

"The boat? What boat?"

"This way!" said Leo, pulling Gisèle through a hole in a crumbling wall.

They then descended a flight of old stone steps covered with moss.

"Hurry!" said Leo.

They arrived in a bare room covered in hieroglyphs with a single-panel, reinforced metal door at the far end.

"We got here just in time," said the Nyctalope, sounding relieved.

He opened his briefcase.

"I know the damn thing's in here somewhere.... Ah... At last!"

He pulled out a key and inserted it in the lock. The door opened, revealing a busy wharf occupied by a mixed crowd of Diurnals and Nocturnals. There were bales of leaves tied together waiting to be loaded and unloaded. Tied to it was a large paddleboat, not unlike the Mississippi Paddleboats, painted in brash and garish colors.

Gisèle gasped in amazement.

"Wonderful, isn't it?" said Leo. "And right on schedule, as always. I love the Polychromatic Paddleboat!"

The Nyctalope and his lady-friend stepped aboard the boat, Leo waving the key at the ticket-taker, who saluted them.

They then settled inside a plush, first-class cabin occupied by only one other passenger, already asleep.

Soon, there was a loud whistle, the sound of steam being released, a last bustle of frantic agitation on the wharf, and the Polychromatic Paddleboat left Choon Ya.

The countryside swept by the windows on both sides of the cabin.

"You might as well enjoy the view, *ma chérie*," said Leo. "It'll take us a couple more days to reach Qotwaa, but, on the other hand, there's nothing like a boat ride for seeing the sights."

Chapter VIII
The Blot

In the streets of Choon Ya, Jaffa M'Deni was examining the still-smoking remains of the mygale. It didn't take long to note for him to the absence of bodies.

Furious, he several some arcane gestures in the air with his wands, then started speaking into the space between the two.

Far to the north, at King Kkal's sanctum, the image of Jaffa M'Deni appeared inside the light column.

"I have *escorned* the French machine, but the Oppressor seems to have *survivated*," he reported.

"That is welcome news," said Lucifer. "I've long desired to again have the hated Nyctalope in my clutches. Bring him to me, Jaffa, I desire to crush him myself, to experience the ineffable joy of..."

But Kkal, interrupting his partner, barked:

"You mean, you've allowed him to escape, you bumbling buffoon?"

Jaffa's expression became apologetic.

"I'm *affligated* to admit so, O Mighty King. The Nyctalope is a sly one and..."

Lucifer finally realized what Jaffa had been saying and was enraged.

"What? You failed? You suffered the Nyctalope to live?" His form began shimmering and was shaken by violent static bursts. "You will pay for your incompetence!"

A small energy sphere formed between Lucifer's hands. He threw it towards the column of light.

"Please, *grafiotous one*..." begged Jaffa.

But the ball had already entered the column of light and rematerialized just in front of the stunned Jaffa.

The ball pulled the hapless Diurnal into itself, then began shrinking, as it rotated faster and faster, until it disappeared with a pop.

Inside the King's sanctum, Kkal and Ddôl exchanged a concerned look. Ppy was cowering in fear. Lucifer turned towards them and shouted:

"You must locate the Nyctalope at once!"

"You heard the great Vôo," said Kkal. "Engage the search. Mobilize all spybirds."

Ddôl started punching in commands while Ppy ran around activating various devices.

"Search commencing, O great King," said Ddôl.

A multitude of images began to flash across the screen...

Meanwhile, aboard the Polychromatic Paddleboat, Gisèle d'Holbach stood at the window, marveling at the strange landscape along the riverbanks.

"This whole area is remarkable. The impression of alienness is overwhelming, and yet it's strikingly beautiful."

"I knew you would like this region. It's quite wonderful. I spent several months charting it during my first visit here..."

But high in the sky, unbeknownst to the Nyctalope and his companion, a spybird glided in the air, as it flew above the boat.

Soon, the image of the Nyctalope and Gisèle standing on the boat appeared inside the column of light in King Kkal's laboratory.

"Ha!" gloated Kkal. "Even the mighty Nyctalope is no match for my spybirds!"

But then, the King suddenly realized what the Nyctalope's presence in the area meant.

"Wait! If he's on the Polychromatic Paddleboat, that means he managed to escape Choon Ya and he is headed directly for Qotwaa! He's coming here!"

He turned towards Lucifer.

"How can we stop him, Great Vôo?"

"Use the special weapon I provided."

Kkal and Ddôl nervously looked at each other, while Ppy found refuge in a corner.

"The Blot? But that's impossible."

"Yes. It's against the Pact."

"Ha! Ha!" sneered Lucifer. "You desire to destroy the Nyctalope, but you're afraid of breaking his laws!"

Kkal grew enraged at hearing this taunt:

"I'm afraid of nothing. I'll release the Blot!"

At the top of the mountain under which Qotwaa was located, a camouflaged double-door slid open, revealing a hangar hidden behind it.

A Nocturnal dressed in a full leather uniform and carrying a skull-like helmet came out of an elevator and walked towards an elongated, egg-like object, black as soot. It looked like a giant drop of ink, liquid, shiny, but strangely not reflecting its surroundings.

Kkal's voice was heard through a loud-speaker:

"Uunan, are you ready?"

"Yes, O mighty King," said the helmeted Nocturnal.

"This is the moment for which you have trained. Release the Blot!"

The drop of ink appeared to shiver as a small undulation rippled across its smooth surface. There was a rumbling sound in the hangar, followed by a low vibration, as the mysterious artifact was activated.

Uunan stepped into the Blot like a man walking into water, and disappeared inside its inky substance.

Then, the Blot began rising above the ground, floating in the air for a few seconds, before bursting out of the mountain like a rocket, despite its apparent lack of propulsion.

"Uunan? Do you hear me?" said Kkal's voice, emerging from inside the inky substance.

"I hear you perfectly, Great King. What are your orders?" replied Uunan.

"Your mission is to destroy the Polychromatic Paddleboat. Understood?"

"Yes, My King!"

The Blot zoomed away towards the south on its mission of destruction.

Unaware of the looming danger, the great Paddleboat was now crossing some wetlands that looked like rice-paddies country.

"Will we be there soon?" asked Gisèle.

The Nyctalope looked at his watch.

"We should be in Qotwaa in... just about six hours."

Gisèle suddenly shaded her eyes with her hand.

"Oh, that is odd... It looks like some kind of flying object..."

"You must be mistaken, *chérie*," said Leo, who was looking in another direction. "The Pact we signed with the Rheans in 1935 specifically forbids the creation of airplanes. It must be a very large bird."

"I told you before not to patronize me," said Gisèle, sounding annoyed. "I'm quite capable of telling the difference between a bird and a flying thing."

In the sky, the Blot dove towards the Paddleboat.

"In fact, I'd say *this* flying thing — whatever it is— is going to attack us!" shouted Gisèle, alarmed.

The Nyctalope looked through the window in the direction she was pointing and said, astonished:

"You're right!"

"I told you so!"

The Blot wooshed past over their heads. Outside, a small band of Diurnal farmers looked at it flying over the Paddleboat in wonder.

"It's not just any flying thing either," continued Leo, identifying the artifact at last. "We've got to get out of here fast!"

The Blot had completed its recon loop over the Paddleboat and Uunan prepared to attack. The flying artifact began to dive again.

Aboard the Paddleboat, the Nyctalope and Gisèle ran through the corridor, past other cabins, until they found an escape hatch, which Leo opened.

"Jump! Quickly!" he told his companion.

Gisèle jumped into the water. The Blot was getting ever closer. Then, the Nyctalope jumped too.

At the end of its dive, the Blot rammed through the Polychromatic Paddleboat, creating a massive explosion, without injuring the mysterious flying thing. The flaming remains of the boat began sinking into the river.

From inside his inky shell, Uunan, looking at the devastation, gave his report:

"Mission accomplished, Great King! The Polychromatic Paddleboat is no more."

On the riverbanks, Gisèle emerged out of the water just as Leo was pulling himself up.

"What was all that about?" asked the young woman.

The Nyctalope watched the Blot zoom away.

"It was the Blot... A tool of death and destruction... Something else stolen from the Builders, I suspect..."

"But why would anyone want to destroy such a beautiful boat?"

"They weren't trying to destroy the boat, *chérie*. They were trying to destroy *me*." Then, after a pause: "So much for getting to Qotwaa that way. We'll have to travel underground now."

"Is that all you can think about?" said Gisèle, horrified. "What about all those poor people?"

"Yes, a bit inconvenient," said Leo, coldly.

The Nyctalope began walking away from the river and towards the hills over the horizon, followed by Gisèle.

"We've got to do something to help them," she insisted.

"We have more urgent problems, Gisèle."

"How can you be so callous? You didn't even try to warn them."

"I may know my way around this world, Gisèle, but even I can't perform miracles. What could have I done? There was barely enough time for us to escape."

"But they wouldn't have been hurt if we hadn't been on that boat."

"Perhaps, but innocent bystanders always get hurt in wars. There's nothing I can do to change that."

"I don't understand," said Gisèle, at last.

"It's like this: it would seem that some as yet unknown enemies have invaded Rhea. If they succeed in breaking into the Core, not only this world, but Earth itself will be in grave danger."

"I see..."

"It's all my fault really. I thought the French colony was safe from all exterior threats, but based on my experience on Mars, I should have known better. In fact, something tells me that my past may well be catching up with me. With a vengeance too." Leo paused for a minute, then continued: "I'm sorry I dragged you here, Gisèle. It was selfish of me."

"Don't be," replied the young woman, smiling. "I don't remember you using force. Monsieur Pichenet insisted that I accompany you, remember? Besides, it sounds like you're going to need some help."

The Nyctalope returned her smile, and put his arm around her.

"So, what do we do now?" she asked.

While talking, they had reached the hills, and the opening of a cave. There was a fountain carved into the rock and a stone post around which were tied two white, stout, llama-like animals.

"These are axicors, the most accommodating species on Rhea. They're like mules used by both Nocturnals and Diurnals for underground travel through the Weeping Hills. They won't mind taking us to Qotwaa."

The Nyctalope whistled three times, with different pitches in a very specific pattern.

One of the axicors answered his call. Leo grabbed the bridle.

"Can we ride them?" asked Gisèle.

"Of course. They're docile as lambs. Aren't you, my boy?"

The axicor harrumphed. Leo then put his hand out to Gisèle to help her onto the beast's back.

"Hop on!"

Once she settled on the animal's back, they began to make their way down the cavern and into the depths of Rhea.

Chapter IX
The Envoy of the Sarvants

The gyrosphere used by Claude Marécourt lay abandoned on the ground. A gasoline puddle leaking from the hole made by Malterre's bullet was a clue as to what had happened to it.

Suddenly, the *Oxus* appeared overhead.

"I think we've found our man," said Frédéric de Soto, looking at a monitor screen.

No.2 also spotted a long trail of footsteps leading from the gyrosphere to the Weeping Hills, a range of low desert mountains with a maze of interconnected caverns. The name was due to the fact that when the wind blew through the hills, it created an eerie sound, not unlike a wail.

De Soto's reasoning was indeed correct, for, at the same time, Marécourt, utterly lost, was wandering through the caverns, muttering to himself:

"I've got to get out of here..."

He entered a cave where a stone altar sat as the centerpiece. Suddenly, his face expressed surprise when a small bubble of light appeared right above it. It grew until it until it turned into a hologram of Frédéric de Soto.

"Marécourt!" said No.2. "I've finally found you."

The young physicist wrung his hands at the hologram.

"It wasn't my fault, Monsieur de Soto. I was careful, I swear. The converter just exploded."

"No need to be afraid, No.9," said de Soto. "We've done some investigating since you, er, left us, and we know you didn't do anything wrong."

Marécourt appeared relieved.

"I didn't?"

"No. It was an act of sabotage."

"But who'd have done a thing like that? And how?"

251

"We found the remains of a cybernetically-modified bug inside the converter. It looks like we were the victim of some kind of plot."

"I'm sorry to say this, but I'm relieved to hear that."

"No.1 is sorry for all the trouble this has caused you," de Soto continued. "Frankly, at this stage, he'd prefer it if you were to leave Rhea and return to Earth. I've arranged for someone to take you back."

"You have? Who...?"

At that very moment, a bullet whizzed by between the holographic de Soto and Marécourt, and hit the rock behind them.

"Ah, I believe she's just arrived," said No.2.

A tall woman with red hair, carrying a six-shooter and dressed somewhat like a character from a Sergio Leone movie, had just appeared out of one of the tunnels.

"Claude Marécourt, meet the Envoy," said de Soto. "Mademoiselle, this is Claude Marécourt. No.1 wants him off Rhea as soon as possible. You know what to do."

And with these words, the hologram switched off. The young physicist was now alone with the strange female *pistolero*.

"You're in good hands now, No.9," said the woman.

With Marécourt in tow, she began walking down a long flight of stone steps.

"You're not part of Koynos's team. I don't recall seeing you on the ship..."

"That's correct. I have been on Rhea from the beginning. In fact, it was I who made contact with Koynos."

"Who are you, really?"

"I'm afraid I can't tell you that. It might endanger the mission."

"What a strange thing to say," said Marécourt, puzzled. "I can't say I like your answers so far, and I'm pretty sure I don't understand them. Why are you helping me?"

"Because both Koynos and I agree that you're not cut out to be a player in this game, Marécourt."

"Is that what it is... a game?"

"No. It's much more than that. The future of Rhea is at stake, and perhaps that of the Human Race as well."

The Envoy, still leading Marécourt, was walking down a seemingly endless flight of stone steps.

"There is a bubble-ship hidden near Qotwaa," she continued. "It's programmed to take its passengers back to Earth. The journey will last just over three months. I'll soon have you out of here."

"I can't say I'll mind leaving this awful planet."

"I know what you mean. It is, after all, the Sarvants' creation."

"Who?"

"The Sarvants. They're the ones who built Rhea. A long, long time ago, they used to be creatures of flesh and blood, just like us. Well, not quite like us, but physical, anyway. Then, they converted their planet into a wandering planetoid in order to travel throughout the galaxy and study the wonders of the universe. Later, they evolved into... something else. Now they're ethereal creatures who exist halfway between space and hyperspace, totally beyond our comprehension..."

"How bizarre... And how do you know all this?"

"A while back, I stumbled into Rhea's Core. I triggered an accident. I was nearly dead, half of my body was gone, but I had attracted the Sarvants' attention, and they rebuilt me..."

"Rebuilt?"

"Yes. They had had some primitive contact with Humanity in 1912,[8] so they knew who we were and how we functioned; they did a decent job on me. We began talking, or rather, they began asking me questions. That's when they found out that Mankind had established a foothold on Rhea, which they had abandoned to the descendents of their slave races, those whom we call Diurnals and Nocturnals..."

"I see."

---

[8] See *The Blue Peril* by Maurice Renard.

"The Sarvants are very concerned about Humanity. Some don't think it should be allowed to spread beyond the Solar System. A few believe it should be eradicated altogether. But they're not impatient creatures. They have all of eternity before them, so they decided to… How should I put it? Set up a commission and study the problem."

"What do you mean?"

"Thanks to my knowledge of recent history, they learned of the French colony on Mars, and the disaster that ensued. They decided to resurrect Koynos…"

"*Resurrect*?"

"Well, rebuild perhaps… Koynos died on Mars in 1911. The Sarvants are masters of time and space. Somehow they plucked him out of the continuum and restored him to life… They have awesome powers beyond human ken. Anyway, they tasked him with the job of surveying Mankind's impact on Rhea. If, after they hear his report, they decide that Humanity is irremediably flawed and dangerous, first they will destroy Rhea before it can spread that 'infection' to other systems in the galaxy, and they may very well end up eradicating all life on Earth as well."

"My Goodness! I wish I'd known all this when…" Marécourt took a look at his surroundings, which he had just noticed, and asked: "Where are we?"

They had reached an esplanade, cut by a deep, bottomless chasm, seemingly made of total darkness, which stretched horizontally to infinity. On the other side, a passageway was visible in the rock. The Envoy walked to the very edge of the chasm.

"This is the discontinuity canyon that exists between the Weeping Hills and Qotwaa. It's the result of an ancient malfunction in the engines. Nothing too serious, but someday I'll have to fix it. In the meanwhile, think of it as a tiny crack in the carburetor, if you'd like. We have to cross it."

"How? There's no bridge?"

The Envoy stepped into the void but, strangely, did not fall. She stood there like a cartoon character walking on air.

"I don't need one. I'm the Envoy of the Sarvants; I'm attuned to Rhea's Core. Small discontinuities are only fractures of reality..."

Suddenly, patches of light appeared beneath her feet, which enabled her to walk a few more steps into the void.

"...If you don't believe in them, they don't exist."

The Envoy then turned towards Claude Marécourt, inviting the young scientist to follow her.

"Well?"

"I don't know," said Marécourt, skeptical. "This pit looks awfully real to me."

"Don't you trust your guide, Claude? Step forward."

Marécourt took a hesitant step, as if dipping his foot into water to test its temperature.

"Okay, if you say so. Here I go..."

Much to his surprise, the same patches of light appeared beneath his own feet.

"Hey! It works... I'm getting the hang of this..."

But the brash physicist had spoken too soon. Walking like a tightrope artist across the void, he nevertheless almost lost his balance a few times.

"Do you need my help?" asked the Envoy, solicitously.

Marécourt, whose pride was wounded, straightened up and put on a brave face.

"Of course not!"

They continued walking across the canyon, until the Envoy set foot on the other bank.

"I'm right behind you," said Marécourt. "Piece of cake."

But, once again, the scientist had been a little too proud of his achievement and bragged too soon. Suddenly, the patch of light under his feet disappeared with a pop. Marécourt looked horrified. Deep beneath him, a huge rip had formed in the dark fabric of nothingness. Through it, crackling tentacles of energy surged upward searching for a prey.

"A plasma leak!" screamed the Enjoy.

Marécourt stumbled in the void, still suspended in mid-air.

"Keep walking! Keep walking!" urged the Envoy.

But the scientist panicked. Below, the plasma tentacles, almost sensing his fear, leaped ever higher. Marécourt began to fall.

"Grab my lasso!"

But Marécourt didn't appear to hear the Envoy. He kept falling until he was grabbed by one the plasma tentacles, which began to engulf his body. Meanwhile, the Envoy, in a smooth, rapid movement, had unfurled a strange, shiny metal lasso and thrown the looped end into the abyss after the young physicist.

Marécourt's body was almost completely enveloped by the plasma, but his arm had remained free, clutching helplessly, when the lasso reached him. At the last moment, he managed to grab the loop with his free hand.

The metal "rope" began pulsating with an eerie blue light which seemed to repel the plasma. Then, the Envoy was able to pull Marécourt up, seemingly without effort. She helped the scientist to set foot safely next to her on the canyon's bank.

"Thank you," said Marécourt, visibly shaken.

"You're quite welcome," replied the Envoy.

She then led the scientist towards another flight of stone steps, hidden in a passageway in the rock.

"Where are we going?" inquired Marécourt.

"I told you: to Qotwaa."

They climbed a few steps, then arrived at a metal door with an enormous lock on it.

"But we don't have a key..." observed Marécourt.

But the Envoy simply pulled the door open.

"I am the key," she said simply.

Chapter X
The Underworld of Qotwaa

Unbeknownst to the Envoy and Claude Marécourt, the Nyctalope and Gisèle d'Holbach were also progressing towards Qotwaa, the capital of the Nocturnals, traveling underground on the back of their axicor.

As they reached a spacious cavern decorated with carvings representing an armadillo-like creature with big claws, Leo got off.

"This is the Temple of the Nightly Evovores; they haven't been worshipped in decades and, as a result, it is rarely guarded anymore..."

Gisèle got off and looked around, while the Nyctalope searched for a door, which he found, hidden behind a big boulder.

"What I love about the tunnels of Rhea are their infinite variety of secret passages."

Gisèle looked that the ancient stone door, which had been decorated with particularly ugly carvings.

"This one seems a bit foreboding," she said.

"I'll admit, it's never been one of my favorite passages, but I've found it very useful in the past."

The Nyctalope took another key from his briefcase, a gnarly, twisted thing, and used it to open the door.

"Still, it will permit us to make a discreet entrance into Qotwaa."

They walked through the door and emerged into what was surely the "underworld" of Qotwaa: a dilapidated slum, overcrowded and reeking with foul odors. They found themselves in the midst of a colorful crowd of Diurnals all singing beautifully to the beat of African-like music.

"Hmm," said Leo, "it looks as if we've arrived in the middle of a religious gathering. These are the sacred songs of

Kkqaua. Let's not dawdle in case someone starts asking questions. Earthmen are not an unusual sight in Qotwaa, but I don't want to press our luck."

They started down a flight of stone stairs, but suddenly, the music and all the singing stopped.

"Please, don't pay any attention to us," said the Nyctalope to the crowd. "We're just passing through."

After a tense minute, the crowd nodded in unison and began singing again.

The Nyctalope let out of sigh of relief. As they made their way through the neighborhood, Leo noticed a frown on Gisèle's face.

"What's wrong, *chérie*?"

"It's all rather... squalid."

"These people are free to live as they please, Gisèle. You can't blame me for all that you see here."

"But you could do so much to improve their lot!"

"In spite of what some people may think, I'm no colonist. We French learned our lesson in Africa and later, in Algeria. When I first came to Rhea, I'll admit I had dreams of turning it onto another colonial outpost, like the one we had built on Mars. But later, I understood the error of my ways. When we returned, I wrote it into the Olbansville Charter that the people of Rhea had to have complete autonomy. If they choose to misuse their freedom, it's not our place to stop them."

"But what's the point of all of this then?"

"You have to think in terms of centuries, Gisèle, something where I have an obvious advantage, of course. Rhea is our path out of the Solar System. If Mankind is ever to spread to other stars, it will be thanks to Rhea. The planetoid accelerates as it pulls out of the Solar System... It may even go into hyperdrive... We haven't figured out the secrets of its interstellar engines, and may take several more decades before we do so, but someday, the descendents of Olbansville will see the light of other suns, will explore other worlds... And it will all have started here."

Behind the Nyctalope, a spybird was perching on a roof-top. Its head rotated slightly and came to a stop when it saw Leo and Gisèle.

Inside King Kkal's sanctum, Lucifer was performing another ritual, involving ribbons of light, under the Nocturnal Monarch's watchful eyes. Ppy, as usual, was zipping around the control deck.

The pattern on the floor swallowed the Vôo's light ribbons. At Rhea's Core, the already-cracked golden control sphere vibrated and shuddered.

The Pattern opened, releasing a flow of golden light.

"This is it!" shouted Kkal. "The Core! We made it!"

But the sphere still held and the warp closed with a snap and a burst of flames.

"I have failed again," muttered Lucifer.

"You try my patience, you alien spirit," roared Kkal. "You came here, offering to rid us of the French, and I agreed to host your mentality in my mighty machines, but so far, you haven't delivered much."

"Use the Blot to destroy the Nyctalope."

"How can I? We don't know where he is, you fool!..."

Suddenly, Ddôl came rushing into the room.

"Your Majesty!"

"Yes. What is it, Ddôl?"

"We've just spotted the Nyctalope in Qotwaa!"

Both Kkal and Lucifer looked stupefied at the news. The form of the Vôo shimmered and wavered in rage. Ppy cowered in a corner.

"What?!" shouted Kkal. "How is this possible?!"

"We must destroy the Nyctalope," roared Lucifer. "Make him die slowly. Painfully…"

"That's all well and good," interrupted Kkal, "but meanwhile, he's here in Qotwaa. How do you propose to stop him before he makes his way into the Core?"

Meanwhile, in another section of Qotwaa, Gisèle d'Holbach was looking at the squalid surroundings with distaste while the Nyctalope, standing in the doorway of a grubby house, was conversing with a portly Nocturnal.

"*Ssponel g'nak dit oz powôo?*" asked Leo.

"*Voss Klaeet*," replied the Nocturnal, shaking his head.

The Nyctalope rejoined Gisèle.

"Are you following a plan, or are we just seeing the sights?" she asked, smiling.

"Don't be sarcastic. I'm trying to find Ludo Corsat, our local agent. This is where he lives, or rather used to live. The housekeeper just told me he moved out yesterday.

"I can't say I blame him."

"It's a bit of a bother," said Leo, "because Ludo's the only one who knows where Professor Henri d'Olbans is hiding these days. And without him, I can't get to Rhea's Core."

"Who is this Henri d'Olbans?"

"A descendent of my ex-wife Véronique, who remarried after I left Rhea. He is a scientist who thought he had discovered a backdoor into the Core. According to Mayor Mitang, he tried several times to test his theories, but without success—quite the opposite, in fact. I was told by Mitang that one of his experiments cost the life of my grand-daughter, Xavière. Ludo found d'Olbans hiding in Qotwaa and sent a report claiming he's had some recent successes, but he's the only one who would know for certain."

"Of all places, why did d'Olbans choose to come here?"

"He didn't—not really. It's the same reason that Kkal chose to make Qotwaa into his capital. The city is built over what may well be an entry point into the Core. A long time ago, it was the site of many strange phenomena which at the time were interpreted as supernatural or religious, like Jerusalem on Earth. You saw the Temple of the Nightly Evovores? The city is littered with sites like that... After his attempt at the North Pole failed, Henri felt this was the perfect location, because, according to him, it is located on top of one of the Builders' very own hatches."

"I see," said Gisèle. "I'll tell you what. Why don't we split up? You keep looking for Ludo, while I make some discreet inquiries on my own. Who knows, I might be able to learn something."

"I don't like that idea," said Leo, frowning.

"Besides, you did want me to see this wonderful world, didn't you?" said Gisèle with her most enticing smile.

"But it might be dangerous."

"I'll be careful. Remember, I'm a French secret agent. I've been in places way more dangerous than this."

"All right. Meet me in two hours at the Orphium Emporium on Oorlak Square. You can't miss it. It's right in the center of Qotwaa."

Gisèle hugged Leo.

"Orphium Emporium. Oorlak Square. Two hours. Got it! And you be careful too, Leo. You may be the great Nyctalope, but you're not invulnerable."

She walked away, waving good-bye, while Leo continued to wander alone through the underworld of Qotwaa.

"Things down here are more confusing than I remember. I seem to be getting lost..." he mused.

Behind him, at some distance, two Nocturnals were watching him from a balcony: Kkal and Ddôl!

"This was a good idea, Ddôl," said the King, smiling nastily. "Now, we've got him."

Chapter XI
Into Danger

In the seedy underworld of Qotwaa, the Nyctalope had just passed a long wall, against which a dozen winged Diurnals were leaning.

Unbeknownst to him, he was being followed at a cautious distance by Kkal and Ddôl.

The Nyctalope stepped under an archway and entered a small, obsidian stone courtyard. At its center was a stone altar sitting on top of a small set of steps. This was another temple left over from Qotwaa's ancient past, when it was the religious center of Rhea.

"A fine explorer I am," sighed Leo. "I can't even find my way through this city..."

Leo put down his briefcase.

"I need to clear my head. I'll just meditate for a few seconds."

He sat in a lotus position next to the altar and closed his eyes.

Kkal and Ddôl then snuck out of the shadows and stepped through the archway, stealthily approaching Leo.

"So this is the famous Nyctalope?" said Ddôl. "I always thought of him as a god. Look at him. He's just sitting there, asleep."

"Yes," said the King. "Completely at my mercy. If I wanted to, I could take my topper..." Kkal removed a strange gun from his pocket and pointed it at Leo's head. "...And— Tang! A slab in the head and no more Nyctalope!"

"Can we do that, O Great King?" asked Ddôl, suddenly afraid. "He *is* the Nyctalope, after all. It could be a trap."

"No! Can't you see? He's just like a babe in his mother's arms."

"I don't know. I wouldn't dare, if I were you."

But Kkal brought the gun very close to Leo's temple.

"I would... In fact, I think I will kill him!"

At that very moment, alerted to the danger by his preternatural senses, the Nyctalope opened an eye.

Kkal immediately repocketed his gun, a look of fear briefly flashing on his face.

The Nyctalope stretched and yawned.

"Ohhh! That's better," he said. "A quick alpha wave tune-up does a body good."

Kkal and Ddôl immediately saluted the Nyctalope, who saluted them back.

"Hum. Good day, stranger," said the King, with a slight stammer, indicating his nervousness. "A rest can be so, er, restful. Allow me to introduce myself. I am, er, Hhaabur and this is my friend Zzolito. It's not often that we see hu-mans in this part of Qotwaa."

Ddôl nodded his head repeatedly, as if to prove the veracity of Kkal's words.

"Pleased to meet you, Hhaabur," replied the Nyctalope. "I'm, er, Pedro Del Campo. Yes, Pedro Del Campo, and I'm from Spain."

"Spain?" said Kkal, affably. "That's to the west of here, isn't it? What are you doing so far from home, Master Del Campo?"

"I seem to have gotten a little lost..."

"Who wouldn't, in the maze of the Lower City?"

The Nyctalope pulled out a pocket watch and looked at it.

"I say, look at the time. I'm supposed to meet a friend at the Orphium Emporium on Oorlak Square and I'm going to be late."

Kkal and Ddôl exchanged a telling glance. They then each took the Nyctalope under one arm.

"I've got an idea, Master Del Campo," said the King. "We'll take you there. We know a few shortcuts, and you can buy us a drink."

"I'd be delighted, Master Hhaabur," replied Leo.

They departed arm-in-arm.

Meanwhile, elsewhere in Qotwaa, in the commercial district, a squadron of armed Nocturnals were chasing after an intruder.

One guard fired his pistol. The shot shattered a statue on a rooftop.

More shots were fired and the crowd began to scatter in panic.

On a neighboring rooftop, hiding from the guards behind a wall, was the target of their fury: Ludo Corsat, the Nyctalope's spy in Qotwaa.

"We've cornered the Olbansville spy in the commercial district, Chief," barked one of the guards into a microphone. "What are your orders?"

Ludo's face began to express consternation; he desperately looked for a way to get away as more guards rushed towards the building on top of which he had been hiding.

"Yes sir, the entire block has been cordoned off," continued the guard reporting to his superior. "He can't escape... Take him alive? I understand. Hark, hark, Chief!"

With a daring leap, Ludo jumped to an adjacent building. He then proceeded to jump and run from building to building, until he finally let himself down into a back alley.

Once there, Ludo took a cautious look before turning the corner.

The alley led onto another street, which itself led into a large avenue. At the end of the street, Ludo spotted a group of four guards engaged in what appeared to be a spot I.D. check.

The person whom the guards had caught was none other than Gisèle d'Holbach!

"You don't have any papers," said the guard. "Come with us quietly, or else..."

"I see," replied Gisèle, coolly, assuming a fighting stance. "Come and get me, monkey-boy."

"My pleasure!" grinned the guard, looking forward to trashing the insolent human female.

But with lightning speed, Gisèle punched the guard on the jaw, causing him to drop like a stone.

"I'm quaking in my boots," joked Gisèle. "Now, are you going to let me go?"

Another guard lunged at the young woman, but before he could lay his hands on her, she turned slightly and karate-kicked him in the chin. He, too, fell to the ground, unconscious.

A crowd of curious onlookers had now gathered and was watching the fight with cautious but unmistakably joyful interest.

"Your kind never learns, does it?" added Gisèle.

She turned towards a third guard, who watched her approach with a mixture of awe and fear. She leapt at him and brought her right knee up, hitting the hapless Nocturnal on the nose.

The third guard joined the others on the ground, down for the count.

But Gisèle had failed to notice the presence of a fourth guard who, stealthily, was approaching her from behind.

The Nocturnal delivered a powerful blow to the young woman's head with his truncheon. She began to fall forward, but he picked her up by her hair.

"Now, we're going to teach you a lesson, you little *lanske*..." the Nocturnal roared triumphantly.

The crowd looked at this turn of events with sorrow.

Suddenly, Ludo Corsat burst forward, pushing people aside.

"Let her go!" he shouted.

Without waiting, he then threw a mighty punch at the fourth guard, who crumpled under the blow.

Gisèle struggled to stand up.

The crowd, immensely pleased by this new development, cheered.

Ludo helped Gisèle get up.

"You're Mademoiselle d'Holbach," said the Nyctalope's spy.

"I beg your pardon?" she replied, surprised.

She dusted herself off.

"I'm Ludo Corsat," explained the spy. "Marc de Ciserat briefed me about Monsieur Saint-Clair and you..." After a pause, he added: "Your photo doesn't do you justice."

"Thank you," said Gisèle, smiling. "You're very kind. But what are you doing here? Leo has been looking everywhere for you."

"The Nyctalope is here? Good! I've got to talk to him. Where is he?"

"We're supposed to meet at the Orphium Emporium on Oorlak Square at..." She looked at her watch. "...Oh, about right now, I'd say. Why don't you come with me and show me the way?"

Gisèle flipped her hair back and the two walk off.

"Now, why don't you tell me exactly what has been going on here?" she asked.

The Orphium Emporium was a large, three-storied establishment located on the southwest corner of the spacious Oorlak Square. The Square was a giant market where tradesmen from the entire Northern hemisphere of Rhea came to sell and exchange their wares. It was filled with a myriad of stalls, ranging from small spice traders to large, complicated cogsellers.

A warm, yellowish light radiated from the small paneled windows of the Orphium Emporium. Customers poured in and out of the swinging doors of its many entrances. The walls were decorated with carvings depicting scenes of banquets and battles.

Inside, one found a luxurious brass and wood-paneled establishment with many chandeliers and wall mirrors. Busy waiters carrying trays loaded with exotic food and drunks smoothly negotiated their way between the throngs of customers.

When they walked in, Ludo and Gisèle were immediately approached by an obsequious waiter. Surprisingly, it was a Diurnal.

"Do you gentlebeings require a table?" he inquired.

"No. We're supposed to meet a friend" said Gisèle, looking around.

A little to the right, the Nyctalope, King Kkal and Ddôl, who had arrived a few minutes earlier, were sitting in a booth, ordering drinks from a waiter.

"A Dra'hund beer," ordered Kkal.

"Blue coffee for me," ordered Ddôl, who prized this delicacy imported from Earth but grown on Rhea.

"A tankard of oldakin wine, southern side, please, and a plate of bromize, light on the sauce," ordered the Nyctalope who liked good food and had missed the many Rhean specialties.

Hearing Leo's voice in the distance, Gisèle spotted the Nyctalope over the top of his booth.

"Ah! I see him over there," she said to the waiter.

Then, followed by Ludo Corsat, she crossed the Cafe towards the booth. When he saw them together, the Nyctalope reacted with surprise.

"Ludo Corsat? What are you doing with Gisèle?"

Ludo's face registered surprise as he recognized the Nyctalope's "companions" behind their transparent disguises. They had managed to dupe Leo who was unfamiliar with King Kkal's likeness, and had never even seen Ddôl, but they couldn't fool his spy.

"Nyctalope! Watch out!" he shouted, pointing at the two Nocturnals. "These two! They're Kkal and..."

"Kkal?" said Leo, astonished. "The King?"

Simultaneously, and before Ludo could complete his sentence, Ddôl suddenly pulled out a topper and shot the spy. The slab went through the Frenchman's skull, bursting out of the other side of his head.

Kkal angrily slapped his Chamberlain in the face.

"You fool! Who told you to shoot?"

He then grabbed Ddôl's arm and dragged him away.

"But, your Majesty, he betrayed us..." whined Ddôl.

"So what? I had them all at my mercy."

They hurriedly pushed and elbowed their way out of the Emporium. Then, Kkal grabbed a passing guard and said:

"This is your King! Emergency! Call all my troops! Surround the Emporium. The Nyctalope must not escape!"

Chapter XII
Henri d'Olbans

Inside the Orphium Emporium, at the booth, unaware of what was going on outside, a crowd of customers had gathered to watch the curious spectacle of the man who had just been shot.

The Nyctalope was still holding the body of Ludo by the shoulders, laying him to rest.

"My poor friend," he said, with great sorrow.

Then, Leo got up and nudged Gisèle towards the kitchens.

"Let's get out of here. This place will be crawling with guards soon."

They went through a set of double-doors and into the Emporium kitchens, which they crossed running, disturbing the careful choreography of chefs and sous-chefs.

"Ludo's death leaves me in a bit of a pickle," said Leo. "He was the only one who could lead me to Henri d'Olbans."

"But I know where to find him. Ludo told me everything on the way to the Emporium!"

The Nyctalope and Gisèle left the Emporium through one of its many back doors. They found themselves in a narrow back alley, lined with trash cans.

"That's wonderful, *chérie!*" congratulated Leo. "We're in the clear now."

"Not yet, it seems."

Indeed, two squadrons of guards, one led by Ddôl, had just appeared, effectively blocking both ends of the alley.

"There they are!" shouted the Chamberlain, pointing at the two humans. "Get them!"

"What do we do now?" asked Gisèle. "There are too many of them to fight. We don't stand a chance."

"Then we'll have to look for another exit," replied Leo.

Moving with lightning speed, the Nyctalope traced a perfect circle on the ground with his right foot. A narrow strip of crackling light appeared where the tip of his boot had touched the ground, created by a miniature laser. He then stomped hard on the pavement.

"Hurry!" said Gisèle, watching the guards approaching.

"Ha! They're done for!" gloated Ddôl.

The Nyctalope kept stomping while the guards moved ever closer. Just as he and Gisèle were about to be captured, the concrete circle suddenly dropped out from under their feet, and they fell through a hole.

"Where did they go?" asked a guard.

"The sewers!" roared Ddôl.

Inside the sewers of Qotwaa, the Nyctalope moved quickly despite the darkness, which did not exist for him. Gisèle, holding his hand, followed right behind him. Together, they moved swiftly along a maze of intestine-like tubes.

On the surface, Ddôl harangued his men:

"They're as good as caught. I know these sewers like the back of my hand. Follow me!"

He then dropped into the hole.

Much later, back at the King's Palace, Ddôl, totally covered in dripping mud, finished making his report.

"I lost them, O Great King," he said forlornly.

"You incompetent, bumbling buffoon!" screamed Kkal. "You're a waste of oxygen!" He then turned towards the "ghost" of Lucifer and asked: "Isn't there any way your magic can stop the Nyctalope, Great Vôo?"

"To confront the Nyctalope in my present form is impossible," answered Lucifer.

"Then what am I supposed to do? Rhea was almost in my grasp. I'll never have an opportunity this good again."

"Use the Blot once more!"

Kkal blanched.

"Here? In Qotwaa?"

"You would rather see the hated Nyctalope win instead?"

King Kkal pondered the question in silence.

Further to the south, the Blot was soaring through the skies. Inside its inky substance, its pilot, Uunan, was waiting. Suddenly a voice rang in his ears:

"Stand by to receive new orders."

It was King Kkal's voice! Uunan smiled a grim, evil smile.

"Understood!" he answered.

The Blot made an abrupt turn in mid-sky.

Meanwhile, the Nyctalope and Gisèle d'Holbach had exited the sewers in the Upper City of Qotwaa, located above ground just above the Nocturnals' city. It was mostly inhabited by Diurnals who worked in the Lower City.

They walked down a busy street towards a seedy-looking hotel.

"We're there," said Leo.

"I suppose I should have expected another flea-trap," said Gisèle, smiling.

"Henri d'Olbans has never been known as being ostentatious," replied Leo, also smiling.

They walked arm in arm into the Hotel. The reception area looked like a Moroccan *souk*. The Nyctalope addressed the Concierge, a Diurnal dressed in a large, green *kaftan*.

"We'd like Room 8, please."

The Concierge seemed overly concerned.

"Are you sure that's the room you want, Hu-man? Not Room 9? People are always getting those two confused."

"You dare question me?"

"No, no, of course not..." stammered the Concierge, looking apologetic.

He rang a bell and Bbri, a small Nocturnal wearing dark glasses to protect his eyes, holding a book in his hand, came out from the back.

"Forgive me, Hu-Man. Bbri will show you the way."

But Bbri showed no sign of moving.

"Bbri, take these two Hu-mans to Room 8," ordered the Concierge.

"Can't I finish my chapter first?" whined Bbri.

"Bbri!" shouted the Concierge.

"All right, all right, no need to shout."

Bbri grudgingly set off, followed by Gisèle and the Nyctalope. They trudged through dingy corridors.

"They exploit us mercilessly," he grumbled. "We get nothing but the dirty jobs, my good masters... An intellectual like myself, forced to carry heavy bags..."

"Um... We don't have any bags," said Gisèle. "We're just passing through."

"Yes, we're merely strangers here," added Leo.

"Strangers, strangers... Everyone is a stranger here. There's no justice, Hu-man, none at all... But the King will soon change all that!"

They almost passed by the door to Room No.8, but the Nyctalope stopped.

"Er, I believe this is it," he said, clearing his throat.

He then handed Bbri a tip.

"I hope you know what you're doing, entering this room," said the small Nocturnal. "The Hu-Man who lives here is crazy."

The Nocturnal then scurried away while the Nyctalope knocked on the door.

"Henri! Professor d'Olbans! It's I, Leo Saint-Clair. Please let us in."

An older man with a kind face, dressed in a blue laboratory overcoat, opened the door. He smiled at the sight of the Nyctalope and they exchanged a warm embrace.

He then welcomed Gisèle.

They settled into comfortable armchairs.

"I have heard a lot about you, Henri," said Leo. "How have you been faring?"

"I was expecting you, Great Nyctalope. I think I have finally achieved our aim—to enter Rhea's Core and take control of the Builders' engines. It wasn't without difficulties, of course. Has Mayor Mitang told you about what happened to your granddaughter Xavière?"

"Briefly. She died in one of your attempts to access the Core, didn't she?"

"Exactly. But I think that was due to our choosing the wrong location. The stress of the Great Transformation was too much…"

"The Great Transformation?" inquired Leo.

"Yes. In order to access the Core, you must undergo a process not unsimilar to that which the Builders themselves went through. It adds an ethereal component to your body; it supercharges it. I call this state becoming an 'overman.'"

"Something like that is bound to send ripples throughout the continuum. Our presence here will be detected. It's a dangerous gamble, Henri."

"Indeed it is, Great Nyctalope. But if you don't do it, Rhea may well be doomed."

"How do you mean?"

"Since I have been here, I've had time to probe the secrets of the Builders. I found I wasn't the only one trying to access Rhea's Core. Someone else, far more devious and with perhaps greater scientific knowledge and resources, was doing the same…"

"I bet he's the entity behind King Kkal's recent actions. I've already seen examples of perverted uses of Builders' technology during our journey here. Mitang's suspicions were correct. Do we know who this entity is?"

"Yes, Great Nyctalope."

"Then speak up, man. Who is our secret enemy?"

"The man whom you once knew on Earth long ago as Baron Glô von Warteck. a.k.a.…"

"…Lucifer!" completed the Nyctalope.

Chapter XIII
The Eve of Armageddon

Meanwhile, the Envoy, still followed by Claude Marécourt, had just emerged from their underground journey into Upper Qotwaa.

They stood on the edge of a vast esplanade, which served as the terminus for loading and unloading the caravans from and to other Rhean cities.

Suddenly, the Envoy raised her head, her face searching the sky for something she could not see.

"What's wrong?" inquired Marécourt.

"I felt... something," replied the Envoy.

Inside King Kkal's buried sanctum, the Nocturnal tyrant paced furiously across the room.

"We've got to find the Nyctalope," he raged. "This is all your fault, Ddôl!"

"Yes, Your Majesty. I'm sorry, Your Majesty!" responded the Chamberlain, sheepishly.

Suddenly, an alarm rang as a new image captured by one of the King's many spybirds flying over the city was broadcast into the column of light.

It was the image of a tank-like vehicle which had just entered Upper Qotwaa—Koynos' battletruck!

"Your Majesty! One of our spybirds has just spotted a Hu-man vehicle entering Qotwaa," said Ddôl, scrutinizing the image. "Wait! It's not from Olbansville. It looks like one of the New Fifteen's!"

"What's it doing in Qotwaa?" said Kkal, concerned. "I don't like it. Is the Blot ready?"

Spookily, the voice of its pilot, Uunan, was suddenly heard throughout the room:

"Destruction imminent."

It was followed by a burst of merciless laughter.

In Room 8, at the hotel in Upper Qotwaa, Professor Henri d'Olbans had taken the Nyctalope and Gisèle to an adjacent laboratory, in the center of which was a complicated chair that resembled a dentist's, but also had a transparent helmet and cables connected to the ceiling and side generators.

"Please, sit in the Aura Polyactivator," invited Henri d'Olbans.

The Nyctalope sat down in silence. Henri started busying himself with the machine's settings, while Gisèle stood by Leo's side.

"Gisèle..." he said.

"Yes, *chéri*?"

"I must prevent the secrets of Rhea from falling into Lucifer's evil hands. There's too much at stake... Things down here may get a bit ticklish, so I want you to get back to Olbansville. Professor d'Olbans will be able to arrange it."

"But I don't want to leave you!"

"I know. I don't want to leave you either. Without you, I would never have made it this far. But you can't follow me further."

"Why not?"

"Where I'm going, I must travel alone. It's my destiny."

Henri lowered a projector from the ceiling.

"Is there anything I can do?" said Gisèle, resignedly.

"There may be. Akira Mitang knows my back-up plan. He'll brief you."

The Nyctalope reached out for Gisèle's hand and squeezed it tenderly.

"Trust me, *ma chérie*. I love you."

"I love you too."

She kissed him lightly, then stepped back as Henri finished plugging the projector to the glass helmet placed over the Nyctalope's head.

"I'm ready when you are, Professor."

"Yes, Great Nyctalope."

Immediately, a torrent of sparks leapt out of the connecting point, while an aura of blinding light surrounded Leo's body.

"Good luck, Great Nyctalope! I suspect the Builders will now be after you like a pack of wolves."

"What's happening to him?" asked Gisèle.

The Nyctalope's body had begun to be consumed by the light.

"Don't worry," said Henri, watching the dials. "It looks like he'll be fine. In fact, I'd say he'll be finer than the rest of us! Ha! Ha!"

Henri then invited Gisèle to follow him.

"Follow me, Mademoiselle."

She did so, after one last look towards the Nyctalope's body, which now seemed to be completely made of light.

Henri opened a door at the far end of the room, and invited Gisèle to enter. On one side was a large spherical machine with a circular central opening, connected by a thick but somewhat corroded cable to a low, round control console.

"What's that?" asked Gisèle, astounded.

"Before the Builders ascended to their present state, they used a limited form of matter teletransportation. This is one of the oldest working units on the planet, which I found in a cavern near the North Pole. I managed to repair it. With it, I can send you back to Olbansville instantly."

Gisèle stepped inside the machine.

"With an emphasis on 'working,' I hope?" she said, smiling.

Henri stood at the console and prepared to pull a switch.

"Watch out for the sparks, I'm ready to activate."

He pulled the switch and Gisèle disappeared in a circle of blinding blue light.

The Professor then walked back into the other room. Where once the Nyctalope sat was now a glowing ball of light. Henri checked the dials again, nodded in satisfaction, and went to sit in an armchair, waiting for the process to be complete.

Outside, people in the street stopped and raised their heads as they saw light pouring out of the hotel.

Inside the King's sanctum, Ddôl suddenly shouted:

"Your Majesty! Come quickly! I think I've found the Nyctalope!"

Lucifer reappeared, his ghostly form hovering around the column of light showing the image of the hotel in Upper Qotwaa with light pouring out of its first-floor windows.

"I sense the Nyctalope mutating," he said. "I feel his energies. He is powerless in this state. You must strike now!"

"Tell the Blot to bomb the target!" roared King Kkal. "No survivors!"

"Understood. Ha! Ha! Ha!" replied the eerie voice of Uunan.

High in the sky, the Blot began its fatal dive towards Upper Qotwaa, passing over its esplanade.

Just below, the Envoy and Claude Marécourt were standing on a platform, when, suddenly, they head the Blot's loud hum filling the sky.

The Envoy looked up again and, this time, saw the Blot.

"The Blot," she said.

"What's that? It looks like a flying egg!"

"That object is an aberration. It was made with technology stolen from the Sarvants. It is evil."

The Envoy pulled out what looked like an old western six-shooter except that it radiated a faint blue light. Without taking aim, she shot a single bullet towards the Blot. The bullet flew through the air and soon turned into a pellet of blue light.

Inside the Blot, Uunan noticed the bullet.

"The Envoy! What is she doing here?" he growled.

The Blot veered sharply to the left, but the bullet turned to pursue it. No matter how many twists and turns Uunan took to avoid the blue bullet, like a heat-seeking missile, it swung and continued its merciless pursuit, until it finally closed in on the Blot, which was starting to fray, dripping a trail of black globules behind it.

The bullet struck the Blot, creating a tremendous explosion.

"What did you do?" asked Claude Marécourt.

"I shot down the evil thing, sending it back to the primal chaos from which it was pulled," answered the Envoy.

However, almost immediately, radiating beams of black nothingness, through which one could glimpse the glimmer of stars, started spreading from the very center of the explosion, splitting and crisscrossing the sky of Rhea.

"One of the Core Engines must have been somehow damaged by the explosion, Your Majesty," said Ddôl, his voice quaking with fear. "The continuum field which protect our planet is breaking apart..."

Kkal pointed an accusatory finger at Lucifer.

"I never should have listened to you, Hu-Man! This is your fault. We're all doomed now!"

Outside Qotwaa, chaos erupted as the energy bolts began to strike the ground in the Upper City. The populace ran in panic—not knowing where to run. Even the Underground City and its Royal Palace were severely shaken.

Kkal almost lost his balance during one of the shockwaves, but Lucifer remained imperturbable.

Inside Rhea's Core, the golden control sphere vibrated uncontrolably, then exploded into a million tiny shards. Darkness fell.

Immediately, a warp opened in the Pattern on the floor of King Kkal's sanctum, releasing another bolt of lightning.

"Look! The hatch is opening!" screamed Lucifer triumphantly. "At last we have succeeded! We can now access Rhea's Core! Plunder the secrets of the Sarvants! Destroy the Nyctalope! Become like unto the gods themselves!"

"At last!" breathed Kkal with a sigh of relief.

The King noticed that his guards were increasingly terrified by what they were seeing, and were making feeble attempts to run away.

"STOP! All of you!" he shouted. "Come back! We've won!"

Shy and fearful at first, but more enthusiastic as they understood the meaning of their King's words, the guards regrouped and gathered.

"We'll begin the Invasion of the Core at once," said Kkal. "I want order and discipline. Ppy, you'll come with me. Ddôl, I'm leaving you in charge. Capture the Nyctalope and bring him to me in chains."

"With pleasure, Your Majesty!" answered the Chamberlain.

Kkal then ordered his men to jump into the glowing hatch.

"Go! Go!"

Finally, unable to wait, he too jumped, shouting:

"Rhea is mine at last! All mine! Ha! Ha! Ha!"

Chapter XIV
Old Enemies Meet at Last

Following the disintegration of the Blot, cracks in the Rhean field had appeared in the skies above Qotwaa.

At the very moment that chaos was spreading amongst the city's inhabitants, the armored vehicle driven by Koynos entered the outskirts of the Upper City.

"No.1 to No.2. Koynos here," said the driver, speaking into a microphone. "Do you hear me, Frédéric? This may well be our last conversation for some time. Events have taken a most unexpected and disturbing turn..." Koynos's hand stopped the engines. "My instructions are for you and all of our men to return to Earth on the *Oxus*," the leader of the New Fifteen continued. Our mission here is finished. Koynos over and out."

A hatch slowly opened on the outside of the vehicle and Koynos stepped out, strikingly handsome, wearing a black leather jacket and pants.

He spent a few minutes surveying the disaster all around him.

"Qotwaa is crumbling under its own fear," he muttered. "How appropriate."

Chaos reigned everywhere as the cracks turned into bolts of "nothingness" that struck randomly. The crowd, comprised mostly of Diurnals, was in a state of utter panic.

"The destruction of the Blot must have short-circuited one of the generators..." mused Koynos.

He then took off, flying towards the devastated city like an angel.

"The time has come for me to face the Nyctalope."

Meanwhile, not far from there, Claude Marécourt was expressing his concern to the Envoy:

"This is terrible. If this spreads, Rhea risks being destroyed. Is there anything you can do? Surely, your masters, the Sarvants, won't allow…"

"Hush! I'm receiving new instructions," said the Envoy, appearing to be listening to an inaudible voice. Then, she said: "The matter is being taken care of. I have a new mission. Follow me."

"Where?"

"Up there!"

The Envoy used her gun to shoot what appeared to be a beam of blue light towards an unseen point high in the sky. Then grabbing Marécourt by the waist, the mysterious woman pulled both of them up into the air.

"Oh, my goodness!" exclaimed the young physicist, more than a little scared.

"Are you losing faith in me?" said the Envoy, smiling. "Hang on; we're almost there."

A small bubble-shaped ship, almost identical to the Blot, but surrounded by blue light, had just appeared above their heads. The Envoy pulled herself and Marécourt onto the ship's strangely solid hull.

"Hold on!" said the Envoy.

At that moment, a bolt of nothingness hit the bubble-ship, slamming Marécourt's body into the hull, rendering the physicist semi-conscious.

Then, another bolt slammed into the ship, its momentum propelling the Envoy towards Marécourt. Their mouths met. They exchanged glances, then kissed passionately.

Without saying anything, they climbed into the bubble-ship, which was being shaken by a giant whirlpool made of space, and then eventually swallowed up by it.

"You've never told me your name," said Claude Marécourt.

"Hold on tight," said the Envoy.

The bubble-ship emerged from the Rhean field in outer space like a bullet being shot out of a gun. They saw the planetoid being wracked by black, cosmic bolts. Space itself seemed to shimmer around Rhea.

"I'm Xavière Saint-Clair," finally said the Envoy.

"Xavière...?"

"Yes. I'm the Nyctalope's grand-daughter."

"But they said you died at the North Pole a long time ago, trying to reach Rhea's Core."

"I told you—the Sarvants rebuilt me—just as they did Koynos. I'll explain later. We're getting out of here," said the Envoy. "I'm engaging hyperdrive."

"Where are we going?"

"Earth."

The bubble-ship vanished.

In the control room at Olbansville, Mayor Akira Mitang and Marc de Ciserat had seen the blip that was the bubble-ship blink out of existence on their viewscreens.

They weren't alone: Gisèle d'Holbach, who had rematerialized safely in the city hours earlier, had joined them.

"What was that?" asked the young woman.

"I don't know," said Mitang. "It looked like a spaceship of some kind, but it couldn't be..."

"We can't tell what's going on in the northern hemisphere," said Ciserat. "Since that strange explosion, most of our monitoring stations have gone down. None of the reports we're receiving are making sense."

"I have faith in the Nyctalope," said Mitang. "He'll pull through; he always does."

"Well, I don't intend to merely sit here and worry, Monsieur le Maire," said Gisèle interrupting.

"But we can't do anything to help him from here, Mademoiselle."

"Wait a minute! Before I left Qotwaa, Leo mentioned a back-up plan. What is it?"

Akira Mitang sighed. Then he began to tell Gisèle what the Nyctalope had planned.

In Room 8 at the hotel in Upper Qotwaa, Professor Henri d'Olbans heard the sound of King Kkal's guards banging on the door.

"Open this door!" shouted Ddôl, leading a fully-armed squadron of Nocturnals. "Otherwise, we'll break it down."

Suddenly, the door opened wide and the guards were repelled by a blinding burst of white light.

The Nyctalope stood on the threshold, appearing superhuman and radiating energy thanks to his polyactivated aura.

In the sky above, Koynos reacted to Leo's emergence in his superhuman state.

"The Nyctalope has successfully mutated the energies of his human shell."

He dived downwards just as the Nyctalope walked out of the Hotel. Leo's head turned towards the sky.

"Show yourself, Koynos," he said. "I know you're here."

Koynos appeared standing in the air a few feet above and before the Nyctalope.

"It's useless to resist me, Leo Saint-Clair," he said. "I carry within me the certainty of victory."

"You speak as if we were at war."

Now the Nyctalope flew up to meet Koynos in the air; it was the meeting of two demi-gods.

"I was your ally once, on Mars," Leo continued. "You saved my life. Can you set that aside so easily?"

"But now I serve the Sarvants who brought me back to life and who are the true Kings of Rhea..." AS they spoke, they continued rising up in the air. "When they found out that you were trying to steal their secrets, they sent me back..."

Beneath them, Ddôl and the guards watched in awe as the Nyctalope and Koynosrose until they were no more than dots in the sky.

"My intentions were ever to use them for good." Leo pointed at the world below. "I gather that you've been secretly surveying Rhea, Koynos. Did you find any evidence of evil intent?"

"You knew I was here?" replied Koynos, surprised.

"I suspected it almost from the beginning, my friend. But what was I to do? Fight you? Run away? No, I preferred to trust in your judgment—and that of your masters. So, what is your verdict?"

Koynos appeared hesitant.

"No, what you set up here is not evil, but the Sarvants are still not sure whether the Human Race should be allowed to spread beyond the confines of its native Earth… A decision hasn't yet been made…"

"I guess we'll both have to wait then. But in the meantime, we've got an urgent matter to attend to. One of my old enemies is back—Lucifer!"

"Lucifer? Glô von Warteck?" said Koynos. "But he's dead!"

"Well, he got better. And if he and that puppet of his, King Kkal, gain access to the Core, they'll use the Sarvants' secrets to commit far, far worse evil than anything you accused me of!"

"See what your pride has wrought, Leo. You've doomed us all. I must contact the Sarvants at once."

"No!" shouted the Nyctalope. "They may decide to destroy Rhea to rid themselves of the problem. Is that what you really want?"

Koynos remained silent.

"Let's fight Lucifer ourselves. There'll be plenty of time to call the Sarvants later."

"I'm not sure I like it, but I yield to your argument," said Koynos, sighing. "The destruction of this world would be a waste. But remember that I don't consider the matter of your ultimate fate closed."

"Fair enough. We can bicker about that after we get rid of Lucifer! Show me the way to the Core!"

The two heroes zoomed off until they were no more than blurs.

In a matter of seconds, they reached the North Pole opening, dove down, and vanished into the great maelstrom that blocked the access to the Core.

Chapter XV
Into the Core

As they descended deeper and deeper into the center of Rhea, the Nyctalope and Koynos found themselves in a world of giant machines, the purposes of which were all but incomprehensible to them.

At some point, Koynos landed on a gargantuan piece of machinery. The Nyctalope followed suit.

"What are we waiting for?" Leo said, sarcastically. "Have you decided that Rhea isn't worth saving after all?"

"You should know me better than that, Leo," replied Koynos, saddened. "I'd risk anything to save this world. We're in the Intermediate Zone. We have to allow for time decompression."

After several minutes, Koynos took the lead again, leaping into a gigantic shaft.

They flew down, deeper and deeper into the maze of machinery, like insects into a god engine.

Gliding down a shaft, they arrived at the location where the small, golden control sphere had once stood: at the center of a shaft, connected on four sides by complex, mechanical arms. Now, the sphere was gone, destroyed, and the metallic arms were covered with a black, thorny substance.

"This is what caused the collapse of the outer fields," said Koynos. "The control sphere was weakened by that matter-antimatter particle explosion at my northern desert base."

"The explosion that my people at Olbansville detected!"

"Yes. I always had the sense that it hadn't been just an accident, or a mistake by my No.9. Later, I found proof that it had been a deliberate act of sabotage orchestrated by those seeking to enter here."

"Kkal and Lucifer…"

Koynos nodded. They descended further.

"We've got to be careful," said the Nyctalope. "They must already have reached the Core."

They flew over an impossibly large room containing enormous spheres, which hummed while radiating a soft, blue light.

"This is impressive," whistle Leo. "I begin to understand why your Sarvants are so reluctant to share their science…"

Koynos looked at a sphere, on the surface of which a single spot appeared to be throwing black sparks similar to the bolts of nothingness they had beheld on the surface.

"There!" pointed Koynos.

They flew closer to the damaged engine.

"This engine was damaged by the destruction of the Blot," said Koynos, "but it should have repaired itself… I wonder…"

Koynos, still followed by the Nyctalope, flew closer to the spot from which the sparks originated and saw a small, rectangular, black metal box attached to it. It contained electrodes and wires, and more disturbingly, what looked like miniature brains made of living matter.

"That's preventing it from rebooting!"

Koynos tore the box from the sphere.

"It looks like some kind of dampener… Or perhaps a reprocessor…"

"This infernal device proves I told you the truth," interrupted Leo. "I've seen that technology before—a long time ago, at Glô von Warteck's Schwarzrock Castle in the Black Forest. This *is* Lucifer's scheme!"

Suddenly, the box sprouted energy tentacles which captured the two heroes in pulsating cocoons. Koynos struggled to free himself, but in vain.

"Another typical Von Warteck trick," muttered Leo.

"I'm starting to regret agreeing to your crazy scheme, said Koynos. "I should have contacted the Sarvants right away."

The cocoons took the Nyctalope and Koynos further down into the Core.

"Calm down, Koynos, we haven't lost yet. And I think your masters are patient. Their time will come."

The Nyctalope and Koynos were now floating along in a totally black space, towards a mysterious destination.

They arrived in front of a huge, oval aperture, behind which shone a bright blue-white light. They soon found themselves inside a small bubble-shaped space, designed to resemble an eden-like world of blue trees, blue flowers, all bathed in a radiant light.

"This is the Inner Core," explained Koynos. "What's left of the Sarvants' original homeworld, preserved in eternity like a perfect jewel in amber."

"This is beautiful," said Leo. "A paradise world. I so wish Gisèle had had a chance to see it," he added regretfully.

They saw their goal in the distance: a stone circle, not unlike that of Stonehenge, built on top of a hill. The heaven-like nature of the place was spoiled by the presence of three of King Kkal's guards waiting for them.

One of the guards grabbed the black box, pulling them down like inflatable balloons.

"You are prisoners of His Supreme Majesty King Kkal, now undisputed master of Rhea."

"What of Luci...?" started saying Koynos.

"Hush!" interrupted Leo.

The guard pressed a switch, causing the cocoons to burst like soap bubbles, freeing the Nyctalope and Koynos.

"Step inside the circle," ordered the Guard. "His Majesty is waiting for you."

They stepped inside, escorted by the guards. They saw a small band of scientists, led by Ppy, exploring and digging up the ground, making a mess of the once-pristine environment.

"Look at what they're doing," whispered Leo. "This Kkal is a disrespectful slob."

Suddenly, the King's voice rang out.

"If I were you, I'd watch my words, Nyctalope. You're no longer the King of the Night. I am."

Kkal stepped out from behind a stone and confronted the two humans.

"I've been looking forward to this meeting for a long, long time, Nyctalope," he said, adding in a megalomaniacal scream: "After all, am I not the architect of your defeat?"

"You're a fool, Kkal," said Leo.

"Your time has come, Nyctalope," continued the King, ignoring the interruption. "Your execution will free Rhea at last!"

"What are you talking about? Rhea has always enjoyed total autonomy. The colonists of Olbansville have always taken great pains to follow my prime directive and never interfere with your two races."

"Leo Saint-Clair speaks the truth," said Koynos. "I have surveyed this world for many months. The Earth people have never behaved like your superiors."

"Bah! His very existence is an affront to us all!" exclaimed Kkal. "We must destroy him to be free."

"You're mad," shouted Koynos. "You don't want freedom. You want to be King of Rhea instead. But I'm warning you: I am an Envoy of the Sarvants…"

"Silence!" shouted Kkal. "You and your damned Sarvants are powerless here. In this place, I am the master of life and death!"

"You're an idiot, Kkal," said Leo, sadly. "You've let yourself be used by Lucifer."

"No! I needed the human Vôo to clip your wings, but now, I'm in charge!"

"He played you for a fool. He'll use the Sarvants' secrets to rule Rhea first, then strike back at Earth… And God knows what else!"

"Listen to the Nyctalope," begged Koynos. "Lucifer only wishes to rule—and to destroy."

"And where will you be then, 'Your Supreme Majesty'?"

"I don't believe you!" shouted Kkal. "You're lying!"

Suddenly, there was a small vibration, a tiny tremor that rippled through the Inner Core, but Kkal seemed to remain unaware of it. Instead, he continued to rant:

"You're trying to confuse me, but it won't work... I'm too smart for you!"

The Nyctalope leaned towards Koynos.

"Did you feel that? I think Lucifer is about to strike."

"SILENCE!" screamed Kkal. "You're only hastening the moment of your demise! I..."

At that very moment, a strange phenomenon occurred, as if reality was folding upon itself, causing Kkal, Ppy and their men to be forcibly ejected from the Inner Core by some all-powerful, invisible force.

They shot into the air from the pattern on the floor of Kkal's laboratory, like tennis balls spat from a tube.

Then the pattern closed behind them, and all was dark again.

The only sound heard in the room was the wailing of King Kkal, as he realized the Nyctalope had told the truth and he had lost his throne.

Chapter XVI
At last—Lucifer!

Meanwhile, Leo Saint-Clair and Koynos found themselves floating inside a smooth, black metallic structure.

"That was a reality shift," said Koynos.

"Yes. Lucifer's last strike. He's gotten rid of Kkal and his men. Now, he's trying to flush us out."

Suddenly, they found themselves face-to-face with Glô von Warteck, dressed all in red, and wearing a silver mask shaped like a demon skull over his face.

The Baron discarded the mask, snapping his fingers, causing it to vanish instantly.

"I no longer need this trinket to impress that fool, Kkal," he said. Then in a burst of savage anger directed at Leo, he added: "I have pursued you throughout the Universe, Nyctalope! At last, you eill know my vengeance!"

"How on Earth did you make it back, Glô?" asked Leo, trying to gain some time. "When I left you for dead at the Pole, you seemed ready to suck the daisies by the roots."

"But I wasn't dead, you fool! Or rather, my matchless mind lived on inside the teledyname where I had already stored my mentality, Do you believe that, otherwise, you could have defeated me so easily? I had planned for some of my faithful servants to return, reclaim the machine and free me, but they never did. The teledyname was instead stolen by the Bolsheviks who took it with them back to Russia. Later, the Nazis tried to steal it. I felt such powerless rage watching you defeat them.[9] The Bolsheviks tried for decades to use my wonderful machine, but always, unknown to them, I thwarted their ends. However, I could not escape for, because of their paranoia, they always kept the teledyname locked inside a

---

[9] See "A Present for Hitler" in *The Nyctalope Steps In*.

magnetic field. But during that farcical comedy they called *perestroika*, the project was abandoned, and I could at last regain my freedom. I didn't know you were still alive then. I no longer had any interest in that petty planet Earth so I projected my mentality into space, until I finally made contact with Rhea…"

"I'm beginning to understand," muttered Koynos.

"Fear not, your turn will come," snarled Lucifer. "I could be hosted by the unloving intelligence that controls this world, but in order to gain entrance, I had to be invited in—which is why I made contact with Ppy and seduced his buffoonish king! But even then, I didn't have full access to the Core; I was in a partition. I could achieve certain things, such as create the Blot, a twisted version of the Rhean bubble-ships, but not gain total mastery. Now that I have it, however, my spectacular plans will at last become reality. I will return to Earth. With Rhea functioning as a giant teledyname, I will enslave its population. I will order hundreds of other Rheas to be built, and at the head of this mighty armada, I will realize the destiny of the human race and conquer the galaxy!"

"Crazy, much, Warteck?" sneered Leo.

Lucifer projected a deadly energy bolt, but the Nyctalope and Koynos avoided it, then joined forces.

"Time to work together again, Koynos," said Leo.

From their eyes, they emitted twin beams of energy which combined and shot towards Lucifer. However, the villain merely captured their energy and reshaped it into a glowing ball.

With a truly Satanic laugh, Lucifer threw the sizzling ball back at them.

It was about to strike Koynos when Leo interposed himself. He received the full brunt and was propelled backwards.

The Nyctalope's body began to smoke. His clothes were in tatters. Koynos' head turned towards Lucifer and energy glowed from his eyes.

"If he dies, I'll..." he growled.

Koynos's blast struck Lucifer in the chest before the villain could do anything to stop it. He had to concentrate all his energy to maintain his cohesion, before he could strike back with another devastating blast.

But Koynos poured out even more energy. Still, Lucifer held strong.

Suddenly, another beam joined Koynos'!

It was the Nyctalope who, although in a frightful state, was still able to fight back.

"You haven't won yet, demon!" shouted Leo.

Their combined efforts sent Lucifer twisting and reeling out of control, vanishing inside the strange, smooth, black metal of the structure in which they fought.

The Nyctalope and Koynos cautiously approached the spot where Lucifer had disappeared.

"Is he gone?" asked Koynos.

"Hard to tell... It may be another trick..."

As the Nyctalope spoke, the evil form of Lucifer: dark, scarlet and enormous, slowly rose up from behind them.

"You will die now!" shouted Lucifer with gleeful laughter.

He released a tremendous beam of energy which sent the Nyctalope and Koynos flying backwards, badly hurt.

"Contact the Sarvants," said Leo, out of breath. "They're our only hope."

"But you said..."

"That was before. There's too much at stake. Rhea must be protected. Earth too."

"What about you? The Sarvants can be wrathful. They might blame you for this. You might lose your immortality... Your life..."

"Don't worry about me," shouted Leo. "Just do it!

Koynos lay down supine, his arms and legs outstretched, in front of Lucifer. A tiny ball of blue light appeared to leave his chest and moved to float above his head. Lucifer appeared to immediately recognize the significance of this.

"The Sarvants!" she shouted. "No! I was so close to triumph! But I can still…"

He released another beam of energy but, this time, when the bolt reached Koynos, it scattered harmlessly.

To the side, the Nyctalope was awed by the Sarvants' power.

Then, a bolt of blinding blue light burst from Koynos and blasted Lucifer. Koynos's face reflected the tremendous toll the battle was making on his very being.

Lucifer appeared to puncture like an inflated balloon, then shrivel and implode, swallowing his own substance into itself.

The Nyctalope, astonished, saw Lucifer begin to be sucked into nothingness until he disappeared, screaming. Leo guessed that the villain had been taken to the otherdimensional realm of the Sarvants. To remain a prisoner forever, or perhaps a pet, or even to be eaten in an incomprehensible feast.

He shuddered.

Inside the Core, a wave of energy recreated the golden control sphere and repaired the mechanical arms that had been damaged. On the surface of Rhea, the black bolts of nothingness that had been spreading throughout the planetoid began to disappear.

Then the Nyctalope and Koynos were carried away by the same invisible force that had earlier removed King Kkal and his guards.

They lost consciousness.

When they woke up, they were lying on the tarmac on the Landing Pad in Olbansville.

Epilogue

The Nyctalope got up with difficulty. His clothes were in rags, and he showed the marks of the battle he has just fought.

He looked over at Koynos, who had remained completely motionless and was still lying on the ground.

He bent to take his pulse. There was none.

"Dead," whispered Leo. "No doubt a victim of the Sarvants' unfathomable will…"

Koynos's body began to shimmer, then disappeared.

The Nyctalope wondered if he was being discarded, like a tool whose usefulness was gone, or taken to join the Sarvants in their mysterious dimension. He shook his head. He probably would never know the truth.

Leo stood up again. As he turned, he saw his reflection in one of the glass windows of the control tower. Whatever transformation had been performed on him by Henri d'Olbans, its effects had totally dissipated. He had retuened to his ordinary human form.

Well, perhaps not so ordinary…

He straightened up and walked towards the control tower, just as Akira Mitang ran out towards him.

"Monsieur Saint-Clair! I wasn't dreaming! It is you! But how…?"

"There will be a time for explanations later, Akira. I assume everything is back to normal?"

"Yes. Whatever threatened to tear Rhea apart is over. All the monitors are back on line and all the signals are green. The Nocturnals and the Diurnals will have some rebuilding to do, depending on where they are, but nothing too dramatic."

"Excellent. Where is Gisèle?"

The Mayor looked somewhat embarrassed, biting his lips, not knowing how to answer.

"Come on, out with it," urged Leo.

294

"Well, er, she chose to go with the back-up plan," he finally said, adding: "I didn't say anything; you're the one who mentioned it to her. When she asked me about it, I had to tell her…"

"You did the right thing, Akira," said Leo, putting his hand on the Mayor's shoulder. "Had Koynos and I failed, the back-up plan would have been her only chance of salvation. I'm glad she took it."

"She left a letter for you, just in case you came back…" said Mitang, handing an envelope to the Nyctalope.

Leo took it and read:

Dearest Leo:

Do not blame Akira for having explained your back-up plan to me. I now know that the three ships, Olb-II, III *and* IV, *that transported the original colonists to Rhea have been refitted with deep sleep capsules for interstellar journeys.*

Your plan was that, in the event of a catastrophic even on Rhea, the colonists would be able to leave the planet and still carry out your dream of space exploration by traveling to the nearest star at lightspeed. It was, and still is, a wonderful plan.

I decided the join this new band of explorers, led by Marc de Ciserat. Marc is a good man, and I know he is not insensitive to my charms. I think I can be happy with him, under the light of another star.

I'm giving this letter to Akira in case you return safe and sound. No one has ever been able to truly defeat you in the past, and I hope this will prove true again.

I will always love you,
Gisèle

During the reading of the letter, Akira Mitang had stepped back, as if to give Leo some privacy. Now that he saw the Nyctalope fold the letter and put it inside his pocket, he approached him and asked:

"Will you be staying on Rhea, Great Nyctalope? The readings indicate the entire planet will be shifting to hyperdrive in a few hours…"

"Good! It means that the Sarvants have agreed to let the Human Race spread its wings beyond the confines of the Solar System. But to answer your question: no. I plan to return to Earth on the *Olb.-1*. There is nothing more for me to do here, while there is still much I can accomplish on our homeworld."

"You do know we'll probably catch up with the other ships in a few months…?"

"I realize that, Akira, but I think Gisèle will be happier with Marc. Wish them both a long and happy life together for me. And always abide by the ideals of our great country as your children and your children's children travel among the cosmos."

"I will, Great Nyctalope. *Vive la France!*"

"*Vive la France!*"

An hour later, the Nyctalope was at the commands of the *Olb-1*. Alone. His destination: Earth. He didn't even turn to watch Rhea shrink in size and vanish in the opposite direction behind him as his ship gained in speed.

Once the automatic pilot was set, he went to his bunk and quickly fell asleep.

And in his sleep, he dreamt of the stars.

Timeline
of the events chronicled in this book

1909. Leo meets Koynos in Africa. ("Dangerous Territory" in *Night of the Nyctalope*)

1910 (Sept.)-1911 (March). The Nyctalope defeats the XV on Mars. Death of Koynos. Leo marries Xavière de Ciserat. (*The Nyctalope on Mars*)

1912 (March). First encounter with the Sarvants. (novelized by Maurice Renard in *The Blue Peril*) (July). Birth of Pierre Saint-Clair on Mars.

1917 (July). Destruction of the French Colony on Mars. Leo returns to Earth, severely traumatized, along with three Martian Agents. ("The Hunters of Mars," "The Children of Heracles" in *The Nyctalope Steps In* and "Justice and Power" and "The Ides of Mars" in *Night of the Nyctalope*)

1921 (March-June). Leo defeats Glô von Warteck, a.k.a. Lucifer. (*The Nyctalope vs Lucifer*) Unbeknownst to him, Lucifer's mentality is duplicated and stored inside his teledyname. (referenced in this volume)

1932. Leo returns to Mars and destroys the first Martian Agent. (*Les Chasseurs de Mystère*; "The Ides of Mars" q.v.).

1934 (June)-1935 (Dec.). First visit of Leo to Rhea. (*The King of Rhea*)

1940 (July). Pierre Saint-Clair joins the Résistance. ("The Lesson of Captain Danrit" in *Night of the Nyctalope*)

1940-41. The Soviets find the teledyname. The Nazis try to steal it, but Leo stops them. ("A Present for Hitler" in *The Nyctalope Steps In*) The Soviets later fail to force Lucifer's mentality to serve them. (referenced in this volume)

1941. Second visit of Leo to Rhea and foundation of the French colony. (referenced in this volume)

1942 (June). Léo helps save Yves Marécourt. (*The Nyctalope Steps In*)

1950. Leo destroys the second Martian Agent in Pasadena. ("The Ides of Mars" in *Night of the Nyctalope*)

1995. After the Dissolution of the Soviet Union in 1992, the Russians abandon the teledyname project and Lucifer is free to project his mentality into space. (referenced in this volume)

2005. Lucifer's spirit finds Rhea, which is on the outer fringes of the Solar System, and manages to be hosted in its Core. The Sarvants take notice. (referenced in this volume)

2008. The Sarvants resurrects Koynos to deal with the situation. Koynos in turn recruits the New Fifteen on Earth. (referenced in this volume)

2011. Koynos arrives on Rhea and begins his mission. (referenced in this volume)

2012. Leo finally defeats the Martian threat. ("The Ides of Mars" in *Night of the Nyctalope*) He receives a mental SOS from Akira Mitang who has become aware of Koynos' presence on Rhea (referenced in this volume)

2014. Leo arrives on Rhea. *The Return of the Nyctalope* begins.

SF & FANTASY

Henri Allorge. *The Great Cataclysm*
Guy d'Armen. *Doc Ardan: The City of Gold and Lepers*
G.-J. Arnaud. *The Ice Company*
Charles Asselineau. *The Double Life*
Cyprien Bérard. *The Vampire Lord Ruthwen*
Aloysius Bertrand. *Gaspard de la Nuit*
Richard Bessière. *The Gardens of the Apocalypse*
Albert Bleunard. *Ever Smaller*
Félix Bodin. *The Novel of the Future*
Louis Boussenard. *Monsieur Synthesis*
Alphonse Brown. *City of Glass; The Conquest of the Air*
Emile Calvet. *In a Thousand Years*
André Caroff. *The Terror of Madame Atomos; Miss Atomos; The Return of Madame Atomos; The Mistake of Madame Atomos; The Monsters of Madame Atomos; The Revenge of Madame Atomos; The Resurrection of Madame Atomos*
Félicien Champsaur. *The Human Arrow; Ouha, King of the Apes; Pharaoh's Wife*
Didier de Chousy. *Ignis*
Jules Clarétie. *Obsession*
Michel Corday. *The Eternal Flame*
Captain Danrit. *Undersea Odyssey*
C. I. Defontenay. *Star (Psi Cassiopeia)*
Charles Derennes. *The People of the Pole*
Georges Dodds (anthologist). *The Missing Link*
Harry Dickson. *The Heir of Dracula*
Jules Dornay. *Lord Ruthven Begins*
Alfred Driou. *The Adventures of a Parisian Aeronaut*
Sâr Dubnotal *vs. Jack the Ripper*
Alexandre Dumas. *The Return of Lord Ruthven*
Renée Dunan. *Baal*
J.-C. Dunyach. *The Night Orchid; The Thieves of Silence*
Henri Duvernois. *The Man Who Found Himself*
Achille Eyraud. *Voyage to Venus*
Henri Falk. *The Age of Lead*
Paul Féval. *Anne of the Isles; Knightshade; Revenants; Vampire City; The Vampire Countess; The Wandering Jew's Daughter*
Paul Féval, *fils. Felifax, the Tiger-Man*
Charles de Fieux. *Lamékis*

Arnould Galopin. *Doctor Omega; Doctor Omega and the Shadowmen* (anthology)

Judith Gautier. *Isoline and the Serpent-Flower*

Léon Gozlan. *The Vampire of the Val-de-Grâce*

G.L. Gick. *Harry Dickson and the Werewolf of Rutherford Grange*

Edmond Haraucourt. *Illusions of Immortality*

Nathalie Henneberg. *The Green Gods*

V. Hugo, P. Foucher & P. Meurice. *The Hunchback of Notre-Dame*

Romain d'Huissier. *Hexagon: Dark Matter*

Michel Jeury. *Chronolysis*

Gustave Kahn. *The Tale of Gold and Silence*

Gérard Klein. *The Mote in Time's Eye*

Fernand Kolney. *Love in 5000 Years*

Paul Lacroix. *Danse Macabre*

Louis-Guillaume de La Follie. *The Unpretentious Philosopher*

Jean de La Hire. *Enter the Nyctalope; The Nyctalope on Mars; The Nyctalope vs. Lucifer; The Nyctalope Steps In; Night of the Nyctalope; Return of the Nyctalope*

Etienne-Léon de Lamothe-Langon. *The Virgin Vampire*

André Laurie. *Spiridon*

Gabriel de Lautrec. *The Vengeance of the Oval Portrait*

Alain le Drimeur. *The Future City*

Georges Le Faure & Henri de Graffigny. *The Extraordinary Adventures of a Russian Scientist Across the Solar System* (2 vols.)

Gustave Le Rouge. *The Vampires of Mars; The Dominion of the World* (w/Gustave Guitton) (4 vols.)

Jules Lermina. *Mysteryville; Panic in Paris; To-Ho and the Gold Destroyers; The Secret of Zippelius*

André Lichtenberger. *The Centaurs; The Children of the Crab*

Jean-Marc & Randy Lofficier. *Edgar Allan Poe on Mars; The Katrina Protocol; Pacifica; Robonocchio; Return of the Nyctalope;* (anthologists) *Tales of the Shadowmen 1-9*

Xavier Mauméjean. *The League of Heroes*

Joseph Méry. *The Tower of Destiny*

Hippolyte Mettais. *The Year 5865*

Louise Michel. *The Human Microbes; The New World*

Tony Moilin. *Paris in the Year 2000*

José Moselli. *Illa's End*

John-Antoine Nau. *Enemy Force*

Marie Nizet. *Captain Vampire*

C. Nodier, A. Beraud & Toussaint-Merle. *Frankenstein*

Henri de Parville. *An Inhabitant of the Planet Mars*
Gaston de Pawlowski. *Journey to the Land of the 4th Dimension*
Georges Pellerin. *The World in 2000 Years*
Ernest Pérochon. *The Frenetic People*
Pierre Pelot. *The Child Who Walked on the Sky*
J. Polidori, C. Nodier, E. Scribe. *Lord Ruthven the Vampire*
P.-A. Ponson du Terrail. *The Vampire and the Devil's Son; The Im-mortal Woman*
Edgar Quinet. *Ahasuerus*
Henri de Régnier. *A Surfeit of Mirrors*
Maurice Renard. *The Blue Peril; Doctor Lerne; The Doctored Man; A Man Among the Microbes; The Master of Light*
Jean Richepin. *The Wing; The Crazy Corner*
Albert Robida. *The Adventures of Saturnin Farandoul; The Clock of the Centuries; Chalet in the Sky; The Electric Life*
J.-H. Rosny Aîné. *Helgvor of the Blue River; The Givreuse Enigma; The Mysterious Force; The Navigators of Space; Vamireh; The World of the Variants; The Young Vampire*
Marcel Rouff. *Journey to the Inverted World*
Han Ryner. *The Superhumans*
Brian Stableford. *The New Faust at the Tragicomique;The Empire of the Necromancers (The Shadow of Frankenstein; Frankenstein and the Vampire Countess; Frankenstein in London); Sherlock Holmes & The Vampires of Eternity; The Stones of Camelot; The Wayward Muse.* (anthologist) *The Germans on Venus; News from the Moon; The Supreme Progress; The World Above the World; Nemoville; In-vestigations of the Future*
Jacques Spitz. *The Eye of Purgatory*
Kurt Steiner. *Ortog*
Eugène Thébault. *Radio-Terror*
C.-F. Tiphaigne de La Roche. *Amilec*
Théo Varlet. *The Golden Rock. The Xenobiotic Invasion; The Casta-ways of Eros; Timeslip Troopers* (w/André Blandin); *The Martian Epic* (w/Octave Joncquel)
Paul Vibert. *The Mysterious Fluid*
Villiers de l'Isle-Adam. *The Scaffold; The Vampire Soul*
Philippe Ward. *Artahe*
Philippe Ward & Sylvie Miller. *The Song of Montségur*

MYSTERIES & THRILLERS

M. Allain & P. Souvestre. *The Daughter of Fantômas*
A. Anicet-Bourgeois, Lucien Dabril. *Rocambole*
A. Bernède. *Belphegor*; *Judex* (w/Louis Feuillade); *The Return of Judex* (w/Louis Feuillade); *The Shadow of Judex*
A. Bisson & G. Livet. *Nick Carter vs. Fantômas*
V. Darlay & H. de Gorsse. *Arsène Lupin vs. Sherlock Holmes: The Stage Play*
Séamas Duffy. *Sherlock Holmes in Paris*
Paul Féval. *Gentlemen of the Night; John Devil; The Black Coats ('Salem Street; The Invisible Weapon; The Parisian Jungle; The Companions of the Treasure; Heart of Steel; The Cadet Gang; The Sword-Swallower)*
Emile Gaboriau. *Monsieur Lecoq*
Goron & Emile Gautier. *Spawn of the Penitentiary*
Rick Lai. *Shadows of the Opera: Retribution in Blood*
Steve Leadley. *Sherlock Holmes: The Circle of Blood*
Maurice Leblanc. *Arsène Lupin vs. Countess Cagliostro; Arsène Lupin vs. Sherlock Holmes (The Blonde Phantom; The Hollow Needle); The Many Faces of Arsène Lupin*
Gaston Leroux. *Chéri-Bibi; The Phantom of the Opera; Rouletabille & the Mystery of the Yellow Room; Rouletabille at Krupp's*
Richard Marsh. *The Complete Adventures of Judith Lee*
William Patrick Maynard. *The Terror of Fu Manchu; The Destiny of Fu Manchu*
Frank J. Morlock. *Sherlock Holmes: The Grand Horizontals; Sherlock Holmes vs Jack the Ripper*
Antonin Reschal. *The Adventures of Miss Boston*
P. de Wattyne & Y. Walter. *Sherlock Holmes vs. Fantômas*
David White. *Fantômas in America*
Pierre Yrondy. *The Adventures of Thérèse Arnaud*

SCREENPLAYS

Mike Baron. *The Iron Triangle*
Emma Bull & Will Shetterly. *Nightspeeder; War for the Oaks*
Gerry Conway & Roy Thomas. *Doc Dynamo*
Steve Englehart. *Majorca*
James Hudnall. *The Devastator*
Jean-Marc & Randy Lofficier. *Royal Flush*

J.-M. & R. Lofficier & Marc Agapit. *Despair*
J.-M. & R. Lofficier & Joël Houssin. *City*
Andrew Paquette. *Peripheral Vision*
Robert L. Robinson, Jr. *Judex*
R. Thomas, J. Hendler & L. Sprague de Camp. *Rivers of Time*

NON-FICTION

Stephen R. Bissette. *Blur 1-5. Green Mountain Cinema 1; Teen Angels*
Win Scott Eckert. *Crossovers* (2 vols.)
Jean-Marc & Randy Lofficier. *Shadowmen* (2 vols.)
Randy Lofficier. *Over Here*

ART BOOKS

J.-M. Lofficier & D. Taylor. *Tongue*Lash*
Jean-Pierre Normand. *Science Fiction Illustrations*
Raven Okeefe. *Raven's L'il Critters; Rave's Faves*
Randy Lofficier & Raven Okeefe. *If Your Possum Go Daylight...*
Daniele Serra. *Illusions*

HEXAGON COMICS

Franco Frescura & Luciano Bernasconi. *Wampus*
Franco Frescura & Giorgio Trevisan. *CLASH*
L. Bernasconi, J.-M. Lofficier & Juan Roncagliolo Berger. *Phenix*
Claude Legrand, J.-M. Lofficier & L. Bernasconi. *Kabur*
Franco Oneta. *Zembla*
L. Buffolente, Lofficier & J.-J. Dzialowski. *Strangers: Homicron*
Danilo Grossi. *Strangers: Jaydee*
Claude Legrand & Luciano Bernasconi. *Strangers: Starlock*